# ALSO BY PAUL

# INFERNO

## THE FROZEN FLAME: BOOK FOUR

PAUL J BENNETT

First Edition: May 2021

ePub ISBN: 978-1-989315-71-2
Mobi ISBN: 978-1-989315-72-9
Apple Books ISBN: 978-1-989315-73-6
Smashwords ISBN: 978-1-989315-74-3
Print ISBN: 978-1-989315-75-0

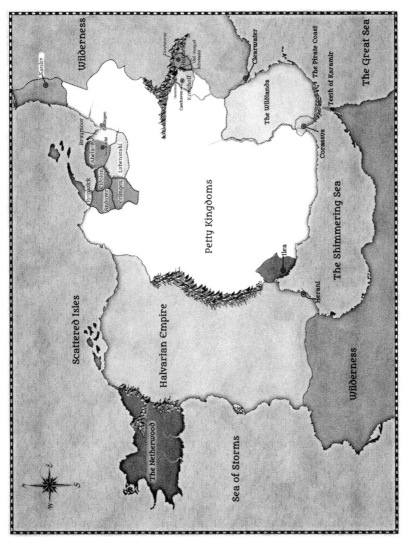

*The World of Eiddenwerthe*

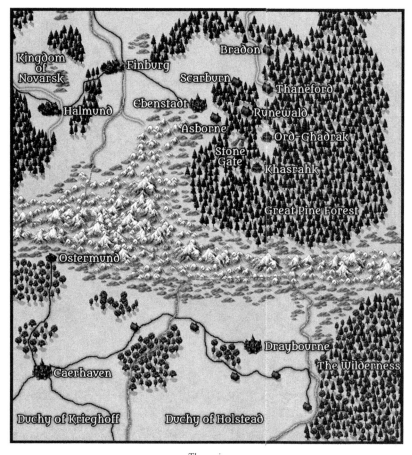

*Therengia*

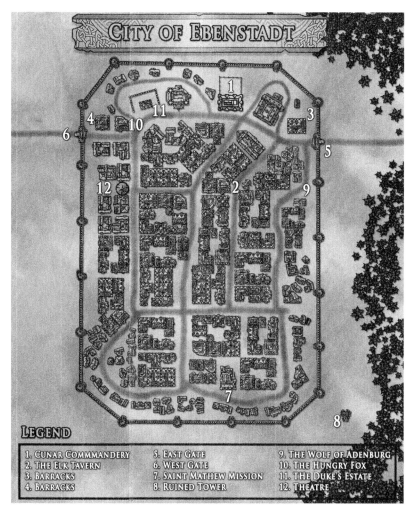

# CITY OF EBENSTADT

**LEGEND**

1. CUNAR COMMMANDERY
2. THE ELK TAVERN
3. BARRACKS
4. BARRACKS
5. EAST GATE
6. WEST GATE
7. SAINT MATHEW MISSION
8. RUINED TOWER
9. THE WOLF OF ADENBURG
10. THE HUNGRY FOX
11. THE DUKE'S ESTATE
12. THEATRE

*Ebenstadt*

# KORASCAJAN

## WINTER 1104

Jendarth Sartellian stared down at the stack of letters spread out on his desk. As head of the Sartellian family, he took pride in overseeing every aspect of their operations, but sometimes even he tired of the endless details. He paused to take a sip of wine, then resolved to get back to his duties, picking up the next letter. It was from the King of Abelard asking for another Fire Mage for his court. It appeared their eastern neighbour, Braymoor, was threatening once again, and the presence of a Sartellian would be considered a powerful deterrent.

He placed the letter on the top of the pile and rose, making his way over to a large, expansive bookshelf. It took only a moment to find the right volume, and then he carried it back to his desk to peruse its contents.

Abelard was on the northern coast of the Continent and therefore should be detailed in this tome. He scanned its pages, smiling, pleased to have found what he was looking for. There, written in his own hand, was an account of the king's court, containing names, places, and dates of import to the family.

Reading through his notes, he frowned. Apparently, the King of Abelard had been somewhat dismissive of the last mage he sent there. His fingers flipped through pages until he found the entry on Braymoor.

"Toras?" he called out.

Moments later, the door opened. "You called, Magister?"

"Braymoor and Abelard, what do you remember of them? Anything we can use?"

His assistant adopted a thoughtful pose, staring up to the ceiling as he was wont to do on occasion. He soon smiled, recalling something of interest.

"There was a civil war there about fifteen years ago," Toras said.

"Was that our doing?"

"It was, Magister. We pressed Prince Maximillian of Braymoor to support the Marhaven's attempt to claim the throne."

"And did they succeed?"

"No, my lord. The rebellion was crushed, as we suspected it would be. It did, however, turn Abelard's attention eastward, allowing its western neighbour, Eidolon, to make a land grab."

"Ah yes, I remember now. It destabilized the entire region. Exactly what we desired."

"I noticed you had a letter from the King of Braymoor," said Toras. "Are they asking for another mage?"

"They are, but I think it's time to sow a little more discontent. Who's our best man in the north?"

"That would be Invidar Sartellian, at the court of Reinwick."

Jendarth pulled forth a fresh parchment and began scribbling a note, making his aide wait. When finished, he handed it over.

"Send this. I'm reassigning him to Braymoor, and I shall expect him there by spring. He is to commence fomenting trouble with Abelard again."

"With an eye to rebellion?"

"No, I believe this time an all-out invasion is best. It will weaken their forces that much more."

"Excellent, Magister." Toras took the note, turning to leave.

"Hold a moment," called out Jendarth as he lifted the next letter in his pile. It bore the seal of the Volstrum. "What's this?" he asked.

"That came in this morning, my lord."

"You should have called it to my attention, Toras. It's not every day we get a letter from our cousins up north."

He broke the wax seal, carefully unfolding the note. Toras waited patiently. Eventually, Jendarth looked up.

"What do you know of this woman"—he gazed at the letter again—"Natalia Stormwind?"

"She's a powerful Water Mage, my lord. The most powerful the Volstrum has ever produced, I'm told."

"And?" pressed Jendarth.

"She fled shortly after graduation and has been on the run ever since."

"It says here she's taken up with a Fire Mage. We don't have anyone involved in that, do we?"

"Not now, Magister, but two of our agents perished trying to apprehend her. She and her companion managed to compromise the operation at Corassus, as well as interfere with our efforts to control the crusade."

"I don't give two sparks for this Stormwind woman. I want to know more about the Fire Mage."

"He's said to be a Therengian, my lord, from a place called Athelwald."

Jendarth looked up in surprise. "Athelwald? I know that name. We have a student from there, don't we?"

"We do. A woman named Ethwyn."

"And how is she progressing in her studies?"

"She has shown remarkable progress, my lord, although there's still much for her to learn. Why? Do you deem her important?"

"If I remember correctly, Athelwald is a relatively small village."

"It was," agreed Toras. "We had our agents burn it to the ground after taking slaves to further our aims in the south. Ethwyn herself was discovered entirely by accident."

"Tell me more."

"She had been sold as a slave to a Kurathian prince. When one of our people visited Kouras, he noted her potential for magic and brought her back here to Korascajan. She's been studying with us ever since."

"How long ago was this?"

"Just this last summer, my lord."

"But isn't she casting already?"

"She is," said Toras. "She has proved to be an incredibly fast study."

Jendarth stared at the letter, seeking more answers, his mind churning.

"Is there a problem, my lord?"

"Not at all." He smiled. "In fact, I believe we may have the solution to the Volstrum's problems."

"I would be cautious, Lord. Remember, we already lost several family members to that pair of rogues."

"Remind me of the details."

"Yes, Magister. First was Nezeroth Sartellian. He perished in Corassus."

"And…"

"Verineth Sartellian. He was organizing our plan to recover godstone near Holstead."

It seems this Stormwind woman has been a particular thorn in our side for some time."

"More like a boil," said Toras. "One that needs to be lanced."

"Agreed. I predict Ethwyn might be just the instrument to take care of that. Have her brought to me here. I would have words with her."

"Surely you don't mean to employ her in service to the family? She has yet to finish her training."

"It's a matter of opportunity. We received word there's a significant settlement of Therengians east of Ebenstadt, I feel it likely Natalia Stormwind has fled there in the company of this Fire Mage they speak of. What else do we know of the area?"

"Very little, Magister. That area falls under the domain of the Volstrum."

Jendarth frowned. "Then we shall keep this to ourselves for the time being." He turned his attention once more to the letter. "It says here, there may be a child. I shouldn't need to tell you what the ramifications of that are."

"We could be looking at an extremely gifted individual once they come of age," replied Toras.

"Precisely."

"But where would the child go? The Volstrum or here?"

"That would entirely depend on what type of magic they manifested, but as you well know, that's years away."

"And in the meantime?"

Jendarth smiled. "I think it would be better cared for here, don't you?"

"And if they manifest the magic of water?"

"Then we would happily send them off to the Volstrum for training."

"Giving us someone on the inside," noted Toras.

"Exactly. You've served the Sartellian line faithfully for decades, Toras. See this operation through, and I see a position on the council for you."

The aide puffed up his chest. "Thank you, Magister. I shall do my best."

"Good. Now go and fetch Ethwyn of Athelwald, and let's see what she's made of."


Ethwyn took a step forward, throwing her hands out to the front, and a streak of flame issued forth, covering a distance of about twenty paces, far greater than her last attempt.

"Good," said Eloran Sartellian, "but keep focused on the target. Your aim was off."

"It's hard work concentrating on power while still hitting the target."

Her instructor chuckled. "You'll get the hang of it, eventually. You've made marvellous progress in a short period of time. Don't let one mistake get you down."

"How long did it take for you to master the magic of fire?"

"Many years, but unlike you, I came here shortly after manifesting."

"Manifesting?"

"Yes, mages typically show an affinity for magic when they mature."

"But I was a full adult. I wouldn't have even known about it had a mage hunter not visited the court."

"I've seen this before. They say that sometimes a traumatic event can unlock the potential in someone's bloodline. Did either of your parents show a particular interest in fire?"

"No more so than anyone else."

"Not necessarily important. It can often skip a generation or two. Have you any brothers or sisters?"

"I had an older brother, Athgar, but he died when the village was attacked."

"Well, we're your family now," said Eloran. "Let's try the spell again, and see if you can't keep the flame from drifting to the left."

Ethwyn took a breath, then stepped forward, once more throwing her hands in front of her. Flames shot from her fingertips, and she felt the familiar warmth as the magic flowed through her. Her pulse quickened as the fire lit the area, then struck the target.

"Very good," said Eloran. She looked at Ethwyn's flushed face. "I see you've experienced the rush. It's fairly common amongst Fire Mages as the spell is released."

"It's as if my entire body is alive."

"Yes, that's the feeling of true power. Kings can rule over men, but only a Fire Mage knows the excitement of controlling one of the elemental forces of nature."

"Do the other elementalists not experience this feeling?"

"No, only the intense power of flame has that effect. You must be careful though. If you don't keep it under control, it can overwhelm you."

"Can I try again?"

"Of course. Now, this time—"

"Mistress Eloran?" interrupted a voice.

They both turned to see the Magister's aide coming towards them.

"Is there something I can do for you, Toras?"

"Is this the Therengian, Ethwyn of Athelwald?"

"Can't you tell from her grey eyes?"

"Yes, of course," he apologized. "I don't mean to interrupt, but Master Jendarth wishes to see her."

"Now?" said Eloran. "We're right in the middle of a lesson?"

"I'm afraid he was most insistent."

"Very well." She turned to her pupil. "You'd best go with Toras, Ethwyn."

"Yes, Mistress."

Toras looked at her closely. She was an attractive woman. Undoubtedly, she would prove a popular choice for breeding once she was fully trained.

Yet, somehow, those eyes unsettled him. He shrugged it off, concentrating on the task at hand.

"Come with me," he said, turning abruptly and walking with purpose towards the office of the Master of Korascajan.


Jendarth stood on his balcony, surveying the students arrayed in the courtyard below. They were the advanced pupils, the ones closest to graduation. Soon they would spread across the Continent, taking up positions in the courts of the Petty Kingdoms. A few select individuals would be elevated to even greater power, but that would typically only come after a few more years of practice. A knock on his door brought his attention back to the present.

"Come," he called, returning inside.

Toras held the door as a woman entered. "Ethwyn of Athelwald, Magister."

"Thank you, Toras. I'll take it from here."

His aide bowed. "Of course, my lord."

Jendarth sat. "Tell me of Athelwald," he said without preamble.

Ethwyn struggled to answer the question. She was obviously nervous but soon got control of herself. "It was a small village located on the border of Holstead, close to the Duchy of Krieghoff."

"How many people lived there, do you think?"

She shrugged. "A few hundred. Most were carted off into slavery, but the rest were put to death."

Jendarth stood, coming around the front of the desk to gaze into her eyes. "Remarkable," he said.

"What is?"

"The eyes. I've never actually seen a Therengian up close. Tell me, is there anything else that distinguishes a person of your race?"

"Race? I'm a Human, just like you."

He smiled. "So you say, but your people are shunned by most of the inhabitants of the Petty Kingdoms. Why do you suppose that is?"

"I haven't a clue. We once had a kingdom of our own. Is it something to do with that?"

He nodded. "What you refer to as a kingdom was, frankly, an empire. It occupied a significantly large portion of the Continent."

"How large?"

"Almost a third of what's now known as the Petty Kingdoms. It was the major political force in the land for generations."

"What happened to it?"

"It was destroyed," said Jendarth, "ripped apart by internal strife. That would have been the end of it, but for the fact its people were easy to identify. It's the eyes. No other Humans have grey eyes."

"And because of that," said Ethwyn, "they persecute us?"

"They do. It's fear, you see. Fear the Old Kingdom will be reborn."

"Old Kingdom?"

"Pardon me," said Jendarth. "I should explain. People in that part of the land tend to be superstitious. They believe invoking the name of Therengia will somehow bring about its return. It's a completely ridiculous concept, of course, but people believe what they're told, and the tales have been around for generations."

"And that's why I was sold into slavery?"

He shrugged. "Who can say what motivates a slaver? I suspect it had more to do with coins than anything else. Your isolated village was a plum target, off the beaten track, and far from what is considered civilized society. I doubt the people of Holstead even knew Athelwald existed."

"We were a protectorate of the duke," said Ethwyn.

"I sympathize with your plight, I really do, but I'm afraid there's little that can be done about it. In any case, WE are now your family. Now, how have you found it here at Korascajan?"

"The lessons have been more than adequate."

"And the rest?" pressed Jendarth. "Are you making any friends?"

"The others students are dismissive."

"They resent your power. You have a natural gift, Ethwyn. You came late to magic, which makes you take on your studies with the attitude of an adult. I see great things in your future." He recognized the pride in her eyes, yet still, there was something else. Defiance, perhaps?

"Do you like wielding magic?" he asked.

"I do," she replied.

There it was again, not defiance, but joy—the sense of wonderment that could only be discovered by remarkably few.

"You crave power," he said.

"Don't we all?"

"You might not believe this, but most of our graduates are content to spend the rest of their life at court."

"Surely a waste of their power?"

"Indeed, yet here we are. You have that inner something which sets you apart. I know the feeling well. I was once much like you, struggling to fit in. Only when I realized the importance of that power did I grow into my full potential. I see that same potential in you, Ethwyn."

Jendarth waited, letting his words sink in, then made his way back to take his seat behind his desk.

"How would you like to serve the family?" he asked.

"I already serve the family, don't I?"

"You do, but I had something else in mind. It has come to our attention that a… situation has developed in the north. We need someone to go and take care of it. Someone with your particular heritage."

"You mean a Therengian?" she said.

"I do. Apparently, a renegade spellcaster has taken refuge with some of your people. Who else could go amongst them unnoticed?"

"To what end? Am I to kill this person?"

"Why? Would it bother you if you were?"

She gritted her teeth. "No."

He stared at her for a moment, judging her response. "Good to know, but no, you're not being sent to kill someone. Rather, your task will be to abduct someone and return them here."

"So I am to rescue someone?"

"Yes, you are. A small child."

"How small?"

"An infant, to be exact. You see, the woman in question, Natalia Stormwind, fled her duties to the family. Her child represents the culmination of generations of selective breeding."

"I'm to steal a baby?" she said in astonishment.

"No, you're to liberate one. I can assure you it is a child of inestimable value to us. You would be amply rewarded for your service."

"Rewarded, how?"

He leaned back in his chair, sensing her surrender. "Well, for one thing, I would allow you to master more complex spells. You would also have your pick of assignments once you graduate."

"I'm told all graduates are expected to produce children."

Jendarth nodded. "They are. It is a duty we must all participate in if we are to prosper, even me."

"Then I would wish permission to pick the father of my child."

"Do this, and you may have whatever you want." He leaned forward, resting his elbows on his desk. "Become my agent, and the resources of the entire family shall be at your disposal. Perhaps you'll even sit here one day, overseeing this very institution."

"I'm an outsider," said Ethwyn.

"So was I when I was inducted into this academy."

"I'll do it."

"Good," said Jendarth. "I hoped that would be your answer. Toras?"

The door opened. "Yes, Magister?"

"Ethwyn may return to her lessons." He returned his attention to her. "You shall be hearing back from me in several days. There are preparations to be made."

"And in the meantime?"

"Continue with your studies. I suspect they will prove crucial to you in the coming months."

"Months?"

"Yes, this mission will take you a significant distance from here. But don't worry, others will help you along the way."

She bowed her head. "Yes, Magister."

Toras led her out, then returned, closing the door behind him. "Will she do?" he asked.

"I believe so. She has a strong will about her, and her desire for power is admirable."

"Did you tell her of the other mage from her village?"

"No," said Jendarth. "Let's not overwhelm her."

# RUNEWALD

## SPRING 1105

I nside the hut, Skora shivered as she put another log on the fire. It was not that she was ill, but Natalia Stormwind was decidedly chilled, and it was best for a birthing mother to be as comfortable as possible.

The old woman looked over at Athgar. The Therengian held his wife's hand while he uttered soothing words that seemed to fall on deaf ears. Another scream issued from Natalia's mouth, and Skora tried to comfort her.

"There, there," she soothed. "It'll soon be over."

"It's freezing in here," said Natalia. Even as she spoke, frost appeared on the walls. Athgar looked up in alarm.

"It is her power," said Shaluhk. "It is becoming uncontrollable."

"Are we in danger?"

"No, it will pass once the youngling is born."

Skora chuckled. "Only Athgar would marry a woman with such power."

"It's not her power I love," he replied, "but rather the woman who embodies it."

"Well said," noted Shaluhk. "Let us hope the child does not display any mastery of fire on the way out."

A look of alarm crossed Athgar's face. "You think that likely?"

"No," replied Shaluhk, her green features darkening. "It was meant to lighten the experience only. Children of mages, even powerful ones, are not known to manifest such things."

Athgar gazed at the ceiling. "And this?"

"This is all Nat-Alia's doing. In the throes of delivery, her control over her powers has weakened."

"Are you saying she's losing her magic?"

"Only her control over it. Do not worry. She will soon be back to her old self."

"Tell me, Athgar," said Skora. "Do you wish for a boy or girl?"

"Only for a healthy child."

The old woman nodded her head. "I wish more thought as you. It was always like that back in Athelwald."

"And it's not here?"

"King Eadred desired men to take up arms."

"Therengian women have always taken up arms beside their men," said Athgar. "It was one of the founding principles of Therengia."

"Look at you," said Skora. "I swear you spend more time with the bard than you do making bows these days."

Natalia squeezed Athgar's hand in a viselike grip. "It hurts," she said through gritted teeth.

"How much longer?" he asked.

"Not long, now," said Skora. "The birth pangs are coming closer together."

Shaluhk moved closer. "I would soothe her pain with magic, but I fear it might affect the child. Human births are much different from Orcs."

Natalia looked up from where she lay, the sweat dripping off her forehead despite the frost on the walls. "Different, how?" she managed to spit out.

"Agar's birth was much quicker. We have been here half the night, yet still, your youngling has not put in an appearance."

"Trust me, I'm as ready as you are to see this baby out of me." She grimaced as another surge of pain lanced through her.

"I'm here," said Athgar, although he wondered if the blood would ever flow back into his hand.

Skora moved to the end of the bed, switching places with Shaluhk.

"It will soon be here," she said. "Let me know when you get the urge to push."

"I've wanted to push all night!" shouted Natalia.

The air grew even chillier until their breath hung in the air.

"I can't deliver a babe like this," said Skora. "My fingers are numb."

Athgar tore his hand from Natalia's grip. "One moment," he said, then uttered a few words of power. He touched the old woman's arm, and the magic flowed into her, warming her to her bones.

Natalia began flailing her hand about. "Athgar," she screamed. "Where are you?"

"I'm here," he called out, desperately trying to grab it before she hurt herself.

Skora knelt. "Here it comes…"

Laruhk approached the hut to see Kargen waiting outside.

"Any news?"

"Not yet," replied the Orc chieftain. "Shaluhk is inside, in case she is needed, but Nat-Alia is a strong female. She will be fine."

"Then why are you so nervous?"

"What makes you assume I am nervous?"

"I know you, Kargen. You only pace when you are worried. Are you worried for Nat-Alia?"

"Never have I heard of a youngling born to two such powerful mages. I am merely curious to see the result."

A snort echoed from the edge of the village.

"Your tuskers grow impatient," said Kargen.

"They are interesting creatures, vicious in attack, yet in their own way, they are as playful as a wolf pup."

"A wolf pup that is larger than a horse."

"Very true, but Rugg, the master of earth, is able to communicate with them. It has made training them so much easier."

"It looks like you found your calling, Master of Tuskers."

Laruhk straightened his back. "Master of Tuskers, I like that. I must tell my sister." He moved to enter the hut, but Kargen held him back.

"I would wait if I were you."

"Nonsense. She will want to know of my elevation."

"I have been listening to the events within. That is not a place I suggest you try braving."

"Nonsense," repeated Laruhk. He opened the door, only to be assaulted by a blast of frigid air. He stumbled back, shivering, while Kargen simply looked at him with a smile.

"On second thought, maybe I shall wait."

"A wise choice," said Kargen.

Agar ran by, chasing a Human child. The young Orc caught him, touching him on the shoulder, then turned and ran off, the Human in hot pursuit.

"Your son does you proud," said Laruhk.

"He is growing fast. Note how already he treats the Humans as equals."

"Would that the Humans returned the favour. There are many who still hold us in contempt."

"That will change in time," said Kargen. "Just as the young accept each other without reservations so, too, will the adults. It simply takes time."

"King Eadred was no friend."

"True, but he is gone, and in his place, Athgar rules Runewald as thane."

"And one day he will become king, then he can rule over us all."

Kargen shook his head. "No, I know Athgar. He would never agree to such a thing. He believes, like us, it is the will of the tribe that should rule, not an individual."

"Yet you are chieftain of the Red Hand?"

"Yes, but a chieftain is merely the caretaker of the tribe. They rule only for the betterment of all."

"And you believe Athgar feels the same way?"

"Do you doubt it?" countered Kargen.

Laruhk shook his head. "No, I suppose not, but if he is not to rule, then who? The Humans would never accept an Orc."

"Then we need a better way."

"We have our own ways."

"As do the Humans, but if we are to make this work, we must all make concessions."

"What of the men in the west? They are our distant allies."

"True," said Kargen, "but their situation is far different. The Humans there already had a kingdom and welcomed our people as allies. Here, we are building a country from the ground up."

"Building a country?"

"Do you believe the Ancestors guided us here to continue with life as it was? I tell you, Laruhk, there is something greater going on here, a chance for our people to finally emerge from the shadows."

"Emerge from the shadows?" said Laruhk. "Humans will never allow it. It is one thing to get these Therengians to accept us, but the entire Continent is quite another matter."

"Minds can be changed," insisted Kargen.

"I hope you are right, but I fear old hatreds will rise again. Most Humans fear what they do not understand, and our ways are foreign to them."

"You surprise me, Laruhk. I would never have thought of you as a wise elder."

Laruhk grinned. "Do not speak of such things. I have many years, yet, before I consider myself as such."

"Nonsense. You are well into your twenties by now. Speaking of which, when are you going to settle down and find yourself a bondmate?"

Laruhk turned a lighter shade of green. "Let us talk of other things."

A scream echoed from the hut, causing both Orcs to look at the door with compassion.

"She is having a difficult time," said Kargen.

"Still? How long do Humans take to birth a youngling?"

"Days, it would seem."

A small shape ran from behind the hut and careened into Kargen. The chieftain looked down to see his son, Agar, clutching his leg, a look of concern on his face.

"All is well, Agar," said Kargen. "Your tribe sister will soon be amongst us."

Another scream, and then all went quiet. Kargen and Laruhk held their breath until the sound of a crying infant emerged from the hut.

"It is done!" said Kargen.

"Yes, and not so different from an Orc after all. He has healthy lungs, this newborn Human."

The door opened, revealing Shaluhk, who smiled as she looked at her bondmate. "Nat-Alia has delivered a healthy youngling, a girl."

"And how is the mother?" asked Kargen.

"Resting. It was quite the ordeal. Once it was delivered, I used my magic to help Nat-Alia rest. She now sleeps."

The door opened again, and Shaluhk stood to the side, revealing Athgar. Kargen moved closer, clasping him on the arms.

"Congratulations, my friend!"

"Thank you," Athgar replied, "though I believe I should get some sleep. Natalia will expect me there when she wakens."

"What will you call this new daughter of yours?" asked Laruhk.

Shaluhk shot him a look of disgust. "Do not pester him with questions, Brother. He is tired."

"No," said Athgar. "It's fine."

"Then the name?" pressed Laruhk.

"Natalia and I discussed the matter some time ago. We'd like you to conduct a naming ceremony, Shaluhk, providing that wouldn't break any rules?"

Shaluhk's smile gave away her answer. "I would be delighted to, but such things are not usually done for sometime after the birth. Are you sure you can wait for that?"

"Yes, we can."

"Excellent," said Kargen. "Then we can welcome her to the tribe."

"The tribe?" said Laruhk.

"Of course. Is not Athgar our master of flame?"

"But he is the leader of Runewald."

"Can he not be both?"

Laruhk shook his head. "It is difficult to keep up with you sometimes, Kargen."

"Do not worry," soothed Shaluhk. "I shall explain it to you, Brother."


Later that day, having rested, Natalia looked much better: the colour, what little of it she normally had, was back in her face. She cradled the infant as she lay in her bed, Athgar sitting by her side.

"How are you feeling, Nat-Alia?" asked Kargen.

"Much better, thank you. Shaluhk has been of great assistance. And, of course, I couldn't have done it without Skora."

"It was my pleasure," the old woman replied. "You know I was there when your husband was born."

Natalia smiled. "And how did his birth compare to our daughter's?" She glanced at Athgar to see a worried look.

"It was rather unremarkable, if truth be told. His sister's, though… now that was an entirely different matter."

"Ethwyn?"

"Yes, she didn't want to come out! If we hadn't pulled her from the womb, she would've stayed in there for weeks."

"Sounds like my brother," said Shaluhk.

"Natalia mentioned something about a naming ceremony," said Skora. "What is that?"

"It is a ritual we Orcs carry out," explained Shaluhk. "We sit around a fire, and the shaman contacts the Ancestors to ask what name shall be endowed on the youngling."

"And is it binding?"

"Binding?"

"Yes," said the old woman. "What if they don't like the name?"

"Why would they not like it?"

"They may prefer to name their daughter after her grandmother?"

"That has never come up before," said Shaluhk. "Why do you ask?"

"It seems like a logical question. After all, the Ancestors are Orcs, aren't they? What do they know of Human-naming conventions?"

"More than you might realize. Our people were once part of the Therengian Kingdom."

Kargen looked at her in surprise. "How do you know that?"

"I have learned much since Khurlig possessed me. I have come to believe I inherited many of her memories."

The concern on the chieftain's face was easy to see. "Are you sure that is safe?"

Shaluhk smiled. "I am perfectly fine. I just know more than I did before. I am still the same person I was when first we bonded."

"Oh no, you are not," said Kargen. "You are so much more beautiful now."

She blushed, turning a darker shade of green, leading the others present to chuckle.

"That's so sweet," said Natalia.

"It seems Kargen is a master of words," said Athgar. "Would that I could sound as charming."

In answer, Natalia reached out, taking his hand. "You are perfect for me," she said.

"Your timing is good," said Kargen. "Word is the other thanes are coming to Runewald."

"Oh yes," said Athgar. "I'd forgotten the moot."

"Moot?" said Natalia.

"It's the old Therengian name for a gathering of leaders. I should like the Orc chieftains to be there, if possible."

"They shall be," promised Kargen. "I have already taken the liberty of contacting Zharuhl and Kirak, and they both promised to be in attendance."

"The Orcs are not yet part of the moot," noted Skora, "and there will likely be opposition to their inclusion."

"Why is that?" asked Natalia.

"They are men who crave power. Adding the chieftains will diminish their own hold over the realm."

"I'd hardly call us a realm," said Athgar. "We're really no more than a collection of villages."

The old woman smiled. "You've been busy comforting your wife, so I will forgive you your distraction, but the truth is more Therengians join us every day."

"From where?"

"Some come from farther east while others flee the Petty Kingdoms, seeking refuge amongst us. Word of your victory over the Church is spreading quickly."

"It wasn't the Church, only a corrupt order of Temple Knights."

The old woman shrugged. "It matters not. Word is spreading that a new Therengia has risen. You can do little to stop it."

Athgar felt the weight of his people on his shoulders. "God's teeth, all I ever wanted was for us to be left in peace. Now others will come seeking to crush us."

"It's not your fault," said Natalia. "It's the way of the Petty Kingdoms. They're all nice and friendly until someone starts to the get the upper hand, then they all band together and go to war."

"But we don't have the upper hand. True, we won against impossible odds, but we lack the people to fight an extended campaign."

"It matters little to them," said Skora. "War is coming, Athgar, whether you want it or not."

"You bear the same curse as the Orcs," said Kargen. "There is always someone to covet what is yours."

"No," said Shaluhk. "If this land is to survive, then we must act as one people, not Orcs and Humans. The first step to doing that is for the moot to accept the tribes as their own."

Kargen smiled. "My bondmate speaks the truth."

"A good point," said Athgar, "and I'm in full agreement. The real question is, how can that be managed? I am but one thane amongst four."

"But you have influence," added Natalia. "The people see you as the victorious leader."

"You led the army, not me."

"I care not for accolades, only that we have a home together. Let them call you the victor. I am content with that."

"Even so, I would still face an uphill battle. Old minds are not so easily swayed."

"Then we must take action," said Shaluhk.

"What do you have in mind?"

The Orc shaman smiled. "We start by increasing trade, taking goods to the other villages. Runewald has prospered by our presence. Why not Thaneford, Bradon, or Scarburn?"

"She makes a good point," said Natalia. "And with prosperity will come acceptance."

"There is more," said Shaluhk. "Although perhaps it is too early to consider the possibility."

"Go on," urged Athgar.

"As you know, our shamans can communicate over long distances. It occurs to me there are tribes of Orcs scattered throughout the region. What if we can convince them to come here?"

"Would the land support them?" asked Natalia. "There would need to be enough game for hunting."

"The great pine forest is unending. A hunter could likely walk there for months without exiting its boughs."

"So you're saying we would expand eastward?"

Shaluhk nodded. "Yes, and as the tribes expanded, so, too, would the villages of Humans. I propose that what we did here in Runewald could be duplicated elsewhere. Humans and Orcs living side by side in mutual trade and protection."

"A grand vision," said Kargen.

Natalia sat up. "It is, isn't it, but we'd need to lay the groundwork now before we grow too big to govern efficiently."

Athgar looked at her in surprise. "I'm not sure I understand."

"At the moment, we have only four villages and three tribes to work with. The greater the population grows, the more voices will be added to the moot, making it much harder to reach consensus. If we establish an efficient system of governance now, it will serve us well in the future."

"And what kind of kingdom would we form?"

"I don't know," said Natalia. "What did the Old Kingdom do?"

"I'm not sure," said Athgar, "but Dunstan would likely know. He's the bard."

"Then seek him out, and discover what he knows about how the Old Kingdom ran. It could be the answer to our own future."

"Not so fast," said Athgar. "I'm no expert, but even I know Therengia fell apart. They say it dissolved because of internal strife."

"Then we shall build a solid foundation."

"I'm not sure I understand what you mean."

Natalia's eyes brightened with excitement. "You told me when you learned to control your inner spark, you started with the basics, correct?"

"Yes."

"Imagine a country along similar lines. We plan for growth, much as a master prepares their student to learn more complicated spells. That way, once they are capable of learning such things, everything is in place to ensure success."

"You have me intrigued," said Kargen. "How do we build this foundation you speak of?"

"We start by learning as much as we can about how others rule."

"But all we have is a bard," said Athgar.

"True. Perhaps we should consider building a hall of knowledge? Then we could attract scholars."

Now it was Athgar's turn to smile. "What if we could get a message to Corassus? I'm sure Tonfer Garul would relish the chance to oversee such a project."

"Tonfer Garul?" said Kargen.

"Yes, he's an Orc who works at the great archives in Corassus."

"An Orc scholar? I have never heard of such a thing. Why does he have such a strange name?"

"Tonfer was the name given him by his Human colleagues."

"I'm sure we could find someone in Ebenstadt to take a message," said Natalia, "though it would likely be expensive."

"What about by boat?" said Kargen. "You sailed from the Duchy of Holstead to Corassus, did you not?"

"We did," said Natalia, "but that would require crossing the mountains to the south, a dangerous journey."

"My people know the path," said Kargen. "It would, however, take a Human to enter the city and negotiate with the boatmen."

"Let us not get ahead of ourselves," said Shaluhk. "All of these ideas are good, but we must deal with the here and now first, and that means convincing the moot of our vision."

# EBENSTADT

## SPRING 1105

Stanislav Voronsky edged around the corner of the building, his eyes alert. Off in the distance, a rough-looking man had stopped at a fruit stall and was making a show of examining some apples. In reality, he was glancing around, alert to any potential danger that might lurk nearby.

Stanislav cursed his luck. He was, by training, a mage hunter, but his old employer had turned against him, forcing him to seek employment elsewhere. Now he roamed the streets of Ebenstadt, eking out an existence as a mere bounty hunter. In any other city of the Petty Kingdoms, he would have thrived, but the recent defeat of the Church in the last crusade had left the city abandoned, and a band of soldiers had seized power. Things had only gotten worse after that.

He moved into the street, nodding a greeting to a fellow citizen. Closer to his target he drew, watching for any sign of flight.

"Stanislav? Is that you?" He turned at the distinctly feminine voice. A woman with long, brown hair and a smiling face stood, staring at him.

"Evira? What are you doing here?"

"Well, that's a fine question," she replied. "Can't a person go shopping? I can't spend ALL my time serving drinks to men like you."

He stared back at her, his quarry now forgotten. "Then perhaps you might join me for dinner sometime, instead?"

"I would like that."

Movement off to his side drew his attention. "I'm sorry, Evira, I must go. I'll catch up with you at the Elk to make arrangements."

"I look forward to it."

The target had tossed his apple to the side and was now running away.

"For Saint's sake!" called out Stanislav as he broke into a run. His target was quick, but the bounty hunter was wily. When the man went down a street that ran in a loop, Stanislav cut across a side street, emerging ahead of his quarry.

He drew his sword. "Give it up, Sadron. It's all over."

The man pulled out his own blade, a long, serrated knife. "And face the noose? I don't think so."

Sadron charged forward while Stanislav brought his sword up, quickly blocking the blow. He had been raised in the streets of Karslev, little more than a thug himself until he found a new life under the apprenticeship of a mage hunter. The old moves came back to him despite his advanced years. Sadron struck again, this time slicing through the air to give Stanislav a light cut across the arm.

"Really?" said the bounty hunter. "That was my good shirt!"

He struck out, jabbing the tip of his sword into the fellow's thigh. Instead of backing up, Sadron moved in closer, wielding the knife with lightning speed. Stanislav was at a distinct disadvantage and dropped his sword, grabbing his opponent's forearms in an attempt to hold him at bay. He felt the weight bearing down on him and then fell backwards, the wind knocked from his lungs. Sadron quickly straddled him, raising a knife for an overhead stab.

Stanislav punched the man in the throat, using an old technique from his street days. His foe fell back, gasping for air, and clutching his neck while the bounty hunter got to his feet. He loomed over his target, watching for any signs of surrender, but it was not to be. Instead, the fool struck out with his fists, a blow easily avoided.

"Do that again, and I'll stick you," said Stanislav, drawing his dagger. He waited a moment as Sadron struggled to breathe.

"Now, are you done?" The prone man nodded. "Good, then get up. I've a bounty to collect." The bounty hunter looked around, noting the onlookers. "Everything is fine," he said. "This man is a wanted criminal."

The interaction nearly cost him his life. Sadron, using the distraction, had somehow retrieved his knife and reached out, sinking the tip into Stanislav's calf. The bounty hunter fell to his knees, feeling the jarring impact of the cobblestones. Another slash cut his arm, and then pain shot through him as the flesh tore open.

He struck back, forcing his own dagger forward, feeling it scrape along bone until it sank into the man's chest. Blood gushed forth, and then Sadron's eyes rolled up into his head, and he fell back with a loud thud.

"NO!" screamed Stanislav. He crawled forward, attempting to stem the flow of blood, but it was too late. The man was gone, and with him, a substantial bounty. The bounty hunter stumbled to his feet, his leg throbbing, then looked around, getting his bearings. The Brothers of Saint Mathew had a mission some two blocks away. The real issue was getting there.

The altercation had drawn a large crowd, including a familiar face. "Evira?" he called out.

The woman came closer. "What happened?"

"This man is a criminal. He resisted my attempts to bring him to justice." She paled as she saw blood on his leg and arm, "You're hurt!"

"I must get this body to the guardsmen if I am to collect my reward."

"You're in no shape to be going anywhere, let alone carrying a body."

"There's little choice if I'm to eat. Coins don't grow on trees."

"Well, at least let me help you," she said as she ripped the hem of her skirt. "I'll bind your wounds, and for Saint's sake, sit down before you pass out. You're as pale as a ghost!"

He sank down to rest beside the body of Sadron while she bandaged him up.

Grifken Skylar looked up as the door flew open, not an uncommon occurrence as fate would have it. Officially, he was a member of the warrior's guild, a particularly grandiose name for what amounted to the gang of soldiers who had seized control of Ebenstadt. He was also the man responsible for disbursing bounties, clearly something that would be occupying a portion of his time this day.

"Stanislav," he said in greeting. "Who have you there?"

The bounty hunter limped into the room, depositing a body onto a nearby table. "This is Sadron."

Skylar frowned. "We wanted him alive."

"Not my fault. He resisted arrest."

"He's of little use to us as a corpse. We hoped to recruit him."

"Recruit him? The man's a murderer."

"Yes. The perfect enforcer for collecting taxes."

Stanislav shook his head. Was there no end to the greed amongst these people? "At least he's off the street. That must be worth something, surely?"

"A few pieces of silver at most."

"Silver? The man was worth plenty more than that when you raised the bounty."

"Yes, but as I said, that was for bringing him in alive."

"Fine, I'll take the silver." He waited as Skylar counted out a dozen coins, then scooped them off the table.

"There's another bounty if you're interested?"

Stanislav winced. "No. I've had enough excitement for today."

"You could join the guild. We're always looking for tough individuals."

"To force more coins from these poor townsfolk? No, thank you."

"Your loss."

"I believe I can live with that." He turned, leaving the room as quickly as his sore leg would permit.

Stanislav sat at the Elk, nursing a tankard of ale. He was in a foul mood, made all the worse by the paltry amount of coins he'd earned this day. As a mage hunter, he had made a decent living, but here, in this Saints forsaken city, he could barely feed himself.

"Another ale?" He looked up to see Evira.

"I'm sorry," he said. "I can't. I need to watch my funds."

Her eyes swept the room, always on the lookout for new patrons, but seeing none, she sat.

"You know, you don't always need coins to find companionship." She smiled, something he found contagious.

"You're right, of course. My apologies."

She continued. "You never told me how you came to be in Ebenstadt. Where did you come from, originally?"

"I was born and raised in Karslev, but I wasn't always a bounty hunter. In fact, I used to make a living working for the Volstrum."

"What's that?"

"It's a magical academy."

"Are you saying you're a mage?"

Stanislav chuckled at the thought. "No, although I was good at finding new talent."

"Is that what brought you here, to Ebenstadt?"

"In a sense," he said. "Years ago, I befriended a young girl who I had found, and now she's as close to a daughter as I'll ever have. Anyway, this girl completed her training as a mage and then ran away."

"And you came here looking for her?"

"I did, although not for my former employer. I'm afraid it's a complicated story."

"Did you find her?" Evira asked.

"I did, as a matter of fact, but she isn't in Ebenstadt anymore. It was far too dangerous for her."

"Then why did you remain here?"

"I worried those searching for her might return. My duty now is to watch for anyone seeking information about her."

"But in the meantime, you still need to eat."

"Precisely. That's why I became a bounty hunter—the only profession I could think of that would let me keep an eye on things."

"Listen," she said. "I know you said coins were in short supply. What if, instead of taking me out for food, you come to my house for dinner?"

"You own a house?"

"Well, I rent a room upstairs, but I do get free food from the kitchen."

"I shouldn't like to take advantage of you."

"Even if I really want you to?" Evira said. "You know they say two can live as cheaply as one."

"Are you asking me to move in with you?"

"Would that be such a bad thing?"

"But you know next to nothing about me."

"Then you can tell me all about yourself tonight unless you've something better to do?"

He smiled. "In that case, how can I refuse."

"So you'll move in?"

"Well, let's not get carried away. We'll start with dinner, and see how things progress from there, shall we?"

"I look forward to it." She rose. "Now, you'll have to excuse me. There are other customers to attend to." Stanislav watched her walk away.

"Is that your woman?"

He turned to see a familiar face.

"Brother Yaromir, what brings you here today?"

"Temple Knights still have to eat."

"Yes, but I thought you'd do that at the mission."

"Have you tasted the stuff they serve there? A warrior needs meat!"

"But don't you need to stand guard?"

Yaromir laughed. "There are only two of us, Stanislav. We can't be on duty all the time."

"Then why did they send you to Ebenstadt?"

"They had to do something to protect our interests, especially now that all the Cunars have fled."

"Well," said Stanislav, "you might as well join me, although I won't be here much longer."

"Why? Are you moving on?"

"No, but my purse is not bottomless. I must seek further employment or starve."

"Well then, let me at least extend you the courtesy of a drink, compliments of the Church."

"Now, that, I would gladly accept."

Yaromir called out for two tankards of ale, then sat. "I don't mind telling you I'm worn out."

"Trouble?"

"Yes. Apparently, the leaders of this city decided to tax the Church."

"The Church is exempt from taxes, isn't it?"

"Tell them that!" said the brother. "They keep sending thugs to make threats. I don't believe they truly grasp the implications should they continue."

Evira leaned close to Stanislav to place two ales before them, close enough that he could smell her scent.

"There you go," she said.

Brother Yaromir gave her some coins. "Thank you, good woman."

"My pleasure," she said, although her eyes were on Stanislav the entire time.

"She likes you," said the Temple Knight.

"And I, her, but it takes more than passion to survive, and coins are scarce these days."

"That's because that so-called guild is hoarding everything they can get their hands on. Why don't you join them and line your pockets?"

"No," said Stanislav. "I'd end up having to kill them all. I can't stand people like that."

"Be assured you're in good company."

A cool breeze blew across the table. Stanislav turned his gaze towards the door only to notice that a trio of Dwarves had entered and were now deep in conversation with Evira.

"What's that all about?" he wondered aloud.

"What, the Dwarves? Who knows? It's rare to see them this side of the mountains though. Say, you don't suppose they work for the family, do you? You did mention they were looking for you."

"That was ages ago," said Stanislav. "They've most likely assumed I'm dead by now."

"Might they be seeking your friends?"

"Possibly. I'd best keep an eye on them."

The trio was shown to a table then Evira disappeared into the kitchen, likely to fetch them a meal.

"Strange folk, aren't they?" said Brother Yaromir.

"I suppose so. I've never really had much reason to interact with them, truth be told."

"I hear they can be stubborn."

Evira reappeared carrying three bowls, which she quickly deposited on the table. She turned to leave, but one of the Dwarves caught her attention. Stanislav couldn't make out what they were talking about, but it seemed serious. There certainly no mistaking the coins they passed on to the woman, far more than was necessary for the meal.

"Why do you think they're here?" asked Brother Yaromir.

"Merchants, I would expect, possibly seeking new trade opportunities? I hear it's a common enough practice amongst them. In any case, I suspect they're relatively harmless."

Evira appeared out of nowhere, taking a seat. Stanislav looked at her in surprise.

"Something wrong?" he asked.

"Not particularly, but I remembered you said you were short of funds." She nodded at the trio. "Those Dwarves over there are looking for someone. I thought they might hire you on to help."

"Who are they looking for?" asked Brother Yaromir.

"Someone named Athgar. Do you know him?"

"Not I," said the Temple Knight. "What about you, Stanislav?"

The bounty hunter had gone pale. "Did you say Athgar?"

"I did," said Evira.

"Did they say anything about Natalia?"

"No, but they did mention he was travelling with a woman. Why? Is that important?"

"Do you remember that young girl I mentioned earlier?"

"You mean the one you considered like a daughter?"

"Yes. Her name is Natalia."

She leaned in close, lowering her voice. "Are you saying those Dwarves are looking for her?"

"It certainly looks like it."

She cast a glance at her new patrons. "What will you do?"

In answer, he looked at Brother Yaromir. "They must be working for the family. Why else would they be looking for Athgar and Natalia?"

"Dwarves? Working for the family? Are you sure?"

"It wouldn't be the first time they've hired outside help. It appears I shall have to do something about them."

"Would you like a hand?"

"This is not a Church issue," said Stanislav.

"True, but I do consider you a friend."

"I may need to kill them."

"Come now, murder will do no good. They'll only send someone else. Better to learn the truth of the matter, surely?"

"What would you suggest?"

"Why don't you talk to them?" suggested Evira.

Stanislav looked around, seeking faces in the crowd. "This is not the place for such talk. It would draw too much attention."

"You could wait until they leave?"

"She makes a good point," said the knight. "And I could back you up in case they prove hostile. Not many would willingly take on a Temple Knight, even if only a lowly Mathewite."

"I'll gladly take you up on that offer, my friend," said Stanislav.

"And what about me?" asked Evira. "What can I do to help?"

"Keep an eye on them, and let us know when they're about to leave."

"I can do that."

He saw the look of eagerness in her eyes. "Be careful. We don't want them to suspect anything."

"I'll be as discreet as possible. This is just so exciting!" She returned to her duties, a noticeable spring in her step.

"It appears you made her day," said Yaromir.

"So I have," replied Stanislav. "I only hope it doesn't lead to trouble for her. The family can be extremely unforgiving."

"Take a deep breath, my friend. We don't know for sure they work for the family."

"Don't we? What other explanation could there be?"

"What if this is a different Athgar? People do have the same names from time to time."

"You and I both know Athgar is not a common name—it's Therengian. How many of those folks do you see in these parts?"

"Quite a few to the east," said the Temple Knight, "or so I'm told. Wasn't it Therengians who defeated the Holy Army?"

"You tell me. You're the one who's taken Holy Orders."

"That's not fair," said Brother Yaromir. "I only arrived AFTER the fact. Whoever it was, though, put the fear of the old Gods into the Brothers of Saint Cunar. They cleared out of Ebenstadt as if they were being chased by denizens of the Underworld."

"Yet your order stayed?"

"We did, and we shall continue to do so, despite the hostility of the new rulers."

"Have you thought of sending for reinforcements?"

"I have, as a matter of fact," said the knight. "Unfortunately, our order is stretched to the limit in this region of the Continent. Thus, we have only two Temple Knights assigned to the mission when there should, by all rights, be more than half a dozen."

Evira passed by, carrying a tankard. "They're leaving," she whispered.

Stanislav looked over at the trio of Dwarves. They had stood and were throwing on their cloaks. The taller of the three tossed some coins onto the table, and then they made their way outside.

"Come," said the bounty hunter, wincing as he stood. "It's time we found out what these three are up to."

# THE MOOT

## SPRING 1105

As Laruhk urged the tusker forward, the rope grew taut, and then the massive timber lifted into position and slid into the hole. Men ran to fill in the space with dirt and stones, locking it into place.

Kargen grinned. The work was progressing much faster than he had hoped, helped, no doubt, by the presence of these massive beasts. The palisade now covered fully one quarter the perimeter of Runewald, including the portion occupied by the Orcs. Their plan was to encompass both settlements with a single wall, with two separate gates for ease of access.

Being familiar with the defences of Ord-Kurgad, the Orc chieftain had been asked to supervise the construction, a task he'd embraced with great enthusiasm. He first organized the workers into groups. The Orcs, being physically stronger, were employed to move the massive timbers into place, while the Humans cut down timber and filled in the base as the wall was constructed.

The first few wall sections had been a disaster, but they soon learned from their mistakes, and now the process was running smoothly. Very likely, the entire palisade would be in place by the summer, assuming nothing else interrupted their progress. He noticed Natalia coming towards him, her tiny youngling held tightly against her.

"I see things are going well," she called out. "You've made excellent headway."

"Agreed, yet there is still much to be done."

She looked at the work in progress. "Is that where the gate will go?"

"One of them," he replied. "The other will be farther north, where the trail heads to Scarburn."

"You've thought this through quite thoroughly."

Kargen grinned. "I have, but you are the one who deserves the credit."

"Me? It was your idea to build a palisade."

"Yes, but you convinced the villagers it was in their best interests."

"Will it be large enough, do you think?"

"Yes. We moved it back from the edge to make room for future growth. The crops will still need to be grown outside the walls, but I understand that is normal for Humans?"

"It is," Natalia said, "although we'll need to build a storehouse inside the walls."

"There is much to keep us busy."

"And is that a bad thing?"

"No, not at all," said Kargen. "Quite the reverse. Busy hands make for progress, and the more Orcs and Humans work together, the greater the bond between them. You have earned well the title of High Mage."

"High mage? Who came up with that?"

Kargen blushed, turning a darker shade of green. "My apologies. I was to keep it a secret."

"Let me guess. It was Athgar's idea?"

"Yes, but he wanted it to be a surprise."

"Then I shan't disappoint him," promised Natalia. "High Mage! You know I rather like it."

"It was either that or Warmaster. Also an apt title considering your presence won us the battle."

"It was all of us working together that defeated the enemy. I only made suggestions."

"And yet," said Kargen, "it was your plan that won it for us."

"All right, that's enough flattery for now. I came out here to tell you the thanes are arriving. Assuming you can be spared, can you gather the chieftains?"

"I can. Kragor will take care of things here."

"Good, then we'll meet at the thane's hall whenever you're ready."

"I shall be there directly."

Athgar took a seat. It was strange sitting at a table, for a change, but he had to agree it was easier to see everyone without smoke getting in one's eyes.

Across from him sat Galan, Thane of Scarburn. While it was the closest village distance-wise, not so much in terms of outlook. Galan was a stubborn man, portly of stature with a hunger for food Athgar thought insatiable. Wynfrith, the sole woman amongst the thanes, sat to Galan's right, her long hair in two braids that fell over her shoulders to hang to her front. She was the most moderate of the Therengians present, although that certainly didn't stop her from voicing her opinion on everything she could.

Aswulf of Thaneford rounded out the Therengian delegates. He was a great uncle to Harwath, but that didn't make him any more reasonable in Athgar's eyes. The man was old, far older than anyone thought possible for a Human. Rumour was he was almost sixty, but then again, maybe he only appeared that age because of his nearly white hair.

The door opened, admitting Kargen and the other chieftains. Zharuhl and Kirak, both imposing figures, loomed over their Human counterparts.

All sat as Skora placed cups before them. Kargen nodded his thanks, but everyone else ignored her, concentrating instead on Athgar.

"Well?" said Wynfrith. "Are we to begin or sit here drinking all day?"

"We are waiting," Athgar replied.

"For what?"

"For the arrival of our High Mage."

"High Mage?" said Galan. "Don't be preposterous. We don't have a High Mage."

"We do now. I appointed her this morning."

"This is a moot, not a social gathering."

"Precisely why I invited her here. Did you forget we owe our very existence to her victory?"

"Nonsense," said Aswulf. "You led the battle."

"No, I led the Runewald fyrd. Natalia was the one who oversaw the battle, and her plan allowed us to defeat the enemy."

Aswulf sat back, obviously upset with the delay.

The door opened, and Natalia entered, drawing all eyes. "Sorry," she said. "I had to feed our child." She looked at Athgar. "She's with Shaluhk."

"You left your daughter with an Orc?" said Galan.

"Why wouldn't I? She is a member of the tribe, as am I."

The statement stunned the Thane of Scarburn. His mouth flapped open, but nothing came out as he lapsed into silence.

"Thank you, High Mage," said Athgar. "Come. Sit with us that we may benefit from your experience." He indicated the seat beside him. She strolled past the other thanes, taking her rightful place. Skora soon placed a cup before her.

"Goat's milk," she said. "We don't want to spoil your own."

"Now," said Athgar. "There is much I'd like to discuss, but I thought I'd open the opportunity for anyone to bring up concerns they might have."

"I would like to know why they're here?" said Galan, pointing at the Orcs.

"They're our allies, and as such, should be included in any decisions we make."

"But their contributions are only military. This is a meeting of civil leaders, not the fyrd."

Natalia cleared her throat to get their attention. "Any discussion of the villages would, of necessity, include measures to protect them, and therefore must include our allies."

"Yes," added Athgar, "and the presence of their tribes are likely the only reason the Petty Kingdoms have not retaliated for their recent loss."

"Are you saying we're facing invasion?" Galan asked.

"Not at this exact moment," said Natalia, "but it would seem inevitable. The Church, in particular, has suffered a terrible loss. They'll be eager to avenge themselves."

"Even against the tuskers?" said Wynfrith.

"That threat will hold sway for a while yet," said Kargen, "but eventually, people will forget how devastating they were and begin to talk once more of war."

"When will all of this finally end?" asked Galan.

Athgar looked around the room. "When we gain recognition as an independent kingdom."

"We are only four villages," said Aswulf. "Hardly a kingdom."

"You forget the Orcs," replied Athgar. "They swell our numbers."

"That's all well and good, but we're still vastly outnumbered by the skrollings in Ebenstadt."

"This is true, but time is on our side. Even as we speak, more of our people are joining us."

"Tell me something I don't know," said Wynfrith. "Bradon is already full to bursting. We need to do something about it."

"What would you have us do?" asked Galan.

"We must start a new settlement," suggested Aswulf.

"And where would we do that? The area is thick with pines."

"Ashborne," said Aswulf.

"Ashborne was burned to the ground years ago, as well you know."

"A fact of which I'm well aware. I'm suggesting we rebuild it."

Galan grumbled. "Is that the best you can come up with?"

"No, wait. Hear me out. We know the land is fertile, and there's plenty of fresh water nearby."

"Yes, and it sits close to Ebenstadt. Resettling that place will only antagonize the new city rulers."

"Not if we protect it," said Kargen.

"And how would we do that?" asked Wynfrith. "You're not suggesting we build a palisade there, in the middle of nowhere?"

"No," replied the Orc. "At least not quite yet. Instead, we build huts. My hunters will keep the area under careful watch, intercepting anyone who might come to do us harm."

Galan snorted. "And why would Orcs do that for Humans?"

"Because we are your friends."

"Yes," said Athgar, "and we would do the same for them if it came to it."

"The idea has some merit," said Wynfrith, "although it would open up a whole new host of problems."

"Such as?"

"Well, for a start, a new village means a new thane."

"Easily done," said Athgar. "What else?"

"There's also the matter of the local fyrd. We can't leave Ashborne's defence solely the responsibility of the Orcs. Do we then strip our own villages to protect this new one?" She looked at Natalia. "You're the master of battle. What say you?"

"In the short term," replied Natalia, "I would recommend each village send a delegation of fyrd members to Ashborne. Let's say a dozen each. Of course, once the village begins to grow, they can train their own warriors."

"What of crops?" said Wynfrith. "It's getting late in the planting season, and the fields will be overgrown with weeds and trees."

"We can provide game," offered Kargen.

"Yes," said Natalia, "and the fields can be marked off and cleared for planting next year."

"And if they're attacked?" continued Wynfrith.

"We will build a keep."

They all stared at her.

"A fortification," Natalia explained. "Initially made of wood, but raised up on a mound of earth."

"That would take too long," said Galan.

"Not so," said Zharuhl. "My shamans are more than capable of moving earth and setting stone. With the High Mage's supervision, we could build a workable defence in a few months. It would, no doubt, pale in comparison to other lands but would provide a place of refuge to the villagers should they be attacked."

"Can we not negotiate with the skrollings?" asked Wynfrith.

Natalia winced. The term skrollings was used to describe any non-Therengian, yet she still found the word offensive. "And who would we send to negotiate?"

"You," said Galan. "They would be more inclined to talk to one of their own."

"She is one of us," insisted Athgar. "I would not put her life in danger."

"In any event," said Kargen, "she can not go. She is still needed here to feed her child."

"There's another problem," said Wynfrith. "With whom would the Humans of Ebenstadt deal? It's a fine thing to send Natalia, but she lacks the authority to act on our behalf. We need to pick a king."

"No," said Athgar. "Eadred was king, and look where that got us? Why should a man rule solely based on who his father was?"

"That's simple," said Galan. "Royal blood."

"Royal blood is no different from ours," insisted Athgar. "And we are thanes, chosen by our villages to rule on their behalf, not here by right of birth. That was always the custom in Athelwald. I would hope the same holds true here."

"But we cannot have everyone in all our villages elect a king. The feat would be nigh on impossible."

"True," said Kargen, "but the thanes are the chosen representatives of their villages, are they not? Why not let them choose the next king?"

"He makes a valid point," said Wynfrith.

"I might suggest a slight modification to that," said Natalia. "The thanes vote to elect a new leader, but that leader should be approved by a majority of the Orc chieftains. That way, their interests are guaranteed to be looked after."

"A good idea," said Athgar.

"Why involve the Orcs at all?" said Galan.

Kargen growled, a low, rumbling sound that filled the room. "Because whoever they choose would also represent US. We must stand united or be picked apart. Can you not see that?"

"Yes," added Natalia, "and whatever method we use would continue going forward, so future generations wouldn't be cursed with another Eadred."

"And how long would such a leader rule?" asked Wynfrith.

Athgar looked at Kargen. "I believe the Orcs' system would work well, don't you?"

Kargen turned to address the thanes. "Orc leaders rule until they die or choose to step down. However, should the tribe desire it, they can remove a chieftain by a simple casting of the stones."

"Casting of stones?" said Galan. "I don't think I follow."

"It's the method used to select their leader," explained Athgar. "It works particularly well."

"It's an interesting concept," said Wynfrith, "but I'm not sure it's something we're ready for just yet. Let's put this whole idea of a king off the table for a while. That will let us go back to our respective villages and see what others think."

"An excellent idea," said Galan. "What about you, Aswulf?"

The old man nodded. "A wise decision, I believe. Now, Athgar, you spoke of something you wanted to talk of earlier. What was it?"

"The fyrd, actually. I thought we needed something more permanent."

"In ancient times, there was a thane guard," said Galan. "A select group of warriors who were well-armed and equipped with the finest armour available."

"But we have no armour," said Aswulf.

"Not exactly true," noted Athgar. "We captured quite a bit on the battlefield. The real problem is we lack the knowledge to maintain it."

"We have smiths."

"True, but none skilled in the maintenance of armour."

"Could we not buy some in Ebenstadt?" asked Wynfrith.

Galan was incensed. "You want us to go to the exact same city that wants us destroyed?"

"What other choice do we have?"

Natalia stood, gaining everyone's attention. "It's not practical at this time to consider anything but the crudest of armour. I would suggest, however, we give serious consideration to a permanent, trained group of warriors. Call them a thane guard if you like or a hearth guard, but they would be trained for battle, not used as the personal bodyguards of rulers."

"And who would train them?" asked Galan. "You? You're not even a warrior yourself."

"I never claimed to be. I am, however, a battle mage, trained in the art of managing war, both magical and material. You select the people, and I'll arrange for their training."

"How many would you require?"

"I would suggest a dozen from each village. Send them here to Runewald."

"And the Orcs?" said Kargen. "Would they, too, receive this training?"

"If you wish, although I believe them better utilized as skirmishers. That way they can work to their strengths."

"Which are?" said Galan.

"Deadly accuracy with the bow along with the ability to close with the enemy when needed. They also have the tuskers, and that, my friends, gives us a distinct advantage in battle. Speaking of which, I should like to increase their numbers."

"I can talk with Rugg," said Zharuhl. "We can have hunters searching for more within a ten-day."

"How long does it take to train those beasts?" asked Wynfrith.

The chief of the Stone Crushers smiled. "We do not train them. Rather, we use magic to communicate with them."

"Are you saying you can talk to them?"

"Not me personally, but our masters of earth are capable of a sharing of emotions and thoughts. I have heard it described as more of a collaboration."

"How many of these tuskers are at our disposal?"

"It is not the tuskers that limit our numbers, but the number of masters of earth. At present, we have only three, and we need to utilize them elsewhere."

"So much for the tuskers," grumbled Galan.

Natalia was not to be deterred. "We still have the masters of flame, and that gives us the advantage in terms of magic. Few of the Petty Kingdoms could boast of more than a single mage, yet we have many."

"How many?" asked Wynfrith.

"Nine, if you want an exact count."

All the thanes showed surprise. "That many?" said Galan.

Natalia smiled. "Including the Orcs, we have three Earth Mages, three Life Mages, or shamans as they call them, two Fire Mages, and, of course, myself, a Water Mage. They were used to great effect at the Battle of the Standing Stones. And I believe, with a little practice in cooperation, they could become an even greater threat to our enemies."

"Could we not have some mages of our own?" asked Aswulf.

"It takes years of training to master the arcane arts," explained Natalia, "and not everyone shows potential. The Orcs have their own traditions with such things. We Humans, however, do not, at least not here amongst our villages. Could we change that in the future? Of course we could, but it would take time and effort we can't afford at this moment. For the present, we should concentrate on what we CAN do—build a standing army. The hearth guard, or whatever you want to call it, would be the first step."

There were nods all around the table.

"I like this idea," said Wynfrith, "although it will take some effort to convince others. I suggest we each send a dozen of our best warriors for training here in Runewald. What say the rest of you?" She looked around, seeing nodding heads. "It appears we have our answer."

"Good," said Galan. "Now, let us adjourn the moot and celebrate the progress we made this day. I don't know about you, but I'm famished!"

# COUSINS

## SPRING 1105

Stanislav stepped from the Elk into the busy street, struggling to spot his targets. As chance would have it, a wagon rolled by, narrowly missing the trio, forcing them to jump back in alarm. Stanislav waited as Brother Yaromir exited the tavern and joined him.

"Over there," he said, keeping his voice low.

"You lead," said the Temple Knight. "I fear my armour will make me too conspicuous."

Stanislav looked at the archaic chainmail. The Temple Knights of Saint Mathew eschewed the plate armour favoured by other orders. Instead, they wore the iron links to symbolize their humility. In addition, they carried axes, not only as a weapon but to represent their vow of poverty. He shook his head, clearing his mind of such thoughts. His targets had moved up the street, oblivious to the fact they were being tailed.

The Dwarves didn't appear to be in any hurry, stopping at stalls and peering into shops to see what might lie within. Stanislav suspected they were getting the lay of the land— though, for what reason, he had no idea. They found themselves at a crossroads and turned left, leaving the two Humans to hurry up or risk losing them. Stanislav rounded the corner, followed by the Temple Knight, and they both scanned the crowd.

"There they are," said Yaromir, pointing. He started to move, but Stanislav caught him by the arm.

"Hold. Something's wrong." The bounty hunter stared a moment. "I only see two. You?"

"It's as you say. By the Saints, they're slippery folk, these Dwarves. Where did the third one go?"

"Let's get closer. Perhaps our view of him is simply obstructed. Take your time though. We don't want to draw attention."

"I'll take the right side of the street," said Yaromir. "You take the left."

They split up, moving amongst the locals at a slow pace. The two Dwarves they could see were busy looking at a merchant's goods, ignoring all around them. One of them turned towards Stanislav, forcing the bounty hunter to duck into a doorway.

"Looking for me?"

He turned in surprise. The third Dwarf, now brandishing a pickaxe, emerged from the store, his eyes locked on the Human.

"I haven't the foggiest idea what you're talking about."

"Come now, do you take me for a fool? I saw you eyeing us at that tavern. What is it you're after, coins?" The Dwarf chuckled. "You Humans never learn, do you? You can't separate a Dwarf from his wealth."

Stanislav reached for his sword, but his opponent took a step closer. "I wouldn't if I were you, else I'll be forced to use this pick. Now, out with it— why are you following us?"

"I heard you're looking for a pair of mages."

"What's it to you?"

"They're friends of mine, and I would not see them harmed."

"What makes you think I want to harm them?"

"You're strangers here."

The Dwarf stared back. "Of course we're strangers. We're Dwarves!"

"No, I mean you're outsiders, asking suspicious questions."

"Suspicious, is it? Well, where I'm from, we like to be direct. You say you know these mages? How do I know YOU don't mean them harm?"

Stanislav ignored the question. "Who are you?"

"The name's Belgast, Belgast Ridgehand."

"And how do you know Athgar and Natalia?"

The Dwarf lowered his pick. "Now that is an incredibly long tale."

Stanislav glanced about. "We appear to have lots of time unless, of course, you're in a hurry to be somewhere?"

"Not at all, but there are far more comfortable places to talk than in a doorway." Belgast moved aside as a patron left the building. The woman paused, looking nervously at the two of them, then hurried on her way.

"What are you suggesting?"

"Well," said the Dwarf, "for one thing, you can let me know your name."

"Stanislav Voronsky."

"Well then, Stanislav, why don't we go and get that friend of yours, then find someplace we can talk, all civilized like?"

The bounty hunter stepped out from the doorway and waved over

Brother Yaromir. Belgast, in turn, motioned for the other two Dwarves to join them.

"This is Brother Yaromir," said Stanislav. "He's a Temple Knight of Saint Mathew."

Belgast looked him over carefully. "At least you're not a Cunar." He extended his hand. "Well met, Brother Knight, and may the good Saint watch over us all."

"Blessings to you also, Sir Dwarf."

The Dwarf smiled at the greeting. "As I was saying to your friend here earlier, my name is Belgast Ridgehand, and these are my cousins, Kieren Brightaxe and Targan Hardhammer."

"What brings a trio of Dwarves to Ebenstadt?" asked Brother Yaromir.

"I'm looking for some friends of mine."

"Here?"

"I guess I'd best start at the beginning?"

"That would be appreciated," said Stanislav.

"I was part of a mining expedition working out of Ostermund."

"Never heard of it."

"It's a small village in the duchy of Krieghoff. It lies south of the mountain range. Now, this is going to sound a bit far-fetched, but some... people... arranged for my cousins to be killed, staging it to look like an Orc attack."

"Let me guess," said Yaromir. "The Temple Knights of Saint Cunar?"

"Yes, although we didn't know that until much later. It turned out they were seeking an excuse to wipe out a group of Orcs, a tribe known as the Red Hand."

"Why?" asked the Temple Knight.

"I'm not sure I should say."

"Come now. If you can't trust a Mathewite, who can you trust?"

"To be honest, I'd be happier if you were a Sister of Saint Agnes."

Stanislav knitted his brow. "Why would you say that?"

"They helped us root out the plot, but I digress. We successfully defeated the Cunars, then I had to return my cousins' belongings to their families. I left with the intent of eventually returning, and then things took an unexpected turn."

"Which was?"

"Give me a moment, and I'll get to it. I ran across my cousins here, Kieren and Targan. They're both smiths. I thought to myself, here's a chance to make some coins and benefit my new friends. The idea was to return to the Orc village and have them set up smithies. The Orcs love to trade for

Dwarven goods, you know, and I figured since they had just fought off an attack, they might want weapons or armour."

"And the unexpected turn of events?" pressed Stanislav.

"Ah, yes. Well, in my absence, the Duke of Krieghoff decided to wipe out the Orcs once and for all. He was, by the way, also implicated in the original assault."

"So the Orcs were all killed?"

"No, many of them escaped, fleeing eastward. By the time I got there, the Duke of Holstead had decided he couldn't stomach the presence of so many foreign troops on his land, and an all-out war had erupted."

Stanislav frowned. "I still don't see how that brought you here, to Ebenstadt?"

Belgast fidgeted. "I'm getting to it! Now, where was I? Oh yes. We arrived at what was left of the Orc village and headed east, hoping to track them down, figuring Athgar and Natalia were likely with them. Now Holstead was at war, remember. Luckily, they had little fear of a trio of Dwarves. In any event, I managed to determine the Orcs went north through the mountains. Now, I don't know about you, but I don't fancy crossing peaks in the middle of winter. So we decided to travel west and circumnavigate them."

"Bringing you to Ebenstadt."

"That's correct. Mind you, we intend to go farther east to pick up the trail north of the mountain range."

"You'd have a hard time," said Stanislav. "That area is thick with trees."

"Clearly something we hadn't anticipated. In any event, we're here now, and that's our story. Why don't you tell us yours?"

Stanislav smiled. "Now that, as you're fond of saying, is a long story. I used to be a mage hunter."

"You hunted down mages? That's barbaric!"

"Not to kill them! I would find those with the potential to learn magic and take them for training at an academy called the Volstrum. That's how I met Natalia. She was only a young girl at the time, but she grew up to be a powerful Water Mage. Then things took a dark turn, and she wanted out. I helped facilitate her escape."

"And Athgar?"

"I didn't meet him until much later. I was sent by a group called 'the family' to find her but was captured by a rival. He used me as bait to capture Natalia. Obviously, we escaped, but then the Holy Army marched eastward, intent on destroying the Therengians."

"Therengians?" said Belgast. "Here? Those are Athgar's people, aren't they?"

"They are, or at least distant cousins. They forged an alliance with Orcs, including those who fled the village you spoke of. There was a battle last autumn where they faced off against the warriors of the crusade."

Belgast was utterly enthralled. "What happened?"

"Our friends defeated a Holy Army if you can believe it. The Church calls it the Battle of the Wilderness, but the Therengians refer to it as the Battle of the Standing Stones."

"Then where are they now?"

"Farther east," said Stanislav, "in a village called Runewald, or at least they were, the last I heard."

"It was a tremendous loss for the Church," noted Brother Yaromir, "but maybe even worse was the aftermath. The Temple Knights of Saint Cunar suffered horrible losses and soon after abandoned Ebenstadt, leaving it to the mercy of rogues and mercenaries."

"Yes," added Stanislav, "and now the city is plundering the lands to the west, in the Kingdom of Novarsk. It can only lead to war and even more suffering. It seems you picked a bad time to visit."

Belgast shrugged. "It couldn't be helped. Now, how far to the east lies this place, Runewald?"

"I'm told no more than a couple of days, but it's within the great forest. You'd also need to get past the Orcs and Therengians. They don't like outsiders much."

"I have no quarrel with Orcs," said the Dwarf, "but I know little of these Therengians. Still, if Athgar and Natalia are there, I'm sure they'd vouch for us."

"I could take you there," offered Stanislav.

"You'd do that?"

"Why not? It's becoming increasingly difficult to make ends meet here."

Belgast turned to Brother Yaromir. "And you?"

"I'm afraid my duty to my order prevents me from joining you, but should you ever find yourself back in Ebenstadt, I would be glad of a visit."

"I'll keep that in mind."

"When would you like to leave?" asked Stanislav.

"Tomorrow morning," said the Dwarf. "We have some business to attend to first."

"Business?"

"Yes, we'll need to purchase some supplies. After all, we intend to set up a smithy."

"I doubt you can buy a smithy here."

"Don't be daft, man," said Belgast. "We have what we need for that in our wagon. No, we need other supplies, like food. There's no telling what we might find out in the wilderness."

"There are villages out there."

"Yes, but we don't know how prosperous they are. We might arrive to find they have no coins with which to pay for our services, then where would we be?"

"I suppose that's a valid concern," agreed Stanislav. "Are you a smith, too, like your cousins?"

Belgast laughed. "Me, a smith? No, I leave that to my cousins here. I'm more of a supervisor, freeing them up to work the forge. By the way, how much do I owe you for taking us to Runewald?"

"I wasn't expecting payment."

"Come now, you must have expenses, and I've plenty to spare. Perhaps you have outstanding debts here in Ebenstadt?"

Stanislav thought of Evira. "I do have some commitments."

Belgast dug out his purse and counted out some coins. "Here, take this, and don't ever let it be said Dwarves aren't generous." He dropped the gold into Stanislav's hand.

The bounty hunter looked down at the coins. "That is most generous of you."

"Consider it an investment. If things go well, I might have further use of your services."

"What services are those? You hardly know me."

"I know you're friends of Athgar and Natalia. That means you're trustworthy."

"I could be lying?"

Belgast looked him in the eyes. "I'll take that chance. I'm a pretty good judge of character. Now, where shall we meet tomorrow?"

"How about the Elk?" suggested Stanislav. "It's the place where we first spotted you."

"The Elk it is, then. We'll be there at first light, loaded and ready to depart. Assuming that's all right with you?"

"That would be fine."

"I'll come by and escort you to the city gates," offered Brother Yaromir, "in case the local guards give you trouble."

"Thank you," said Belgast. "Would a donation to your order be acceptable?"

"Though not required, it would be greatly appreciated. I'll see to it every coin makes it to the mission."

"Well, now. It seems today hasn't been so bad after all. Good day to you,

Stanislav, and you, too, Brother Yaromir." He bowed respectfully. "May your forefathers look down on you with favour."

Stanislav watched as the Dwarves made their way down the street. "What did you think?" he asked.

"An interesting bunch," said the Temple Knight, "although the cousins didn't say much."

"That may be a language issue. Belgast definitely knows the Human tongue well, but Targan and Kieren didn't seem to take in much."

"Agreed," said Brother Yaromir. "You had concerns they might work for the family. Do you trust them now?"

"I detected no deceit. Doubtless, they have their own agenda, but I rather suspect that has more to do with making a living than anything else. I also have a hard time believing the family would employ Dwarves to do their dirty work."

"Why is that?"

"They tend to believe magic is everything."

"Who's to say the Dwarves can't use magic?"

Stanislav looked at him in surprise. "I hadn't considered that, but I think it unlikely."

"Because they're Dwarves?"

"No. Dwarves are known to have spellcasters, but to my knowledge, none has ever set foot in the Volstrum. They also appear to be smiths."

"We only have their word on that."

"Not so," said Stanislav. "Did you note the heavy musculature and calloused hands? Those are not typical of a mage. They might not be smiths, but they definitely perform some type of manual labour."

"You're a remarkably astute individual."

"It comes from being a mage hunter. My training taught me to look for clues concerning magical affinity, and I saw nothing amongst those Dwarves that would indicate such a thing."

"And if you're wrong?"

Stanislav smiled. "He claims to know Athgar and Natalia. I'll know soon enough if that's true."

"Well," said Brother Yaromir, "I wish you well on your journey, Stanislav. If you're ever back in Ebenstadt, look me up."

"You'll still be there in the morning, won't you?"

"Of course, I gave my word."

"Good. I'll see you then. I have some business of my own to attend to."

"Oh yes? And would that business have something to do with Evira?"

Stanislav blushed. "Perhaps."

"I'll leave you to it, then. I must return to my post."

. . .

All was quiet in the Elk as was often the case mid-morning. Stanislav took a seat, then waited for Evira to come over and take his order.

"The usual?" she asked.

"I wondered if you might join me for a moment or two instead."

She looked around the room, but seeing no one else waiting for drinks, she sat. Stanislav struggled for words, his face holding a melancholy expression, something the woman quickly picked up on. "Is something wrong?"

He forced a smile. "Yes and no. I need to leave town for a while, but I will be back. I promise you."

"Is this something to do with those Dwarves?"

"It is, as a matter of fact. They engaged my services to take them eastward."

"Into the Wildlands? That's dangerous, isn't it?"

"Not as dangerous as you might think. My friends are there."

There was no mistaking Evira's look of sadness. "Oh, I see."

He reached across, taking her hand. "I don't intend to stay long, most likely only a few days, but I really can't say for sure. I DO want to return here, though, if only to see you."

Her face brightened considerably. "When do you leave?"

"Tomorrow morning."

"Are we still on for tonight?"

He grinned. "That's what I wanted to talk to you about. I've come into some coin."

"You should save it."

"I'll put some of it away, but I'd like to treat you to a nice meal, one you don't need to scrounge from the kitchen."

Stanislav stared into her eyes, noting some hesitation. "Look," he continued, "I know I'm an old man. If I'm being too forward—"

"No, it's not that," she said. "It's only that I haven't felt this way for many years. The truth is I feel out of my depth."

"As do I. I tell you what, let's take this slowly, all right? Just dinner, no expectation of anything else."

She nodded. "I would like that."

"I also wondered if you might do something for me?"

"If I can. What is it?"

"I don't want to take all this with me into the wilderness. I hoped you'd look after it for me."

"You want ME to look after your coins? Surely there are others better suited to such a task?"

"Perhaps, but I need someone I can trust. I don't expect trouble, but these are dangerous times. If something were to happen to me, I'd at least have the comfort of knowing you'd be looked after."

"Don't say that," she said. "It doesn't bear thinking. I'll hold your coins for you, but you must come back to get them, agreed?"

He gazed into her eyes, seeing the commitment, then smiled. "Agreed."

# THE NAMING

## SPRING 1105

Athgar watched as the Runewald fyrd lined up, the men and women eager to show what they were capable of. Many had taken part in the battle last autumn, but others were new, not yet of an age to know the horrors of war.

Natalia came to stand beside him. "They look impressive."

He shrugged. "I'd like to see a bit more discipline. Note how ragged their line is?"

"They'll get there in time."

"Where's the baby?"

She nodded to her left. "Over there with Shaluhk. Agar is quite taken with her. I suppose I can't blame him. She's the closest thing to a sister he has."

"Not to change the subject, but have you had a chance to look over all that armour we recovered from the battle?"

"I have," said Natalia, "and we've managed to scavenge some decent pieces, but we lack the skill to repair most of it. I'm sure, in time, our smiths will be up to the challenge, but for now, we need to limit ourselves to helmets and greaves."

Athgar kept his eyes on the fyrd. They were advancing now, shields held together in an overlapping manner. "I suppose a shield wall is an old tactic by today's standards."

"It is," she replied, "but still effective from time to time. The real trick to using it is discipline, like you said earlier."

Athgar gazed off to his right. "Ah," he said. "Here comes Laruhk."

"Laruhk? He's not part of the fyrd, is he?"

"No, but I thought it might prove worthwhile to get our men and women used to the tuskers."

"I must admit they're fearsome beasts," said Natalia.

"You managed to wield them well enough. They won us the battle."

"It wasn't easy. None of my training prepared me for such creatures. I had to improvise."

"Well," said Athgar, "your instincts were spot on."

"You had a fyrd back in Athelwald, didn't you?"

"We did. Why?"

"I was merely curious as to how often they practiced."

"Once a month, usually. Not that it proved any use when the slavers attacked."

"You mean the Cunars?" said Natalia. "I doubt anything could have stopped them."

"Here we practice twice a month, although maybe we should increase that?"

Natalia shook her head. "We can't. In the end, these people still have crops and animals to tend to."

"Do they not use fyrds in the Petty Kingdoms?" he asked.

"Many kingdoms have something similar called a regional levy. It calls up all the men capable of bearing arms to handle an invasion or predatory bandits."

"Only the men? Can women not fight too?"

She laughed. "Apparently not, except for the Temple Knights of Saint Agnes, of course."

"That would cut their potential army in half, wouldn't it?"

"I guess that's one way to look at it, but they believe it's a woman's duty to care for the young."

"Their loss, I suppose," said Athgar.

They both watched as the fyrd completed its advance. Then, as they halted, their spears came down, presenting a formidable obstacle.

"Do they always use spears?" asked Natalia.

"Only to ward off horsemen. Those in a shield wall who've closed with the enemy would prefer to use long knives or axes. Swords would work, too, although I suppose they wouldn't be too effective against plate armour."

"And they would typically have archers?"

"They would," he said, "but as you know, here we rely on the Orcs for that."

"I'm well aware," said Natalia. "The other tribes are starting to adopt Kargen's warbows."

Athgar laughed.

"Something funny?" she asked.

"Yes. I was the one who designed those bows."

"Ah, yes, I remember now," said Natalia. "Perhaps I should refer to them as Athgar's bows?"

"Warbows is fine."

The fyrd took a break, the men and women drifting apart to talk or get a drink. Athgar turned to Natalia.

"So?" he asked. "What did you think?"

"They have a lot of potential, but we're in desperate need of some kind of armour we can maintain. I wonder if we could hire out a smith from Ebenstadt?"

"I'm not sure that would be well received. Can you imagine the look on those people's faces if Therengians showed up to hire an armourer?"

"I suppose that's true," she said. "I had thought about selling all that captured armour in Ebenstadt, but it just feels wrong, like we're arming our own enemies."

"What about all the horses?" asked Athgar.

She frowned. "Most of them are the property of the Church. Any reputable horse trader wouldn't touch them. We have some hooked up to ploughs, but they're warhorses, ill-bred for such tasks. In the meantime, they eat us out of house and home."

"I wish there were some Church members around here we could trust, then we could return them. That might buy us some goodwill."

"And have them used against us again? No, thank you."

Athgar gazed at the fyrd scattered across the field. Many were chatting away, caught up in the fraternization that was common with such gatherings. "It feels as though we're trapped."

"In what way?" asked Natalia.

"We have the people—we even have goods, in this case, armour and horses, yet there's nowhere for us to sell them. We really only have one border, and those who live there are hostile towards us. No matter how successful we are, that will never change."

"What you say is true," she agreed, "but we must concentrate on what we CAN do rather than what we can't."

"I suppose you're right."

"You suppose?"

"All right," he said. "I agree with you."

She smiled. "I knew you'd come around, eventually."

Athgar gazed at the sun. "It's almost noon. Shaluhk will be expecting us."

"Yes, we'd best get going." She took his hand, giving it a squeeze. "Just think, we're about to learn our daughter's name!"

. . .

Athgar stared into the flames. They were inside the new chieftain's hut, a large building that could house the entire tribe when needed. At one end was a separate room for the Orc chieftain, while at the other end of the immense structure sat Athgar and Natalia's living space. Beside him was Natalia, their newly born infant in her arms. On his other side sat Kargen and Shaluhk. Rounding out the group were Laruhk, looking quite pleased with himself, and Skora, taking everything in with interest.

Shaluhk was chatting with the old woman. "We will start by saying a blessing and passing around the milk of life, then I shall invoke the Ancestors. You will not be able to see or hear them, but I will."

"And they will give you a name?" asked Skora.

"They will."

"And this 'milk of life', what is it, exactly?"

"A milky-white liquid brewed from a selection of plants. I am told it is similar in taste to some of the stronger mead your people brew, so you might find it quite potent."

"Strong drink doesn't scare me."

"In any event," said Shaluhk, "you only take a sip, then pass it on to the next person."

"And will you conduct the ceremony in Orcish?"

"Yes, but I shall repeat it in the common tongue of Humans in honour of our guests." The shamaness looked over at Natalia. "Ready?"

"You may begin," the Water Mage answered.

Shaluhk took a cleansing breath, letting her eyes wander over the small group. "Since time immemorial, our Ancestors have watched over us, enriching our lives with their advice and experiences. Today we offer a sacrifice to you"—she looked up as if beseeching the sky—"that you might bestow your wisdom on us once again."

Reaching behind her, she pulled forth a bowl filled with the milk of life. It touched her lips briefly, then she handed it to Kargen. He, too, took a sip, then passed it on, and it continued in this manner until all had partaken. Shaluhk then placed it down and began the ceremony.

Words softly flowed from her lips, indistinct at first, then growing in intensity and clarity. The air buzzed with energy, and then Shaluhk's eyes briefly glowed with a white light.

She uttered words first in the Orcish tongue, then repeated them for the Humans in the room. "We seek your guidance this day," said Shaluhk with a tilt to her head. Clearly, she heard something, but the room remained silent.

"This daughter, born to Athgar and Natalia, is a member of our tribe. By what name shall she be known?"

There was a pause, and then she broke into a smile. "A most appropriate name."

The light faded from her eyes as she scanned the group once more. "The Ancestors have spoken."

"And by what name shall our daughter be known?" asked Natalia.

"Her name shall be Oswyn."

"Oswyn?" said Skora.

Athgar grinned. "It means Orc friend."

"I love it," said Natalia. She peered down at the tiny bundle. "Hello, Oswyn."

"The Ancestors are wise," said Kargen. "Her name bridges both our cultures."

Athgar, overcome with emotion, teared up as he leaned forward, kissing his daughter on the forehead. Natalia reached out, taking his hand. "Our daughter has a name!"

The door opened, and Agar rushed in, halting as he saw everyone sitting around the fire.

"Hello, Agar," said Natalia. "Come take a look at your tribe-sister. Her name's Oswyn."

The young Orc stepped closer, leaning in to see better. Agar was only eighteen months old, yet in Human terms, he was closer to that of a three-year-old in both size and development. A smile broke out on his face. "Oswyn, friend," he said.

"That is right," said Shaluhk. She held out her arms, and her son moved to be enfolded by them. "Now, you must mind Oswyn, Agar. Human children need our protection. They do not grow as fast as we do."

"Agar protect Oswyn," shouted the youngling.

The shamaness looked at Kargen. "It looks like your son already knows his duty."

Kargen stood. "As chieftain of this tribe, I proclaim Oswyn, daughter of Athgar and Nat-Alia, a member of the Orcs of the Red Hand. Now, let us repair to the other chamber so the tribe can welcome its newest youngling."

They made their way into the main room, where most of the tribe had gathered. A great firepit ran the length of the place, and Natalia moved to its end, holding their child out for all to see.

"I present to you the newest member of our tribe," said Kargen. "Oswyn."

The Orcs thumped the ground.

"What are they doing?" asked Skora.

"It's their way of showing their approval," said Athgar. "Much like clapping."

"Now," said Shaluhk, "we feast in celebration of this naming."

She sat, allowing the rest to do likewise. Other Orcs soon entered, bearing platters of food.

"I hope you are hungry," said Kargen. "The tribe has been cooking all day in preparation."

"For one child?" said Natalia.

"Oswyn is more than just a child. She represents the future of both our peoples. She is also the daughter of a master of flame, not to mention a master of water. Such a thing is rarely seen amongst my people."

"Such a thing is NEVER seen," added Shaluhk. "I do not recall ever hearing of a union of this type."

Agar squeezed in between his mother and Natalia. "Oswyn, protect," he said, clutching his wooden axe.

Kargen leaned forward to look at his son. "He grows so quickly. We shall soon need to replace that axe of his with something better."

"His bow?" said Laruhk.

"No," said Shaluhk. "As I have told you before, he is too young for a bow. Kargen means a flint axe. Once he masters that, we will move him up to weapons of iron, or better yet, steel."

"We have plenty of those," said Natalia, "but they're made for full-grown Humans."

Laruhk plucked an apple from a nearby platter as it passed by. "When will Oswyn be able to use an axe?"

"Not for many years," said Athgar. "Human children progress much slower than Orcs."

"Then we shall have to rely on Agar to keep her safe."

"I believe WE can manage that," said Natalia.

Laruhk blushed, turning dark green. "Of course, I apologize. I did not mean to offend."

"I can see we still have much to learn from each other," said Kargen.

"Yes," agreed Shaluhk. "It will be interesting to see Oswyn mature. Will she take after her mother, do you think?"

"She has Natalia's eyes," said Athgar.

"Yes, but your complexion," added Skora. "She's a beautiful child, and Oswyn is such a lovely name."

Natalia held her out towards the old woman. "Would you take her, Skora? I think she'd like her grandmother."

"Grandmother? Me?" Tears ran down her face as she took the child.

"Of course, you're the closest thing to family Athgar has."

Natalia turned to Shaluhk. "Now, there's something I want to ask you both."

"What is it?"

"Athgar and I have been talking, and if anything should happen to us, we want you and Kargen to take care of Oswyn."

"Are you sure? We are Orcs. A Human child's development is unknown to us."

"There are others who can assist," continued Natalia, "but I know you would have the best interests of Oswyn in your hearts."

Shaluhk looked at her bondmate, and an understanding passed between them.

"We would be delighted," said Kargen, "but that is no reason for you two to go off and die."

Natalia laughed. "Don't worry, we have no intention of doing so."

The Therengian villagers, drawn by the commotion of the celebration, entered the hut. They were welcomed with open arms, causing the numbers to swell even more. By nightfall, the place was so crowded many continued the festivities outside. After all, it wasn't every day both Humans and Orcs had something to celebrate.

Athgar and Natalia finally made their way to bed, but the noise of all the revellers made any thought of slumber impossible. Instead, they stayed up, talking into the wee hours of the morning, until sleep finally claimed them.

The sun fell across Athgar's face, momentarily blinding him. Raising his head, he looked about the room. Natalia was there, fast asleep on his right, while a sound to his left made him turn back. Then a small green face suddenly appeared above him.

"Agar protect!"

Athgar's heart almost stopped. "Agar, what are you doing here?"

In answer, the young Orc held up his wooden axe. "Protect Oswyn."

"She's sleeping," he said, placing his finger to his lips.

"Oswyn sleep?"

"Yes, Oswyn sleep. You must be quiet. Now run along and see what your mother is up to."

Agar ran off, slamming the door as he went. The action caused Natalia to stir. "Athgar, is that you?"

He leaned over her, caressing her arm. "Go back to sleep, my love. Everything's fine."

"I thought I heard someone."

"That was just Agar checking in on Oswyn."

Natalia sat up, trying to get her bearings. She reached out, taking Athgar's hand, and he noted how it trembled.

"What's wrong?" he asked.

Her eyes sought their daughter, but the infant was still fast asleep in her bed. "I had a strange dream of Oswyn as a young girl, running from Orcs."

"Running FROM Orcs? Are you sure she wasn't running WITH them?"

"I'm not sure," she said. "It's all so foggy."

"What else can you remember?"

"A thick mist blanketed the ground, and I could see her breath frosting in the air. The sounds of battle surrounded her."

Athgar looked at their child, but Oswyn rested peacefully. "The sounds of battle, you say?"

"Yes, the clash of steel, the yells of warriors, that sort of thing."

"You mentioned seeing her breath. Was there snow on the ground?"

"I think so," said Natalia, "but I can't be sure. Why? What is it?"

"I'm not certain, but I had a similar dream some nights ago."

"How can that be? Two of us having the same dream?"

"I don't know," said Athgar, "but it can't be a coincidence, can it?"

"We should talk to Shaluhk. Maybe she can shed some light on it."

Natalia rose, collecting Oswyn and moving towards the unlit firepit. She spared a glance for her husband. "Would you mind?"

"Of course," he said, digging deep to call up his inner spark. Moments later, the fire burst to life, warming the hut.

Athgar watched as she fed their daughter, then rose from the bed, fetching a cloak to place around her shoulders. He then took a seat beside her, his attention on the flames.

"What are you thinking?" she asked.

He looked up, meeting her gaze. "I remember someone telling me once my mother had prophetic dreams. I didn't put much faith in it at the time, but now I have to wonder if there wasn't some truth in it."

Natalia stared down at their child. "Are you suggesting Oswyn's future is already determined?"

"No, but maybe it's inevitable?"

"Why would you say that?" she asked.

"We're both members of the Red Hand, as is Oswyn now. It only makes sense she would develop strong bonds with the Orcs."

"But if that's the case, why would they be chasing her? And, more importantly, why would I be dreaming about that?"

"I don't believe they were chasing her," said Athgar. "I think she was leading them. Perhaps one day she'll become a great military commander, like her mother."

"That still doesn't explain why we both had the same dream."

"Doesn't it? We both care deeply about our daughter's future. It only makes sense we would dwell on it, even in our sleep. What else could it be?"

"Your idea has merit," said Natalia, "but I suspect there's more to it. What if someone is trying to send us a message?"

"Through a dream?"

"Do you remember why we travelled to Ebenstadt in the first place?"

"Shaluhk recommended it, didn't she?" replied Athgar.

"She did, but she was only passing on the wisdom of the Ancestors. They were the ones who wanted us to come north. What if they're trying to reach us now?"

"Through our dreams? It seems unlikely. And even if that were true, couldn't they be more direct? It's not as if this dream is easy to interpret."

"You must remember," she said, "the Ancestors are all Orcs. Their thoughts may not work the same as ours."

"Well, if they are trying to reach out to us, it would be easy enough to discover. We can have Shaluhk contact them. That should give us the answers we seek."

# THE JOURNEY

## SPRING 1105

Belgast heaved the last sack into the wagon. "That's everything."

Stanislav stared at the sheer bulk of it. "Are you sure? I imagine there's still room for a twig or two if you should desire."

"It's good to be prepared." He noticed the smirk on the Human's face. "Are you mocking me?"

"Only in a friendly manner. Do all Dwarves travel with such a load?"

"Ah, you forget. We intend to remain at our destination for some time. We can't keep coming back to Ebenstadt for things we've forgotten." Belgast nodded to one of his cousins, who had climbed up to drive the team of horses. "Let's get going, shall we?"

Kieren flicked the reins, and the mighty beasts began straining at the yoke. At first, Stanislav worried if the weight might be too much for them to bear, but slowly, the wagon crept forward.

Belgast and Targan walked to the left while Stanislav and Brother Yaromir took the right, urging people to move aside as they went. Such a burden was, after all, difficult to stop in a hurry, and no one wanted to see anyone crushed under its weight. They soon picked up speed as the horses settled into a comfortable gait.

"Clear skies," noted Brother Yaromir. "You should make excellent progress by nightfall."

"Let's hope so." Stanislav glanced over at the wagon. "I'd hate for this thing to get bogged down in the mud."

As the group headed up the street, making their way towards the city's eastern entrance, they garnered considerable interest, for Dwarves were a rare sight in Ebenstadt. Eventually, the gatehouse came into view, and the wagon slowed.

A group of ill-equipped soldiers inspected anyone leaving, leading Stanislav to suspect something else was going on here other than simply preventing smuggling. As they rolled up to the guards, his suspicions were quickly confirmed when a burly individual wearing a thick gambeson approached Kieren.

"What have we here?" the man demanded.

The Dwarf merely stared back.

"He doesn't understand you," called out Stanislav. "He knows little of our language. Can I be of help?"

"Certainly," the guard responded. "I need to know the value of the goods this wagon carries."

"Why?"

"So I can levy the appropriate tax."

"You tax people to leave?" asked the baffled mage hunter.

"In or out, it makes no difference to me," the guard replied. "I'm just doing my part to keep the city running."

Stanislav moved closer, placing his left hand on the side of the cart, while his right rested on his hip beside his sword.

"Most of this is refuse," he replied.

"Refuse?" said the guard. "I doubt it. It looks heavy if the horses' efforts are any guide."

"Take a look if you like, but it's mostly stone."

"Why in the name of the Saints would they be transporting stone?"

"Who knows?" said Stanislav. "They're Dwarves."

Brother Yaromir moved closer. "These Dwarves are working for the Church," he added.

The guard sneered at the Temple Knight. "Oh yes? And what would the Church be doing with a wagonload of stone?"

"It's for construction of a church if you must know. They're masons, renowned for their working of such material."

"And where is this church to be built?"

"Are you familiar with this area?"

"Can't say that I am," admitted the guard.

"There's a small village," said the Temple Knight, "just to the east of here. That's where the foundation is to be laid."

The guard looked at the wagon again. "Why a stone church? Isn't wood more plentiful?"

"It is," continued Brother Yaromir, "but stone is easier to fortify." He moved closer, lowering his voice. "After all, we know Orcs are in the area."

"True enough," the man replied, "but I still need to levy a tax."

Belgast pushed his way into the conversation, producing two golden coins. "Will this satisfy your curiosity?"

The man stared at the crowns. "I don't know..."

"What's there to think about?" said the Dwarf. "You collect a coin for your masters, and keep one for yourself. Who's going to say otherwise?"

The gleam in the man's eyes confirmed his greed as he snatched up the coins. "Very well, you may proceed." He turned to his comrades. "Open the gate!"

Kieren urged the team of horses onward once again, and they slowly passed beneath the stone gatehouse.

"This is where I leave you," said Brother Yaromir, "but I wish you safe travels."

"Won't you get into trouble, lying like that?" asked Stanislav.

"Who said I was lying?"

"You claimed the stone was destined for a church, but you and I both know the Dwarves are going to make a forge out of it."

"Do we? For all we know, that very same stone might find its way into a church's wall... eventually."

Stanislav laughed. "I'll let you have the victory this time. Goodbye, Yaromir."

The sun above was bright, the warm wind coming from the north a welcome respite from the southerly breeze that typically blew off the mountains. Stanislav pined for a horse, but such an expense was no longer within his means. Instead, he concentrated on the countryside, breathing in the fresh air.

There were several buildings outside the wall, mostly those necessary to allow the tilling of the fields. A little farther on, however, saw an end to such things. The countryside here was flatter, replacing the farmland with fields of tall grass and weeds. It was an idyllic scene. Stanislav wondered why the ground had not been planted, for it appeared to be rich soil if the abundance of weeds was any indication.

By mid-morning, they well on their way, the city gone from sight. Now bored with the serene countryside that had previously captivated him, Stanislav chose instead to engage Belgast in conversation.

"Earlier, you mentioned Kieren and Targan were your cousins. Do you have any brothers or sisters?"

"No," replied the Dwarf, "but I understand your confusion. You Humans like to give complicated labels to relatives, but Dwarves are far more practical."

"In what way?" asked Stanislav.

"Well, you have second and third cousins, don't you?"

"I don't, personally, but I'm familiar with the term, yes."

"Now," said Belgast, "you tell me, what is a first cousin?"

"Someone who traces their direct lineage back to your grandfather."

"Precisely. And a second cousin?"

"Shares a great-grandfather."

"Now, imagine how complicated that would get if your race lived to the ripe old age of, oh, I don't know, three hundred and fifty or so?"

Stanislav gave it some thought. "I suppose you could have eighth or ninth cousins, couldn't you?"

"You could, and that's not including the relatives of uncles, great-uncles, and so on. In Dwarven society, we still use terms such as grandparent, uncle, and aunt, not to mention brothers and sisters, of course, but anyone else who's related is simply referred to as a cousin."

"That does make it easier, but it must make for large, extended families."

"It does," agreed the Dwarf, "although bear in mind it's rare for us to have more than one child at a time. Also, our women can bear children for many more years than Humans. A good thing, considering their fertility is low."

"What do you mean by that?"

"It can take many attempts before our women are with child. Not only that, but only about a fifth of the population is female."

"Why are you telling me all this?"

Belgast shrugged. "I don't know. Perhaps I'm just bored. I'm used to using my mind. I was a Royal Advisor once, you know."

"Royal Advisor to who?"

"The King of Kragen-Tor, a fellow by the name of Haglarith."

"Never heard of him," said Stanislav.

"Nor would I expect you to. In any case, he died some years ago, and that's when I took up the life of a trader. Mind you, my first endeavour didn't work out so well."

"And what was that?"

"I tried setting up an iron mine in the mountains. All that brought me was grief, although I did meet Athgar and Natalia, so it wasn't a complete waste of time."

"And now?" asked Stanislav.

"I'm hoping this idea of smithing works out."

"How do you know Athgar's people need smiths?"

The Dwarf stared back in shock. "Why wouldn't they?"

"What if they already have their own?"

"Come now, my cousins are not ordinary smiths. Kieren has been forging swords for decades, and Targan, well, you should see some of the armour he's crafted over the years."

"Ummm"—the bounty hunter took a moment to think through his response—"my understanding is these Therengians are not a prosperous people."

"Ah, but they will be one day. You must look at the big picture."

"The big picture?"

"Yes," said the Dwarf. "With Athgar and Natalia behind them, they're bound to prosper, and prosperity means potential profits."

"Profits you might not realize for years, decades even."

"I'm a Dwarf," said Belgast. "I'm in no hurry."

"So you would set up a business that will need to wait decades to reap its rewards?"

"Of course, it makes perfect sense. We call that getting in on the ground floor."

"That's a strange expression."

"It comes from the design of Dwarven cities. We tend to dig down into the stone for our homes and businesses. The ground floor is where a city begins. Thus, it's a longer-term commitment, but it usually carries bigger profits down the road."

"You seem to have given this some thought."

Belgast smiled. "I have, indeed. Mind you, I expected to carry out this plan within an Orc village, not a Human one, but the results should still be the same."

"Have you dealt with Orcs before?"

"Briefly, in Ord-Kurgad, but Athgar's told me all about them. By the way, how was he the last you saw him?"

"In fine health," said Stanislav.

"And Natalia?"

"Her, too, especially considering her situation."

"What situation was that?" asked the Dwarf.

"The last time I saw her, she was pregnant."

"Pregnant? Are you sure?"

"Quite," said Stanislav. "It even interfered with her spellcasting."

"How far along was she?"

"I'm not sure. She wasn't even showing, but I rather suspect she would have delivered by now."

"That's grand," said Belgast. "A little baby spellcaster. I wonder what they called it?"

"It?"

"What other term can I use? I would have no idea if they had a boy or a girl. You?"

"Not the kind of thing I'm familiar with."

"Well, we'll find out soon enough. How far did you reckon this village of theirs was?"

"At this speed?" replied Stanislav. "Likely two or three days."

They lapsed into silence. The wagon rolled by some old ruins, prompting Belgast to comment.

"Now, that's interesting," the Dwarf said.

"What is?"

"Those stones over there. Are there many structures like that in these parts?"

"Not that I'm aware of," said Stanislav. "Why?"

"It speaks to the history of this region. Any idea who might have built it?"

"Not really, but then again, I'm not from around here. My original home's farther north, in a place called Karslev. And yes, before you ask, that's the same place where Natalia was trained in the arcane arts."

"What do you know of this family of hers?" asked Belgast.

"Quite a lot, actually. I used to work for them. What would you like to know?"

"Well, for a start, why are they so nasty towards her?"

Stanislav smiled. "Nasty, a very appropriate word. Natalia was a gifted child. Most potential spellcasters first exhibit signs of their magic when they mature. We use the term manifesting to describe the signs."

"Signs?" asked Belgast.

"Yes, effects on the natural order of things. In Natalia's case, she would cause water to smooth against the wind or fish to gather near her, only she was much younger than was normally the case."

"So you're saying she's gifted?"

"Not so much gifted as bred," replied Stanislav.

"I'm not sure I follow."

"The family matches powerful mages for the purpose of producing children with extremely strong magical potential. Of course, we didn't know it at the time, but Natalia's father was one such mage."

"And her mother?" asked the Dwarf.

"Only a peasant woman as far as I know, but who can say for sure? It's not as if a woman in her place could trace her ancestry, although we do know magic runs in the family."

"So they have a breeding program?"

"They do. Shocking, isn't it?"

Belgast shook his head. "And just when I thought Humans couldn't get worse."

"Don't go grouping all of us together. We're not all bad."

The Dwarf slowed. "Did you hear that?"

Stanislav ceased walking, but his ears could pick out little, other than the groaning of the wagon. "What was it?"

"Horses, if I'm not mistaken, and I don't mean ours." Belgast hurried to catch up to the cart. "Stop the wagon, Kieren. There's trouble afoot!"

Targan appeared from the other side of the wagon, crossbow in hand. He placed the butt on the ground and began winching the string back. It took the wagon nearly a hundred paces to come to a complete halt, then Kieren dug behind his seat, pulling forth a hatchet.

Stanislav looked around but still saw nothing. Then it came, the distinctive sound of horseshoes on the hard-packed dirt.

Kieren pointed eastward. "They come."

Stanislav glanced farther up the road to a rise, and then the road curved to its left. Around that rise rode three horsemen, their armour mismatched, their surcoats dirty and faded.

"This looks like trouble," grumbled Belgast as he pulled his pick from the back of the wagon and stood defiantly, his eyes locked on the newcomers.

The three men kept coming until they were only a horse's length from Kieren's team.

"Well, well," said one with dirty, grey hair. "What have we here?"

"That," said Belgast, "is none of your concern."

"None of my concern? I'm afraid you're wrong there. Any who travel this road are of concern to me, for it is MY road!"

Stanislav stepped forward, his hand resting on the hilt of his sword. "By what right do you lay claim to this thoroughfare?"

"We serve Tybalt Kemp, High Lord of Ebenstadt. It's our job to enforce the collection of taxes. Now, come, hand over your coins, and we shall let you be on your way."

"We already paid a tax when we left the city," insisted Belgast.

The man smiled. "And now you'll pay to use the road. Consider it a toll if that makes the thought of it any more palatable."

"And if we refuse?"

"I can just as easily kill you and take all your coins. It makes little difference to me."

"How many coins would that be?" asked Stanislav.

In answer, the grey-haired man stared at the wagon for a moment. "I figure twenty might be sufficient, don't you?"

"No, I don't."

Before Stanislav had even moved, the riders drew their weapons. At the same time, a bolt sailed out from beneath the wagon, striking the grey-haired man solidly in the chest, puncturing the padded jacket he wore. He slumped over in the saddle, then tumbled to the ground while his horse just stood there. Stanislav drew his sword, running forward, eager to close the distance as quickly as possible.

The remaining riders, stunned by the sudden change in their fortunes, struggled to react. The smaller of the two spurred on his mount while the taller turned tail, determined to put some distance between himself and the crossbow.

Stanislav dove out of the way as the rider galloped past, narrowly avoiding being trampled. The enemy rode straight for Belgast, but as he closed, a flash of silver caught his eye. He turned his head just in time for a hatchet to bury itself into his shoulder. The man screamed, and then Belgast was there, burying his pick into the fellow's leg.

A sword came down, narrowly missing the Dwarf. Stanislav regained his feet, rapidly closing the distance. The rider's horse was in a panic now, struggling to be free of its burden. The bounty hunter's blade struck out, taking the rider in the lower back. The now lifeless body fell to the ground.

The third one raced up the rise, eager to get away, but Targan was already taking careful aim. Stanislav heard a click as the trigger released the string, and the bolt sailed forth, striking its target dead centre of the fellow's back. His horse slowed as the rider swayed in the saddle but somehow remained upright.

Stanislav grabbed the reins of the beast before him, hauling himself into the saddle, and then he was off, galloping after the taller man.

As he closed the range, the injured rider's horse began nibbling at a tuft of grass. Stanislav drew alongside only to see the bolt sticking out of the man's chest. It had likely penetrated his heart, killing him instantly, but in a bizarre twist of fate, he remained upright. The bounty hunter gave him a push, and the body fell to the ground.

He looked back towards the Dwarves. Belgast was stripping a body of anything valuable while Targan reloaded his crossbow yet again. Kieren, being lazy of nature, simply sat on the wagon, his eyes gazing longingly at the hatchet he'd thrown.

"Well," said Belgast, "that was interesting."

"What do you want to do now?" asked Stanislav.

"Do? Why continue, of course."

"And this lot?"

A groan escaped the Dwarf's lips. "I suppose we'd better bury the bodies. We don't want them sending more riders after us."

"And the horses?"

"We take them with us. They're bound to be worth something." He gazed around at the bodies. "Say, you don't suppose there's more of them out here, do you?"

"It's unlikely," said Stanislav. "We're getting closer to the land of the Wildlings."

"Wildlings?"

"Sorry, I suppose I should say Therengians. It's only that I'm getting used to the local parlance."

"Just out of curiosity," said Belgast, "what else do they call Athgar's people?"

"I've heard them called Easterlings, or even heathens, both of which are technically correct, given where they live and who they worship."

"I couldn't care less who they worship. If Athgar and Natalia are with them, they must be trustworthy folk."

"You think so?" asked Stanislav.

"Of course, don't you?"

# A GATHERING OF FRIENDS

## SPRING 1105

The next day the roadway simply ended, forcing them to find their own way across the fields of grass and shrubs. The distant pines grew closer until they passed beneath the boughs.

There had been no other people in sight since the attack, although there was certainly plenty of wildlife about. Once within the forest, their progress slowed, hampered by the thick blanket of needles that covered the ground, threatening to stall the wagon by allowing its wheels to sink into hidden ruts.

The only solution was to periodically halt so they could dig themselves out. This proved to be a labour-intensive task, and Stanislav began to wonder if this entire trip had been a mistake.

It was during one such stop they discovered they weren't alone. Stanislav and Belgast were on their knees, scooping handfuls of pine needles from beneath a wheel when a deep, rumbling voice boomed out.

"What brings the mountain folk to these woods?"

Belgast stood up abruptly, smashing his head against the underside of the wagon. He let out an expletive-laden curse, then turned around, seeking the source of the greeting.

An Orc stepped out from behind a tree, a nocked bow in his hands. He held it low, its string loose, but kept his eyes on the group.

"Answer my question," he demanded.

"Are you Orcs of the Red Hand?" asked Belgast.

"We are. Why?"

Belgast moved closer. "Do you not recognize me?"

The Orc's face broke into a broad grin. "Belgast Ridgehand?"

"That's me. Your face looks familiar. Give me a moment, and I'll recall your name." He hummed and hawed for a bit. "Kragor, isn't it?"

"It is. We are a long way from Ord-Kurgad, my friend. What has brought you here?"

"We seek Athgar and Natalia."

"Then you have come to the right place." Kragor let out a whistle, and three more Orcs stepped from cover. "What is this?" He pointed at the wagon.

"A gift of sorts. I had originally intended to return to Ord-Kurgad, but found it in ruins. I'm glad to see you made it out alive."

Kragor moved closer, although by now, he had put away his bow. He lifted the tarp on the wagon, gazing within. "It looks like stones."

"And so it is, amongst other things. Allow me to introduce my cousins, Targan Hardhammer and Kieren Brightaxe. They're both smiths."

"And the contents of the wagon?"

"The items needed to build a Dwarven forge."

The very mention of it brought a smile to the Orc's face. He moved around the back of the wagon, then spotted Stanislav. "And who is this?"

"Stanislav Voronsky," answered the bounty hunter, "at your service."

"That is a name I do not know."

"Are you familiar with Natalia Stormwind?"

"Of course," said Kragor.

"She can vouch for me."

The Orc looked him up and down, gauging the threat. "What of you, Master Belgast? Do you speak for this Human?"

"I'm led to believe he's a trustworthy sort. He's certainly given me no reason to think otherwise."

"In that case, I will take you to Runewald."

"How far away is it?" asked Stanislav.

"Some distance yet," said Kragor, "but we should make it by nightfall. We will, however, need to adjust the path you take. If you proceed eastward from here, you will miss it entirely."

"We'll need some help," said Belgast. "The wagon has sunk into the pine needles again."

Kragor walked around to the spot indicated and examined the wheel, then nodded his head sagely. "So it has, but with the help of my hunters, we should soon be able to dislodge it. Now, stand back and have someone ready to lead the horses forward…"

Shaluhk looked at Natalia. "You say you both had the same dream?"

"As near as we can tell. Some small details differ, but the imagery was consistent."

Athgar leaned forward. "Could the Ancestors be responsible?"

"Anything is possible," replied the Orc shamaness. "Yet I would have to ask why they would do such a thing?"

"Wasn't it at their urging we travelled to Ebenstadt?"

"It was, and I thought it strange at the time, but that is a far cry from sending you dreams."

"Yet look where it brought us," said Natalia. "We have a home now, as does your tribe… OUR tribe. None of that would have come about without the urging of the Ancestors."

"They are not gods," Shaluhk reminded her. "They are the spirits of the deceased who linger between worlds. Their collective wisdom guides us, but ultimately, the living decide their own fates."

"Then why send us north in the first place? Clearly, they must have suspected something."

"Perhaps there is an explanation for that, one which only now comes to mind."

"Go on," urged Athgar.

"When I seek the Ancestors' advice," explained Shaluhk, "the spell allows me to connect to the spirit realm. In that strange world of shadows, there is no such concept as distance. The spirit who answers my call might not even be from the area in which the spell is cast."

"Meaning?" asked Athgar.

"We were in Ord-Kurgad when they urged you to travel north, but what if the Ancestors answering the call were from this very region? They would be well aware of the troubles brewing in the area, thanks to the shamans of the Black Axe and Stone Crushers."

"So it was essentially a call for help?"

"That is one interpretation," continued Shaluhk, "but it is mere speculation at this point."

"And the dreams?" asked Natalia. "You're not suggesting it's a coincidence that they matched?"

"I wonder if it might not be an attempt to contact you through spirit magic."

"Like you do with the Ancestors?"

"Yes," agreed Shaluhk. "We shamans communicate over long distances using a spell called spirit talk. It uses the realm of spirits to act as a connection between distant points. However, in my experience, it only works between shamans."

"But when you use that spell," said Natalia, "doesn't it work both ways?"

"It does, and I always believed in order for it to work, the shamans must know each other."

"Then how does that explain the dreams?"

"When I was possessed by Khurlig," said Shaluhk, "I saw glimpses of other possibilities. At the Battle of the Standing Stones, I was able to tap into her memories, unleashing a spell called warriors of the past, but there was so much more waiting to be remembered. I believe it might be possible to contact ANY person, using a form of spirit talk, regardless of whether or not they are a shaman."

"Wouldn't we then hear voices?" asked Athgar.

"Not necessarily. I never heard tell of the spell used between Human and Orc. Could our brains be interpreting the magic in different ways?"

"It's an interesting supposition," noted Natalia. "Is there any way to test it?"

"I can ask the Ancestors," said Shaluhk, "but like us, each one has different experiences and knowledge. It might take some time to find one with the answers we seek."

"I think it worth pursuing, don't you?"

"Very well, then, I shall start immediately."

"Right now?" said Athgar. "Are you sure?"

"I have no other pressing duties at present. Shall I proceed?"

Athgar looked at Natalia, who simply nodded. "By all means," he said.

Shaluhk closed her eyes, focusing her mind on the spell. She blanked out all around her, calling forth the words of power that would connect her to the spirit realm. The magic built within her while the air buzzed with energy, then she snapped her eyes open, feeling the presence of others nearby.

"*I am here,*" she said aloud in her native tongue. "*Come, Ancestors, heed my words. I am Shaluhk, Shaman of the Red Hand, and I call on you to guide us with your wisdom and experience.*"

A shadowy figure appeared before her, then slowly took shape as an elderly Orc.

Shaluhk felt her throat constrict. "*Uhdrig, is that you?*"

The image smiled. "*It is, Shaluhk. It is good to see you again.*"

"*And you, Master.*"

"*Now, now,*" said Uhdrig. "*Your powers have now surpassed mine. The time for such titles is long past. What guidance do you seek, my friend?*"

"*I would seek the answer to a riddle.*"

"*You have me intrigued. Come, tell me more.*"

Shaluhk took a breath, steadying her nerves. Uhdrig had been her mentor in life until the spirit of Khurlig had stolen that life from her. Now, seeing her like this was almost too much to bear.

"*Calm yourself, Shaluhk. I know it pains you to see me after witnessing my death, but I am here to help you. How can I do that?*"

"*You remember Athgar and Nat-Alia?*"

The old Orc nodded sagely. "*Of course, I carry with me all I knew in life.*"

"*The spirits sent them north to a place called Ebenstadt.*"

"*I am well aware.*"

"*How did they know to do so?*"

"*The Ancestors have little to do in death other than think. As such, they are always pondering what was and what might be. The fortunes of our race are improving in the west, and so they have been waiting for an opportunity to do the same here in the east. The shamans of the tribes in these parts have been having trouble with Humans for some time. We, the dead, are well aware of the Therengian presence. When Athgar came along, a new opportunity presented itself, one they could not resist. It was hoped he might bridge this gulf between the races, much as his Ancestors did long ago.*"

"*You speak of the old Therengian kingdom?*"

"*I do,*" said Uhdrig. "*It did not rival the great Orc cities of antiquity, but it let our people live in relative peace for a good many years. There is always the belief it shall be so again in the future.*"

"*So they urged Athgar and Natalia north?*"

Uhdrig nodded. "*They did. The hope was they would broker a peace between the races. Never did they imagine their actions would see a rebirth of that which came before. You and Kargen share credit for that.*"

"*They say they shared a dream. Are the Ancestors responsible for that?*"

"*I am unable to say for sure, but I think it likely.*"

"*How can you not know?*" asked Shaluhk. "*Are you not a spirit yourself?*"

"*Of course I am, but just as you are not able to hear the thoughts of others living near you, so I am in ignorance of the thoughts of the spirits which surround me. Tell me more of these dreams.*"

"*They see their daughter, Oswyn, running with Orcs in her wake. She is no longer an infant, but rather a young woman.*"

Uhdrig nodded. "*The Ancestors wish a future for our race, a future likely tied to the success of the Humans. The events in the west have borne this out, and now Athgar and Natalia have, by their joining, produced a child who is of both worlds— Orc and Human.*"

"*Are you saying she is destined to lead us?*"

"*There is no such thing as destiny, merely possibilities. Oswyn is in a unique position, or at least she will be. The Orcs accept her as one of their own, as do the*

Therengians. She can complete the bridge between our people that was started by her parents, but it is her choice to make."

"And the dreams?"

"A manifestation of their wishes, nothing more."

"I had no idea the Ancestors could do such a thing."

"Nor did I, but you must remember, Shaluhk, amongst our numbers, are some of the greatest shamans who ever lived." Uhdrig grinned. "Even I pale in comparison to their knowledge."

The old Orc took a breath, then continued. "When I first arrived here, amongst the spirits, they talked only of the past, of how the great cities were the epitome of Orc culture and accomplishment. Since the birth of Oswyn, however, they look to the future, a future full of possibilities. I see a bright future for both Humans and Orcs, Shaluhk, but I fear it will be a long and difficult path, fraught with peril."

"Thank you, Uhdrig. You gave me much to think on."

"Be well, Shaluhk, and give my regards to Kargen and Agar."

"I will." The image faded, leaving the shaman staring into the flames.

Athgar and Natalia both looked at her, eager to hear what had transpired.

"How much of that did you hear?" asked Shaluhk.

"Enough to get a general idea," noted Athgar. "So it was the Ancestors?"

"It may have been, although even Uhdrig could not say for sure. One thing is for certain, however—Oswyn is the key to all of this."

"She is here to serve the whims of fate?" said Athgar.

"No," replied the Orc, "but she comes at a fortuitous time. You began the process of uniting Orcs and Humans, Athgar, but your daughter will have the opportunity to complete that task. It is for her to decide if that is what she truly desires."

"I'd be happy just to keep her from the clutches of the family," said Natalia.

"Let us not get carried away," said Shaluhk. "She is still an infant."

"An infant who, it appears, might hold the future of both our people in her hands," noted Athgar. "I'm sorry, Shaluhk. I know this wasn't your idea. I feel as though we're being… what's the word?"

"Manipulated?" said Natalia.

"Precisely," he agreed.

"Once again," said Shaluhk, "the Ancestors can only advise. She is free to choose her own destiny, as are you."

Natalia took a cleansing breath. "Well, I suppose that gave us an answer, even if it wasn't the one we were looking for."

"Would it be so bad?" said Athgar. "Our daughter uniting our people? It worked for the Therengian kingdom."

"True," replied Natalia, "but I might remind you it was, in turn, conquered by the Petty Kingdoms."

"Then we'll have to make sure this time we get it right. Our daughter's future depends on it."

"If there is nothing else," said Shaluhk, "I must seek out Agar. I left him in my brother's care, and I fear he may be running around and terrorizing the tuskers."

Athgar laughed. "He's very brave."

"But bravery must be tempered with reason."

"I have to go too," said Athgar. "It's time I began taking a proper accounting of all those weapons we captured."

They rose, Natalia turning to Shaluhk. "Shall I come with you?"

The shaman smiled. "Of course, Nat-Alia. I would relish the company."

They stepped outside the hut, Natalia and Shaluhk walking towards the pens where the tuskers were kept while Athgar sought out Harwath. He had only just found him when an excited warrior ran up to him.

"My lord," the young man spat out. "We have visitors."

"Describe them."

"A wagon and horses, Lord, led by a skrolling."

Athgar winced. "You mean an outsider," he corrected.

"Is that not what I said?"

Harwath turned to the young man, pointing a finger. "How many times have I told you, Weyland, the term skrolling is rude?"

"Sorry, but what else do you call Dwarves?"

"Dwarves?" said Athgar. "Now that IS interesting. Take me to them."

"As you wish." The warrior turned, leading them towards the edge of the village.

They passed by the palisade workers to see the distant wagon being escorted by Orcs. Athgar halted, waiting as they drew closer and then broke into a grin as he recognized the visitors.

"Belgast!" he called out.

"By the Gods," the Dwarf replied. "I thought we'd never find you."

"How did you find us?"

"It's a long story, best told with a mug of ale. The short of it, though, is Stanislav here brought us."

Athgar looked at the sole Human amongst the group. "Good to see you again," he said. "How have things been in Ebenstadt?"

"Not terribly good," replied the bounty hunter. "I'll fill you in later after you've welcomed your friends."

"Now," said Belgast, "before we get any further, let me introduce my cousins. This is Kieren Brightaxe and Targan Hardhammer. They're pretty quiet, mostly because they don't speak your language particularly well."

"And this wagon?"

"Ah, now that's something I can't wait to show you." Belgast moved to the back and lifted up the tarp. "This," he explained, "is the making of a Dwarven forge."

"You brought a forge here?"

"I did."

"How are we to use it?" Athgar asked.

"Did I not mention my cousins here are both smiths?"

"No," said Athgar, "you did not."

"I suppose I just got caught up in all the excitement of finding you. Speaking of which, where's Natalia?"

"She went over to the tusker pen with Shaluhk."

Belgast screwed up his face. "The what?"

"Sorry, I forgot how much you missed. I'll show you later. Let's get you inside, shall we?"


Natalia leaned against the fence. A simple structure, little more than a few pens and far too weak to stop the tuskers should they choose to ignore it, but the beasts seemed content to graze the nearby grass.

"I still can't get over how docile they seem," she said.

"It helps to have a master of earth who can talk to them," noted Shaluhk. "All they really want is food and water. Give them those, and they are happy."

"What do we have here?" called out a familiar voice.

Natalia turned. "Stanislav? What are you doing here?"

"I can come for a visit, can't I?"

She gave him a hug, then stepped aside to make introductions. "Stanislav, this is Shaluhk, my tribe-sister."

"Greetings," said the shaman. "I have heard all about you."

"Nothing bad, I hope?" he said.

"He is quick, this one," noted the Orc.

Stanislav looked at Natalia's stomach. "I see you've had your baby. Where is it?"

"SHE is having a nap. It's the only thing she does these days other than eating."

"And does SHE have a name?"

"Oswyn. It means Orc friend."

He smiled. "A marvellous name."

"Did you see Athgar?" she asked.

"I did. He just went inside with Belgast."

"Belgast?"

"Of course," said Stanislav. "I couldn't just show up without a surprise now, could I?"

She took his arm. "I can see we have a lot to catch up on. You too, Shaluhk. Why don't you hunt down that son of yours and meet us inside?"

"I should be delighted," said the shamaness.

# SUMMER

## SUMMER 1105

The arrival of the Dwarves was initially met with some skepticism, especially amongst the Therengian smiths who plied their trade in Runewald. They were seen as a threat to their business, but once it was made clear they would only deal in weapons and armour, most objections were withdrawn.

Belgast was also instrumental in smoothing out relations, even offering to teach some Dwarven techniques to any Human smiths who might desire it. There was resistance at first, but once they saw how superior the Dwarven forges were, they quickly took them up on their offer.

After a few weeks to get things set up, Kieren and Targan quickly got to work. The first order of business was making something useful out of all the captured armour and weapons. The Therengian smiths, unused to working with such high-quality steel, had done little other than sharpening swords. The Dwarves, however, were able to smelt down the steel, producing new goods custom-made for the members of the fyrd.

So it was on a warm summer's day, Athgar was found looking over some chainmail links.

"This is fine work," he noted.

"That's Targan's doing," said Belgast. "I wanted him to make you plate armour, but he insisted on this instead. Said it's quicker."

"It's just as well. None of our people are used to wearing such protection, and where would we store plate?"

"Don't worry, you'll get it eventually. The plan is to provide chain for some of your men, then start upgrading them to chain and plate."

"Which is?" asked Athgar.

"Metal plates worn over chainmail to protect the vital regions. Now, do your men have gambesons?" asked the Dwarf.

"Only those we captured, why?"

"They'll need something to wear under the chain. Otherwise, it'll chafe."

Athgar chuckled. "It looks like you thought of everything except profit. I'm afraid we're a poor people, Belgast."

"We're Dwarves, my friend. We see the long picture. I'm sure in a decade or two, we'll be rolling in coins. For now, we only need to establish ourselves."

"By working used armour?"

"In due course, we'll produce our own goods, but it's a place to start. The real problem will be sourcing good quality iron."

"You don't happen to have more cousins who can mine, do you?" Athgar asked.

"I do, as a matter of fact, but let's not get ahead of ourselves. This lot here will keep us busy for months, if not years."

"How do the weapons look?"

"Not bad," said Belgast. "It's mostly been a matter of sharpening blades and re-wrapping handles. The biggest problem, in my opinion, is the lack of conformity."

"I'm not sure I follow?" said Athgar. "Why would that matter?"

"Purely from a smith's point of view, it doesn't, but when it comes to training, it's a different matter entirely. Each weapon has a distinct style in terms of use, making it harder to standardize your practice techniques."

"Do the Dwarves standardize their weapons?"

"They do, as a matter of fact," confirmed Belgast. "They group their warriors together based on fighting styles. Axes or hammers are the preferred choices for equipping a company, although, of course, our archers all use arbalests."

"And if you were going to equip our fyrd, what would you suggest?"

"Spears would work well for the majority of them, but I hear you're looking into forming something called a thane guard. I assume they'd be better equipped?"

"They would," said Athgar.

"And how many of those would be we looking at?"

"A dozen from each of four villages to begin with."

"I'd suggest axes, then. We Dwarves are good at making them, and I noticed your people tend to use them a lot. They're also much easier to make than a sword and more effective against the kind of armour your enemy would use. I'm assuming, of course, the troops in Ebenstadt are the biggest threat?"

"They are."

"I'd put your thane guards into chainmail for now, but you'll need to get people sewing padded gambesons. That would give your fyrd at least some protection."

"And what would that take?" asked Athgar.

"A gambeson is basically a quilted jacket, made of wool. The actual stuffing can be almost anything, even horsehair."

"Could you show us how they're constructed?"

"I'm no expert," said Belgast, "but I can point you in the right direction. Of course, you're talking months before any of this could be produced in any significant numbers."

"That's fine," said Athgar. "Like you, we're looking at the long-range picture here." He looked over to where Belgast's cousins were pounding away at the forge. "I wonder if you'd do me a favour?"

"If I can," replied the Dwarf. "What is it?"

"We're gathering the moot again to discuss a whole range of things, including the current status of our warriors. Would I be able to call on you to explain all this to the other thanes?"

"I'd be delighted. When are they arriving?"

"In a few days. It's meant to coincide with the summer equinox."

"Is that significant to your people?"

"That's what I'm told," said Athgar. "People come from the other villages to socialize, play games, and generally have a celebration. The real reason for the get-together, however, is for matchmaking."

"So people come looking for husbands or wives?" Belgast shook his head. "What strange customs you Humans have."

"How do you find a wife in Dwarven society?"

"Ah well, that's just it, we don't. Female Dwarves are rare, so it's them who do the choosing, not us males."

"Truly?" asked Athgar. "I had no idea. That must be very difficult for you."

"Not really. We don't have the drive Humans do. Most of us concentrate on increasing our skills and advancing in the guild."

"Guild?"

"Never mind," said the Dwarf. "I'd have you here all day trying to explain its complexity. Suffice it to say, as a long-lived race, there's plenty to keep us busy."

"And how have you and your cousins found Runewald? Apart from your smithing, that is."

"It took a while to be accepted, but you've got some decent folk here.

They're much more welcoming than some of the Petty Kingdoms I've visited."

"Well," said Athgar, "we're glad to have you here. Now, you must excuse me. I need to make arrangements for the gathering of the moot."

Athgar stared across the table, trying not to yawn. The thanes had been in discussion for most of the afternoon, during which Wynfrith had droned on and on about the need for greater trade opportunities.

"Come now," Galan was saying. "We've wasted enough time on the matter. Let us move on to something else. What do you say, Athgar?"

Startled awake, he fought down the urge to flee. "Yes, I would agree. What would you like to discuss?"

"I'd like to talk about Ashborne. I hear tell we've had some success there?"

"The land is good," replied Athgar, "and there's plenty of water, but we've had some problems with bandits of late, riding out of Ebenstadt."

"Haven't the troops we sent there been keeping things safe?"

"They have, but the fyrd was meant to serve for a short period, not spend months on our border."

"What about those thane guards of ours?" asked Galan.

"An effective force," said Athgar, "but under-equipped. We're taking steps to change that, but even Dwarven smiths have their limitations. No offence, Belgast."

"None taken," replied the Dwarf.

"And are you an expert in armies?" asked Wynfrith, eyeing Belgast suspiciously.

"As a matter of fact, I am. Amongst my many accomplishments was acting as military and trade advisor to King Haglarith of Kragen-Tor."

"If you were so good at serving your king, why are you here now?"

"He died, as kings are prone to do," said Belgast. "Mind you, he lived to the ripe old age of four hundred twenty-three, a remarkable achievement considering his eating habits."

"And in that capacity," said Wynfrith, "you learned all about the armies of man?"

"I did."

"Then tell me," said Galan, "what do you make of our army?"

"They have spirit," answered Belgast, "but they're woefully unprepared for war."

"Nonsense," said Aswulf. "They won us a victory at the Standing Stones, and they'll do so again."

"That victory was mainly due to the Orcs," added Athgar. "Or did you forget about the role the tuskers played?"

"Then perhaps it's those very same tuskers we should send to Ashborne?"

"Ashborne doesn't have the wherewithal to support them," explained Athgar. "They require a lot of fresh meat, and that means lots of hunters. Ashborne can't even support itself at the moment. To expect them to feed our mounted troops is too much to ask of them."

"So you're saying we're vulnerable?" said Aswulf.

"To a war, yes," said Athgar, "but we can handle any bandits the city might send our way."

"What makes you assume they won't invade?"

"The city is run by a group of renegades. They lack the manpower for an all-out war."

"That might be," said Wynfrith, "but there's always the danger the Church might get involved again. We need a powerful army as a deterrent, not to mention a king."

"Are we on to that again?" said Athgar. "There must be more important things to discuss?"

"What about a treaty?" asked Galan. "If we could send a representative to Ebenstadt before the Church returned, we could secure our safety."

"And who would we send?" asked Wynfrith.

"Natalia, of course. As a skrolling, she'd have a much better chance of reasoning with them."

"From what I've heard," said Athgar, "the leaders of Ebenstadt care little about anything but lining their own pockets."

"It's true," added Belgast. "Stanislav told me as much."

Wynfrith grimaced. "And you would trust the word of an outsider?"

"I have no reason not to," said Athgar. "Stanislav helped us escape the clutches of the family, and Natalia's known him for years."

"Would he be willing to carry word to Ebenstadt on our behalf?"

"I don't think that a wise idea. We have no strength from which to bargain."

"What about a bluff?" suggested the Dwarf.

"That would put him in a precarious position," said Athgar, "especially if they realize it's a ruse."

"And of what consequence is that to us?" said Wynfrith. "He is an outsider whose loss would affect us little. I say it's worth the risk."

"And you expect me to put him in danger, with that attitude? I think not."

"Then what would you have us do?" said Galan. "We're open to suggestions."

"We're all equals here," said Athgar. "Why is it MY responsibility to contact Ebenstadt?"

"It was you and your wife who convinced our people to take a stand and fight in the first place. This situation is of your making, Athgar, thus it falls to you to find a remedy."

"Then it's my decision we do nothing," said Athgar. "Risking a bluff might only make things worse."

"In what way?" asked Wynfrith.

"The city believes we have a strong army. Were they to learn otherwise, they might convince other Petty Kingdoms to band together to eliminate us."

"And what other Petty Kingdoms would those be?"

"Novarsk," replied Athgar. "It lies just west of Ebenstadt."

"You honestly believe they would invade after that disastrous crusade?" said Wynfrith.

"If they feel threatened, they could raise their entire army to the cause, easily outnumbering us."

"Then we would defeat them just as we defeated the Church."

"At what cost?" said Athgar. "We can't afford another victory like that, Wynfrith. We came close to being annihilated."

"And so we sit here and do nothing?" said Wynfrith.

"For now," suggested Athgar, "I propose we keep an eye on things. If we see any signs of a threat, we'll move to intercept it."

"And if they march in force?"

"Then we muster our allies and fight for every plot of land we have."

"That sounds good enough for now," said Wynfrith. "I see no reason for further discussion on the subject. Shall we adjourn?" They all nodded their assent, and she continued, "Then I propose the moot assemble again in three months, in Bradon. Is that to everyone's agreement?"

"Yes," said Aswulf. "Now, let's go round up some drinks before the ale is all gone."

They filed out, leaving Athgar and Belgast alone.

"Well, that was definitely interesting," said the Dwarf. "Are your meetings always like that?"

"More or less," replied his Human companion, "but sometimes the conversation gets REALLY heated!"

· · ·

"… And so Stanislav was the only one to clap at my induction into the family," said Natalia.

"It's true," added the bounty hunter. "The rest were too full of themselves to recognize true talent."

"What was she like back then?" said Athgar. "I have a hard time thinking of her as a young girl."

"Very quiet." Stanislav grinned. "You'd never know it now, of course, but she had quite the hard time making friends."

"Difficult with that crowd," explained Natalia. Oswyn let out a gurgle, drawing smiles from their guests.

"And now you have a daughter of your own," said Stanislav. "I feel like a proud uncle."

"You know you're welcome to stay with us as long as you like," said Athgar. "You're the only real family Natalia has. Don't get me wrong, she has lots of friends, and we count Kargen and Shaluhk as siblings, but you're the only connection she has to her past."

"And I appreciate that, but I have friends of my own back in Ebenstadt, and I've already been away for far too long."

"When will you leave?" asked Natalia.

"Not for a bit, yet. Belgast is making a shopping list of things he needs to be arranged."

"Such as?"

"Mostly letters to send off," said Stanislav. "It seems our Dwarven friend has cousins everywhere."

A young Therengian man wandered over, a woman of similar age on his arm.

"Who's this, Harwath?" said Natalia.

"This," the man replied, "is Bergwith. She hails from Bradon."

"Down for the summer festival?" asked Athgar.

"I am. I was part of Wynfrith's delegation." She looked at Harwath and smiled. "Not that I intended to find a husband or anything, but I'm glad I came. It's quite nice here in Runewald."

"Perhaps you'll be able to tame him," said Natalia. "He's a little rough around the edges."

Harwath blushed, but Bergwith was enjoying the attention. "I shall be sure to keep an eye on him. Is there anything else I should know?"

Athgar was about to speak but saw the look of utter fear on the young man's face. "No, he's a pretty decent fellow and a good friend. He stood with me when we challenged King Eadred."

"I heard about that," she replied. "Did he really try to kill you?"

"Try?" said Natalia. "He almost succeeded! I must have aged ten years that day."

"She exaggerates," said Athgar. "It wasn't that bad."

"It was," added Harwath, his voice low.

Athgar looked at him in shock. "And here I thought you were MY ally."

Harwath blushed. "I am, Lord. You know I would die for you."

"That won't be necessary, and I'm not a lord."

"You're a thane."

"He's got you there," said Stanislav.

Athgar smirked. "I can see I'm outnumbered here."

"True," said Natalia, "so you might just as well surrender to the inevitable."

He made an exaggerated bow. "Then I do so now, in full view of these witnesses."

Bergwith laughed, joining in the merriment. "Is he always like this?"

"On occasion," said Natalia. "More so since Oswyn was born. Father-hood suits him."

"Tell me," said Athgar, "what's Bradon like?"

"It sits at the edge of the forest rather than within it. Other than that, it's very similar to here."

"And does it have a palisade?" asked Natalia.

"Not at the moment, but after seeing what you've done in Runewald, Wynfrith is considering having one built."

"We'd be happy to lend her our expertise," offered Athgar.

"I'll be sure to pass that on to her."

"Do you know her well?" asked Stanislav.

"I would certainly hope so. She's my aunt. And yes, before you ask, she's always been argumentative, but it comes from a place of caring."

"She definitely livens up the moot," said Athgar. "Do you have any ambitions yourself? Aside from spending time with Harwath, I mean?"

"I may follow in Wynfrith's footsteps eventually, but I'm in no rush. I'd like to settle down first, maybe even have some children?" She looked at Harwath, who blushed profusely.

"Well," said Natalia, "it's best to get childbirth over with quickly while you still have life in you. I couldn't imagine having all that responsibility if I were much older."

"Oswyn wearing you out?" asked Stanislav. "She's only an infant!"

"An infant who constantly needs feeding. I swear all she does is eat, cry, and… well, you get the idea. Athgar helps when he can, but let's face it, he's not exactly equipped for the role of feeding."

"It'll get better in time," said Bergwith. "As they grow older, they get less dependent on their mothers."

"I didn't know you had children?"

"I don't, but I have younger siblings. They're all grown up now, of course, but I still remember my mother's exhaustion. It took everything she had just to look after us."

"Just how big IS your family?" asked Natalia.

"Six children if you include me."

"And are you the oldest?"

"I am now," said Bergwith. "I had an older brother, but he passed away three years ago."

"And what does your father do?"

"He farms. One of the reasons he had such a large family was to help with all the work. If you ever find yourself up at Bradon, you'll have to come and visit us."

"That would be wonderful," said Natalia. "What do you think, Athgar?"

"It might be sooner than you expect," he said. "We've called for the moot to reconvene there in three months."

# CONFLICT

## SUMMER 1105

K ragor stretched his arms, enjoying the warm summer's day. The sky above was clear, bringing a fresh breeze from the west. From the east drifted the sound of axes hewing wood, and he turned his gaze to watch the Therengians at work.

Several huts were already framed, and the process of thatching had begun, while others shaped timber for more houses. In total, more than a hundred people worked to build this new settlement, and that didn't include those standing guard.

The Orcs under Kragor's command were a mixed group consisting of hunters from all three tribes. However, the one thing they had in common was their mastery of the warbow, Athgar's gift to their people. He looked at his own bow, laying nearby, unstrung, and considered its impact on their way of life. Though it could be used for hunting, it was far more effective at penetrating armour. At the Battle of the Standing Stones, it had proven decisive, for little else, save the tuskers, had proved capable of penetrating the heavy plate armour of their adversaries.

A crow cawed off to his right, and he immediately recognized the danger. "*String your bows,*" he ordered, using his native language. "*Someone is coming.*"

He rose, taking care of his own bow before moving north, his small party following in his wake. Three hundred paces he travelled, then knelt beside Grundak, another of his tribe. "*You saw someone?*"

"*I did,*" the hunter replied. "*A group of riders, coming from the west. If you watch closely, you will see them through the trees from time to time.*"

"*Could they be unaware of our presence?*" asked Urughar.

Kragor shook his head. "*They do not need to see us. The sound of axes is more than sufficient to alert them to our presence.*"

"*Shall we attack?*"

"*No,*" said Kragor. "*Kargen wants us to avoid antagonizing them. If they come in peace, then we will leave them alone.*"

"*And if they come to raid?*" asked Urughar.

"*Then we punish them for their aggression.*"

The road ran north-south just behind the trees, then curved around the end of the woods to come eastward once more. Kragor spotted them through the leaves, a dozen riders, each wearing armour, although not the full plate expected of a Temple Knight.

"*It looks like warriors from Ebenstadt,*" said Kragor.

"*Shall I confront them?*" asked Grundak.

"*No. I know their language best. The rest of you stay here but remain alert.*"

He moved closer to the road, waiting for the riders to appear from around the northern edge of the forest. The Humans were armed with a variety of weapons, including axes, swords, and spears. Those in the front looked to be wearing more impressive armour, identifying one of them as the group's leader.

Kragor, satisfied they were all now within sight, stepped from the trees, holding his bow on high to gain their attention.

"Halt!" he shouted, using the common tongue of Humans.

The riders slowed but did not stop. Behind their leader, others drew weapons—a bad sign from Kragor's point of view.

"We would speak with you!" he called out.

This time the horsemen stopped. "Who are you to block our way?" came the reply. "You are trespassing in the lands of Ebenstadt. Stand aside and give way."

"This land belongs to the free people of the Alliance. We do not recognize your claims. Turn back now, or I shall be forced to use arms."

Their leader urged his mount closer, although he did tell the others to remain in place. He trotted to within twenty paces, then stopped, eyeing the Orc.

"Who is your chieftain?" he asked.

"Kargen of the Red Hand," said Kragor.

"Then take this message to Chieftain Kargen. Tell him all the land hereabouts lies within the dominion of Ebenstadt. Your presence here is an affront to the warriors guild."

"Guild?"

"Yes," said the man, "an association of fighting men, not that I'd expect someone with your thick skull to understand."

"I understand more than you might think," said Kragor. "Now, are you going to turn around and ride off, or do I have to teach you a lesson?"

The rider laughed. "You? Teach ME a lesson? I think you have that backwards." He drew his sword but remained in place. "Now, stand aside, greenskin, or I shall be forced to slay you."

Kragor reached into the quiver that hung from his belt, selecting a bodkin arrow. On seeing the Orc's action, the rider spurred his horse forward, intent on closing the distance as quickly as possible.

Kragor rolled to the side at the last moment, then came up into a kneeling position and let loose with an arrow. It wasn't a full draw, but then again, it didn't have to be. It sank into the horse's rear quarter, and the beast let out a terrible wail. The rider, denied his target, fought to keep his horse under control.

"Kill him!" screamed the Human.

The other riders urged their mounts forward. Two went down immediately as Grundak and Urughar hit their targets. The remaining riders raced towards the distant villagers who were still hard at work, unaware of the danger that threatened them.

Kragor sent another arrow sailing forth to bury itself in a rider's back, toppling him from the saddle. But before he could nock a third, they closed in on the Therengians.

Grundak and Urughar were now running, their bows discarded in favour of their axes. Kragor screamed at the top of his lungs to warn the villagers. Several turned from their work, axes in hand, but the riders were upon them, stabbing out with spears and crushing skulls with swords.

From Kragor's viewpoint, at least five villagers were taken down in the initial contact. The riders then split up, chasing down anyone they could catch. The Orc let loose with several more arrows, but, concerned that he might accidentally injure his allies, he started running towards them. As he closed the range, a rider came out from behind a half-finished hut, spear at the ready. Kragor stopped, took his time to line up his target, and then let fly from a full draw. The arrow punctured the man's chest. The spear dropped to the ground while the horse kept going but careened off to the left, its dead rider no longer in control.

Screams echoed throughout the village as smoke began billowing from one of the huts. Kragor ran towards it, only to see a dismounted rider there, torch in hand. The Human had evidently seen fit to grab a timber from the nearby fire and set the thatch alight, even as workers took refuge on the roof above him.

An arrow sunk into the raider's head, and he pitched forward, the burning timber still held tightly. The rest of the riders now fled, their job complete. Kragor kept his bow strung, but no other targets presented themselves.

The settlers climbed down, but the carnage had been done. Only the one roof was afire, but at least half a dozen Therengians had been cut down, and three more wounded.

"Where is the fyrd?" shouted Kragor.

"Here," answered an old man. "We were helping the workers lift timbers."

"Your duty was to remain alert, not assist in the construction. Your actions this day cost us lives."

"There was little we could do against such a force, and what of your role? You were supposed to provide a warning!"

Kragor, fighting to control his temper, found himself wondering what Kargen would do. "Gather the wounded," he finally said, "and bury the dead. I will send word to Runewald of what has befallen us here this day. Let us hope they will send more warriors."

"Why bother?" the man replied. "They'll only come back in greater numbers. This place is now doomed. We should abandon it."

"If you would run at the first sign of resistance, then go ahead. We Orcs will remain to defend what is ours."

"A fine sentiment, but we can't finish construction under constant threat of attack."

"We should create a palisade first," suggested Kragor, "then put thought to the huts within."

"That would require a lot more people than we can currently spare."

"The palisade at Runewald will soon be complete. Once it is, the workers will be freed up for other tasks."

"And in the meantime?" asked the man.

Kragor looked over the wounded. "You are correct. We must wait until we can return in force. Let us bury the dead and leave this area until we are better prepared to defend it."

"And how many did you say attacked?" asked Athgar.

"Only a dozen," replied Kragor, "but they were all mounted."

"What were our losses?"

"Six dead and five wounded, although with our shamans' help, they are expected to make a full recovery."

"You were wise to bring them back to Runewald," said Kargen. He turned to Athgar. "It appears the city folk are getting serious about claiming land."

"I don't see why," replied Athgar. "The area's been abandoned for years."

"What if they intend to expand?"

"Stanislav seems to think they're only concerned with coins."

"Possibly," said Kargen, "but if that were the case, would they not want to subjugate us instead of driving us from our land?"

"I suppose that would lend credence to your idea that they want to expand. It IS prime land after all."

"Are there many people in Ebenstadt?"

"Yes," replied Athgar. "Far more than we have in all our villages combined."

"Then how do we stop them from claiming our land?"

"The people who live there are city dwellers. I doubt many of them crave the life of farmers."

"They still need to eat," said Kargen. "Do they have farms to the west?"

"I would assume so, else how could they feed themselves? I would imagine a city like that would require a lot of crops."

"Then that could be the opening we need. What if we offered to sell them the food they require?"

"We don't have any excess food," said Athgar. "And it's far too late in the year to plant more."

"True, but if they let us prepare the village, we could have the fields seeded by next spring, could we not?"

"How do you know so much about crops? I thought Orcs were hunters."

"And so we are," said Kargen, "but since living beside you Humans, we have learned much. There are even those amongst us who are willing to take up tilling the soil. Is that the right expression?"

"It is. You surprise me. I never thought there would be an interest in farming amongst the Orcs."

"We must have farmed long ago when we lived in great cities."

"I suppose that's true," said Athgar.

"Of course, we will need to improve your methods."

"Our methods? How?"

"Easy," said Kargen. "Through the application of Earth Magic. Rugg tells me there is much that could be done to increase the yield of your crops."

"Such as?"

"Something about drainage, but it is beyond my understanding. He assures me, however, that a few relatively minor changes could easily lead to a greater harvest."

"It sounds like Ashborne is the place to put such ideas to the test."

"I shall talk further with Rugg," said Kargen.

"What am I to do in the meantime?" asked Kragor.

"We will send more hunters, and this time, Laruhk and some of his tuskers will accompany you. If those Humans return, we will be ready for them."

"And I'll send the thane guard," added Athgar, "with strict instructions to remain on watch and NOT help with the construction."

Natalia put Oswyn down to sleep. Skora hovered over her, ready to leap into action should the child prove troublesome, but all was quiet.

"There," said Natalia. "Finally, a moment of rest."

"You should take a nap," suggested Skora. "You look worn out."

"I'll be fine."

A knock on the door led Skora to open it, revealing Stanislav. "Mind if I come in?"

"Not at all," said Natalia. "What brings you by?"

"I'll be heading out to Ebenstadt tomorrow. I just thought I'd drop by in case there's anything you need."

"I do hope you'll be coming back at some time."

"Of course," he said.

"In that case, could you keep an eye out for some decent cloth?"

"You seem to have ample here in Runewald."

"Yes," she said, "but not in blue. Dyeing is not very popular in these parts."

Stanislav grinned. "I'll keep my eyes open, I promise. How's Oswyn doing? Is she sleeping through the night?"

"Most of the time. Luckily Skora here is good at soothing her, else I'd never get any sleep at all."

"It'll pass in time, you know. One day you'll wake up, and she'll be running around the house screaming in glee."

"I can hardly wait," said Natalia. "That reminds me; are you taking a horse?"

"I am. Athgar tells me you have plenty. I thought I might sell some of them for you. They should bring a fair price in Ebenstadt."

"Aren't you afraid someone might recognize them?"

He shrugged. "Not particularly. I doubt the members of the guild care about such things as previous owners."

"It's a pity you can't take all those warhorses we captured from the Temple Knights."

Stanislav smiled. "Warhorses? Hmmm, give me time, and I might be able to arrange something."

"Truly?"

"It's not guaranteed, of course, but I DO have a connection with the

Temple Knights of Saint Mathew. Perhaps they can arrange something? How many do you have?"

"More than a hundred," she said.

"That many? You surprise me."

"We had even more," said Natalia, "but a few were wounded. Some we had to put down, while others were put to the plough."

"You hooked a warhorse up to a plough?"

"We did. Several, in fact. It wasn't a great match, but better than doing everything by hand. The bigger problem is keeping them fed. They take a lot of resources."

"I can understand why you'd want to get rid of them. I tell you what," he said, "if I can't find a way to dispense with them in Ebenstadt, I'll send word to Novarsk. I'm sure they'd be willing to overlook the question of previous ownership."

"What makes you so sure?" asked Natalia.

"The price of horseflesh has risen considerably since the Cunars left. I imagine it's the same in Novarsk."

"Why so?"

"It's all a matter of supply and demand. The Temple Knights didn't just ride horses—they bred them. When their order fled, they took all the breeding stock with them."

"Leading to higher prices for what remains," said Natalia.

"Precisely."

The door opened, admitting Athgar and Belgast.

"Stanislav," said the Therengian, "I was just looking for you. I have a proposition I was hoping you might consider."

"Go on."

"We need someone to approach the people in charge of Ebenstadt."

"To what end?" asked Stanislav.

"To see if we can make an arrangement with them."

"I'm not sure if I would trust them, but tell me what you have in mind."

"Kargen and I were talking," said Athgar, "and we wondered if they might consider buying some of our crops. It would give them the food they likely need and us some coins to spend."

"I'll consider it, but I'll need to see what's changed in my absence. There could be new rulers by now."

"You think that likely?" said Natalia.

"The people who run the place are thugs. I wouldn't put it past them. And, if I AM to approach them, I'd need an official letter of introduction stating I'm negotiating on your behalf."

"Easy enough to arrange," said Natalia. "I'll get right on it."

"Might I suggest I accompany him?" asked Belgast.

Athgar was taken aback. "You? Why on the Continent would you want to return to Ebenstadt?"

"To get word to more of my other cousins. Eventually, we're going to need miners, and these things take time to arrange."

"I assume Kieren and Targan would remain here?"

"Of course," said the Dwarf. "I have no need of them in the city."

"It's fine by me, but ultimately it would be Stanislav's decision."

The bounty hunter looked at the Dwarf, then broke into a grin. "It would be my pleasure to have you accompany me."

"Good," said Natalia. "Now, all that remains is for me to write this letter of introduction." She stared at her husband. "This IS with the permission of the moot, isn't it?"

"Not exactly," he replied. "Kargen and I only just came up with it."

"I don't suppose it would matter much," she added. "It's not as if the leaders of the guild will be able to check its authenticity."

"Still," said Athgar, "you'll need to take great care presenting it. There's no telling how they might take the offer."

"I'll stick by him," said Belgast. "That way, someone has his back."

"Are you sure the two of you will be enough?" said Natalia.

"Maybe not," said the Dwarf, turning to Stanislav. "What was the name of that other fellow we met back in Ebenstadt?"

"You mean Brother Yaromir?"

"That's him. Do you think he might be persuaded to join us?"

"It couldn't hurt to ask."

Belgast looked at Natalia. "Would that suffice?"

"Let's see," she replied. "A Dwarf, a mage hunter, and a Temple Knight? I think you'll be fine."

"I don't know," said Stanislav with a smirk. "It sounds like the beginning of a joke to me."

Natalia laughed out loud, but Athgar failed to see the humour in it. Instead, he just looked at her, trying to figure out what had gotten into her.

She suppressed her laughter and glanced at him apologetically. "I'll explain it later," she said.

"Will you take the wagon?" asked Athgar.

"No," said Belgast. "I'll ride one of the horses if that's all right with Stanislav."

"Fine by me, but I will be selling it once we're in town, so the trip back might be a bit slower."

"That's fine. I've got my feet and a good pair of boots. I'll manage."

# FAMILY

## SUMMER 1105

Wynfrith glanced up to see a familiar face standing before her. "Galan? What brings you to Bradon?"

"I wish to talk to you about naming a king."

"Athgar has refused the title."

"Athgar is not the only one who could be offered the Crown."

She leaned forward, setting her elbows on the table. "Go on," she urged.

"I came here by way of Thaneford. Aswulf is of the opinion it's time we took matters into our own hands."

"Meaning?"

"If Athgar refuses the Crown, we should offer it to one of us."

"Us meaning YOU?"

"You misread my intentions," said Galan. "I certainly have no desire to see myself on the throne. Rather, I would be the power behind it, as I suspect you would prefer to be as well."

"So you're suggesting we give the Crown to Aswulf?"

He grinned. "Why not? Does he not have experience in leading?"

"Being thane is not the same thing as being king."

"True, but what better way to prepare for such a responsibility? And, in any event, we would be there to advise him."

"And have you sought out his thoughts on this scheme?"

Galan's face fell. "I have, unfortunately."

"And?"

"And it appears there's some work ahead of us to convince him of the wisdom of it."

"I can hardly say I blame him," said Wynfrith. "Being king is a heavy responsibility. What about Athgar, then?"

"What about him? There's nothing he could do about it, is there? After all, it would be a majority of thanes who elected our new king."

"There's still the matter of the Orc chieftains."

"Now, that," said Galan, "is something we'd need to work on. What's your take on them?"

"It doesn't matter what you say. Kargen will follow Athgar's lead."

"So he will, but I might remind you there are two other chieftains with which we can deal."

"Do you speak Orcish?" asked Wynfrith.

"No, but then again, I don't need to. Both Zharuhl and Kirak began learning our language some time ago."

"And you believe they might be swayed?"

"In truth," said Galan, "I don't really know, but Athgar keeps reminding us of how similar our races are, so perhaps there's hope. The real trick, I imagine, will be offering them something they desire."

"Which is?"

"Wealth? Power? Influence? Or maybe they'll see reason?"

"This sounds a bit weak, don't you think?"

Galan pouted—there was simply no other way to describe it. "There must be something they covet above all else?"

"They're Orcs," said Wynfrith, "not Humans. To think of them in any other terms would be a crucial mistake."

"What other choice do we have? We can't keep going on like this, trying to reach a consensus on everything!"

"Oh, I don't know, it's worked for us so far."

"Yes," said Galan, "but if war breaks out, decisions will need to be made in a hurry. We won't be able to wait on a consensus."

"Your proposal has merit, but I feel our energies would be better spent on convincing Athgar to take the Crown. After all, he's the one people look up to."

"No, that skrolling woman of his led us to victory, not Athgar."

"Yet," said Wynfrith, "he was elected thane, a result you were more than satisfied with at the time."

"It was convenient, and how could I know he would refuse the Crown? By all rights, he should already be king."

"With you behind him? I doubt that would've worked out the way you hoped."

"What's that supposed to mean?"

"Only that Natalia is content to let him rule. She is the real power here."

Galan gave it some thought. "Are you suggesting we remove her from the picture?"

"No," said Wynfrith. "I'm suggesting the way to have Athgar made king is to convince Natalia of its necessity. Once she's in agreement, he'll have no choice but to acquiesce."

"A clever concept, but flawed."

"Why would you say that?"

"Because she loves him. She'd never force him to do something he wasn't comfortable with. There might be another way though. What if we found some way to control her?"

Wynfrith laughed. "Control her? She's a battle mage, you fool. What could we possibly use to control her?"

"A battle mage she may be, but she's also a new mother."

Wynfrith felt an icy hand grip her heart. "Don't even suggest such a thing."

Galan shrugged. "It's only idle speculation. You're right, we should work on making Athgar see the necessity of a king. And if we're lucky, he might insist one of us take the Crown."

"Would you accept the Crown when HIS influence is so great? No, it must be Athgar. The people will accept no other."

"Careful what you wish for, Wynfrith. That would make a skrolling our queen."

"Do you think so little of Natalia? She is a powerful mage and a brilliant military leader. We need her, whether she be queen or not."

"I'm surprised to hear you say that," he said. "You haven't been shy in your opposition to some of her ideas."

"That's only because I want what's best for our people. I respect Natalia, both as a woman and as a leader. Why can't you?"

"Because, despite everything else, she's still an outsider, with strange ideas about what it means to live amongst our people."

Wynfrith smiled. "You're upset because she suggests we adopt a lot of the Orc customs."

"They are not our ways!"

"And what have our ways done for us in the past? I'll tell you what— absolutely nothing! Our glorious king, Eadred, kept running eastward at the first sign of trouble. If we'd followed him, we'd have been destroyed by the Orcs. Instead, they're standing by our side, helping to protect our people. Our future lies with the Orcs, Galan, as was so visibly demonstrated at the Battle of the Standing Stones. Now, I've heard enough of this… discussion. I think it best if you leave."

"Of course," he replied. "I shall leave you to enjoy the rest of your day."

She watched as he turned and exited the room.

"Bergwith?" she called out.

Moments later, her niece appeared. "You wanted me?"

"Have someone keep a discreet eye on Thane Galan, would you? He's been stirring up some trouble."

"I shall take care of it immediately, my lady."

"How many times do I need to tell you it's Wynfrith, not 'my lady'?"

"But you're the thane."

"A thane who is chosen by the people to govern for them, not born to it. We have no nobility amongst our people, Bergwith. You would do well to remember that."

"But Eadred was a king?"

"Yes, but still chosen by the moot. Let us not forget that important detail."

"Of course."

"Good. Now go and find someone to watch Galan before he disappears from sight."

"Yes, Thane Wynfrith."


Thane Galan climbed onto his horse, an impossible luxury until the defeat of the Holy Army. It had taken some time to grow accustomed to the saddle, but in the end, it had been worth it, for the trip from Scarburn was far more enjoyable on horseback. He turned to his aide, a young warrior named Magran.

"You're an adventurous sort," Galan said. "How would you like to be a member of the Thane Guard?"

"I would be honoured, my lord. What would be expected of me?"

The thane smiled. "I need you to go to Runewald on a little fact-finding expedition."

"Fact-finding, Lord?"

"You need to find something to give me leverage on Natalia Stormwind."

"Leverage?" asked Magran.

"Yes. Something I can use to force her to do what I want. Do you understand?"

"I suppose so, but I'm not from Runewald. How, then, would I get close enough to learn anything?"

"Simple," said Galan. "You travel to Runewald and convince them to join the local fyrd. Since Athgar is training them himself, you'll already be close."

"And what am I looking for, precisely?"

"I can't really say for sure. Something we can use against her. A secret she doesn't want to be revealed, for example."

"Am I to leave right away, Lord?"

"No," replied the thane. "We'll ride back to Scarburn first, then you can make your way to Runewald. Once you find what we need, I will have the power to make you the captain of the Thane guard.

"Captain? I would be honoured to serve you, my lord."

Galan smiled. "Good. I hoped that would be your response."


Stanislav gazed at the distant gates. "Ebenstadt," he said. "Not a place I ever thought I'd end up missing."

Belgast grinned. "Something tells me it's not the city you're missing."

"Is it that obvious?"

"Apart from the fact you've talked about nothing else the last few days? No, not at all."

"Tell me, Belgast, do you have a woman back home?"

"There was one, once, but she chose to forge with a guild master instead."

"Forge?"

"Sorry, I forgot you Humans use different terms. That would be marriage to you."

"May I ask why?"

"Dwarven culture is all about status," said Belgast. "And a guild master outranks a lowly member of the traders guild."

"I thought you were an advisor to a king?"

"That came later."

"So what does a trader do?"

"We travel the Continent looking for opportunities to sell Dwarven goods."

"And did you enjoy that?" asked Stanislav.

"I enjoyed the travel, as well as meeting people, but advancement in the guild is incredibly difficult."

"So how was it you came to be an advisor to the king?"

"Well now, that's a very interesting story. You see, King Haglarith's predecessor was a Dwarf named Nodrim. He'd risen through the ranks of the warriors guild some years before to become an important part of Kragon-Tor's army. Now, I know in Human society, the line of kings is measured by bloodline, but we do it differently. A given king chooses his own successor. Sometimes it's a blood relative, but more often, it's a trusted friend, someone who will carry on ruling in a similar manner. Now in

Nodrim's case, he died before naming an heir, creating a very troublesome situation."

"So what did they do?"

"They assembled all the guild masters and chose a new king. Of course, it took months, with everyone wanting their own representative on the throne. In the end, they compromised, naming Haglarith the new king. He was young as far as kings go but ended up being a great leader."

"And how did you become his advisor?"

"We had a trade dispute with one of our neighbours, a Human realm, and I was called in to explain the situation. Of course, by then, I was a little higher up in the guild. I so impressed Haglarith, he made me his advisor on Human matters. Eventually, the role expanded to include other duties, but that all ended when he died."

"Did you go back to the guild?"

"No, I'd had enough of that. The guilds are... what's the word?"

"Set in their ways?"

"I'd say set in stone," said Belgast, "but I suppose it's almost the same thing. You need to understand how the guilds work. Advancement is based on seniority, and since Dwarves live for hundreds of years... well, I'm sure you can see the problem."

"Is that when you decided to strike out on your own?"

"Yes. I'd spent a lot of time amongst Humans, so it was only natural I'd seek my fortune there."

"You mentioned the mining venture where you met Athgar and Natalia. Was that your first expedition?"

"As a matter of fact, it was. Mind you, I'd wandered amongst your people for a few years to get an idea of what I'd like to do."

"How did you survive?" asked Stanislav.

"I'd saved up a tidy sum as a Royal Advisor, so funds were never an issue, although I do need to go home once in a while when I start running a little short."

"So you're wealthy?"

"I suppose I would be considered so by most Humans. You must remember, by Human standards, I'm ancient, but as a Dwarf, I'm only middle-aged."

"Well," said Stanislav, "I'm glad you decided to accompany me. It's been a most pleasant trip."

"It has, hasn't it?" agreed the Dwarf. "Now, if only the city was a bit more welcoming."

Stanislav urged his horse forward, and they continued on towards the distant gate. "That reminds me," he said. "Do you have a place to stay in Ebenstadt?"

"I thought I'd find a nice inn somewhere. Can you recommend one?"

"They have rooms over the Elk."

"Sounds good to me."


Raleth watched the fyrd fall into line. There was a slight drizzle in the air, enough to plaster his hair to his face, but at least the day was warm. Off in the distance echoed the familiar sounds of axes on wood as the villagers were back at work, cutting timber for the new palisade, assisted in their endeavours by some Orcs. Ashborne boasted only two completed buildings, longhouses used to house the workers, but many more were planned. However, since the last attack, priority had switched to the defences, so the construction of a palisade had been put into motion.

Each of the other villages contributed a quarter of their fyrd on a rotating basis. Presently, it was Runewald's responsibility to guard the workers, and Raleth, as one of its veterans, was in command of the detachment.

He walked down the line of warriors, observing the men and women with a critical eye. They lacked much in the way of armour, but since the coming of the Dwarven smiths, their shields were improved, now being lighter in weight and sturdier in their construction than their predecessors.

All eyes were on him as he examined the formation, all except for Hilwyth. She focused on something beyond him, causing him to halt before her.

"What are you looking at?" he asked.

"Someone's coming," she replied.

He turned around, spotting the distant figure instantly. The stranger walked at a brisk pace, altering their direction to coincide with the location of the fyrd.

Raleth looked to the north to see a trio of Orcs watching intently, their bows nocked yet not drawn. They'd likely seen the newcomer some time ago, but a single person represented little in the way of a threat.

"You stay here," he ordered.

"Raleth," said Hilwyth. "You shouldn't go alone."

He looked at her, noting her smile. "And I suppose you feel you're the best person to accompany me?"

"It couldn't hurt, could it?"

Raleth tried to keep himself from smiling, but he found it challenging.

He and Hilwyth grew up together. It felt strange having her under his command, or anyone else, for that matter.

"All right," he relented. "Come with me, but keep your weapons close."

They began walking westward, towards the approaching newcomer. As they drew closer, he realized the stranger was a woman, and she wore a smile that could melt ice. There was a spring in her step that spoke of youth and vigour, characteristics Raleth greatly admired.

"Who do you suppose that is?" asked Hilwyth.

Raleth blushed, his thoughts returning to his duty. "I have no idea, but I aim to find out."

"Oh yes?" she remarked, a playful edge to her voice. "You think she's pretty, don't you?"

His face turned a darker shade of crimson. "Why would you say that?"

"Come now. We've known each other for years. You never look at me that way."

He halted, turning to face her. "What way is that?"

"You men are all the same," she said. "You can't see what's right in front of you. Do I need to point out the obvious?"

Raleth was at a loss for words and could only stare back.

She tried to lessen the blow, smiling, but it looked forced. "I don't want to see you hurt…" Her voice trailed off.

"What are you talking about?"

"Greetings!" called out the stranger.

Raleth tore his gaze from his companion. The woman who approached was like a dream come true, with her brown hair hanging in braids and piercing grey eyes, which identified her Therengian heritage.

"Good day," he finally answered. "I am Raleth, commander of the local fyrd."

Hilwyth coughed.

"Oh yes," he added, "and this is Hilwyth, one of my warriors."

"Greetings," the stranger replied, her voice soft and silky.

Hilwyth nudged him, breaking the spell.

"What brings you to Ashborne?" he asked.

"Ashborne?" She gazed at the construction off in the distance. "Is this a Therengian settlement?"

"It will be, soon," he replied, "though we have other villages farther east. Do you come seeking a home?"

"As a matter of fact, I do. Long and far have I wandered, and then I heard tell of a great battle. A battle in which those like me defeated an army from the Petty Kingdoms. I knew then, I was close to finding a place to settle down."

"Are you travelling alone?" asked Raleth, hope evident in his voice.

"I am, but then again, you already knew that. Your people have been watching me for some time." She pointed at the distant Orcs. "I see you have allies."

"Indeed. Are you familiar with the Orcish race?"

"I am, although I don't understand their language."

Raleth smiled. "I can teach it to you—"

"I'm sorry," interrupted Hilwyth, "I didn't get your name."

"It's Ethwyn," the woman replied. "Ethwyn of Athelwald."

# SETTLING IN

## SUMMER 1105

Raleth led the way into Runewald, a broad grin on his face as people turned their way in greeting. Their welcome was soon replaced by wonder at the new arrival.

Ethwyn, gracious as ever, made sure to return the waves, then spotted a familiar face. "Melwyn? Is that you?"

The woman looked up, breaking into a smile. "Ethwyn? We thought you dead!" She ran over, grasping her in a warm embrace. "By the Gods, look at you!"

"How ever did you come to be here?" asked Ethwyn. "The last thing I remember, you were being chased by those slavers."

"Skora and I managed to evade them. We wandered around the wilderness for some time before we stumbled into this place. What about you? How did you escape?"

"My opportunity only came after they sold me off. I was managing on my own well enough, but then I heard of Therengians massing in the east. I came here looking for them, but never, in my wildest dreams, did I expect to see you here!"

"Have you seen Athgar yet?"

"Athgar? I thought him dead?"

"He's alive, all right, and living here in Runewald." Melwyn lowered her voice. "I'm afraid he's taken up with a skrolling though."

"A skrolling?"

"Yes, an outsider. A woman who's not a Therengian. I'm sure you'll hear all about her."

"My brother has a woman?" said Ethwyn. "Was he not to marry you?"

"He was, but when he failed his hunt again, I was promised to Caladin. Remember him?"

"Is he here as well?"

"No, I'm told he died in Corassus. Did he not travel with you?"

"No," said Ethwyn. "After we left Athelwald, they broke us up into smaller groups and sent some of us south. Who's this woman he's taken up with?"

"A spellcaster by the name of Natalia Stormwind."

Ethwyn did her best to look surprised. "A spellcaster, you say?"

"Yes, and a mighty powerful one at that."

Just then, an Orc came out from behind a hut carrying some wood. It was nothing out of the ordinary for those who lived here, but it shocked Ethwyn. "Why are there Orcs here?"

"They helped us defeat an attack," said Melwyn. "You might know some of them, in fact. This bunch is from the Orcs of the Red Hand."

"Should that mean something to me?"

"They used to live near Athelwald. Do you remember Kargen?"

"Oh yes. He was one of Athgar's customers. Why? Is he here?"

"Here? I'll say he's here. He's the chieftain of his tribe." Melwyn's face grew grave, and she moved closer, talking in low tones. "Much has happened in your absence, Ethwyn. Your brother was taken in by the Orcs."

"What do you mean, 'taken in'?"

"He became a member of their tribe, and they taught him Fire Magic."

"Truly?"

Melwyn nodded. "And that's not all. He and Natalia have a child, a girl named Oswyn."

"Marvellous," said Ethwyn.

"Excuse the interruption," said Raleth, "but the thane will be waiting."

"That's Athgar," added Melwyn.

"My brother's the thane?"

"He is," said Raleth, trying hard to suppress a grin.

"What about our reports?" asked Hilwyth. She'd made the trip with them, along with the returning fyrd members.

"You can deal with that. Dismiss the fyrd, and then report to the thane when you're done."

"And what will you be doing?"

He smiled. "Reacquainting our thane with his sister."

Hilwyth turned to the men and women who followed the small group. "What are you looking at?" she barked out.

"Now," said Raleth, "I hate to interrupt, but if you'll come this way, I'm sure Athgar will be pleased to see you."

"I'll catch up with you later," said Melwyn.

"No, come with us now," pleaded Ethwyn. "I insist."

"I doubt he wants to see me. He has a wife now."

"Then he's obviously made a mistake. Come on, Melwyn, I need you by my side. It's not as if I know anyone else in this place."

"Very well."

Ethwyn turned to Raleth with a smile. "Would you do us the courtesy of leading the way?"

The man beamed. "Most certainly. If you'll follow me?"

Ethwyn suppressed a giggle. He was positively giddy with excitement, something she could use to her advantage.

They passed by several huts, similar to those she was familiar with back in Athelwald. However, the ultimate destination was a much larger structure, easily the largest longhouse she'd ever seen, although it paled in comparison to the buildings that made up Korascajan.

Raleth halted at the entrance, speaking softly to the warrior who stood watch. The guard opened the door and poked his head in, then turned back to Raleth. "You may enter," he announced.

Ethwyn followed the man inside to where a small group was deep in discussion. It took a moment for her eyes to adjust to the dim interior, and then Athgar's voice boomed out.

"Ethwyn!" He stepped close, giving her a hug. "I feared you dead. It's so good to see you."

"And you, Brother," she replied.

He released her, holding her at arm's length. "How in the Continent did you find us?"

"It's a long story. I hear you've been busy though." She turned to the pale, dark-haired woman at his side. "Who's this?"

Athgar stood back, his cheeks tear-stained. "Where are my manners? Allow me to introduce Natalia Stormwind, my bondmate."

"Bondmate?"

"Sorry, I meant wife."

"Greetings," said Natalia.

Ethwyn eyed the woman she'd been warned about. So this was the rogue Stormwind? She didn't look particularly powerful, but then again, appearances could be deceiving.

"Well met," she finally replied. "I'm sorry, it's only that this has been such a shock to me. I didn't even know my brother survived the attack on Athelwald, never mind that he's got a wife."

"And a daughter," added Natalia. "Would you like to meet your niece?"

Ah, there it was, the very object of her mission here. "Yes, by all means."

Natalia turned, calling out, "Skora? Could you bring out Oswyn, please? Her aunt would like to see her."

The door opened a moment later to reveal the old woman carrying an infant. "Her aunt? What nonsense is this?" She halted as she spotted the woman. "By the Gods, Ethwyn. I thought you dead."

"Glad to see you too, Skora. Is this my niece?"

Skora moved closer, revealing the babe. "This is her. Oswyn's her name."

"Oswyn? I don't believe I've heard that name before."

"It means Orc friend," explained Athgar.

Melwyn shot her a look, but the inference was clear—Athgar had been thoroughly corrupted by the greenskins. Ethwyn made a mental note to follow up with Melwyn sometime soon. The woman might have more information that could be used to her advantage.

"She has your eyes, Brother, although, luckily, your wife's nose."

"You must come and sit," insisted Athgar. "There is much to catch up on."

"Most assuredly. Call for some mead and let the tales begin." Ethwyn let her eyes roam the room, coming to rest on Harwath. "And who is this handsome fellow?"

"Harwath," said Athgar. "He leads the fyrd here in Runewald."

"I thought Raleth had that responsibility."

"My brother commands a small detachment," said Harwath, "nothing more."

Ethwyn noted the look of disdain from his older brother and smiled. "Well, it's nice to be looked after by a pair of such good-looking men."

"Have you any belongings?" asked Natalia.

"Only the clothes on my back."

"You must stay with us," said Athgar.

"I couldn't."

"You're family," said Natalia. "It's only right."

"You have a new family to look after," said Ethwyn. "I'd only get in the way."

"But you must stay somewhere?"

"She can stay with me," offered Melwyn.

"There," said Ethwyn, "you see? All taken care of. Now, let's have some of that mead, shall we? I have a lot of tales to tell."

Hilwyth absently scraped the stone across her blade, her attention on the distant hut. "What in the Gods' name are they doing in there?" she said aloud.

A shadow loomed over her. She looked up to see a woman of a similar age staring down at her.

"Who's 'they'?" the newcomer asked.

"I don't believe we've met. I'm Hilwyth. And you are?"

"Bergwith. I hail from Bradon."

"Well, Bergwith, it appears Ethwyn of Athelwald has arrived."

"And she is?"

"The sister of our thane," said Hilwyth.

"You don't look too happy about that."

"I suppose I should be, but then again, the woman's dangerous."

"Dangerous, how?" asked Bergwith. "Does she carry weapons?"

"No, although I imagine she can fight if she needs to. No, she's dangerous in a different way. She has the looks of a goddess, and she's cast her spell over everyone."

"Everyone?"

"Well," said Hilwyth, "probably not everyone."

"But someone you wish she hadn't."

The woman looked up at Bergwith. "Is it that obvious?"

"So, who's this man you've fallen for?"

"His name's Raleth."

"Harwath's brother?"

"Yes, why?" said Hilwyth. "Do you know him?"

"He's the reason I'm here!"

"Oh? Are you a fyrd commander?"

"No," said Bergwith, "but he and I met at the summer equinox. I hoped we might settle down together."

Hilwyth nodded her head in the direction of the longhouse. "Not with Ethwyn around."

Bergwith chuckled. "I doubt she's that bad."

"You haven't met her yet."

"And you have?"

"Oh yes. I travelled in her company all the way from Ashborne."

"Was she rude to you?"

"Not exactly, but it's almost as if I weren't there at all. Raleth only had eyes for his precious Ethwyn." She sneered as the words escaped her mouth. "I'd keep a close eye on Harwath if I were you. There's no telling what that woman might get up to."

"I'll bear that in mind," said Bergwith.

· · ·

Ethwyn settled in quickly, for it wasn't much of an adjustment. After all, she'd spent most of her life in Athelwald, living a similar lifestyle. However, her recent past far outshone her early years, and she found fault with almost everything around her. Instead of a home, she saw it as a prison, a situation she was forced to endure in order to accomplish her mission.

Fortunately, Melwyn proved a veritable fountain of knowledge and was quick to introduce her to everyone. Ethwyn always found it easy to make friends, but the Orcs proved remarkably resistant to her charms. To her, they all looked the same. She had a hard enough time telling Kargen apart from the other Orcs even though she'd met him years before. He presented an obstacle to her plans but not an insurmountable one. She must, she thought, take efforts to learn more about these Orcs and their influence over her brother.

As for Raleth and Harwath, she took great pains to flatter them as often as possible. They, like many of the other men in the village, proved susceptible to her charms. She had no doubt that, given the right incentive, she would have them firmly in hand.

Her orders had been very clear—the only person of consequence was the child. If she could spirit away Oswyn, her future would be secured.

Natalia patted Oswyn's back to be greeted by a burp. Agar, who was inside the longhouse, thought this hilarious and began running around, imitating the sound.

"He likes his tribe-sister," she remarked, looking over at Athgar, who sat, staring at the embers, poking them with a stick.

"What's wrong?" she asked.

"Nothing."

"I know you too well. It's not nothing."

"It's not important."

"Is it Ethwyn?"

"No, not at all. She fits right in."

Natalia sensed trouble. "But…"

He looked up at her. "It's just that she's distracting everyone around her."

"In what way?"

"At her insistence, I put her into the fyrd. It's not like she hasn't done it before. We used to train together back in Athelwald."

"And?" prompted Natalia.

"She flirts shamelessly with everyone."

"Everyone?"

"Well, all the men, at least. Nothing seems to get done when she's around. It's almost as if she's purposely sabotaging things." He held up his hand to stop her interruption. "I know. I should have expected this. She's always been popular, far more so than me."

"Is that what this is about, a bruised ego?"

He smiled. "No, I have you. It's just that when she showed up here, I expected her to have matured. Instead, I have that same annoying, younger sister I grew up with."

"Don't take it so hard. She's only popular because she's new around here. Once she's settled in, things will calm down. Who knows, she might even find someone and get married?"

"That'll be the day," said Athgar. "My sister, married. I'll believe it when I see it."

Natalia rose, moving closer to him. "Here, take your daughter. She wants her father."

He reached out, a smile creasing his face as he took Oswyn. "There you are, my darling. Daddy's got you."

"Good," said Natalia. "Now, I've got work to do."

"You do?"

"Yes. The fyrd is practicing, and I wanted them to experience magic."

"I'm not sure I follow."

"It's simple, really. I want them practicing their manoeuvres while I cast spells nearby. It lets them get a feel for what to expect in battle."

"Let me know how it goes. I'll be here with Oswyn"—he heard a scream echo through the hut—"and Agar, of course."

"Good," said Natalia. "Shaluhk will be along shortly to collect him. She was just meeting with some of the other shamans."

The Water Mage stepped outside, breathing in the fresh air. The fyrd was formed up on what was known as the common—a field left undeveloped in the middle of the village. Here they were supposed to be practicing with weapons, but, instead, all she saw was a group of men gathered around Ethwyn, all paying close attention to her words, particularly Harwath, who was obviously smitten. Ethwyn looked at the man as she tucked a strand of hair behind her ear. Behind them, Raleth stared at them with a look that could kill. Natalia made a mental note to keep a close eye on the brothers in the future.

Skora used a stiff-haired brush to spread fat over the chicken as it dripped onto the fire, filling the room with a mouth-watering aroma, making even her own stomach yearn to be filled.

"That smells delicious," said Natalia as she entered the room. "You're very gifted when it comes to food."

"Thank you," said Skora. "It's nice to be appreciated, but let's not get carried away. I've made this particular meal plenty of times. What is it you wanted to see me about?"

"Can't I just come to chat?"

"Of course, but although we've only known each other a short time, I can already tell when something's on your mind. Out with it, girl, and don't hold back. Nothing shocks me anymore." She waited, then looked at Natalia, who was obviously in turmoil. "Is it Ethwyn?"

"Yes, how did you know?"

"What else has happened of late?"

"Lots," said Natalia. "Our people were under attack in Ashborne, and the thanes continuously argue over forcing Athgar to become king."

"Yes," said Skora, "but none of that would upset you like this. Now tell me, what is it you wish to know about Ethwyn? That's why you came to see me, isn't it?"

"I suppose it is. You lived in Athelwald. I thought you might have some insight into her character."

"Character? Well, I imagine I know her as well as anyone else. Anything, in particular, you're looking for?"

"I noticed her paying attention to the men hereabouts. Is that something she used to do back in Athelwald?"

"You mean flirting? The girl was born to it. She's always been a shameless tease. But then again, if I had her looks, I can't say I'd be any different. Her mother was a great beauty too. That's the reason Rothgar married her in the first place. Athgar took after his father, but Ethwyn, well, she got the best features of both her parents."

"Did she ever show the slightest interest in settling down? Athgar told me it was common for couples to wed young."

"There were plenty who would have obliged," said the old woman, "but Ethwyn was having none of it. She wanted to live life on her own terms, not be defined by her husband."

"I thought Therengian women were considered men's equals?"

"Yes, they are, but Ethwyn had no skills to speak of. She never showed any interest in the trade of bows, like Athgar did, and her cooking was absolutely horrendous."

Natalia smiled. "And that's when you stepped in."

"It was. Someone had to feed the two of them."

"Were they close? Athgar doesn't speak of her much."

"Very close in their youth, although less so as they grew older. You need to understand, after the death of Rothgar, Athgar became responsible for looking after her. That's a lot of pressure on someone so young."

"You make him sound like a child."

"Well, he didn't make his first kill until he was twenty summers, well past the usual time for such things. Kargen was the one who taught him how to hunt, you know."

"Yes," said Natalia. "I've heard the tale plenty of times, believe me. Did Ethwyn have much interaction with the Orcs?"

"No, she never showed the slightest interest in such things. All her attention was on the young men of the village. She could have her pick of any of them had she wanted. Instead, she wasted her time doing frivolous things."

"You disapproved?"

"I understand the passion of youth," said Skora. "After all, I was young once, too, but Ethwyn… it's like she had no desire to grow up at all."

"She's only slightly younger than Athgar, isn't she?"

"Yes, about a year. Why?"

"Shouldn't she have participated in her first hunt?"

"She did, almost a year before Athgar was successful. Many wondered why she didn't wed, but I think part of her didn't wish to abandon her brother." She brushed some more fat over the chicken, listening as it sizzled. "Anything else you'd care to know?"

"No," said Natalia. "That explains a lot. Thank you, Skora."

"My pleasure," the old woman replied.

# THE CITY

## SUMMER 1105

Stanislav looked up at Evira. "You have no food at all?"

"Well," she replied, "not for sale, anyway. We have plenty of ale though."

"Do you have any food for yourself?"

"For now, but it's getting increasingly difficult to find. I hear people in the lower quarter have taken to eating rats."

"That's terrible," added Belgast. He turned to Brother Yaromir. "How are things down at the mission?"

"There's enough grain to last at least another week, but more and more people are coming to us, desperate for food. It can't go on much longer."

"How did things get so bad?" asked the Dwarf.

"In a word," said the Temple Knight, "Kemp."

"Who's that, when he's about?"

"Tybalt Kemp is the self-styled High Lord of Ebenstadt," explained Stanislav. "If you remember, the guards mentioned him when we left the city in the spring."

"So where did this fellow come from? And why would he be the cause of this food shortage?"

"As to your first question, he was a soldier in the employ of the Duke of Erlingen. When the Duke died in battle, his men fled, but Kemp decided to set himself up as ruler of the city. By then, of course, the Temple Knights of Saint Cunar had already abandoned the place. I believe he's got his palace at the old Cunar commandery."

"He does," confirmed Brother Yaromir. "Though I daresay they haven't kept it up to its usual standards. They are a slovenly crew, these men of the warriors guild."

"And no one stood up to them?" asked Belgast.

"Who could? Most of the soldiers of Ebenstadt marched off with the Holy Army, and those who remained after the battle took up with Kemp."

"But what of those who stayed behind to man the walls?"

"Only a few did," said Stanislav, "and they were soon outnumbered by their new masters."

"This is what happens without a ruling class," grumbled the Dwarf.

"I might remind you they don't have such a thing in Runewald either."

"True, but at least they chose someone to tend to things. Leading a kingdom, or a city, in this case, requires someone with the dedication and perseverance to look after its people."

"A noble sentiment," said Yaromir. "I wish more thought as you do."

"That explains how this Kemp fellow became High Lord, but what about the lack of food?"

"That's his doing as well," continued the knight. "He sent his men out raiding all the local farms, gathering the resources to feed his army. The problem is, he has no concept of how farming works. He left nothing behind. Rather a short-sighted plan, if you ask me."

"Nothing at all?"

"No, half the fields now lay barren. He ruthlessly killed any of the farmers who tried to tell him of his mistake."

"And now everyone must suffer," grumbled the Dwarf. "It's just not right."

"On the brighter side," said Stanislav, "it means Athgar's grain will have a ready market."

"True, but that won't be in place until next year. What are the people to do until then?" Belgast eyed the rest of the group, but they'd all fallen silent. "Just a moment," he continued. "Did you say he hoarded food for his army?"

"What of it?" said the Temple Knight.

"Perhaps he could release some of his grain? Where is it stored?"

"Good question," said Stanislav.

"I might have an idea," added Brother Yaromir.

"Go on," urged Belgast.

"He guards the old commandery as if it were his palace. I would suspect that's where we'd find the grain. Likely in the courtyard."

"The courtyard? Surely not! It would get ruined in the rain. Even the dimmest of folks knows not to do that."

"Ah, but the courtyard in the commandery is covered. My Cunar cousins used to practice their horsemanship there in wintertime."

"That still doesn't help anyone," said Evira. "The fact remains it's guarded by the High Lord's men, and I doubt he'd be willing to share it in any case."

"We could try appealing to his humanity?"

"I admire your faith, Brother," said Stanislav, "but I've run across men like Kemp before. He'll not soon part with all that food. It's what gives him power over his men."

Belgast smiled. "Could we leverage that?"

"I'm not sure I follow?"

"He wants to remain in power. If we can assure him of future shipments of food, he might be willing to make a deal."

"It's the people who need the food," said Evira, "not Kemp."

"I understand that, but there's nothing we can do about it with his people in charge. We can, however, achieve our own objectives."

"And leave the rest of us to starve?" said Evira.

"You won't starve," said Stanislav. "I won't let you."

"I doubt there's much you can do about it."

"I could take you away from here. We could move to Runewald. I'm sure they'd accept us?"

She reached across the table, taking his hand. "That's sweet of you, but this is my home. I have friends here. I can't just abandon them."

Brother Yaromir shifted in his seat, leaning forward. "We must at least attempt to make the man see reason. I propose we seek an audience. At the very least, we can get the measure of him."

"I'm in," added Belgast. "When do we go?"

"Hold on a moment," said Evira. "You can't just walk in and talk to the High Lord of Ebenstadt. You need to get past his men, and that means you'll need coins."

The Dwarf grimaced. "Are you saying we must buy our way to him?"

"That's what I've heard, and it won't be cheap. Everyone you talk to is going to have their hand out. It's how the entire city works now."

"Fine," said Belgast. "I'll front us the funds, but I expect to be paid back, eventually."

"Then I suggest we dally no longer," said Brother Yaromir.

"You want to go right now?" said Stanislav.

"I see no reason to delay it, do you?"

"No, I suppose not."

"Then let's get it over with," said the Dwarf.


The old commandery of the Temple Knights of Saint Cunar was an immense stone structure, built more than a hundred years ago. At its height, it housed a full ten companies of Temple Knights, not to mention all their horses. The Holy Warriors abandoned the place after their defeat at the hands of the Therengian-Orc Alliance, but it was still an impressive sight.

Stanislav, Belgast, and Brother Yaromir had left the Elk mid-morning, making the short walk at a brisk pace. They now stood on the opposite side of the roadway, watching the comings and goings.

"What do you make of it?" asked Stanislav.

"I say we storm the place," said Belgast. "Look at those guards. Have you ever seen such slovenly soldiers?"

"I admit they look ill-equipped," said Brother Yaromir, "but I suspect they more than make up for it in numbers."

The Dwarf sighed. "I suppose you're right. So if a frontal assault is out of the question, how do you suggest we proceed?"

"The first step will be gaining entry to the building," said Stanislav, "then we'll need to ascertain where we can find Tybalt Kemp."

"I suspect that won't be too hard," suggested Brother Yaromir.

"Surely you jest?" said Belgast. "Look at the size of that place."

The Temple Knight smiled. "Most of that building is dedicated to small cells which used to house the brothers of the order. I doubt Kemp will want to use one of those. Instead, he'll likely take the Knight Commander's quarters, which are on the top floor on the western side of the building."

"You've been there before?"

"No, but all commanderies follow the same principle of design. By tradition, the commander of the detachment has a window that faces west, towards the Holy City of Herani."

"But Herani is to the south, isn't it?" said Stanislav.

"More southwest than due south," said the knight, "but such calculations would prove far too difficult to master in the real world. Thus, we have this simple tradition."

"Any other traditions we should be familiar with?" grumbled the Dwarf.

"If it were Temple Knights we were up against, I would say plenty, but at a guess, the present occupants do not follow the same strictures of their predecessors. In any case, we are here to talk, not fight."

"Not even a little?"

"No, my friend. Such an altercation could well spell the doom not only of us but of your friends to the east as well."

"That means you must behave," added Stanislav.

"I know what it means. I just don't have to like it. Don't worry, I'll keep my temper in check. Now, where do we enter?"

"Over there," said Brother Yaromir, pointing. "There's a gate where the knights would ride in and out. If you look closely, you'll see a wicket gate. That's the smaller gate used to allow individuals entry."

"You mean the one with the two guards?"

"Precisely. Shall I lead?"

Belgast swept his hand and made a small bow. "By all means."

They walked across the road, the guards quickly noting their approach. Hands went to weapons, but no steel was drawn; instead, they gave the trio suspicious looks.

"Greetings," said the knight. "My name is Brother Yaromir, Temple Knight of Saint Mathew. My companions and I seek an audience with His Lordship, Tybalt Kemp."

"Do you, now?" replied the burlier of the two men. "Well, I'm afraid you'll go away unsatisfied. The High Lord is not seeing anyone today."

"No one at all?"

The guard shook his head.

"A pity," said Belgast. "And here we were, ready to make a donation to the guild."

"A donation?"

The Dwarf held out a golden coin. "Yes, for the betterment of warriors everywhere. I don't suppose I could leave it in your care?" He could almost see the man drooling.

"I can let you in, but I can't guarantee he'll see you."

"Understood," said Brother Yaromir.

Belgast took a step closer and dropped the coin into the man's palm. The guard stared at it a moment, then closed his hand. "You may enter."

"Thank you," said the Dwarf.

They passed through the wicket gate and then proceeded down a tunnel. The far end sported another pair of doors, but Brother Yaromir directed them to an archway on the side. "This should get us inside the dormitory. From there, we'll be able to find a way upstairs."

They entered to see a long hallway, doors along the sides at regular intervals. There'd been tapestries hanging here at some point, but many had been torn from the walls. Others had their lower halves cut off, likely to feed a fire or serve as some proof against the cold and dampness of the place. Refuse was strewn about the corridor, everything from spoiled food to Human waste, and Stanislav struggled not to gag at the stench.

"Disgusting," said Belgast. "Have they no sense of decency?"

Warriors watched them walk by but, otherwise, paid them little attention. Eventually, they reached a large, two-storey room with a wide set of stone steps leading to the upper floor.

They began to ascend, the Temple Knight leading, but they encountered two more guards as they neared the top landing. One of them, an older man with a thick, blond beard, heard them coming and moved to intercept.

"You can't come up here," he announced. "This area is off-limits to non-guild members."

"And if we want to join the guild?" asked Stanislav.

"Then you'll need to arrange a meeting with the guild master."

"And how do I do that?"

"Beats me, but you won't find him here."

Brother Yaromir ignored the comment. "We come seeking the High Lord of Ebenstadt."

"And I came here searching for fame and glory," replied the bearded guard. "We don't always get what we want."

"Can we not reach an understanding?"

"Understand this," the man added, placing his hand on the hilt of his sword. "You're not going any farther."

Belgast pushed his way past the Temple Knight. "Come now," he soothed. "Surely we can come to an agreement?" He held up a coin.

"You'll need to do better than that."

"This is robbery," grumbled Belgast, pulling a second coin from his pouch.

The guard watched him closely. "Keep going," he urged.

"This isn't a bottomless purse, you know." The Dwarf pulled the third coin, then held them out. "Will that suffice?"

The man took the coins, tossing one to his companion. "You may pass," he said, "but don't say I didn't warn you."

They moved through the landing into a long corridor. The layout of the commandery was essentially a rectangle, with the courtyard smack dab in the centre. This corridor appeared to run all the way around the building, making navigation a simple matter.

"This way," said Brother Yaromir. "We'll soon be able to see the commander's offices."

The upper walls were built of the same stone, but the wooden floor beneath their feet creaked with every step.

"This is shoddy work," muttered the Dwarf. "You'd think they'd take greater care."

"The Church doesn't build its own structures," defended Brother Yaromir. "Rather, it hires out experts in such things."

"Well, your experts here weren't worth the coin. This floor feels like it would collapse at a moment's notice."

"Nonsense. It's quite sturdy."

"Not by Dwarven standards, it's not."

"Come now, you two," said Stanislav. "Let's not bicker."

Belgast halted, examining a portrait that hung on the wall. "Who's this?" he asked.

"Likely a past commander," noted the Temple Knight. "The Cunars celebrate their leaders."

"Does your order do the same?"

"No, we value humility."

"A pity," said the Dwarf. "You'd look good in a painting like this. The artistry is impressive."

"How much farther?" asked Stanislav.

"I'm not sure," said Brother Yaromir, "but we must be close. There are more paintings down this way."

"This is quite the building," mused Belgast. "I wonder what it would take to capture such a place?"

"This place is a fortress, built for the express purpose of holding off attackers. You'll note the double doors every thirty paces. They might be open at the moment, but each can be barred should the need arise, and those doors are solid oak. They would prove difficult to breach."

"But not impossible," said Belgast. "My people have ways of dealing with such obstacles. I'll admit the place is impressive, but it's no Dwarven fortification."

"How many men do you figure it would take?" asked Stanislav.

"Why?" asked the Temple Knight. "Have you an army nearby?"

"No, merely curious."

"A hundred, maybe a few more," replied Brother Yaromir. "It really depends on exactly how many men Kemp has here and whether or not they know their business. From what I've seen so far, I would say their reputation far exceeds their quality."

They turned a corner, placing them in the westernmost section of the building. Clearly, this was where they wanted to be, for two men stood guard outside a door, looking smart in matching armour and weapons.

"Well, now," said Belgast. "It looks as though we finally found the man in charge." He began rummaging through his purse.

"Greetings," said Brother Yaromir. "We come seeking an audience with Lord Tybalt Kemp."

"Wait here," ordered the shorter of the two guards. He stepped inside, leaving the door slightly ajar while his companion kept a close eye on the visitors.

The guard soon reappeared. "There will be a fee for the privilege of conversing with His Lordship."

"Of course there will," complained the Dwarf. He extracted some gold, but as he held them out, the man shook his head. "That's for His Lordship, not us." He opened the door the rest of the way, allowing them access.

They stepped through, with Brother Yaromir in the lead. The large room they entered was far bigger than the common room at the Elk, and the western end held a series of narrow windows depicting scenes in stained glass. One such window was open, allowing a fresh breeze to circulate through the room.

Beneath the windows, behind an immense desk, sat a plain-looking man with thinning hair and a clean-shaven face. He looked up from a pile of parchments and papers upon their entrance. Brother Yaromir halted some three paces from the desk, then bowed respectfully.

"Greetings, High Lord," he said.

"Your Grace," said Kemp.

"I beg your pardon?"

"You will address me as 'Your Grace'. Is that understood?"

"Of course, Your Grace."

Kemp tapped an empty spot on his desk. "You may place your payment here."

Belgast stepped up, spreading the coins out before Kemp.

The High Lord stretched his neck as he examined the funds. "You've only paid for the privilege of a short audience," he said. "What can I do for you?"

Brother Yaromir continued. "It's more about what WE can do for YOU, Your Grace. We are led to understand there's a food shortage at present."

"Of what concern is it to you?"

"We come representing an alternate source of grain, Your Grace."

"Crops?" said Kemp. "Where is this food?"

"To the east."

"Preposterous. The only thing to the east is wilderness and wild men. I've seen it myself."

Stanislav cleared his throat. "It's those very wild men who we represent, Your Grace. They wish to trade with you, food in particular."

"What makes you think I won't just send soldiers east and take what we need?"

"Do that," said Stanislav, "and the crops will burn."

"You wouldn't dare! Your own people would starve."

"No. Personally, I wouldn't, but I'm not the one making the decisions. I represent the Thane of Runewald, and he can be extremely ruthless when the occasion requires."

"And what, exactly, would he want in return?"

"A peace pact and access to your markets."

Kemp pursed his lips, clearly thinking things through. The room remained silent, a silence that went on a little too long, until the High Lord of Ebenstadt finally turned to Brother Yaromir. "What does the Church have to say on the matter?"

"We are always eager to keep the peace, Your Grace."

"I'm sure you are." Kemp's eyes swivelled back to Stanislav. "This Runewald of yours, how far away is it?"

When no one answered, he pressed the issue. "Come now. If we're to send wagons, we must surely know the distance?"

"Wagons? Two days," said Belgast, "maybe three if they're heavily loaded."

"That close? You surprise me. I expected to need to go much farther afield."

"So you agree?" asked Stanislav.

In answer, Kemp looked at the papers that littered his desk. "Do you see all this? They're from people asking me for help. I only have one rule when it comes to such things—payment. Now tell me, what will you pay me to take your food?"

"Pay? Your townsfolk are starving. You need this food to feed them."

"I need no such thing. Do you think I care one way or the other whether they starve?"

"So, just to be clear," said the Dwarf, "you don't want the food?"

"Oh, I want the food, but I'm not willing to pay for it. Your only hope is to grease my palm. Do that, and your food will have a ready market."

"I cannot, in good conscience, agree to that," said Stanislav.

"Then it appears we are at an impasse. I suggest you go home and prepare for war, gentlemen. It's your only hope."

"I don't think you realize your mistake," said Brother Yaromir. "This is the same group who defeated the Holy Army."

"Is it?" said Kemp. "Good. I look forward to the challenge."

"They destroyed the Cunar presence in these parts. Surely you don't mean to fight them?""

"The Cunars were fools. I, on the other hand, am not bound by Holy Orders. Now leave, gentlemen, before I have you clapped in irons."

# SUBTERFUGE

## SUMMER 1105

"So tell me again how is it you didn't end up married to my brother?"
"When he arrived in Runewald, he was already with Natalia," said Melwyn. "I tried to convince him it was wrong, but he wouldn't listen."

"My memory's a little hazy about my time in Athelwald," said Ethwyn. "Something to do with the head wound I took when the village was attacked. Didn't you end up promised to someone else?"

"I did. You remember Caladin?"

"Of course," said Ethwyn. "You mentioned him earlier. He was quite the catch—everything my brother wasn't. You should count yourself lucky. You could've done a lot worse."

"It's not that we had much of an opportunity to see where it would go. We were attacked shortly after that."

"Did you get a chance to… you know, try things out?"

Melwyn blushed, although she obviously enjoyed the attention. "No, I'm afraid not."

"So, in essence, you waited for Athgar."

"I suppose that's one way of looking at it. To be honest, I was convinced he was dead. When he showed up here, I thought it had to be the work of the Gods."

"How do you know it wasn't?" asked Ethwyn.

"He didn't want me anymore."

"I doubt that. He probably felt trapped."

"Trapped? How?"

"I've seen what it's like out there in the Petty Kingdoms first-hand. The women there will spread their legs for anyone."

"And you believe that's why he married Natalia?"

Ethwyn smiled, her trap complete. "Why else would he do such a thing? He hardly knows her."

"I suppose I never thought of it that way, but it matters little. I've lost him now."

"Oh, I don't know about that."

"Meaning?"

"I know my brother," said Ethwyn. "He still loves you, Melwyn. I see it in his eyes. Of course, he can't act on those feelings. I mean, how would it look, a thane carrying on behind his wife's back?"

"You think he still loves me?"

"I know he does. If that skrolling of his weren't around, I'm sure he'd be with you right now."

"She's a powerful mage."

"She'd need to be. Look at her. She's pale as a ghost and can barely carry her own child. Why, I bet a stiff wind would knock her down. It's not as if she has any meat on her bones."

Melwyn laughed. "I suppose you're right."

"I bet if we put our minds to it, we could push those two apart."

"We can't. We need her magic to help protect us."

"Nonsense. We're more than capable of looking after ourselves. It's not as if I'm suggesting we do away with the Orc alliance entirely, merely render Natalia less... influential."

"All right, I'm in," said Melwyn. "How do we proceed?"

Ethwyn smiled. This was proving far easier than she'd imagined.


That evening she sat across from Athgar, listening while he related all that had befallen him. She feigned interest, occasionally asking for clarification, but her real focus was on the others gathered around the fire. Skora was there, of course, but the old woman held little interest to her. Natalia sat to Athgar's right, Oswyn held tightly in her arms, while to his left sat the Orc chieftain, Kargen, and his bondmate, Shaluhk. Harwath rounded out the little group. He'd been reporting on the fyrd's progress when Ethwyn arrived, and, sensing a potential ally, she'd insisted he remained. Now he sat beside her, and she made sure to reach past him from time to time to remind him of how attractive she was.

"And that's how we ended up here," said Athgar.

"A fascinating tale," said Ethwyn. "And you say she tried to kill you in Draybourne?"

Natalia laughed. "Not intentionally."

"It all worked out for the best in the end," he added. "After all, she DID nurse me back to health."

"Yes, and now we have a beautiful daughter together."

Ethwyn suppressed the urge to tell the traitor to shut up. The Stormwind woman was dangerous, after all, and she couldn't risk an overt display of her own abilities. "You must find it difficult, living life amongst our people after spending so much time in the larger cities of the Petty Kingdoms."

"This is my home now," answered Natalia. "I wouldn't want it any other way."

"Yes," added Shaluhk, "and she is a full member of our tribe, the same as her bondmate."

"Surely not?" said Ethwyn. "Gods know I love my brother, but he's definitely no Orc."

"One does not need to be an Orc to be a member of the Red Hand," said Kargen. "Who knows, perhaps one day you, too, shall be inducted into our tribe?"

"That would certainly be an honour," said Ethwyn. "Tell me, how was it you knew he could be a Pyromancer?"

"That was not my doing, rather it was the wisdom of Artoch. He discovered your brother's affinity for fire."

"Yes," added Athgar. "He was a great mentor. I miss him dearly. He taught me how to harness my inner spark."

What nonsense is this, thought Ethwyn. Inner spark? Was her brother truly insane? A real Fire Mage must understand the primal element of flames, not work with tiny sparks.

Natalia picked up on her confusion, misreading it for ignorance. "The Orcs' approach to magic differs significantly from what we learned at the Volstrum."

"I assume that's a magical academy?" said Ethwyn.

"It is, and the place where I trained."

"You have me intrigued. In what way are the two different?"

"We Stormwinds were always taught to release the full power within us, even when using minor spells. Only after meeting Athgar did I learn there was an advantage to occasionally holding back when casting."

"Holding back? That sounds dangerous."

"Not in the least, although it can be difficult at times. Since I met him, I've learned a certain degree of"—she looked at her husband—"finesse."

"I've heard you're a very powerful caster, Natalia. Is that true?"

"I developed my powers at an early age, if that's what you mean, but I'm sure there are others more powerful than I."

"She is being modest," said Shaluhk. "I have seen her in battle and would not want to face her. She even stopped Athgar from immolating."

The words shocked Ethwyn. At Korascajan, they'd been warned about the possibility of being consumed by their own magic. It was considered the worst possible fate, yet they were told there was nothing they could do about it.

"Immolating?" she managed to squeak out.

"Yes," the shaman explained. "If a master of flame uses up all their inner spark, they can draw on their physical body to supply the energy they need to sustain the spell. This approach, however, comes with substantial risk. If not controlled, the magical flame will consume the caster."

"And you say Natalia stopped this from happening? How is that even possible?"

"That I can not say," said Shaluhk. "I saw it with my own eyes, yet still, I do not understand how. Artoch said, together they are greater than they are apart. That situation was evidence of that very truth."

"It's hard to believe my own brother is a Fire Mage."

"Not a Fire Mage," corrected Athgar, "a master of flame."

"Aren't they the same thing?"

"The difference is in the training," explained Natalia. "The Orcs don't use what we Humans would refer to as traditional training techniques. Instead, they take a more measured approach."

"Meaning?"

"At the Volstrum, students spend years learning the history and basics of magic before they're allowed to cast their first spell. The Orcs, on the other hand, teach one spell at a time, advancing in knowledge only as each is mastered."

"And does that make their approach better?"

"That's difficult to say," said Natalia, "but it's certainly a different way of looking at things."

"It also means a master of flame can grow quickly in power," said Kargen. "In essence, they are limited only by their capacity to learn."

"Yes," added Natalia, "yet they don't cover nearly so much theory as we did at the Volstrum."

"All that's true," said Athgar. "Natalia isn't just a Water Mage—she's a battle mage. And she didn't learn just spells, but strategy and tactics as well."

Ethwyn looked at her sister-in-law with new respect. Back at Korascajan, they hadn't told her she'd be facing a battle mage. Now she wondered what else they'd failed to mention.

"Just how many mages are here?" she asked.

"Aside from Athgar?" said Natalia. "Only two, Shaluhk and I, but there are more within the other tribes. They all helped out at the Battle of the Standing Stones."

"But I thought Shaluhk was only a healer? How would she help in battle, other than helping the wounded, I mean?"

"There is much a shaman can do to influence a battle," said Shaluhk. "I called on the spirits of the Ancestors to lend their aid."

"So you prayed?"

"No, I invoked their spirits to assist in the fight."

Ethwyn was dumbfounded. "Are you saying you conjured the dead?"

"No," said Shaluhk. "I called on the spirits to manifest in this world to aid us. You might call it a ghost army."

Ethwyn turned to Harwath and gave him a winning smile. "And what of you? Were you there?"

"Yes," the man answered. "I was part of the select fyrd."

"Select?"

"Yes," explained Athgar. "The more seasoned warriors were kept as a reserve used to turn the tide of battle, Harwath amongst them."

Ethwyn touched Harwath's arm. "How exciting. You didn't tell me you were a hero."

He blushed. "I'm not. I was only doing my part to fight for my people."

"Well, you definitely have the body for it." He turned an even darker shade of red, and she smiled, her grip over him now complete.

"I'm glad everything worked out well in the end," Ethwyn continued, then let out a yawn. "My pardon, I didn't realize how late it was. I'd best turn in for the night."

"And leave us?" said Harwath. "You can't mean it?"

"I'm afraid so," she said, watching his face fall. "I tell you what; why don't you walk me home?"

His face lit up. "I'd be delighted"—he looked at Athgar—"providing that's all right with you?"

"Why would it bother me?"

"She's your younger sister. I just thought..."

"My sister is more than capable of looking after herself."

"So I shouldn't escort her home?"

Athgar shook his head in wonderment.

"Go take her home," said Natalia, "before she changes her mind."

Ethwyn waited for Harwath to stand, then took his offered hand, leaning on him as she stood. She made sure to bring her face close to his. "Come," she whispered. "It's getting late, and I would be abed."

Natalia watched them leave. "Not the quickest at picking things up, is he?"

"Who?" said Athgar. "You mean Harwath?"

Shaluhk smiled. "It seems males of both our races are similar in many ways. Amongst them, not recognizing the obvious."

"What are you suggesting?" said Kargen.

"Nothing, my love," she replied, standing. "Now, take me to bed. It's getting late."

Kargen turned a deeper shade of green. He turned to Athgar, but all he saw was a smirk. "What are you smiling at?"

"I'm just happy. Why, is there something wrong with that?"

The Orc cleared his throat. "No, there is not. Now, I am off to bed with my bondmate. See that you do not disturb us."

"Oh, we won't," said Natalia. "We've plans of our own."


Magran surveyed the village. Runewald was the first of the Therengian villages to receive a palisade, and he wondered how long it would be until all were protected in this manner. He'd come here seeking information about Natalia, but now that he'd arrived, he had little idea where to begin.

A trio of Orcs edged past him, speaking in their guttural tongue. It still felt strange seeing the greenskins amongst his own people, but they'd come to their assistance when the invaders attacked. Perhaps their presence wasn't so bad after all?

Natalia Stormwind had been named the High Mage, making her responsible for the training and equipping of the army. It, therefore, made sense for Magran to seek out her underlings, the better to judge her character. He spotted two guards by the great hut and walked over to them.

"Excuse me," he said. "Could you tell me who commands the fyrd here?"

"That would be the thane's responsibility."

"Does he oversee all their training?"

"No, why? Do you wish to join?"

"I do, as a matter of fact. Who would I see about that?"

"Seek out a man named Harwath. You can find him over yonder." The guard pointed.

Magran followed his gaze to see a trio of men standing around an odd-looking smithy. "Which one is Harwath?" he asked.

"The shorter one."

"In that case, I shall talk to him directly. Thank you."

He moved closer, listening as his target talked. One of the men moved slightly, revealing a Dwarf wearing a leather apron.

"How long does it take you to forge a blade such as this?" asked Harwath.

"Not long," replied the Dwarf, "but I've other priorities at present."

"Excuse me?" called out Magran. "Are you Harwath?"

"I am," replied the man, turning to face the newcomer. "What can I do for you?"

"I came here from Scarburn. I wish to join the fyrd."

"Scarburn has its own fyrd."

"True, but Thane Athgar's fame is known far and wide. It is he who I wish to serve—a true hero."

"He is but a man," said Harwath. "You'd do well to remember that."

"I meant no offence."

"And I took none. Tell me, have you any experience with arms?"

"Of course. Like all good Therengians, I learned the axe and shield."

"Done any spear work?"

"A little."

Harwath looked him over. "You look to be reasonably fit. Have you your own weapons?"

"Only an axe. Everything else belonged to the Scarburn fyrd."

"And you informed your own thane you were coming here?"

"Of course."

"Good," said Harwath. "What's your name?"

"Magran."

"In that case, welcome, Magran. The fyrd assembles once every fifteen days, the next occasion being two days hence. Where are you staying?"

"That I've yet to determine."

"Any family here?"

"I'm afraid not."

Harwath frowned. "I'll let you stay with me until we can find somewhere else for you to call home." He pointed. "See that hut over there? That's mine. Inside, you'll find a woman named Anweld—that's my mother. She'll find you some food."

"Thank you, Harwath."

"Don't thank me. You've yet to see the kind of training we do here."

"I shall endeavour not to disappoint you."

"See that you don't. Now, you must excuse me. We're in the middle of a transaction with Kieren here."

Magran bowed his head. "Of course, forgive me for the interruption."


That evening he sat across the fire from Harwath, watching the man as he warmed his hands.

"It's a bit chilly tonight," said Harwath.

"Your mother tells me you were at the great battle."

"So I was."

"What was it like?"

"I could lie and tell you it was heroic, but the truth is it was absolutely terrifying."

"How did the battle progress?"

"Not a clue," said Harwath. "From my point of view, we stood around endlessly, then charged into battle for a fierce melee. You'd need to talk to Natalia Stormwind to really get a feel for the ebb and flow of it all."

"She's the mage, isn't she?"

"She is, and also wife to the thane."

"Do you know her well?"

"I count her amongst my friends, if that's what you mean. Why?"

"I know so little of her," said Magran. "I'm told she's an outsider. Is that true?"

"It is, but that doesn't make her any less dedicated to our cause."

"I must confess my knowledge of magic is fairly limited."

"As is mine," said Harwath, "not that it matters. Natalia is a Water Mage, but her understanding of all the arcane arts is impressive, especially on the battlefield."

"So it was her magic that saved us?"

Harwath chuckled. "That's oversimplifying the matter, but true to a certain extent."

"Meaning?"

"Her tactics of organizing all our spell casters proved decisive in the end. Well, that and the tuskers."

"Interesting," noted Magran. "What do we know of her background? She's obviously not a Therengian."

"True. She's actually from a place called Karslev, which, I'm told, lies to the north, but she travelled with Athgar for some time before settling down here."

"And you trust her?"

"Of course," said Harwath. "Why wouldn't I?"

"No reason at all," said Magran. "I just find it strange an outsider has been accepted so readily."

"Only because you don't know her."

"It's true, I don't, but I hope you'll introduce me someday. I'd love to meet the saviour of our kingdom."

"We'll see," said Harwath. "She keeps pretty busy, what with their new daughter and everything else going on."

"Everything else? What's that supposed to mean? Are we in danger of attack?"

"There's always a threat lurking somewhere. For now, you need to concentrate on honing your martial skills. Who knows, you might need them at some point in the future."

# PLANNING

## SUMMER 1105

Raleth halted the warriors and called for a brief rest. They flopped to the ground, content to soak up the sun and relax, all except for Hilwyth. She, alone, strode over to their commander.

"Well?" she asked. "How did things go with Ethwyn?"

"That's none of your business," he snapped.

"Has this got something to do with your brother Harwath?"

He glared back at her. "What do you know about Harwath?"

"Probably nothing."

"Out with it, Hilwyth."

"It's only that I had an interesting chat with Bergwith. Do you know her?"

"Bergwith? Of course, my brother's seeing her."

"Not for much longer, unless I miss my guess."

"What's that supposed to mean?"

Hilwyth smiled. "I hear he's taken a liking to our thane's sister."

Raleth's face turned crimson. "Preposterous!"

"I'm only relating what I've heard."

"But he can't. He's as good as married."

Hilwyth shrugged. "Don't blame me. I'm only the messenger. Do you want to talk about it?"

He glared at her, giving her a sense of doom, but then he shook his head. "I'm sorry," he said at last. "I didn't mean to upset you. It's just that…"

"You liked Ethwyn."

"I did. She's like no woman I've ever seen before."

"And now?"

"I see her as nothing but a temptress."

Hilwyth had seen him in a foul mood before, but today she wasn't willing to offer any pity. "Pull yourself together, for Gods' sake. Do you think you're the only one to lose out on love?"

He looked as though she'd slapped him. "What are you talking about?"

"I don't want to sit here listening to your blathering anymore, Raleth. If you can't see what's right in front of your nose, then I'm done with you!"

"I…"

"I, what?"

"I never knew you felt that way."

"Well, now you do," she said. "Now that I've embarrassed myself, I'm going to march ahead to Scarburn."

"No, wait," he pleaded. "I'm sorry. I got carried away. Let me escort you."

"You need to march the warriors," she said, "or did you forget your duty?"

"No, of course not. Look, I'll be the first to admit I've been a fool. When I set eyes on Ethwyn, she was all I could think about."

"Well, that doesn't make ME feel any better."

"Can I make it up to you?"

"How?"

"I beg your pardon?"

"How will you make it up to me?"

"Any way I can," he replied. "Just give me another chance. I beg of you."

"I will, but no more talk of Ethwyn."

"Agreed," said Raleth. "Now, can I escort you?"

"Don't be silly. The fyrd still needs you."

"Then will you accompany us as we march?"

She smiled. "I most assuredly will."

He called the fyrd to their feet, and they resumed their march westward, Hilwyth now at his side.

They walked in silence for half the morning, then she began her interrogation. "Tell me, why were you so infatuated with Ethwyn?"

"That's easy. She's a great beauty. Few women have that sort of presence."

"And what makes her beautiful?"

"I'm not sure. I suppose it's a combination of things."

"Such as?"

"Her face, her hair, the way she smiles at me… I mean, everyone."

"So you're saying she's a shameless flirt?"

He reddened. "I guess I am."

"And just because she bats her eyes at you, you believe the Gods sent her here to reward you? I'm afraid real life doesn't quite work that way, Raleth."

"Meaning?"

"That the very thing you find attractive in her would also drive you to distraction."

"I'm not sure I follow."

"Let's put it another way—you like the fact she flirts with you. What would you do if she flirted with everyone else in that same way?"

"I don't think I'd like that."

"So there you have it. The thing that attracted you to her in the first place is working against you. She's using you, Raleth, likely to get at your brother."

"And why would she do that?"

"I'm not sure," said Hilwyth. "Maybe to get closer to controlling the army?"

"But that's Athgar's responsibility."

"You know as well as I do, Athgar doesn't concern himself with the day-to-day details."

"But what about Bergwith?"

"What about her?" she replied. "Bergwith is a grown woman and more than capable of taking care of her own affairs."

"Yes, but I don't imagine she'll be too pleased to learn Harwath has been spending time with Ethwyn. Should I tell her?"

Hilwyth thought about that before answering. "No, it's best she learns for herself. In any case, I think she already suspects."

"You do? Why?"

"No reason in particular." She glanced at the fyrd, following along in their wake. "How much farther, do you suppose?"

"We've got a while to go yet. Why? In a hurry?"

She smiled. "Not anymore."


"Pass the ale," said Athgar. "I'm building up a massive thirst."

"You know," said Natalia, "just because Belgast has returned from Ebenstadt doesn't mean you need to get drunk."

"I'm just speaking a lot, and it makes my throat dry." He returned his attention to the Dwarf. "Sorry, you were saying?"

"I'm afraid this Lord Kemp fellow didn't take kindly to our suggestions. It's likely he'll send troops after us."

"When do you figure he'll make his move?"

"Soon, if he wants to keep his soldiers happy."

"Surely he'll wait till the autumn," said Natalia. "That way he can capture the harvest."

"I doubt he's that forward thinking," said Belgast.

"In that case, maybe we should educate him?"

The Dwarf snorted, causing him to choke on his ale. "Sorry, but I don't think he'd listen. He appears to have only one thing on his mind—instant obedience. Stanislav elected to remain in the city. He'll try to send word if the army marches."

"Any idea how many men he can muster?"

"Not accurate numbers, no. We do know he has some horsemen, although not the same quality as the Cunar knights we defeated. I doubt he could put much into the field when it comes down to it. We know he's been hoarding food, but even that can't last forever."

"That only makes him more dangerous," said Natalia. "A warrior who's starving will take desperate chances to survive."

"I can't say I like the timing," said Athgar. "We're supposed to leave for the meeting of the moot soon. I can't very well do that with Ashborne being threatened."

"You're not the only thane," said Natalia. "The others can take steps to halt them."

"I wish it were so, but we're the closest to Ashborne."

"I don't believe sending troops there is the answer," said Belgast. "He must realize he can't defeat us in open battle. His men simply don't have the discipline."

"Then what is it you think he intends?"

"Are you familiar with Elven tactics?"

"No," said Athgar.

"I am," said Natalia, "and I think I see where you're going with this."

"Then can you explain it to me?" said Athgar.

"I'll let Belgast continue. I'm interested to see his take on things."

"Very well," said the Dwarf. "When the elves get involved in a conflict, they'll often start by sending out forest wardens to learn all they can about the enemy."

"You mean like scouts?" said Athgar.

"Similar but much more deadly. They don't just learn the terrain, they also attack randomly, forcing their enemy to deploy warriors to protect their villages and farms."

"To what end?"

"It weakens the enemy by making them have to hold warriors in reserve. Then, when their foe is stretched to the limit, they'll advance their army in one massive push, overwhelming all defences."

"And you believe this is what Kemp intends?"

"I do," said Belgast, "though perhaps he feels this type of raiding will be sufficient to convince us to accept his offer."

Athgar turned to Natalia. "How do we counter that?"

"We'd need to remain vigilant, not only at Ashborne but the other villages as well. Runewald has the advantage of the palisade now, but I'm worried about Scarburn. It's the next closest village to Ebenstadt, and it also lies in open terrain, easily located by our enemy."

"Wouldn't that make it easier to defend?"

"Not necessarily. If Belgast's theory is correct, Kemp will use hit-and-run tactics, likely using horsemen to speed their retreat. If their aim is to instill fear, then they'll attack at night, at least for a while."

"Meaning?"

"If their tactics prove successful, they'll become bolder, massing in larger numbers and attacking during the day."

"You seem to understand a lot about this," said the Dwarf.

"We learned about this at the Volstrum. It's how insurrection usually starts."

"Insurrection?" said Athgar. "Are you suggesting they want to overthrow us? I doubt that would work."

"On that, we can agree. Therengians have a strong cultural bond. If anything, the attacks of outsiders will only bring them closer together."

"Yes, but would Kemp understand that?" said Belgast. "I imagine he's operating under the assumption everyone is just like him."

"It's a valid argument," said Natalia, "but the fact remains we must still do something against this type of raiding, however irregular it might be."

"What did your instructors at the Volstrum suggest?"

"Ruthless suppression of anyone who spoke out against the ruling elite, but I'm afraid that approach won't work here. These are outsiders." She grinned. "You might say it's the skrollings we have to blame."

"Could we counter with the same tactic ourselves?" asked Athgar.

"I suppose we could. I never would've thought of that."

Now Athgar was the one to smile. "You would've gotten around to it sooner or later."

Belgast snapped his fingers. "That's it! The Orcs are experts at this type of warfare, don't you see? It utilizes all their hunting skills."

"We can't just send the Orcs off to do all the fighting."

"True," added Natalia, "but they can show our people how to go about it. I would propose we form smaller groups of a dozen—half would be Orcs, the rest Human."

"It would take time to train them," said Belgast, "time we likely don't have."

"He makes a good point," said Athgar.

"We must start somewhere," she replied, "and even if we don't use them here and now, they'll be ready to carry out orders should a full-blown war erupt."

"You don't need to convince me. You're in charge of our army."

"Yes, but you're the head of our government. Well, you and the other thanes."

"I'll meet with Kargen and see what he thinks. If he agrees…"

"You know he will," said Natalia.

"Then, WHEN he agrees, we'll create a few of these groups and see how things progress. That way, we only involve Runewald and the Red Hand Orcs."

"Good," she added. "And then, when it DOES work, you can tell the other thanes all about it."

"That's good in the long run," said Belgast, "but what of the short? You can't keep sending men to Ashborne, especially now with the threat of raids hanging over all the villages."

"We must rely on the Orcs to protect us," said Athgar. "The fyrd is trained to stand in a line of battle, not fight in this manner."

"That's a good point," said Natalia. "What if we approach this from a different perspective?"

"Meaning?"

"We should be thinking like the enemy. What do they know of our land?"

"Very little," said Athgar. "The leaders of the Holy Army had no decent maps."

"True, but they marched to battle near the stone gate, so they more or less know that area."

"They never actually found any of our villages."

"Except for Ashborne," noted Athgar. "They raided it, remember?"

"Put yourself in Kemp's boots. If you were the leader of Ebenstadt, how would you proceed?"

"I don't think I could without knowing the area."

"Then how would you learn more about the region?"

"Send out patrols?" suggested Athgar.

"And what would a patrol consist of?"

"Horsemen, so they can move quickly."

"And how many would you send?" she asked.

"That's a good question. I suppose there'd have to be enough to stay safe, especially now they're aware we've got people on watch. Say a dozen?"

"That would certainly be consistent with the size of the group who raided Ashborne." She turned to the Dwarf. "When you were in Ebenstadt, what did you see in terms of warriors?"

"Quite a motley bunch, mostly footmen. Then again, that's what you'd expect in a city, isn't it?"

"We know from Stanislav that horses have grown much more expensive. That would seem to indicate there's a desire for more of them."

"What makes you say that?" asked Athgar.

"It's simple," she replied. "The cost of goods goes up with demand. The price of horses is high, meaning there must be a corresponding demand for them."

"Couldn't that mean a shortage of horseflesh?"

"It could, but that would take longer to affect prices. After all, if no one were buying, it would matter little how many were for sale."

Athgar shook his head. "I don't know how you can remember such things. I have trouble remembering how to fletch an arrow."

"You forget, I spent years learning theory. The family spent generations perfecting their teaching techniques." She smiled. "And, for the record, I've watched you making arrows, and I've never seen you doubt yourself."

"She's got you there," added Belgast.

A distant cry interrupted them.

"It looks like Oswyn has woken up," said Natalia. "If you'll excuse me a moment, I'll fetch your daughter."

Athgar watched her disappear into the next room. "What do you think, Belgast?"

"About the horses?"

"No, I mean about everything. Am I right when I estimate the strength of their patrols?"

"It's as good an estimate as any."

"But what if I'm wrong?"

The Dwarf shrugged. "Life is a gamble, my friend. We can make all the guesses we like, but in the end, we'll only know if we're right when the enemy appears."

"Yes, but am I making the right choices? People's lives are at stake here."

"Given the circumstances, I'd make the same decision as you," said Belgast.

"Thank you, that helps."

"I can see the burden of command weighs heavily on your shoulders. Feel free to call on me whenever you need advice, my friend. It's what I did for King Haglarith."

"I'm no king," insisted Athgar.

"Maybe not in name, but the way these people look at you says otherwise."

"Nonsense. I'm just another thane."

"Is that what you think? Have you not seen the reverence in the way they talk to you? It's a good thing you've got friends here to keep you humble, Athgar, else you'd need to widen the doors."

Athgar knitted his brows. "Widen the doors?"

"Yes, so your head would fit through."

"Why would my head not fit?"

"Never mind, it was a poor jest, anyway."

Natalia re-entered the room, Oswyn in her arms. "Did I miss much?"

"Athgar will fill you in," said Belgast. "I'm afraid I've got other things to see to."

"I hope we haven't kept you overly long?"

"Not at all, but I promised Kargen and Laruhk I'd meet them at the smithy."

"Kargen and Laruhk?" said Athgar. "What are they up to?"

The Dwarf smiled. "They've identified a potential weakness with the tusker riders—they're particularly susceptible to arrows. My cousins believe armour would solve the problem, but they're not familiar with Orcs' physiques."

"I didn't know you could design armour?"

"I don't, but my cousins don't speak the Human tongue very well, nor do they speak Orcish. I'm needed to translate."

"Well," said Natalia, "in that case, we won't keep you. Will you join us later for dinner?"

"Of course," said Belgast, bowing deeply before leaving.

Natalia sat and began feeding Oswyn while Athgar stared at their daughter.

"I wonder what the future will hold for her?" he mused.

"No one can predict the future, but we all make it."

"Isn't that a contradiction?"

"Not at all," she replied. "I sometimes like to ponder what might have happened had I made different choices, but the fact of the matter is it was precisely the choices I DID make that led me here, and I wouldn't change that for anything." She looked up from their daughter. "What about you? Having regrets?"

"No, it's not the past that concerns me, but the future. How do I know I'm doing the right thing?"

"That's a question philosophers have been asking for hundreds of years."

"Philosophers?"

"Yes, men and women of learning who spend their entire lives pondering things."

"And this earns them enough to eat?"

She laughed, lightening the mood. "In a sense, I suppose it does. They typically have a wealthy patron, some noble or person of influence who likes to show off his wealth by sponsoring such people. Philosophers are one name for them, but they might also be called sages, intellectuals, or even just thinkers."

"And what, exactly, do they ponder?"

"Anything and everything. Some might study magic, even though they're incapable of casting it. Others study animals. Remember Tonfer Garul—his position at the archives was essentially that of a philosopher."

"I guess when you put it that way, it makes perfect sense. What about our bard?"

"Dunstan? Yes, in a sense, he's a type of scholar as well."

"Scholar? Another name for them," said Athgar.

She laughed. "I expect one of the things they think about is what else they can call themselves. We often make fun of them, but they perform an important role in society."

"Which is?"

"They are repositories of knowledge."

"You make them sound like an archive."

"And they are," said Natalia. "It's much easier to ask someone for an answer than to research it yourself."

"How does one research an answer?"

"By reading old tomes and papers, by observation, especially in the case of nature, and lastly, by talking to witnesses."

"Witnesses to what?"

"Whatever it is you're researching. At the Volstrum, there were many accounts of the use of magic in battle. Do you know why?"

"To help you learn battle magic?" suggested Athgar.

"No, I meant where do you suppose they came from?"

He shrugged. "I haven't the faintest."

"Our ancestors took pains to record important events. You know, there's an old saying that those who don't learn their history are doomed to repeat it. Think about your own life. Have you ever cut yourself while making a bow?"

"I have, but not seriously. Why?"

"You learned your trade from your father. In a sense, he was a type of scholar, his expertise being the making of bows. You also learned Fire

Magic from Artoch, making him a scholar as well. I imagine one day you'll pass on your skills to someone else, possibly even your own daughter."

"Making me a scholar?"

"Precisely. Knowledge is most valuable when it's passed on from generation to generation. Of course, not every scholar spends ALL their time pondering things, but like anything else, things get better with practice."

"So the more I think about things," said Athgar, "the easier it will get to find solutions?"

"That's certainly the idea."

# MANIPULATION

## SUMMER 1105

"His name is Magran," said Harwath, "and he comes from the village of Scarburn."

"And he came here to serve my brother?" said Ethwyn. "I find that hard to believe."

"You shouldn't. Athgar's seen as a hero in these parts."

"But he wasn't even in charge of the battle, or so I'm told."

"It's true he wasn't in command, but he fought with the fyrd, and they well remember his axe swinging beside them."

Ethwyn frowned. "And you say this Magran contacted you?"

"He did. Apparently, he wants to join the local fyrd, although I suspect he'd prefer a position in the Thane Guard."

"So, then, why bring this to my attention?"

"He's been asking a lot of questions of late."

"About what?"

"Mostly Natalia, but he asks after Athgar as well."

"And his opinion of our Water Mage?"

"I don't know," said Harwath. "He keeps his personal opinions to himself."

"Could he be working for someone else?"

"Undoubtedly, but who? He's a Therengian. It's not as if he'd be employed by our enemies."

Ethwyn smiled at the thought. "No, I suppose not. It seems, then, the only logical explanation is he works for one of the other thanes."

"I'm not sure I follow," said Harwath. "Why would the other thanes need to do such a thing?"

"Could they feel threatened? Athgar is, as you say, perceived as the true leader of the Therengians. I'm sure they'd pay handsomely to learn what he's up to."

"Are you suggesting they're plotting to take over?"

"No, merely staying well informed about what's happening in this land."

"What do we do about him? Should I inform Athgar?"

"No," said Ethwyn. "We may be jumping to conclusions. It would be best if you brought Magran here to meet me. Then I can have a word with him and see what he's really up to.

"Excellent idea," said Harwath. "I shall seek him out."

"Good, but don't tell him why."

"I must tell him something."

"Then tell him you'd like to introduce him to your woman."

Harwath's eyebrows went up. "My woman?"

Ethwyn forced a smile. "Of course, better to start with the truth, don't you think?"

"Indeed," said Harwath.

"Where would he be right now?"

"He's not on duty at the moment, so I suspect he's watching the Dwarven smiths."

"Then go and find him and invite him to eat with us tonight."

"I shall." He dashed off without so much as a goodbye.

Melwyn stepped into the room from the back door. "He's a fool," she snapped.

"True," replied Ethwyn, "but he's our fool and may yet serve a useful purpose."

"I doubt it."

"Come now, you must learn to be more charitable. We can't do this all by ourselves, Melwyn. If nothing else, he'll provide a convenient alibi."

"What is it you're suggesting?"

"Me? Nothing at all, why? Have a guilty conscience?"

Melwyn frowned. "Not at all. Natalia deserves to suffer for the indignation she's caused me."

"And she will, I promise. But we must bide our time till the opportunity presents itself. If we act too soon, the whole thing will come crashing down on us, and everything will be for naught."

"And this stranger? What was his name, again?"

"Magran."

"I've never heard of him."

"Nor I," said Ethwyn, "but we are both relatively new to this place, and he's from a completely different village, or so he says."

"I'd know if he was local, for I have an excellent memory for faces. What do you suppose he's really after?"

"I suspect it's all about power. My brother has unwittingly placed a target on his back."

Melwyn gasped. "You think Athgar's in danger? I don't wish any harm to befall him."

"I'm sure he'll be fine. After all, he's surrounded by friends."

"Yes, including that skrolling woman. I wish I'd never met her or, better yet, that HE'D never met her."

"Come now," said Ethwyn. "She'll get her comeuppance in due course. In the meantime, we must present the appearance of the perfect family."

"He's not my family," said Melwyn.

"Not yet, but get Natalia out of the way, and it'll only be a matter of time."

"You really believe so?"

"I know so," declared Ethwyn. "Now, let us put our minds to the task at hand."

"Which is?"

"How do we put Natalia in her proper place? Has she any weaknesses?"

"None that I'm aware of."

"There must be something?"

Melwyn shook her head. "No. As far as Athgar's concerned, she's perfect."

"I very much doubt that."

"What's that supposed to mean?"

"Every relationship has its weaknesses," said Ethwyn. "All we need to do is find theirs, apply a little pressure, and watch as it crumbles."

"What about jealousy?"

"Who would we make jealous—Athgar? I don't think that would work. He's too confident that she loves him, and in any event, we don't want to do anything that might turn him against you, Melwyn, or this whole idea will sink."

"Sink? What a strange turn of phrase."

"It is, isn't it? I picked it up somewhere on my travels." The answer appeared to mollify Melwyn, and Ethwyn took a sigh of relief. It was challenging to maintain this façade, but so far, it was working. All that remained was to secure Oswyn and take her away from here. But the real question was how?

"What else do we know about Natalia?" she continued.

"She's from a place called the Volstrum."

"Yes," said Ethwyn, "and it lies within a city called Karslev, which is apparently ruled by her family. Strange, isn't it?"

"What?"

"Well, here she is, claiming to be one of the Continent's most powerful Water Mages, yet her family is out to get her? I find that a little hard to believe, don't you?"

"I'm not sure what you're suggesting?" said Melwyn. "Are you saying there is no family?"

"What if she works for this very family she refers to?"

"Then why would they be hunting her?"

"Who says they are?" asked Ethwyn. "We have only her word for that and no way to corroborate it."

"If that were true, why come here to Runewald? What could possibly be of interest to them here?"

"What do we know of her family?"

"Not much," said Melwyn. "She claims they consist of both Fire and Water Mages."

"Perhaps that's the secret," said Ethwyn.

"What is?"

"What if the family is trying to recruit Athgar?"

"By having a child? I find that difficult to believe. Even if it were true, why create such an elaborate story concerning her family? No, I think she sees him as an opportunity to advance her own status."

Ethwyn smiled inwardly. Melwyn had not even batted an eyelid when her betrothal to Athgar had been broken. Now that he had come back into her life, she was doing all she could to be with him. Clearly, she was the one looking to advance her own status, but it mattered little to Ethwyn, providing she could accomplish her own objectives.

"Other than Athgar, what does she hold dear?" she asked.

"Who knows?" said Melwyn. "She came to Runewald with little."

"And how does she spend her days?"

"Visiting with her friends, primarily those two Orcs, Kargen and Shaluhk. When she's not gushing over that brat of theirs, that is."

Ethwyn watched as the seed took root in Melwyn's mind.

"That's it," Melwyn continued. "Oswyn is the key."

"What is it you're suggesting? Surely you don't mean to harm my niece?"

"No, of course not, but that's Natalia's weakness. You've seen the way she looks at that half-breed. She'd do anything to keep her safe."

"I don't see how that helps us. If something were to happen to Oswyn, Athgar would be devastated."

"He would, but what if he blamed Natalia for it? I'm not saying to kill her or anything, but what if she was injured somehow?"

"Injured, how?" asked Ethwyn. "You forget that Orc friend of hers is a shaman. She's more than capable of healing even the worst type of injury."

"Oh yes, I'd forgotten. Still, I can't help but feel we're on the right track. What do you think of Oswyn?"

Ethwyn shrugged. "I don't have feelings one way or the other, to be honest. My brother abandoned me to the slavers. I have no pity where he's concerned." She leaned across, placing her hand on Melwyn's forearm. "Not that I want him killed or anything, but he deserves to be punished for his treatment of you."

"Then I shall give it further thought," said Melwyn. "I'm sure I can come up with something, eventually."

"Not to put too much pressure on you, but it should be sooner rather than later. The longer we wait, the stronger Natalia's grip on Athgar."

"Maybe this new fellow can help. What do you think?"

"I might remind you we don't as yet know his true motives."

"Then let's make finding out our top priority."

"Agreed," said Ethwyn.

That evening, Harwath, Ethwyn, and Magran sat near the fire. Many of the villagers had adopted the new habit of using tables. However, the old ways died hard, and the traditionalists still stuck to the simple gathering around the flames.

"So what brings you to Runewald?" asked Ethwyn.

"Your brother," replied Magran. "His fame is spreading far and wide."

Ethwyn chuckled. "And by far and wide, you mean the other three villages."

"I do."

"Would it surprise you to know not everyone worships the ground he walks on?"

"Really? Do tell."

"I don't know if I should," she replied. "After all, it's only hearsay."

Magran rubbed his hands. "Come now, what's a little gossip between friends?"

She looked at Harwath, but the man only shrugged. "Well," she said, "there are some who believe he's grown a bit arrogant of late, acting like he rules over everything."

"You know they offered him the Crown," said Harwath, "but he refused it."

"If I know my brother, he'll change his mind eventually, especially with that... woman by his side."

"You don't like Natalia?"

"Oh," said Ethwyn, "she's all right, for a skrolling, but do we really want an outsider telling us what to do?"

"Athgar's the thane," defended Harwath, "not Natalia."

"Do you truly believe she has no influence? The woman bore him a daughter. He'll do whatever she wants."

"So you're saying she's a strong influence?" said Magran.

"Most definitely. Not that there's anything wrong with that, mind you. I mean, if she were a Therengian like the rest of us, I should have no objection at all. It's just she has some rather strange ideas about how things should be done."

"Yes, I'd heard that. Tell me, what could be done to... temper her judgement?"

"I haven't the foggiest idea."

"Come now, you're his sister. You must have some idea?"

"Well," said Ethwyn. "He was once promised to a woman named Melwyn. Under the right circumstances, I'm sure he could be made to appreciate the affections of one of his own race."

"And you think he'd be amenable to that?"

"Not without some outside influence."

"Such as?"

"Copious amounts of alcohol, for one thing. It would also help if he mistook her for that wife of his."

Magran frowned. "That sounds difficult. I hear he only drinks to excess in the company of that Dwarf."

"Then we must learn more about Natalia," suggested Ethwyn. "He told me all about how they met, but I must admit to some astonishment. My brother was never an outgoing person."

"All the more reason to believe we might be able to find some way to control him, but Natalia must be out of the way first."

"I'm sorry," said Ethwyn. "Are you suggesting we conspire to remove her from power?"

"I am," replied Magran. "Is that not why we've met this evening? Don't look so surprised, Ethwyn. I've met people like you before."

"Well then, let's drop the pretences, shall we? Yes, I'd like to see Natalia Stormwind out of the picture, as do you, clearly. What I need to know is who you're working for?"

"Let's just say there are others who feel as you. Men and women whose influence would be greater were Natalia out of the way. We're not proposing she be killed, of course, merely discredited, or at least controlled in some way so we can keep her from exerting undue influence."

"In that, we are in agreement," said Ethwyn. "The real question is, what can we do about her? Have you any thoughts?"

"Could someone seduce her?"

"No," said Harwath. "She's hopelessly in love with Athgar, and he with her."

"She's a mother," said Magran. "Could we use that against her?"

"I don't see how," replied Ethwyn. "We can't very well abduct the child."

"Can't we? Think on this a moment. Athgar and Natalia are travelling to Bradon for a meeting of the moot. If we demonstrate how easy it is to get hold of the baby, we can force them to our will."

"Easier said than done," said Ethwyn. "They're both powerful mages."

"I'm not saying it would be easy, but a critical vote is being brought forth at that meeting. If we can force his hand there, we can break his hold on the moot. It would likely be our only chance."

"You'd need someone he trusts to get close to the child," said Harwath.

"What about you?"

"No, I'm a warrior, nothing more. I'd never be able to get close enough without Athgar or Natalia in the room. It would need to be Ethwyn."

"Me?" said Ethwyn. "Surely you jest? I can't just go in and steal away a child? What of the guards?"

"Harwath commands the guards," said Magran, "and there won't be many of them there, in any case, what with everything going on with Ebenstadt."

"He has a point," said Harwath. "I can make them turn the other way, enabling your escape."

"And then where would we go?" asked Ethwyn.

"I'll arrange safe passage to Scarburn," said Magran. "You and the child can hide out there until we've seized control."

"I don't like it," said Harwath. "It won't take long for Athgar and Natalia to realize who's responsible."

"Agreed, but by then, it'll be too late. We'll have stripped him of his power, and she'll be voted out of her position as leader of our army, disgracing her."

"Are you sure you'll have enough votes?"

Magran smiled. "Positive. Now, do we have agreement on this?"

"We do," said Ethwyn.

"Good. Then all you need to do is get you and your companions to Bradon. Hopefully, this will all be over by the end of next week."

"In that case, we'll see you there."

Magran left, but it was clear Harwath had more to say on the matter.

"Can we trust him?" he asked.

"You tell me—you're the one who brought him to us. Are you having second thoughts?"

"I feel as though we're stepping over a cliff with this. Perhaps it's too much?"

"It takes bold steps to make progress," said Ethwyn. "I know the situation isn't ideal, but it's the only option we have if we want to control Natalia."

"But to take her child?"

She moved in closer, staring into his eyes intensely. "We can do this," she said, "but only if we act together. You know she has to be controlled. It's the only way to keep out the influence of the Petty Kingdoms."

"Athgar won't like it," said Harwath.

"No, he won't, but in the long run, he'll see the right of it. Natalia doesn't belong here, plain and simple."

"This will crush him."

"It will," she agreed, "and when he falls, he'll need someone to lean on, someone like you."

"Me?"

"You're the commander of the Runewald fyrd. Who better to become his right-hand man, the man he turns to in his time of need?"

He nodded, although she sensed his heart wasn't in it. "Look," she said, "your part is simple. When the alarm is raised, all you must do is send the search party in the wrong direction. It's not as if you're the one actually taking the child."

"I suppose."

She grasped him by the shoulders. "Harwath, we're in this together, you and I. I know it's difficult, but imagine our future together. The two of us will be the power behind the throne. We'll have wealth beyond our wildest dreams."

"From stopping Athgar?"

"Yes. You were there when they defeated King Eadred, weren't you?"

"I was. Why?"

"Do you not remember the riches that had been accumulated? They sit there still. My brother showed them to me. All of that could be ours."

He stared back, unblinking. "And all we need do is discredit the both of them by forcing them to our will. Doesn't that bother you?"

She decided on a new tactic. "Of course, but to lead our people to a brighter future, we're forced to make tough decisions. If you feel bad about it, then maybe we should reconsider. You can return to being a guard captain, and I'll search for someone more decisive to advance our plans."

"No," said Harwath. "I'm with you."

Ethwyn leaned in close, kissing him, feeling all his opposition melting away. "I knew you'd come around," she said, her voice low and husky. She knew, in that instant, he would do whatever she wanted.

"What now?" he asked breathlessly.

"You go back to your duties as captain while I go and visit my brother. It shouldn't take much to convince him to bring me to Bradon with him. Now, remember, not a word to anyone. We won't talk again until we arrive at the moot."

# CONFLICT

## SUMMER 1105

Stanislav opened his eyes as sunlight flooded the room. Evira stood at the window, the shutters wide open to let in the fresh air.

"Is it morning already?" he asked.

She turned, displaying a smile that was a constant of late. "Something's happening out there. I thought you might like to see."

"Oh? You have me intrigued." He rose from the bed, making his way to her side.

"I suggest you put some clothes on. What would the neighbours think?"

"That you've taken a lover," he said. He kissed her, then held her tight, enjoying the smell of her.

"There'll be plenty of time for that later," she giggled. "You need to take a look outside."

He tore himself away, then leaned on the windowsill, looking at the activity below. Several men were grouped together, armed with an odd assortment of weapons and armour. They stood listening to another individual clad in a surcoat who looked much more professional.

The fellow was chatting away, although from his vantage point, Stanislav could make out nothing of what was being said. Moments later, more soldiers arrived, and then they started marching towards the eastern gate.

Stanislav leaned out the window, twisting to see farther up the road where even more men were assembling. It could mean only one thing—the High Lord of Ebenstadt was going to war.

He turned, intending to recover his clothes, but Evira had beaten him to it, holding them out for him to dress quickly. A swift kiss was all he had time for, and then he was scrambling into his clothes and hurriedly pulling on his boots.

"Stay here," he said, then disappeared through the door, leaving Evira with the sound of his receding footfalls. She moved back to the window, spotting him a moment later as he ran up the street, following in the soldiers' wake.

Brother Yaromir reined in his horse. The street was packed with warriors assembling for the march eastward. Typically, such men would take what they wanted from the local merchants before leaving, so the Temple Knight stood by, ready to ensure the townsfolk's safety as best he could.

As the great doors of the city opened, the men flooded out onto the field beyond. This was no organized army—it was a mob. A familiar voice called out from the city's streets, and he turned to spot Stanislav making his way towards him.

"I'm surprised to see you here," said the bounty hunter.

"I'm doing my job keeping everyone safe. Soldiers often steal food before leaving, the better to survive while on the road."

"Has Kemp provided no food?"

"Not from what I can see."

"How many do you reckon there are?" asked Stanislav.

"I'd say about three hundred in this lot, although he did send out more this morning."

"Any horsemen?"

"No more than about two dozen, and they had little in the way of armour. This army is nothing more than the dregs of the city."

"What does he hope to achieve?"

"Who knows?" said Brother Yaromir. "These men are desperate, and desperate men will do terrible things. I'd hate to see that lot unleashed on poor farmers."

"Any sign of who's in charge?"

"None whatsoever. It's as if he really doesn't care what happens to them."

"Maybe he's using this as an excuse to thin out his ranks?"

"He must have something in mind, else why send them eastward?"

"An excellent question," said Stanislav. "They'd stand little chance against any opposition."

"I don't know about that," said the Temple Knight. "Have you ever witnessed an uprising? When people get upset enough, they'll take on anything."

"But this is a completely different matter. They're not rising up against their sovereign; they're marching on an enemy."

"Perhaps Lord Kemp is not as experienced as we thought." Brother Yaromir watched as the last of the soldiers passed through the gates, then turned his attention back to his companion. "What will you do?"

"I need to ride to Runewald and warn them," said Stanislav. "This army might be disorganized, but it can still be dangerous if it catches them by surprise."

"I'd offer you my horse, but I doubt you'd get to Runewald in time. They've had men on the road since early this morning. There's no way you'd be able to get safely past them."

"But I can't just watch them go and do nothing."

"I know it's difficult," said the Temple Knight, "but your presence here might prove more beneficial to your friends in the long run."

"Beneficial, how?"

"Your friends defeated the Cunars. I doubt this group will give them much trouble. Give it half a week, and most of this lot will be screaming to be let back into the city. That might provide us with an opportunity to move against Kemp."

"Do my ears deceive me, or did a Temple Knight just advocate for a change in rulers? I thought the Church frowned on that kind of thing?"

Brother Yaromir smiled. "I'm only speculating on what might occur. There's no harm in that, is there?"


Kragor stood atop the palisade, admiring the progress. A good hundred paces of logs had been sunk into the ground, as well as a walkway along its top, but there was still much more to do. He shifted his gaze to the buildings in the east, watching as axes hewed the trees into logs.

A distant roar caught his attention, and he turned around, looking westward. Whatever it was, the sound came from the trees, growing louder by the moment, and Orcs were running back towards him, their legs carrying them as fast as they could. Following almost right behind them, men rushed out from beneath the trees.

"To the wall!" called out Kragor. He strung his bow, then nocked an arrow, but his eyes remained firmly fixed on the Humans running towards him. He took careful aim, then let fly, sending the arrow sailing into the mob. His arms worked by memory, stringing and loosing arrows without watching to see if his aim was true.

A crossbow bolt sailed past him, and then he realized the danger. The central mass of Humans had come from the woods, yelling at the tops of their lungs while their companions, a group of horsemen, had headed farther north. Now these riders had looped around behind the completed wall section, putting them all in danger.

"Fall back," he called out, then jumped from the wall, landing and rolling to avoid damage. He was up on his feet in no time, sprinting towards the buildings. The fyrd, led by Raleth, had formed a line, but it looked woefully thin compared to the approaching swarm.

"Back!" shouted Kragor. "There are too many of them!"

Raleth hesitated, and that was his undoing. The Human footmen starting streaming around the ends of the completed wall, aiming straight for the small formation of Therengians. Meanwhile, the horsemen descended from the north, cutting off any chance of retreat. Raleth called for a shield wall, but it was a futile gesture. The enemy quickly lapped over their sides, and the defenders disappeared in a chaotic melee.

Kragor halted every ten paces or so, turning to loose off an arrow before continuing his retreat. His own Orcs were doing likewise, using whatever cover was at hand to help protect themselves. Even so, the men of Ebenstadt moved quickly.

Kragor heard the horse's hooves just in time to avoid being trampled. He transferred his warbow to his other hand, then pulled forth his axe, prepared to fight for his life when a horse careened into him, knocking him from his feet. He struck out with his weapon, but his loss of balance worked against him, and his blade missed the mark. He rolled, then sprang to his feet, striking out with his axe, feeling it sink into horseflesh. His target reared up in pain, and he struck again, driving the head of his weapon into the rider's thigh.

Another horse ploughed into him, knocking the wind from his lungs as it cracked a rib. Breathing suddenly became painful, and he struggled to get his bearings as a sword lashed out, cutting into his scalp. Blood ran down his face and into his eyes, temporarily blinding him.

A spear stabbed his arm, and his axe fell from his grip. Kragor staggered back, reeling from the wounds, desperate to clear his vision. The ground began to rumble, and for a moment, he wondered if more horsemen had arrived. He clawed the blood from his eyes, only to see a rider looming over him, spear raised, ready to end his life.

The next thing he knew, a spear tip exploded from the Human's chest, right as the horse's legs were torn asunder by the great teeth of a tusker.

"*Here,*" called out a voice in Orcish. "*Take my hand.*"

Kragor reached out and felt a firm grip haul him up onto the beast's back. Men and horses screamed in fear and pain, filling the field with the sound of slaughter. Before him, Laruhk stabbed out with his spear, taking a Human in the neck.

"*It is no use*," Laruhk said. "*They simply melt around us. We must cover the retreat.*" He turned his tusker around, calling out to his fellow riders. They surged eastward, past the now-abandoned buildings and straight on towards the forest.

The raiders, stunned by the sudden change in their fortunes, halted, milling around the buildings as they tried to avoid the Orc riders.

Kragor, now able to see clearly, cast his gaze about. The Orcs were falling back to the treeline, using their skirmishing tactics to keep up a steady hail of arrows as they made their way eastward. A few Therengians had joined them, but it looked like the bulk of the fyrd had been killed or captured.

"*We must get word to Runewald*," he said.

"*I shall send a rider*," said Laruhk, "*but the rest of us will need to buy him some time.*" They rode into the forest.

"*Drop me here*," said Kragor, "*and I shall take command of the archers.*"

"*Watch for those horsemen*," warned Laruhk. "*They move much faster than we do and will probably try to get around you.*"

"*Then they shall pay a steep price.*" Kragor dropped to the ground. "*Ride, Laruhk, and warn our people of what comes.*"

"*I must remain to see you to safety.*"

"*Then let us hope the Ancestors are with us this day.*"


Kargen watched as the great door was dragged into position for the third time this day. They had built it out of sturdy timbers, but hefting it into place was proving far more difficult than he had anticipated. It galled him, for the door was the last thing needed to complete the village's defences, yet it simply would not fit.

He turned to Grundak. "*Go and fetch the Dwarf, Belgast. He will know what to do.*"

The Orc hunter ran off to the smithy, leaving his chieftain to further ponder their situation. The doors had been a great idea, but the Orcs of the Red Hand had little experience with this type of structure. Back in their old home, Ord-Kurgad, they had managed to put together a temporary door, but Athgar and Natalia had been there to supervise. Now, with both of them on their way to Bradon, Kargen was left to sort things out, something for which he readily admitted to being ill-suited.

"What have we here?" said Belgast. He halted, looking at the great door with a critical eye.

"It is stuck," said Kargen, "and nothing we do will dislodge it."

"I see that. Only one of the pins is in place. The other one is misaligned." He moved closer. The Dwarves had produced two metal pins that would slot into rings attached to the wall, acting as large hinges. It appeared one of the pins had been bent somehow and wouldn't line up correctly.

"It'll need to come down," the Dwarf said, "then we can straighten it."

"Somebody is coming," came a shout from the top of the wall.

They all turned their attention westward. A trio of tusker riders approached, moving slowly, spread out into a widely spaced line. Kargen thought it a strange tactic, but then other Orcs and Humans followed in their wake, spaced apart like the riders, running for all they were worth.

"We are under attack," shouted Kargen. "Man the walls, and get this door out of the way." He turned to Belgast. "We need to block up this doorway."

"I'll take care of it," said the Dwarf. "You there," he called out. "Get that wagon over here, and somebody bring those barrels to the entrance."

A horn blew, alerting everyone to take up arms. Soon, dozens of Orcs and Therengians rushed to the walls with bows, spears, and axes in hand.

The tuskers drew closer, and even in the fading light, Belgast could make out the figure of Laruhk.

"Bring those tuskers here," he shouted. "We'll use them to dislodge this door." He began gathering rope, directing others to tie it to the gate.

Laruhk led the riders through the entrance, pulling his own mount off to the side. Behind them streamed in the survivors from Ashborne, exhausted from their ordeal. Many collapsed to the ground, while others sought water to slake their thirst.

"Where is my sister?" asked Laruhk. "We have many who need healing."

"Gone to Bradon," replied Kargen. "We shall have to make do without her skills this day. How many of the enemy come?"

"Hundreds! They race across the ground like a swarm of insects. Most are on foot, but their horsemen are swift, and we are unable to chase them down."

Belgast tied off the rope to the tusker. "Haul away," he called out, "and be quick about it. We need to clear this door."

Laruhk urged his mount forward, feeling the strain as the rope went taut. Moments later, there was a loud crack, and the bent pin broke off, freeing the door. It fell to the ground to be dragged into the village. Belgast ordered the cart moved up to block the door, but their own people were still making their way inside.

"*They are coming!*" called out an Orc.

Kargen stepped outside, pushing his way past the refugees to get an unobstructed view. A pair of Therengians, distinctive in their brown tunics, left the woods. One limped, while the other, trying to help, had her arm around him. Behind them came the sounds of screaming. Then the attackers came into sight, moving in small groups, brandishing a variety of weapons. They appeared to be in high spirits, but the presence of the palisade was clearly a surprise for them, for they halted all of a sudden rather than pursuing their prey.

Kargen ran flat out, heading straight for the two Therengians. As he drew closer, he recognized Raleth, who bled from a head wound along with one of his legs that was bound by a tourniquet. The men of Ebenstadt, frustrated by the defences set before them, yelled and screamed, building up the courage for a charge.

Kargen rendezvoused with the injured Therengian. "Let me help," he called out, then halted, taking a quick look at the distant troops. "I will carry him on my shoulders." He stooped, lifting Raleth's arm and draping it over his shoulder, then he twisted, grasping the man's legs and hauled him up like a prize doe. "Run," he shouted as he began loping towards the distant gate.

Belgast ordered the wagon tipped up but left a small opening. Into this, he would eventually roll some barrels, but there was no hurry. The enemy attack had paused to gather their courage.

Kargen, Raleth, and the woman staggered through the gap, collapsing onto the ground. The barrels were then rolled into place, with spearmen placed behind them. Now they had little to do but wait.

"Take the injured to the great hut," ordered Kargen. He turned to the woman. "What is your name?"

"Hilwyth."

"Take charge of the fyrd, Hilwyth. Your task is to hold the gate. My hunters will man the walls, along with the few archers amongst your people. Should the enemy push you back, we shall reinforce you. Do you understand?"

"I do."

"Good. If you need help, Belgast here will be of assistance. Now, I must get to the wall if I am to assess our enemy's strength." He found the nearest ladder and climbed up onto the platform to survey the attacking warriors.

They had gathered at the edge of the woods but were now preparing to charge. Mounted men rode back and forth in front of them, exhorting them to launch the assault.

"*Where is Kragor?*" Kargen called out, switching to the Orcish tongue.

"*Injured at Ashborne,*" replied Grundak. "*One of Laruhk's riders carried him back.*"

"*Have someone see to his wounds,*" Kargen ordered, then turned his attention back to the army of Ebenstadt. "*The enemy has no ladders. They must attack the gate to gain entry. I want our hunters lining the wall on either side of the gate.*" He looked out into the village. "*Laruhk, gather the rest of the tuskers. I want them massed behind the Dwarf's makeshift gate. If the enemy breaks through, you are to charge.*"

"*Yes, Kargen,*" the Orc called back.

"Here they come," yelled Hilwyth.

The Humans of Ebenstadt, now roused to a great fervour, rushed forward, screaming defiance as they ran.

Kargen raised his hand. "*Hold your arrows,*" he called out. The enemy drew closer until the entire village echoed with their cries. "*Loose!*"

Arrows flew forth, decimating those in the front. The Warbows of the Orcs sang out again, penetrating armour and felling even more. A few brave individuals made it to the gate, but Hilwyth's spears soon made quick work of them.

# THE FEAST

## SUMMER 1105

Wynfrith raised her cup. "Here's to Runewald," she proclaimed.
Cheers erupted all around the great firepit. Most of the village
was present, ostensibly to welcome Athgar's delegation to Bradon, but the
reality was few knew of such things. To them, this was merely an excuse to
eat, drink, and make merry, and they were going to make the most of it.

Athgar toasted the other thanes, then food was brought out, carried on
heaping platters.

"This is quite the celebration," said Natalia. "I've never seen anything
like it."

Athgar had to yell to be heard over the din of the festivities. "Did they
never celebrate things at the Volstrum?"

"Of course, but they were all stately affairs. As students, they taught us
all to be quiet and respectful. Here, however, everyone is boisterous."

"Can you blame them? It's not every day they get to host a moot." He
noted her fidgeting and looked down to Oswyn, who was fussing.

"It's too loud for her," said Natalia. "She needs some quiet time."

"You can't leave now. The speeches are about to begin."

"But I thought they already spoke BEFORE the food got here?"

Athgar looked insulted. "Those were only the introductions."

"But the food's coming out. Surely they'll wait till the end of the meal?"

He shook his head. "That's not our way. The truth is if we waited that
long, half those in attendance would be passed out from the drink."

"Shall I take her?" offered Skora.

"If you would," replied Natalia. "She's ready for a nap. Thane Wynfrith
made a hut available for us."

"I'm well aware," the old woman replied, turning her attention to the infant. "There, there. It's much too noisy here for you, isn't it? Let's take you somewhere nice and quiet, and you can have a little nap." She rose, making her way through the noisy villagers.

Natalia watched her go, her eyes locked on Oswyn.

"Are you all right?" asked Athgar.

"It gets harder and harder to be parted from her," she replied. "I suppose it's only natural, but I feel like I'm abandoning her."

"Nonsense. You just want her near you. Don't worry. By tomorrow night, this moot will be over, and we'll be on the way home. Then we can spend as much time as we want with her."

"Will we though?"

"Of course we will," he said. "Why wouldn't we?"

"It's only that everything seems to be falling apart. I thought we'd found a home here, a nice place to settle down and raise a family, but instead, we must deal with Ebenstadt all over again."

"The Church gave us grief last time, not Ebenstadt."

"You know what I mean," she replied. "Why can't they just leave us alone to live out our lives?"

"Greed," said Athgar. "Greed and fear."

"Care to elaborate on that?"

"The rulers of Ebenstadt covet what we have. Look at the food at our disposal. I bet the city folk would love to partake of a feast like this."

"I would say that constitutes envy rather than greed, but I'll let you have that one. What about fear?"

He shrugged. "That's easy. We live differently than they do, electing our leaders. Those who rule the Petty Kingdoms are afraid our ideas will spread to their lands. What would a noble be without subjects to rule over?"

"I hardly think a few Therengians could threaten the realms of the Petty Kingdoms," said Natalia.

"It only takes a small spark to start a great inferno," said Athgar. "We're both living examples of that. Had we not stumbled upon the plot of the Cunars, Ord-Kurgad and all those in it would have been completely destroyed."

"Yes, and all for some metal that fell from the sky. Whatever happened to the godstone?"

"Kargen and Shaluhk brought it with them when they came north."

"We should probably tell Belgast about it," said Natalia. "Doubtless, he'd know what to do with it."

"I hadn't thought of that. I'm sure his cousins could smelt it. I wonder what they'd make?"

"I would suspect that largely depends on how much of it they have."

"Well," mused Athgar. "It must be a substantial amount, else why would the Church have risked war over it?"

She smiled. "You make a compelling argument. You're becoming quite the master of speech."

"What can I say? I learned from the best."

Natalia looked across at Ethwyn, who sat beside Harwath, the two of them engaged in an intimate conversation despite the noise surrounding them. She couldn't make out any of their words, but the intent was certainly clear if Harwath's blushing had anything to show about it.

"It looks like your family might be growing sometime soon."

Athgar followed her gaze. "Who? You mean Ethwyn? That would be a surprise." He watched the pair smile and laugh. "Then again, it shouldn't shock me. My sister's been through a lot lately. I suppose it's inevitable she settles down at some point."

"They certainly look like a happy couple," said Natalia. "I wonder how Bergwith is taking it?"

"Bergwith?"

"Yes, you remember her. We met a few months ago. She's Wynfrith's niece."

"Oh yes, I remember now." He knitted his brows. "Wasn't she involved with Harwath?"

"She was," said Natalia. "Hence my remark. I doubt she shares Harwath's infatuation with your sister."

"They're sitting a fair distance apart. That should help prevent any altercation."

"You feel that likely?"

"Therengian women can be quite possessive at times."

"As can their men," said Natalia, looking him squarely in the eyes.

He stared back, stung by the remark, but his wife couldn't maintain the stern image. Instead, she lapsed into a smile.

"You're teasing," he said.

"I am. Now, come," she said, eyeing a platter as it made its way towards them. "Let's eat."


"We must make sure there's plenty of mead for tomorrow," said Wynfrith. The lack of response caused the Thane of Bradon to direct her gaze to her niece. The younger woman was fixated on a couple sitting some distance away.

"Bergwith? Is everything all right?"

"I'm… not feeling well. I fear I might have indulged in a little too much mead. Would you mind if I took my leave of you?"

"No, of course not. I hope you'll feel better in time to join us later?"

"I'll do my best," promised Bergwith. She stood, her eyes locked on to the form of Ethwyn. There was unfinished business between them, and this was the night to settle such things. Bergwith forced herself to unclench her fists, then began making her way through the crowd towards the object of her scorn.

Ethwyn had watched as the old woman took Oswyn away. The plan was to take the infant later tonight when everyone was heavy with sleep, their senses dulled by the mead. To do that, she must first gain entry to the hut in which they stayed. She disentangled herself from Harwath's arms and stood, casting a quick glance in the direction Skora had walked.

"Stay here," she ordered. "I have work to do." Content no one was paying her any attention, she followed Skora.

Her target wound through the village to a spot well out of earshot of the great firepit. Here sat a modest hut, set aside for Athgar's delegation. Skora went inside, as was expected, but before Ethwyn could follow, a hand gripped her elbow, causing her to turn.

"Not so fast," followed the voice of a woman.

"Who do you think you are?" demanded Ethwyn.

"My name is Bergwith, and my aunt is the Thane of Bradon."

"And my brother is the Thane of Runewald. Now get your hands off me!"

Bergwith released her elbow but watched her closely. "You have no idea why I'm here, do you?"

"No," said Ethwyn, "nor do I care. Now leave me alone. I have other things to keep me busy."

"I'll leave you alone when you take your hands off of Harwath."

Ethwyn's brows shot up. "Harwath? What in the Gods' name are you talking about?"

"We were to be betrothed until you got in the way."

Ethwyn turned, intending to leave, but Bergwith grabbed her by the arm once again. "Where do you think you're going?"

"Wherever I want. So leave me alone while you still can."

"Not until I've had it out with you," the woman persisted.

Ethwyn had meant to simply flee, but now, her plans threatened, a fury raged inside her. Words of power suddenly issued from her mouth and then a streak of fire shot out from her hands, striking Bergwith and sending her sprawling to the ground. The woman stared back, horror filling her eyes.

"You're a Fire Mage!" she said, her voice quivering.

Ethwyn knew then her plans were spoiled. She couldn't afford for word of her magic to get out, so she advanced to stand over Bergwith and draw her knife.

"I'm sorry, I truly am, but I'm afraid I can't let you live now." Ethwyn plunged the blade into the woman's chest, again and again, sending a spray of blood up towards her. Bergwith let out one last gasp of breath, then lay still. The blood dripped from Ethwyn's hands as she stared at the dead body at her feet.

"Fool," she said. "Now I must hasten my plans." She looked around for any sign of alarm, but thankfully, the place was empty, the distant sound of merriment masking the killing.

She lifted Bergwith's legs and began dragging her to the edge of the forest. It was difficult work, hampered further by the fact someone could discover her at any moment. Finally, she dropped the corpse, covering it with loose foliage. Bergwith's body would, no doubt, be found soon enough, necessitating immediate action. Ethwyn resolved to carry out her task before she lost the opportunity.

The hut Skora had entered was only some sixty paces away from the scene of the attack. There was the possibility Skora had heard their argument, but that was a risk Ethwyn had to take if she were to win through this day.

She moved closer, treading as quietly as she could. Soon, she had her ear pressed up against the door, listening for any signs that might indicate what was happening on the other side. Skora's voice drifted back, singing a soothing lullaby, presumably to put the child to sleep.

Ethwyn opened the door, and as silently as possible, stepped in. The hut was a single-room dwelling, with a central firepit edged by small stones. The old woman stood across from the door, her back turned towards Ethwyn as she stooped to put the infant to bed.

"Stop where you are," demanded Ethwyn.

Skora turned, her charge forgotten for the moment. "Ethwyn? What are you doing here?"

"I've come for Oswyn. Natalia wants her."

"I doubt that," replied the old woman. "She's only just sent her to bed."

"Give her to me, you old hag."

"And why should I?" demanded Skora.

Ethwyn took a step forward, her patience lost. Arcane words issued from her mouth and her hands began to glow with energy. As the magic built, so too did her temper.

"Give her to me!" she screamed.

"Never!"

"You fool!" Ethwyn pointed to the side, aiming a streak of fire into the floor of the hut. It flashed out, scorching the wood and filling the room with an eerie green light.

The old woman recoiled as the flames receded.

"Now pick up the child, or I'll immolate the both of you!"

"You wouldn't dare!"

"You have no idea what I'd do. My orders were clear, you old crone. Either I come back with Oswyn or make sure she's dead. Which option I take is entirely up to you."

Skora turned briefly to pick up the baby, then stood, clutching her to her chest.

"Don't harm her," she begged. "I'll cooperate, I swear."

"That's better," said Ethwyn. "Come over here, and don't even think about running, or I'll burn you down where you stand."

The old woman shuffled across the room. "Where are we going?"

"Anywhere I choose. Now, step outside, and don't try anything foolish."

"You won't get away with this."

"That's not for you to worry about. I have powerful friends, Skora. Trust me, they'll help me."

"Take Oswyn, and there won't be a safe place left in all the Continent. It's not too late, Ethwyn. Cease this madness!"

"Stop trying to tell me what to do!" She pulled her knife, waving the bloody weapon menacingly. "Let's get going and keep your voice low. I don't want anyone raising the alarm."

Slowly, ever so slowly, they made their way northward. Just as they entered the shadows of the forest, a figure stepped from the darkness, causing Ethwyn to almost jump, but it was only Melwyn.

"You're early," the woman hissed at them.

"It couldn't be helped. I ran into a bit of trouble."

Melwyn's eyes locked on Skora. "What's she doing here?"

"There were complications."

"Complications? Are you mad? It's bad enough stealing away Oswyn, but Skora? She'll be able to identify us!"

"It was either that or kill her." Ethwyn turned her attention to her prisoner. "It's still not too late to change my mind."

"No," begged Melwyn. "She's done nothing."

"You live only as long as you're useful to me," said Ethwyn.

"I shall have no part of this," said Melwyn.

"You have no choice. You're here with me, and you're part of this plot whether you want to be or not."

"I shall not be a party to murder."

"Too late for that." Ethwyn held out the bloodied dagger.

Melwyn paled. "Whose blood is that?"

"Some fool who chose to get in my way. Do you want to suffer the same fate?"

"No, of course not."

"Then lead on," insisted Ethwyn. "We must make haste to be free of this place."

Branches rustled off to the south, causing both of them to glance in that direction. Skora remained where she was, clutching Oswyn as if her life depended on it.

"Who's there?" shouted Ethwyn.

The leaves rustled some more, and then a small Orc youngling burst onto the scene, wooden axe held high.

"Agar protect!" he cried out in the common tongue as he rushed past Skora, heading straight for Melwyn. So sudden was his advance that there was no time to react. The axe dug into Melwyn's shin, drawing blood. The woman fell to the ground with a scream, and then Agar turned to threaten Ethwyn.

The young Orc was fast, but the Fire Mage was quicker. She raised her hands, spoke the words of power, and then sent a streak of flame across the clearing to strike the youngling in the chest. A dull thud accompanied the hit, knocking little Agar from his feet. But he jumped right up, screaming out in defiance as he resumed his charge.

"Agar protect Oswyn!"

Ethwyn thrust her hands out once more, and this time a much larger flame engulfed her target. Melwyn looked away, unable to bear the sight of it. Even the sound nauseated her as flesh bubbled and cracked.

Agar lit up the forest like a pillar of fire. But as the flames took his eyes, he could no longer see his target. His legs kept pumping, and he rushed off, leaving a trail of soot and burned underbrush.

Ethwyn ran to her co-conspirator, shaking her violently. "Run, you fool!" Melwyn stared back in horror, only to receive a slap. "Get moving, for Gods' sake!"

Melwyn plunged into the woods, desperate to put the gruesome sight behind her. Ethwyn turned on Skora.

"You too, old woman." She pointed with the knife. "I shouldn't need to tell you I know how to use this."

"They'll hunt you down," said Skora, "no matter how far you go. You'll spend the rest of your life looking over your shoulder, fearing their vengeance."

"Don't be absurd. Once we're clear of this place, I'll go where they can never follow."

"There's no such place."

"You fool!" shouted Ethwyn. "Do you think I learned the magic of fire all by myself? I have powerful allies, Skora, allies who can make short work of my brother and his skrolling wife."

"And would they be Sartellians?"

Ethwyn, taken by surprise, simply stared back.

"Oh yes, I've heard it all. Natalia tells me that's where the family trains their Fire Mages. How did they get hold of you, Ethwyn? Did they buy you from the slave markets?"

"You know nothing of my history."

"I know more than you think. Athgar tried to find you after Athelwald was destroyed. He travelled halfway across the Continent in the hopes of locating you. Did you know he found the man responsible for your capture?"

"You lie," said Ethwyn.

"I do no such thing. He hunted him down in Corassus and killed him, nearly dying in the process. And now you come here to steal his child? What kind of person does that?"

"Enough of this prattling. One more word from you, hag, and I'll silence you permanently. Now, move, and not another word out of you."

Skora clung to Oswyn but was wise enough to know when she was outmatched. She moved farther into the forest.

# SEARCH

## SUMMER 1105

"I must tell you," said Wynfrith, "there are those who would see you fall from grace."

"I'm not sure I understand," replied Athgar.

The Thane of Bradon leaned in closer, lowering her voice. "Galan plots against you."

"Why would you say that?"

"He told me so. He believes if we offer the Crown to Aswulf, he can be controlled."

"Why doesn't Galan take the throne himself?"

"He's no fool. He knows he lacks the popularity to rule."

"I shall remember to keep my wits about me," said Athgar. "Although I must admit I AM curious as to why you're telling me."

"You've refused the title of king, but our people need someone to look up to. We're growing, as you well know, and we won't be a collection of four villages for much longer. We'll have no choice but to form a country, and that requires a king."

"Holstead and Krieghoff are duchies."

"They are, but do you truly believe Therengians would settle for a ruler who styles himself on the Petty Kingdoms? We have a rich tradition amongst our people, a tradition which includes the position of king."

"Then name Aswulf king. He's likely more suited to it than me."

"No, he's not," said Wynfrith. "Athgar, I know you and I have had our differences in the past, but people look up to you. You've earned their respect, not through birth, but by action."

"I am no king!"

"All I'm asking is that you might consider the possibility of ruling. If you don't like the title of king, then call yourself something else. I've heard you're a big believer in the Orcs' method of choosing a leader. Could it be adapted to our own needs? You could call yourself a High Chieftain, for example."

"I'll consider it," Athgar replied, "but I'd like to get Natalia's opinion."

"Of course, as you should. She has a level head on her shoulders, despite what others may think."

"What others? Is someone trying to undermine her?"

"I probably shouldn't be telling you this, but Galan seeks to find some way to control her. He fears her outsider influence."

"That's ridiculous. She wants only what's best for everyone."

"You and I both know that, Athgar, but Galan is a proud man. And, I might add, he used to be a fervent supporter of King Eadred."

"Eadred was a fool."

Wynfrith smiled. "It seems, on that matter, we are in complete agreement."

A hue and cry arose, causing both to look in the direction of the commotion. Villagers moved aside, desperate to get out of the way of a column of fire. As more cleared a path, Athgar beheld a small figure engulfed in flames rushing towards them. He immediately brought his hands up before him, letting his inner spark build. The energy surged within him, and then the flame vanished, extinguished by his magic. As the body collapsed, there could be no denying it was a young Orc, and there was only one it could be.

"Agar!" he screamed. He ran towards him as the youngling fell, letting out a wail of pain when he hit the ground. In moments, Athgar was there, looking for signs of life, but the charred body lay motionless. Then Shaluhk appeared by his side, words of power flowing from her lips. Her eyes began to glow as she gazed at her child, and then she laid her hands upon him. Athgar heard a sudden intake of breath.

"He lives!" she cried out.

Natalia ordered everyone back, giving Shaluhk room to work. The shaman's casting began anew, calling forth arcane powers to heal her son. Athgar felt like someone had punched him in the stomach. He turned to Natalia to see tears streaming down her face.

"Who could have done this?" he demanded.

"That was a magical flame," she replied. "Did you notice the green tinge to it?"

"I did, but who has such power? I thought I was the only master of flame here?"

Athgar thought back to Kargen's injury of last year. The Orc chieftain had been engulfed by magical fire at the hands of Verineth Sartellian. He had managed to recover, thanks to the ministrations of Shaluhk, but it had taken weeks. The smell of burned Orc flesh drifted to Athgar's nose, and he turned to vomit.

Agar opened his eyes, looking straight up at the face of his mother. "Oswyn, danger!" he shouted hoarsely.

Athgar felt a hand grip his heart. "What was that?" he called out.

"Oswyn!" screamed Natalia.

She pushed past the crowd, desperate to reach their hut. Athgar ran after her, his heart heavy with fear. She was barely ten paces ahead of him, racing towards who knew what. He worried someone might be waiting to kill her but put such thoughts from his mind. She was a powerful mage, quite capable of protecting herself.

Natalia entered the hut first, but Athgar had closed the gap between them. He rushed through the door, only to see her staring at the empty furs that marked Oswyn's bed. She turned to him, a look of utter devastation etched upon her face.

"Think," he insisted. "She must be close and alive, or why else take her?"

He saw her struggling, and then the educated mind of the most powerful spellcaster he had ever laid eyes on settled into a look of grim determination.

"There was an altercation here," she said. "Skora would never let anyone take Oswyn unless she had no choice."

"So both were taken," said Athgar, rooting around, looking for anything that might give them some clue as to who was responsible.

"Over here," called out Natalia, crouching down and pointing at a scorch mark on the floor. "It looks like magic was used."

"Yes. Definitely the work of a Fire Mage, but who?"

Natalia looked up into his eyes. "There's only one person it could be."

Athgar fought to control his panic. "That's impossible. Ethwyn was never trained."

"We don't know that. Magic runs in the blood, blood you share with your sister. It only makes sense she has the potential to wield the magic of fire, same as you."

"But this makes no sense. Why would she take Oswyn?"

"It's obvious, isn't it?" she said. "Other than the Orcs, who do we know trains Fire Mages?"

"The family, but how would they have gotten hold of her?"

"That's an answer only she can provide."

"They're probably long gone by now, whisked away by magic."

"I doubt that," said Natalia. "It takes years for the family to train a mage, and ring of fire is a particularly advanced spell."

"Ring of fire?"

"It's a spell used by Fire Mages to travel great distances, but it's said to be difficult to learn. It's more likely she's still in the area somewhere."

"Then we must begin a search as quickly as we can."

"I've called up the fyrd," said Wynfrith. "They won't get far. Did you account for all your people?"

"Not quite," said Athgar. "We're missing four if you include Oswyn. Ethwyn and Skora are gone, but so is Melwyn. I suspect they're working together."

"To what aim?"

"I can best answer that," said Natalia. "There is a group out there known as 'the family' that I used to serve. I believe that's where they're taking Oswyn."

"Why would they do that?" asked Wynfrith.

"Natalia is a powerful spellcaster," explained Athgar, "and her child might be even stronger."

"So you're saying they've stolen your child to raise as their own? That's barbaric."

"And they call us wild!" said Athgar.

"How is young Agar?"

"Under Shaluhk's care," said Natalia. "He'll survive, but it'll be quite the ordeal for him, even with magic to regenerate the burned flesh."

"I should be out there," said Athgar, "looking for Oswyn."

"You'd only get in the way. I know it's difficult, but we're better served by waiting here. It'll allow us to respond to any sightings much faster."

A warrior approached the group, nodding to Wynfrith. "We found Bergwith. I'm afraid she's dead."

Wynfrith paled. "Burned?"

"A little, but the likely cause of death is from a blade of some type, probably a knife. Her body had been dragged to the woods to avoid detection."

"How is her death connected to all of this?"

"I suspect she was simply in the wrong place at the wrong time," said Natalia. "Do you think she stumbled upon Ethwyn's treachery?"

"No," came Harwath's voice. The captain moved closer, offering his axe in both hands. "I yield my weapon to you, Thane Athgar. I am no longer worthy to serve."

"What are you talking about?" said Athgar.

"I was taken in by Ethwyn's charms. Never did I imagine she would murder to achieve her aims."

Natalia rounded on the captain. "You'll do better than that. Tell us everything, or I'll shatter you into a thousand shards of ice."

Harwath shrank under the onslaught. "She tempted me, told me what I wanted to hear."

"I don't care about that," she pressed. "What's her plan?"

"To take Oswyn to force your hand."

"Force my hand to do what?"

"To stay out of the business of the moot."

"Why would Ethwyn care about the moot?"

"I don't know," said Harwath. "Maybe it was Magran's idea?"

"I know that name," said Wynfrith. "He's one of Galan's aides." She shook her head. "I should have known he'd take matters into his own hands. I suspect he wanted you out of the way so the moot could elect Aswulf king."

"This is getting worse by the moment," said Natalia. She moved closer to Harwath, letting frost build up on her hands and holding it before him, allowing him to feel the chill. "Where have they taken her?"

"Originally, the plan was to take her to Scarburn, but she wasn't supposed to kill anyone."

"I'll send men there," promised Wynfrith. "In the meantime, you'd best contact your Orc friends. If we're to find Ethwyn and her hostages, we're going to need all the help we can muster."

"Agreed," said Natalia. "Shaluhk can use her magic to send word. We'll ask them to sweep westward of here."

"Why west?" asked Wynfrith.

"Athgar and I suspect Ethwyn's not fully trained, which means she'll need to rely on more conventional means to escape. With her treachery revealed, she has only one option left to her—Ebenstadt."

"Couldn't she flee northward?"

Athgar shook his head. "No, like me, she doesn't know the area. She came to us through Ebenstadt. She'll stick to what she's familiar with."

"We should send word to Stanislav," said Natalia. "He can keep an eye out for her."

"We'll go ourselves," replied Athgar, "and hope we can intercept her before she makes the city gates."

"And if we can't?"

"Then we'll storm the city if we must. No one's going to stand between our daughter and us! I promise you."

"And in the meantime," said Wynfrith, "what shall we do with this one?" She nodded at Harwath.

"Place him under guard. He may yet hold the key to Oswyn's safe return."

Kargen surveyed the battlefield. Bodies were scattered around the area, but his people had been lucky, for only the enemy had died here. Under other circumstances, it would have been a great victory, but it boded ill for his people nonetheless, for the attack could not be ignored. They were now at war.

"Gather the dead," he commanded. "We will burn the bodies to the west, well out of range of our noses."

Belgast appeared at his side. "What can I do to help?"

"You can get your cousins to work on that gate. Can it be salvaged, do you think? Or must they start from scratch?"

"It's only the hinge that was broken. I'm sure they can have it repaired soon enough."

"Can they complete it by morning?"

"I should think so. As long as you have the people to heave it into place, but we'll need the light to put it in place."

"Then do so," said Kargen. "I will arrange for the tuskers to be at your disposal once the sun rises."

"What if those men come back?"

"I sent hunters out into the woods, so we should have plenty of advanced warning."

"How's Kragor doing?" asked Belgast. "I understand he was badly wounded at Ashborne."

"He was, but he will recover. I sent him on to Ord-Ghadrak. The shaman there, Laghul, will have him back to his old self in no time."

"And the rest of the wounded?"

"They remain here," said Kargen. "Hopefully, Laghul will accompany Kragor when he returns."

"It's too bad Shaluhk wasn't here. She would have proved useful."

"Yes, she would have, but such things are beyond our control. If we are to build a lasting society, we will need more healers."

"A lasting society? You sound like a king."

Kargen grinned. "I am a chieftain, not a king, but the responsibility is the same. We both rule on behalf of our people."

"That's not how Human kings work," said Belgast. "Most of the Petty Kingdoms are ruled by men whose only concern is themselves."

"Athgar is not like that. He has the well-being of all at heart."

"As he should. But then again, he's part of your tribe, isn't he?"

"He is," said Kargen. "He is our master of flame."

"He told me how you rescued him from the ruins of his village. That must have been quite a shock."

"It was."

"Did you ever visit Athelwald before it burned to the ground?"

"I did, on many occasions. Why?"

"I was wondering if it was like Runewald?"

"In some ways, in others, it was laid out more like Ashborne, or at least what was left of Ashborne."

"Ah, Ashborne," said Belgast. "Have you ever seen a place so cursed?"

The Orc chieftain turned to him in surprise. "Do you believe in such things?"

"Curses are real. Ask anyone who knows about magic."

"So you are a mage, now?"

"No," replied the Dwarf, "but witches do exist. Of course, the scholars like to refer to them as Hex Mages, but it amounts to the same thing."

"And you think one of these Hex Mages cursed Ashborne?"

"Look at the evidence. The original village was burned to the ground years ago, and both times we've tried to revitalize it, we've been attacked. What else would you call it other than a curse?"

"It is what Nat-Alia would call politics. Ashborne was built too close to Ebenstadt and was seen as a threat."

"Then why build it in the first place? Didn't its founders realize the danger?"

"Many years ago, Ebenstadt was called Dunmere."

"Isn't that a Therengian name?"

"It is," said Kargen. He called out to a passing villager. "You there, go and fetch Dunstan." He returned his attention to the Dwarf. "I believe you have already met the man. He is a what Athgar calls a bard—some kind of scholar. He can tell you more." He gazed over at the gate. "We must move these wagons back out of the way, but keep them close by, in case we need of them again."

Everyone carried on with their assigned tasks, eager to put the battle behind them. There was still worry in the air, and several times the alarm was sounded out of pure panic. Belgast got his cousins to work, then made his way back to the gate.

"Ah, there you are," said Kargen. "Dunstan is here."

"Greetings," said Belgast. "Kargen tells me you know all about Ebenstadt, I mean Dunmere."

"I do," the man replied. "Are you familiar with the tale of Beothric?"

"No, should I be?"

"He was nephew to the ancient king of Therengia. When the kingdom began to crumble, he set up a provincial capital, hoping to delay the inevitable. He named it Dunmere, but it became better known as the last city of the Therengians."

"So it was built right as the kingdom was collapsing?"

"Yes, but you must remember it took decades for Therengia to finally succumb to its enemies. I have no exact dates, but I suspect Dunmere fell about two hundred years ago."

"What makes you say that?"

Dunstan smiled. "I know the ancient tales, and they make no mention of its fall. That means it comes after the death of the last king. Local legend mentions it was lost within the last few generations, but even those tales use antiquated terms, hence my estimate."

"So your people have always been in this part of the Continent?"

"Not at all, but as war engulfed the Old Kingdom, many fled east. Dunmere was a haven for them, even if only a temporary one."

"And after Dunmere fell?"

"We moved farther east, founding the five villages. Had it not been for Athgar and Natalia's intervention last year, we would have again moved eastward, driving us even farther into the wilderness."

"And what of you?" asked Belgast. "Have you any thoughts on the matter, or are you only here to bear witness to history?"

"There is little I can do to control events," said Dunstan, "but if I am able to help keep the customs and history of our people alive, then at least I would have made a contribution."

"Well, it looks like you'll need to write some more tales."

"I'm not sure I understand?"

"You're a bard, aren't you? Can you not recognize history when it's being made? All around you, change is happening. It's your job to record your account of what's going on here. Who knows, perhaps one day a bard will tell YOUR tales?"

"I never thought of it that way."

"No," said Belgast, "I don't suppose you have. You scholars are all alike, sitting back and letting others do the work for you. Well, it won't work this time. Come with me, and I'll put you to work. Let's hope a little labour will help inspire your prose."

# FLIGHT

## SUMMER 1105

"Get a move on," urged Ethwyn. Skora and Melwyn led the way while their captor followed.

"It's difficult in the dark," said the old woman. "And I've got Oswyn to care for."

"She has a point," added Melwyn.

"Quiet," snapped Ethwyn. "If I wanted your opinion, I'd give it to you."

"What's that supposed to mean?"

"You haven't had a thought worth listening to since you were a child."

"At least I was promised in marriage."

"To my brother? That had nothing to do with you. It was a business transaction between my father and yours. You're like a sack of rotten potatoes—I bet your father couldn't wait to be rid of you."

"I didn't see anyone lining up to marry you."

Skora chuckled.

"You find that funny, old woman?" said Ethwyn. "Get a move on, or I might just use my magic again."

"You wouldn't dare," said Skora. "It would hurt the child."

In answer, Ethwyn grabbed her arm, causing her to pivot around to face the mage.

"I can just as easily make Melwyn carry the brat."

Skora stared back but wavered. "I shall behave," she said at last.

"See that you do. Melwyn? You lead."

"Me? I know nothing of these woods."

"Nor do I, but we shall have to make do. Now move."

They continued on, but after a few hundred paces, Skora began to slacken her pace.

"What now?" said Ethwyn.

"I'm sorry. I'm tired," the old woman replied. "It's been a long night, and we haven't let up at all."

"All right, we'll take a quick rest. Melwyn, come back here. Skora's worn out."

They gathered together in a small clearing, the better for Ethwyn to see her companions. Skora flopped to the ground, still clutching Oswyn, but Melwyn remained standing. She stepped closer to Ethwyn, lowering her voice.

"We should turn around," she urged.

"To what end?" asked Ethwyn.

"It's not too late. We can release Oswyn and turn ourselves in."

"Are you mad? Two people are dead, Melwyn. They won't look favourably on us after that."

"Two? I remember the Orc child, but who was the other?"

"A woman named Bergwith."

A sharp intake of breath revealed Melwyn recognized the name. "Bergwith? Are you sure she's dead?"

"Of course. I killed her with my own knife. Why?"

"She's niece to the Thane of Bradon. Do you know what you've done?"

"I had no choice. She confronted me."

"How did she know about our plans?"

"She didn't," said Ethwyn. "She wanted to talk about Harwath."

Melwyn shook her head. "I knew that was a mistake. You should have left him alone."

"Nonsense. I needed him."

"Plenty of other men would have obliged you."

"Not for that, you fool. He was our inside man. As the captain of the fyrd, he had access to all the arrangements for the very meeting that brought us to Bradon."

"But Athgar is your brother," said Melwyn. "Why wouldn't you ask him for that sort of thing?"

"And arouse suspicion? I think not."

"And so you had to tempt poor Harwath, using your wiles?"

"It's not as if he protested. I didn't exactly drag him into this. He was a willing participant."

"He was besotted with you, and you played on that infatuation to make him do what you wanted."

"What if I did?" said Ethwyn. "He's clearly a man of low moral character; otherwise, how could he be so easily swayed?"

Melwyn gave her a disapproving stare, but Ethwyn was having none of it.

"Don't give me that look. You're not exactly innocent in all of this."

"I didn't murder anyone."

"No, but you were more than willing to go along with the abduction of that child."

"Her name's Oswyn," said Skora. "And she's your niece."

"No," said Ethwyn. "She's a prize, nothing more. Once I'm back in the fold of the family, they'll reward me with riches beyond imagining."

Skora turned pale. "The family?"

"Of course. Who else do you think covets the child? The Church? Don't make me laugh."

"The plan," said Melwyn, "was to use Oswyn to force Natalia to our will, under pain of death."

"That's what I let you believe," said Ethwyn, "but the truth is I've always intended to return her to the family."

"For the reward?" said Skora. "You've disappointed me. I always thought you were better than that."

"Not everything comes down to coins."

"Then what's it about?"

"The most basic element of all—power. Success in this will grant me access to some of the most powerful spells ever discovered."

"Where? In Ebenstadt?"

Ethwyn laughed. "Don't be silly. They trained me in a place called Korascajan."

"Where's that?" said Melwyn.

"It lies to the southwest, beyond the mountains, at the forks of a great river. They train only the greatest Fire Mages there."

"And how did you come to find yourself there?" asked Skora.

They both looked at her in annoyance.

"What?" said the old woman. "I'm not allowed to ask questions?"

"I was enslaved and sold off to a prince's court. If I hadn't been on display when a mage hunter arrived, I would be there still."

"On display?" said Melwyn. "What's that supposed to mean?"

"I was an attendant to Princess Olani of the court of Kouras if you must know."

"Never heard of it."

"I'd be surprised if you had. It's one of the Kurathian Isles."

"Still never heard of it."

Ethwyn stood. "It's not my problem if you're ignorant of such things. In any case, Skora asked, not you."

"Don't look at me," said Skora. "I haven't heard of the place either."

"Fine," said Ethwyn. "Our rest is over, anyway. Get to your feet. We've still much ground to cover."

"Can't we stay a little bit longer?"

"No. Now on your feet, or we'll leave you here, and I don't mean alive."

The old woman rose, her joints complaining. "I can't keep up this pace," she said. "Do you have any idea how old I am?"

"No," said Ethwyn, "nor do I care. The choice is yours, Skora. Walk or die."

They pushed on through the night. The forest was dark, so much so they were lashed by branches and tripped up by twigs strewn around the ground, making even a slow walk quite hazardous.

As the early dawn's light began to filter through the boughs overhead, they rested again, this time by a small stream. Skora placed Oswyn on the ground, using the respite to rub her arms. Ethwyn scooped up water with her hands, but Melwyn just lay there with her eyes closed.

"You should be ashamed of yourself," said Skora. "How could you be party to such a thing?"

"Don't blame me," replied Melwyn. "Athgar was the one who spurned me."

"Spurned you? That's not the way I remember it. Your father, Wulforth, withdrew the offer of marriage."

"And it broke my heart."

"You weren't so heartbroken when you were in Caladin's company," accused Skora. "Athgar didn't spurn you. He was freed of you."

"What would you know of such things? You're nothing but a dried-up old hag."

"I was young once too. Do you think I don't know what it feels like to be rejected?"

"My father was a tough man," said Melwyn.

"Oh please! He doted on you. You never struggled in your entire life. The truth is, you never even completed your first hunt."

"I made my kill the same as everyone else."

"No, you didn't," said Skora. "Your father made the kill, then gave it to you to claim as your own. And to think you made such a big deal about Athgar failing his own."

Melwyn sat up, a look of anger on her face. "Who told you that?"

"You'd be surprised what you hear over the years. Do you deny it?"

The woman looked away in shame. "No, I don't. I thought I'd left all that behind me when we escaped, but I suppose everyone's past follows them, regardless of the path they take in life."

"That's true," agreed Skora, "but it doesn't need to define you. You have a mind of your own, Melwyn. Don't let your actions be dictated by others."

"Quiet, you two," said Ethwyn. She stood before them, but her voice was hushed. "There're noises up ahead. If either of you makes a sound, I swear I'll slit your throat. Understand?"

They both nodded, eager to avoid death.

Ethwyn waved them closer, then pointed to some reeds. "Over there," she whispered, "and keep that baby quiet, or it'll be the last thing you ever do."

They crouched in the reeds, the water up to their ankles. Men's voices grew closer, likely no more than a dozen paces away. Skora thought of calling out, but Ethwyn, sensing that, hovered a knife over Oswyn.

"One false move," she rasped, "and the child dies."

They all held their breath, but the men moved past. The water chilled them to the bones, but still, Ethwyn held them in place, waiting for the voices to fade into the distance.

"Time to go," she finally said, then ushered them out of the reeds. Oswyn began to fuss, crying out.

"Keep her quiet!" said Ethwyn.

"She's hungry," replied Skora.

"Then feed her."

"With what? She's an infant who needs her mother's milk."

Ethwyn drew close. "Then she'll just have to do without, won't she?"

"Then don't expect her to remain silent. She's a baby, Ethwyn. She doesn't understand your threats."

They stared at each other, eyes locked, but Ethwyn wasn't about to back down. "I don't care what you do to silence that thing, but by the Gods, if you don't do something soon, it'll be you who pays the price."

"You can threaten me all you like, but I have no control over an infant's hunger. This is what you get for taking her from her mother."

"Fine," said Ethwyn, drawing her knife. "Then we'll silence her the old-fashioned way."

"No!" screamed Melwyn.

"What did you say?" Ethwyn turned her attention to the woman, but she stood her ground.

"You said you had to return her to the family. Surely they want her alive?"

Ethwyn paused, and Melwyn turned to the old woman. "There must be something you can do? You've been a midwife for years, Skora. Surely in all that time, you've seen mothers die prematurely. What did you do?"

Skora let her gaze sweep over the area. "I suppose we could mix up a paste. Were we back in Athelwald, I would have no problem finding what I need, but this area is unfamiliar to me."

"It will be light soon enough," said Melwyn. "I would imagine a brief search will yield something suitable." She turned to their captor. "What say you, Ethwyn?"

"It's worth a try. We'll rest here until morning but stay alert. Those men were obviously sent from Bradon, and there must be more out looking for us."

Morning brought a chill wind from the north, a warning that the summer months were drawing to an end. Skora stood unsteadily, feeling the cold that had seeped into her bones, but her younger companions suffered no such ill effects.

They began their search under Skora's guidance and soon gathered many plants that the old woman assured them were edible. Ethwyn had never been one to learn such things and was quite willing to starve until they reached Ebenstadt. Still, she knew the real prize was Oswyn, and she could hardly arrive with the child malnourished.

Skora used stones to grind the ingredients, mixing them into a paste with the help of a little bit of water. This she then fed to Oswyn, using her finger to place small amounts in the child's mouth.

"You have a way with children," said Melwyn, a hint of sorrow to her voice.

"I've always loved them," the old woman replied, "but I was never blessed with them myself. That's why I became a midwife."

"How many children have you delivered?"

"Far too many to count, but each experience is up here." She tapped her head.

"Did you help with Ethwyn's birth?"

"Of course, as I did with yours."

"But my mother died," said Melwyn.

"As did many others, but she loved you, nonetheless. I can still remember her smiling as she faded away, a look of bliss to her face after seeing you delivered safely."

Melwyn choked up. "What was my mother like?"

"Freywith was full of hope and always saw the joy in life. You're the spitting image of her, you know."

"I wish I'd known her."

"As do I, but we cannot change the past, only live for the future. Your mother understood that well enough, but I fear you're coming to that realization later in life than she did."

"How old was my mother when I was born?"

"Younger than you are now," said Skora. "Let's see now. I believe she was in her seventeenth summer."

"That young?"

"Of course, and why not? She had recently married your father, and they both wanted children. They were quite the couple back then, strolling through the village hand in hand."

"My father did that?"

"Yes, why? Is that so hard to believe?"

"I suppose not," said Melwyn. "I just have a hard time imagining my father being like that."

"You only remember him when he was older, after he'd spent years looking after you. That kind of responsibility can wear a man down."

"Are you saying I was a burden?"

Skora smiled. "Aren't we all? It takes a lot of work to care for a child, Melwyn, something you'd be well aware of if you'd settled down."

"It's not my fault the slavers came."

"True, but rather than follow your heart, you let your father arrange a marriage for you."

"I loved Athgar."

"No," said Skora, "you didn't. You loved the idea of being married. Athgar had a trade, unlike many in the village, and you wanted a life of ease. If you truly loved him, you wouldn't have been so quick to accept your father's offer to Caladin. If that was even his decision."

"What are you suggesting?"

"I saw how cozy you were with him, not that I can blame you. Caladin was a fine figure of a man and one of the more successful hunters. Tell me, how long had you been pining for him?"

"Enough chatter," barked out Ethwyn. "We need to get moving."

She towered over them, staring down with a glare that brooked no argument.

"Very well," said Skora. She rose unsteadily, her bones creaking.

"Come," said Ethwyn. "We've got a long way to go, and I want us to be well away from this place."

· · ·

They set out at a fast clip, Ethwyn leading them due west. She intended to travel for two days, then cut directly south, hopefully bringing them straight into Ebenstadt. This had the added benefit of allowing them to bypass Scarburn, but Skora wondered if that might be a little too ambitious. She well remembered the last time she was lost in the wilderness when she and Melwyn had miraculously escaped the slavers. They had almost starved as a result, but at least they had eventually found a safe haven in Runewald. This trip, however, promised no such reward, and she knew, in her heart, only death awaited her at its conclusion.

They soon found themselves on a relatively flat plain, with little in the way of cover. Ethwyn, more concerned with being discovered, urged them to an even greater speed, but Skora proved unequal to the challenge. Thus it was that in the late afternoon on the third day, she was unable to rise after a particularly gruelling journey.

To make matters worse, Oswyn was fussing again, and Skora couldn't blame her. The paste she had mixed was a poor substitute for her mother's milk, and the child had eaten little.

Tempers were frayed all round. Ethwyn, finally having had enough, stomped over to tower above the prone, old woman.

"Get up," she demanded.

"I cannot," Skora replied. "I lack the strength."

"Then we leave you behind." Ethwyn drew her knife.

"No!" screamed Melwyn. "Don't do this, Ethwyn. There's no need to kill her. Let's abandon her instead."

"And have her bring word of our position? I think not."

"Be reasonable. What purpose would her death bring?"

"It would allow us to travel faster, for a start."

"And what of the child?"

"You'll take her."

Melwyn placed herself between her two companions. "Don't do this," she begged again. "There has to be a better way."

Ethwyn stared into her eyes for a moment, then relented. "Fine, have it your way." She tucked her knife back into her belt, then turned, intending to continue the trek westward. Melwyn turned her attention to Skora.

"You take her," the old woman said, looking at Oswyn, who wriggled around on the dirt. "Just for a short while. I need a break."

"No," said Melwyn. "I can't."

Ethwyn halted in her tracks, turning as fury filled her. "Do as she says, or by the Gods, I'll burn the old woman to cinders." Strange words tumbled forth, and then she thrust her hands out before her.

Melwyn acted instinctively. "No!" she screamed, standing before Skora in an attempt to face down their captor. Flames streaked out from Ethwyn, splashing across Melwyn's torso, engulfing her face. A horrified scream erupted from the woman's scorched lips, and then she dropped to her knees as the green flames grew in intensity.

Ethwyn fed the fire, the flames licking at the skin even as the stench of burned flesh reached her nostrils. The magic flowed through her, and she felt like a goddess controlling the most primeval of powers. She took a step closer, pouring more of her energy into the flame, watching the flesh writhe and bubble as it separated from the skull.

Finally, the spell subsided, and Ethwyn felt a sense of euphoria. All that remained of Melwyn was a burned corpse and greasy smoke trailing off into the sky. She stared at it, fascinated by the ferocity of her attack.

She turned to Skora. "Get up," she said, "or suffer the same fate."

# PURSUIT

## SUMMER 1105

The warrior knelt before her. "There's no sign of them, Thane Wynfrith," he said.

"And you searched to the west?"

"We have, as well as north and south, but the darkness hampers us. With the rising of the sun, I hope we will have better luck."

Wynfrith turned to Athgar. "The more time that passes, the harder it'll be to find them."

"What should we do?" he asked.

"Scarburn lies on the route to Ebenstadt. I would suggest you go there first. There is still the chance they intend to complete Galan's plan."

"I doubt it," said Natalia. "If the family wants Oswyn, the most logical choice for Ethwyn is to make straight for Ebenstadt, but you're right, Scarburn IS on the way."

"I have some spare horses," said Wynfrith. "I shall have them prepared for you."

Shaluhk approached, along with Agar. The youngling looked terrible, with patches of pale-green skin poking through cracked and charred flesh.

"How is he?" asked Natalia.

"Progressing slowly," replied Shaluhk. "I gave him numbleaf to dull the pain and used regeneration to heal the skin, but it is a slow-acting spell, and more treatments are necessary. How goes the search for Oswyn?"

"Nothing so far. We believe Ethwyn's taking her to Ebenstadt, then into the Petty Kingdoms."

"Agar find Oswyn!" shouted the youngling.

"It appears my son is determined to find his tribe-sister," said Shaluhk. "We shall accompany you."

"Are you sure that's wise?" asked Natalia. "Agar must rest, surely?"

"The numbleaf will keep him comfortable, and I can continue his treatments on the way as easily as here in the village."

Athgar returned his attention to Wynfrith. "It looks like we'll need a third horse."

"You'll need considerably more than that," replied the Thane of Bradon. "I'm sending some warriors with you to keep you safe."

"How long will you need to assemble them?"

Wynfrith smiled, then stood aside, revealing a dozen men some distance behind her. "They're ready now."

Athgar turned to the Orc. "Are you comfortable on horseback, Shaluhk?"

"I have never ridden," she replied, "but I am willing to try it."

"What about Agar?"

"He can ride with me," said Wynfrith, "provided his mother does not object?"

The Orc looked at her in surprise. "You are coming with us?"

"This treachery happened while I was your host. It's only right I help bring Oswyn safely home."

"Then I will allow Agar to ride with you, Thane Wynfrith, providing he wants to."

Agar, who had been watching everyone talk, ran towards the distant horsemen. "Agar ride!" he called out.

Natalia laughed. "It sounds as if he's made up his mind."

They followed him, climbing into their saddles as the sun rose. Someone hefted Agar up before Wynfrith, and then they rode out into the early morning mist.


Natalia gazed across at her tribe-sister. "You seem to have adapted extremely well to the saddle. I wish it had been so easy for me."

Shaluhk chuckled. "It is comfortable enough, and I think I understand now why my brother likes his tuskers. The view from up here is quite pleasant."

"I suppose I never thought of it like that. My chief complaint isn't so much the riding; it's the after-effects."

"Which are?"

"Sore buttocks."

Shaluhk smiled. "Ah, but you forget, I am a shaman. I have magic to soothe such pains."

Athgar laughed. "I wish we had her with us when we rode up from Corassus."

"I am surprised you do not have more horsemen," noted the shaman. "Is it not common amongst the Petty Kingdoms to have such warriors?"

"It is," replied Natalia, "but the Therengian custom is to fight on foot."

"Why is that?"

"I suspect it has more to do with a shortage of horses," said Natalia.

"Not so," said Athgar. "Dunstan tells me the thanes would ride with their personal guards all the time but would dismount to fight."

"Probably due to their stubbornness to accept new ways."

"There's likely some truth in that. Back in Athelwald, we still hunted with spears, even though we had bows available. I questioned it once, but old Gunthar told me it was tradition and couldn't be helped."

"And so you continued with the old ways?" said Shaluhk.

"So it would seem."

"We Orcs have our own traditions but are willing to sacrifice them if they interfere with our lives. You are a prime example of that, Athgar. Had we stuck with our traditions, you would have been left to die in Athelwald."

"Then we must thank the Ancestors," said Natalia. "I couldn't imagine a life without Athgar."

"Nor I without you," he replied. "Now all we need to be complete is the safe return of Oswyn."

"At least we know she is safe," said Shaluhk. "If what you told me about the family is true, they very much want her alive."

"Yes," added Natalia, "but she's still an infant. How will Ethwyn feed her?"

"Skora will find a way," soothed Athgar. "She's a very resourceful woman."

"Let us hope they will both soon be back amongst us," said Shaluhk.

"I wish there was more we could do."

"I have sent word to the other tribes," continued the shaman, "and they will send it on to Runewald. Given what happened, Kargen will send hunters to Ebenstadt in an attempt to intercept Ethwyn."

"Good," said Natalia, "then we can trap them between our two forces."

Kargen examined the gates. The massive doors had been hauled into place and now rested on their hinges, a tribute to Dwarven engineering.

"They look impressive," he said.

"And," said Belgast, "they're perfectly balanced. Even a child could open them once the drop bar is removed. You'll also notice there's a vertical bar on one side. That drops down to keep the door in place should you desire only one to be open. I also have something else in mind, although it'll have to wait."

"Oh, and what might that be?"

"A gear. It would allow the drop bar to be raised and lowered with a minimum of effort."

"How would that work?"

"It's difficult to explain. I'll show you one day, but we'll need more iron to make it. I'm afraid our modest collection of used weapons and armour isn't really appropriate for such things."

"How is it," asked Kargen, "that you Dwarves became masters of innovation, while the other races still do things the old-fashioned way?"

"We have patience," said Belgast. "I suppose it mainly has to do with our long lives. Humans and Orcs, if you'll pardon me, are always in a hurry to get things done."

"By that logic, the Elves should take forever to accomplish anything."

"That IS what they say."

Laruhk's voice cut through the general hubbub of the village. "Kargen, visitors approach."

"Open the gates." Kargen turned to Belgast. "It appears these fine doors are about to have their first real test." He watched as a villager pulled open the gate. A group of Orcs approached off in the distance, yet he needed no help to identify them.

"*Kirak*," he called out in the Orcish tongue. "*Welcome to Runewald. What brings you to our village this day?*"

"*I bring news*," the Black Axe chieftain replied, "*but it is not good. Laghul here has been in contact with Shaluhk. Events have taken a turn for the worse in Bradon.*"

"*As they have here in Runewald*," answered Kargen.

"*It is your son, Agar.*"

Kargen's heart stopped. "*What of him?*"

"*He was injured, burned to be exact. Shaluhk has him under her care, and we are assured he will make a complete recovery.*"

"*Burned? How?*"

"*The question is not how, but rather by whom. He was set afire by a magical flame.*"

"*Surely you are not suggesting Athgar is responsible?*"

"*No*," said Kirak, "*his sister, Ethwyn.*"

"*Ethwyn can command the magic of fire? How is this even possible?*"

"*It is thought she was trained by the Sartellians. I should not need to explain to you the possible consequences of that.*"

"*Where is she now?*"

"*She evaded capture, but it gets even worse. She took the Human child, Oswyn.*"

Kargen struggled to find words. Inside, his gut wrenched, threatening to leave him weak. His face settled into a look of grim determination. "*What can we do to help?*"

"*It was suggested we take hunters to Ebenstadt. They believe the fugitive is headed there.*"

"*I shall send them out immediately,*" said Kargen, "*but they will need to proceed in large numbers, for we now find ourselves at war.*"

"*War? How can this be so?*"

"*Men from Ebenstadt attacked us at Ashborne, then followed our hunters back here, to Runewald.*"

"*Were many lost?*" asked Kirak.

"*Not on our side, but the enemy suffered greatly. They have since withdrawn, but the threat of their horsemen lingers.*"

"*Can we not chase them down with our tuskers?*"

"*No, they are too fleet of foot for our riders to catch. The great beasts are devastating in battle but of little use to us under these circumstances.*"

"*Then let us march,*" said Kirak, "*for I have brought hunters of my own with me. We must teach the people of Ebenstadt that we will suffer their predations no more.*"

"*I would ask your shaman's help first, for we have several wounded from the skirmish at Ashborne.*"

Kirak turned to Laghul, but she had already stepped forward. "*Lead on, Kargen, and I shall do what I can for them.*"

"What's going on here?" called out Belgast.

Laruhk came down from the wall. "It is complicated," he said. "Where would you like me to start?"

"How about the beginning?"

"Well, it all began when Kirak arrived…"


"Something's wrong," said Brother Yaromir.

Stanislav set down his drink. "Can you be more specific?"

"As you know, Kemp sent out a warband several days ago, and now they are returning. I sense they suffered a defeat."

"At the hands of Athgar's people, I hope?"

"So it would seem. I rather suspect Kemp believed they could capture the food he so desires, but it appears his men weren't up to the task."

"Not surprising, given who they were up against. Anything else you can tell me?"

"Yes, the men on the walls grow more concerned by the day. I also hear Novarsk has been making threats."

"How do you know such things?"

Brother Yaromir smiled. "You'd be surprised what people tell a Temple Knight."

"Let me guess: you can't tell me?"

"People forget we're merely Holy Warriors—we take no oath to keep secrets. In fact, quite the reverse. We promise to tell the truth at all times."

"So what else have you heard?"

"Kemp's raiders travelled west, into the land claimed by Novarsk, and the king there is none too happy about it. The rumour is he's sending troops to sort things out, and that's got Kemp worried. This defeat in the east has only added to his woes."

"He doesn't need to worry about Athgar's people," said Stanislav. "They have no desire to take Ebenstadt, at least not as far as I know."

"Could his attack on their homes have changed their minds?"

"I suppose it's possible, but I doubt they've got the manpower to carry out a siege. The King of Novarsk, however, has me worried. What do we know of his forces?"

"They're pretty typical of the Petty Kingdoms, from what I hear. My guess is he'd be able to field a force of about fifteen hundred on short notice. He could raise more, of course, but only for a limited time. They use a form of levy in these parts, and that limits how long he has them for."

"Will Novarsk storm the city or lay siege to it?"

"The smart move would be to surround it, then starve Kemp and his people out. There's already a food shortage, so they wouldn't last long."

"Yes," said Stanislav, "but does the King of Novarsk know that? What if he decides to assault the gates?"

"Not much hope there—they're well built. Have you not seen them?"

"I have, although I confess the details of fortifications are not my area of expertise."

"Well," said Brother Yaromir, "I can assure you it WAS part of my training as a Temple Knight. The city only has the two gates, and whoever built them did an excellent job. They won't fall easily."

"So that leaves the king with the choice of reducing the walls and forcing a breach. A costly tactic."

"Agreed. I suppose it all comes down to how much the king wants this city. To be honest, it's always been a thorn in his side, sitting as it does so near his eastern border. Of course, with the Church in control, there was little he could do in times past. Now that the Cunars have fled, it's a different situation entirely."

"And where does your order sit on the matter?"

"We've no official opinion," said Brother Yaromir. "I am here to guard the property and people of the Brothers of Saint Mathew, nothing more."

"Come now," said Stanislav, "we both know that's not true."

"Well, that's the official story. The truth is, I offered advice to many of the soldiers who defend this city, and I've got a pretty good idea of what it is they want."

"Which is?"

"Leadership they can rely on. Kemp rules over this place with an iron grip, relying more on fear than anything else. It wouldn't take much to tip the balance against him."

The bounty hunter grinned. "Are you urging the city to rise up against him?"

"Of course not. I would never do such a thing. As a Temple Knight in service to Saint Mathew, I'm supposed to remain impartial in such matters."

"Then what are you suggesting?"

"Only that, should an invader breach the walls, there would be little opposition in the streets."

"Have you ever been under siege?"

"No," said Brother Yaromir. "Why? Have you?"

"Yes, as a matter of fact. Years ago, I was sent to a place called Grislagen. Ever heard of it?"

"Can't say I have. Why? What happened?"

"Well, I was there to check on rumours of a Water Mage, but I arrived right as the king started cracking down on dissenters. I heard the local baron had a claim to the throne and was throwing his weight around, but that's neither here nor there. Anyway, when the Royal Army arrived and laid siege to the city, I was trapped inside. It was not a pleasurable experience."

"How bad was it?"

"Let's just say I was there long enough to grow accustomed to the taste of rat. Not something I'd care to repeat."

"Did you find your mage?"

"No, which only made the trip even worse. The siege lasted for nearly six months, during which siege engines were brought in. Eventually, they breached the walls, and then the soldiers poured in. A lot of people died that day, many of them innocent townsfolk. It's enough to make a person sick."

Brother Yaromir rose. "You give me much to think on."

"Where are you going?"

"To the east gate. If we are to be sieged, then I can at least ensure everyone gets safely inside the walls of Ebenstadt before our attackers arrive."

"Then shouldn't you head to the west gate?"

"No, it's already sealed. Anyone who still wishes to enter the city must now go to the east."

"Why?"

The Temple Knight shrugged. "I suppose because Kemp expects the army of Novarsk to march from the west."

"What can I do to help?"

"You can start by convincing the owners of this fine establishment to make sure their shutters are in good order. When the enemy comes, there'll be a thirst for blood, and we don't want these good people getting caught in the middle."

"So they are to barricade themselves in?"

"What else can they do? It's not as if they're trained warriors."

Brother Yaromir, true to his word, headed to the east gate, stopping by the mission only long enough to retrieve his warhorse. Thus it was, that fully equipped, he found himself overseeing refugees as they streamed into the city.

The guards in the gatehouse looked nervous. He fully expected the gates to be closed by nightfall despite the absence of any immediate threat. Farmers crowded the gate, their precious belongings piled high in wagons, their looks of utter terror evident to anyone who cared to take notice.

The afternoon wore on, and still more people pressed through the gatehouse. Brother Yaromir had no idea where most of these newcomers would find shelter, for the city was already overcrowded. No doubt his mission would use up its remaining stores trying to feed the massive influx of humanity, but there was nothing he could do about it.

As afternoon made way to evening, the crowds finally began to thin as the sun sank in the west, turning the horizon crimson. Brother Yaromir turned his horse around, ready to gallop back to the gate, then spotted movement off to his right. A young woman, likely no more than twenty summers, hurried down the road, an infant held close to her chest.

A horn sounded, announcing the gates were about to close. Eager for the woman to find shelter, he rode back, begging the soldiers there to hold off.

The woman hurried on, passing through even as the great doors swung shut. She looked up at Brother Yaromir, nodding her thanks, and he was struck by her grey eyes that seemed to pierce his very soul. She then turned and hurried off into the city proper, leaving him to wonder who this Therengian might be.

# LOCKDOWN

## AUTUMN 1105

L aruhk stared at the distant city. The walls of Ebenstadt were tall, much higher than any Orc structure the hunter had ever seen. Evenly spaced towers would give ample room to rain down arrows on any attackers tempted to storm the walls. It was, in a word, impenetrable, at least to his untrained eyes.

Just as he was about to turn his tusker around and ride back to the rest of the army, a movement in the field to his right drew his attention. Staring at the spot confirmed nothing, so he pulled on his reins, only to see a flicker of movement out of the corner of his eye. He focused on the location again, then edged his mount closer, moving slowly lest he scare off whatever it might be.

At first he took it for a bird picking away at some food, but as he drew closer, he noticed the sprawled form of a Human. Not wishing to startle whoever it was, he dismounted, proceeding on foot at a cautious pace, his hand resting on the knife handle protruding from his belt.

Laruhk parted the long grass to reveal the bloodied countenance of Skora lying there, clutching her stomach, her hands stained with blood, but very much alive.

"Skora?" he called out. "What has happened here?" He knelt beside her, cradling her head as he stared down into her pain-wracked eyes.

"It was Ethwyn," the old woman croaked out. "She has Oswyn."

Laruhk's eyes searched the immediate area. "Where is she?"

"Fled into the city. I slowed her down too much, and she feared she wouldn't make it through the gates in time."

"Hang on, Skora. A shaman is on the way."

She clasped his hand. "She killed Melwyn," she gasped out.

"And for that, she will pay, but for now, you must conserve your strength." He waved at one of his riders, gaining her attention. "*Ushog, go and fetch Laghul,*" he said in his native tongue. "*We have need of her magic.*"

"*I shall do as you command,*" she replied, turning abruptly and riding off, the tusker's hooves thundering on the hard ground.

Laruhk returned his attention to Skora. "Breathe easy, my friend. We shall soon see to your wounds."

He stayed with her, comforting her even as her hold on life grew tenuous. Laghul finally arrived, kneeling down to examine the old woman as Kargen joined the two Orcs. The shaman cast her spell, calling forth arcane powers, then placed glowing hands to Skora's stomach. The flesh knitted as the magic poured into her, suffusing her body with a golden glow. It soon dissipated, leaving her much refreshed and putting colour back in her cheeks.

"It was Ethwyn," said Laruhk. "She turned on Skora when she could not keep up."

"Where is she now?" asked Kargen.

"In the city, far from our reach."

"Mount up and take your riders to the west gate. See if it, too, is shut."

"You suspect something?"

"I do," said Kargen. "It is likely both gates to the city are now locked."

"Because of us?"

"Possibly, although I suspect we are not the only reason. Ride fast, Laruhk, then return to tell us what you discover."

"And if I find anything else?"

"Then investigate, but do not put yourselves at risk. At the moment, it is information we seek, nothing more."

"Then I shall do as you command." He ran off, calling for his riders to assemble.

Laghul now stood, looking down at her patient.

"*How is she?*" Kargen switched back to the Orcish tongue.

"*Weak, but she will recover in time. We should take her to our camp. Her advanced years work against her, leaving her frail.*"

"*Then I shall carry her.*" He knelt, cradling Skora in his arms, then stood, finding her surprisingly light. "*Lead on, Laghul.*"

The rest of their army was busy setting up camp, organized by Kragor, now much recovered from his earlier wounds. He wasn't quite back to normal, for he tired easily, but at least his body was intact. Raleth was there, too, leading close to a hundred warriors from Runewald.

Skora was laid before the fire and covered in furs, then fed an Orcish porridge and given water. The woman ate sparingly but drank as though she were parched. Kargen waited until she finished before questioning her.

"Tell me all that happened since you left Bradon," he said.

"Ethwyn threatened Oswyn, forcing me to go along to spare the babe's life. She took me to the woods where Melwyn met us. I thought at first Melwyn was as guilty as she, but I don't think things went as they expected. Ethwyn mentioned killing two people but provided few details."

"She killed a woman named Bergwith," said Kargen, "and set my son, Agar, aflame."

The pain in her eyes was clear. "Yes, I bore witness to that. Did he survive?" she asked.

"He did, thank the Ancestors, but it was close. Had Shaluhk not been there, it would have been a far different outcome."

"I am glad he survived, although I'm sorry Bergwith died. I only met her once, but she seemed a nice enough person. Where are Athgar and Natalia?"

"On their way here," said Kargen, "or at least they were, the last I heard. Shaluhk sent word by way of Laghul here."

"I'm not sure I understand," said Skora.

"Orc shamans can communicate over long distances, but only to other shamans. Laghul brought word to Runewald."

"And so you marched here to intercept Ethwyn?"

"We did, but it appears we arrived too late to stop her. Is there anything else you can tell us?"

"Like what?"

"How about Melwyn? Is she still with Ethwyn?"

"No," replied Skora. "They fell into an argument. Ethwyn was furious with me, said I slowed them all down. No doubt she was going to kill me with her magic, but as she cast, Melwyn got in the way." She paused a moment, tears coming to her eyes. "She sacrificed her life for mine."

"And she will be remembered for it. We will find Ethwyn. I promise you. And when we do, she shall answer for her crimes."

Laruhk slowed his tusker. Off to the west, sunlight reflected off metal, indicating the presence of warriors.

"*What do you make of it?*" he asked, turning to Ushog.

"*It appears we are not the only army wishing to capture the city.*"

"*Who said anything about taking the city? We are only here to find Ethwyn.*"

"*Yes, but she is safely within the walls of Ebenstadt, so we must now take the city for ourselves. Either that or admit defeat and run home with our tails between our legs.*"

"*We have no tails*," said Laruhk.

She smiled. "*It is merely an expression. I have heard the Humans use it from time to time.*"

"*They have no tails either?*"

"*It matters not. The meaning is clear.*" She looked at the western gate. "*The doors to the city are closed here, too, likely in response to the appearance of this army. What will you have us do?*"

"*There is little we CAN do at this point in time. We should return to Kargen with news of these new arrivals, but let us get a closer look first. He will be eager to know as much detail as possible.*"

They edged closer, taking care to remain well out of archery range.

"*I see plenty of warriors on foot,*" said Laruhk.

"*As well as archers,*" added Ushog, "*though their bows look strange.*"

"*They are crossbows, the same weapons they used at the Battle of the Standing Stones. Do you see any horses?*"

"*A few, although they appear relatively small of stature. Far different from the Temple Knights we fought.*"

"*That is good,*" said Laruhk. "*It means they have no knights to throw against us.*"

"*Knights do not scare me!*"

"*They should. Had it not been for our tuskers, they would have made short work of us.*"

They sat for a moment, scanning the enemy lines.

"*Look,*" said Ushog, pointing. "*There, do you see?*"

He followed her gaze, revealing the approach of a dozen horsemen.

"*Let us turn* around," he commanded. "*Now is not the time to let them see a tusker up close.*"

"*Should we just leave them be?*"

"*They are likely here for the same reason as us—to attack the city. Let us hope Nat-Alia can convince them of the wisdom of joining forces.*"

"*They will never agree,*" she said. "*Humans and Orcs typically do not get along.*"

Laruhk barked out a laugh. "*You forget our allies.*"

"*They are the exception rather than the rule.*"

"*I will agree with your assessment, but let us not tarry here. We have important information for Kargen.*"

"*As you wish,*" she replied, turning, circling her mount to ride eastward.

They trotted across the field that lay north of the city, seeing little but abandoned houses and farms. "*Have you ever considered the cost of war?*" she asked.

"*I am not sure what you mean?*" said Laruhk. "*They came and killed our people. Are you suggesting we let them get away with that?*"

Ushog let her eyes wander over the empty fields. "*It is not the farmers who attacked us. Rather, it is their warriors.*"

"*And it is their warriors who we shall fight. Think you that we would slay innocents?*"

"*No, definitely not, but it is the death of loved ones that perpetuates the hate between our races.*"

"*You have given this far more thought than I,*" said Laruhk. "*Perhaps it is a discussion best left for another time?*"

"*I would welcome the opportunity,*" said Ushog. "*Shall we say this evening?*"

"I…" Laruhk, suddenly bereft of words, looked at his comrade with a new sense of wonder, then cleared his throat. "*Of course. I, too, would welcome it.*" They continued the ride in silence.


Kargen halted his pacing. "*Are you sure of this, Laruhk?*"

"*I am. Both Ushog and I saw the enemy warriors.*"

"*What would you estimate their numbers at?*"

"*Two thousand, maybe more.*"

"*Then they mean to take the city.*"

"*So it would seem,*" agreed Laruhk. "*What do you want us to do?*"

"*Maintain the scouts in their present positions, but if they are forced back, send word immediately.*" He turned to Kirak. "*What think you?*"

"*It puts us in a precarious position, at least until the rest of our army arrives.*"

"*And when will that be?*"

"*I would expect them by morning,*" replied Kirak.

Kargen nodded. "*That would be my estimation as well. When they get here, I would like you to take your hunters south of Ebenstadt. Keep an eye on the wall but also to the west. Let us see if these new Humans intend to encircle the city.*"

"*And the other tribes?*"

"*I shall send the Red Hand north, leaving the Stone Crushers here in the centre to be reinforced by the Therengian fyrd.*"

"*And that, you think, will be sufficient to keep the newcomers at bay?*"

"*I am not sure,*" said Kargen, "*but it is a simple matter to redeploy our forces should Nat-Alia deem it necessary. She is, after all, our master of war.*"

"*And when do we expect our battle mage to arrive?*"

"*It will be a few days yet. She and Athgar have a long trip. In the meantime, we must prepare things as best we can.*"

"*Anything else?*"

"*Yes,*" said Kargen. "*Have Laghul contact Shaluhk and explain what has happened here. It will give Athgar and Nat-Alia time to ponder the situation as they travel."*

King Vastavanitch gazed at the distant city. "Are you sure of this, General?"

General Spanov, unused to being questioned, held back his retort, instead making his voice as pleasant as possible. "Yes, sire, they are massed to the east."

"Who are they?"

"I suspect the same group who defeated the Holy Army last year. I sent riders out to investigate, but so far, all they've spotted are some greenskins lurking in the trees."

"Could they be part of some larger army?"

"From where, sire? The area to the east is nothing but wilderness."

"They must have come from somewhere to win the battle?"

Spanov held his tongue again, though, in truth, he wanted to point out the kings' conclusions were altogether obvious. Did His Majesty think his general a fool? Instead, he tried to be diplomatic.

"Could they be from farther north?" he suggested.

"No," said the king. "There's nothing up that way for several hundred miles, save for wilderness. No, these must be the wildlings that plagued the Church for so many years."

"Let me take some men, and I shall clear the woods, sire."

"No, wait. If they've got a grudge with Ebenstadt, they may be of use to us."

"Are you suggesting an alliance?"

The king grinned. "Possibly, or at least an opportunity."

The general waited, but an explanation was clearly not forthcoming. "Meaning?" he prompted.

"If an enemy army is waiting to storm the walls of Ebenstadt, we should oblige them, don't you think? After all, why lose men assaulting a city wall if our ally is willing to do it for us?"

"But what if they succeed, sire? They would hold the town, and we'd still be outside."

"I'm sure we could reason with them."

"May I at least deploy the army?"

"Of course," said Vastavanitch. "That is, after all, your prerogative."

"And if the men should encounter this new army?" asked Spanov.

"Then have them halt. We shan't risk a conflict with this new faction just yet."

"Did you consider the possibility they might be here to relieve the city, sire?"

"Relieve? Are you suggesting they allied with those brigands?"

"We know so little of the rulers of Ebenstadt, Your Majesty. Who's to say where their loyalties lie? I would urge action now while we have the element of surprise."

"No! Until we know otherwise, we shall treat them with dignity and respect. Better to make friends than enemies, I think."

"And if they attack us?"

"Then, for Saint's sake, you will defend. Now, get on with it, General. I'd like to see the men settled by the time the light fades."

Spanov rode off, leaving the king to survey the distant walls. Even though Ebenstadt was a large city, the walls were relatively new, built up in the last fifty years under the supervision of the Temple Knights of Saint Cunar who, up until last year, had ruled the place.

They had done good work here, but now the king must see to their undoing if he were to gain control of the city. He sat for some time, studying the walls from afar, looking for any signs of weakness. General Spanov eventually returned, finding the king exactly where he had left him.

"The men are in position, Your Majesty."

"Thank you. Tell me, General, what do you make of the city?"

"It's an impressive sight. I fear the walls won't be easy to breach."

"Nor should they be. The Temple Knights oversaw their construction themselves. They are said to be masters of such things, you know."

"So I've heard," said the general, "but that helps us little in this case."

"How tall would you say those walls are?"

Spanov stared at the city a moment before answering. "I should say nearly thirty feet."

"Difficult to climb, then?"

"I'll grant you they're tall, but I'm more concerned with the towers. Whoever designed this place knew their business."

"Come now, they're not all that bad, are they?"

"They protrude from the walls, Your Majesty, just enough to allow archers to cover the base of them. Even if we could punch a hole in the wall, any advance would be flanked by at least two towers."

"Can't we use our catapults to destroy the towers?"

General Spanov rolled his eyes. "How much time do you have, Majesty? It would take weeks, if not months, to do that."

"For Saint's sake, you're my chief military advisor. Surely you have something to offer?"

"I would suggest we focus our energies on the western gate."

"Western? There are other gates?"

Spanov bit back his angry retort. Did the king have no common sense? "Yes, there are two gates, Majesty. This one before us now is the west gate, and there's another on the eastern side."

"But there's no southern gate? Why is that, do you suppose?"

"To where would it lead? Nothing lies to the south save for the mountains."

"The same could be said for the east," said the king.

"Not so. There's farmland in that direction."

"Well, I suppose that makes sense. After all, someone needs to feed all those people."

"Precisely," said an exasperated Spanov.

"Then how do you suggest we proceed?"

"The first step is to isolate the defenders. Normally, I would surround the place, but with these interlopers in our way, that won't prove feasible."

"I shall ask them to send a delegation to us," said the king. "Let's hope they can be convinced to block the eastern gate."

"A fine idea, Majesty. In the meantime, I shall order up the siege engines, and we can get to work on demolishing the city gates on our side."

"How long will that take?"

"That's hard to say," replied the general. "Ordinarily, I'd guess three or four weeks, but knowing the Church designed them... well, it could take significantly longer."

"Then I shall leave it in your capable hands. Now, I want you to summon a dozen men to carry a message to these other warriors. Let's see if our interests align."

# SKIRMISH

## AUTUMN 1105

Natalia's eyes wandered to the far walls of Ebenstadt. The Alliance's army stretched out on either side, taking up positions to prevent anyone from entering or leaving Ebenstadt. They weren't close enough to be riddled with arrows, but their presence couldn't help but be noticed by the defenders.

"Oswyn is in there, somewhere," she said, her voice cracking.

"We'll find her," promised Athgar.

"You don't know that. This city is under siege. Anything could happen."

"Yes, but at least we know she's still here."

"For now, but who's to say Ethwyn won't use magic to leave?"

"If she had that kind of magic, she would've used it days ago. She's trapped, and that means she can be found."

"There are thousands in that city," said Natalia, her tone melancholy. "How in the Saint's name are we going to find her?"

"Oswyn is an infant, and Ethwyn is no mother. She'll need a wet nurse. How many of those do you reckon there are in Ebenstadt?"

"Dozens, likely, given its size."

"Yes, but Ethwyn is a Therengian. Her eyes will give her away."

Natalia turned to him, tears in her eyes. "I understand that, but I can't help this feeling of helplessness. We're out here, staring at the walls, while she's tucked away inside with our daughter. How do we even get inside the city to rescue her?"

"Could your magic get us inside?"

"No. I'd already thought of that, but I've no spells that could help us breach those walls."

"Then we'll build siege weapons."

"We have no expertise in such things."

"True, but Belgast does. I'm certain he'd be willing to help."

She smiled, although it was clearly forced. "I'm sure he would, but the bigger threat is that other army which lies to the west. They didn't come here only to talk. They'll fight their way into the city, and then chaos will ensue."

Athgar moved closer, placing his arm around her shoulder. "She needs Oswyn alive," he reminded her.

"I understand that, but siege weapons can play havoc with buildings. And what if they set fire to the town?"

"Then we must get there before any of that can happen."

"How? Fly? The gates are locked up tight, Athgar. No one's getting in or out."

"We'll find a way. I promise you."

"And in the meantime, what are we supposed to do?"

Athgar straightened his back. "We look after our people. All of them are counting on us, Natalia, and, hard as it may be, we have a duty to see this through to the end."

She turned slightly to hug him, clinging to him as if her very life depended on it. There they stood, holding each other, feeling the warmth of their bodies pressed together. For just a moment, everything around them dissolved, and all that mattered was each other.

Natalia gazed up at him, her features now settled. "Gather everyone," she said. "We must make plans."

"Are you sure? You can take a bit longer if you wish."

"No, I'm ready. Better to be doing something than worrying over what we can't control."

He left her, feeling the weight of the world on his shoulders.

Agar fidgeted, yet Shaluhk remained unwilling to let go of him.

"He looks well," said Kargen.

"His physical wounds are healed, but he is upset Oswyn is not here."

"As are we all, but we are doing everything we can to retrieve her."

"Speaking of which," said Natalia. "Can we get back to the matter at hand?"

They all turned to look at her. She stood, moving around the circle as the others watched. The leaders of the tribes were gathered, along with their shamans, and Thane Wynfrith had brought the captain of her fyrd to offer advice. Belgast rounded out the group, although he spent most of the time focusing his attention on the distant walls of Ebenstadt.

"We must find a way in," said Athgar, "and we need to do so quickly. Anyone have any ideas?"

Wynfrith shook her head. "The walls are far too high to climb, even with ladders. What about storming the gatehouse?"

"I thought of that," said Belgast, "but any attackers would be cut down by those flanking towers. They planned the defences well."

Natalia frowned. "What other options do we have?"

"What about bringing down a wall?" asked Kargen. "Do you think Rugg and his masters of earth can use their magic?"

"A good idea in theory," answered Kirak, "but they would need to get far too close to the wall, putting them in great danger."

"It seems to me," said Athgar, "there are only three options."

"Which are?" asked Kargen.

"We go over the wall, through it, or under it."

"None of us can fly," said Natalia, "and it looks like going through poses its own problems."

"Leaving us with only one option," continued Athgar. "I propose we tunnel beneath the walls."

"That would take forever," said Wynfrith.

"Ah, but you forget, we have the masters of earth." He turned his attention to the Orc. "*Tell me, Master Rugg, how much dirt can you shift using your magic?*" he asked in the Orcish tongue.

"*That depends on many things. How wide and tall would the tunnel be?*"

"*Let's say shoulder width, to the height of an Orc?*"

"*Likely a hundred paces a day or so. The problem is not moving the earth. It is stopping it from collapsing in on itself.*"

Athgar translated all this for the rest of the group.

"I can help with that," said Belgast.

They all looked at him in surprise.

"What? You didn't think a Dwarf could make a tunnel?"

"I thought you were an advisor to a king," said Athgar, "not a miner."

"I'll have you know I've held many positions over the years. Why, when I was a youth, I spent a year in an iron mine."

"Was that by choice?" asked Kargen.

"Of course. When a Dwarf reaches the age of maturity, they spend several years trying different professions. How else would we be able to decide what we wanted to do for a career?"

"And you became a master tunnel builder?"

"Let's just say I had a knack for it."

"In that case," said Athgar, "why didn't you pursue it as a career?"

"The miners guild was far too static for my liking."

"Static?" said Wynfrith. "What does that mean?"

"Dwarves live a long time," continued Belgast, "and promotions within the guild are based solely on seniority. I'd need to be ancient indeed if I ever wanted to make it up the hierarchy. In the end, I joined the traders guild instead."

"And did you find that rewarding?"

"I did. Meeting other races was a challenge at first, what with their strange customs and all, but I soon grew accustomed to such things."

"But you DO know how to stop a tunnel from collapsing?"

"I most assuredly do," replied the Dwarf. "Normally, we'd use stone columns or wooden beams, but I believe Rugg here has other options."

Wynfrith shook her head. "I'm afraid I'm not familiar with this type of magic. What options are you referring to?"

"Masters of earth can turn dirt to stone. At least the Dwarven ones can."

"They can," said Kirak, "but I do not see how that serves us here. We want to tunnel through the dirt, not turn it all to stone."

"Of course," continued Belgast, "but what if, as they dug out the dirt, they turned the walls and ceiling to stone?"

A smile blossomed on the Orc's face. "Ah, I see what you are proposing. A most ingenious idea, my Dwarven friend."

"We'd need to know exactly how long to make it. Too short, and we'd emerge before the walls."

"Agreed," said Athgar. "And if we go too far, we risk exiting into someone's home."

"I can take care of measurements easily enough," said Belgast.

"And how do you propose to do that?"

"I once worked as a surveyor."

"Is there any job you haven't done?"

The Dwarf thought for a moment. "Not that I can think of at this moment, no."

"Right, then," said Natalia. "We'll leave Belgast to work with Rugg and Kirak to devise a plan of tunnelling under the wall. In the meantime, I'd like to see some siege engines put together."

"You can't be serious?" said Athgar. "We have no expertise in such things?"

"They don't need to be perfect, but if we give them the impression we intend a siege, they'll be less likely to suspect a tunnel."

"So they're for appearances only?"

"Precisely."

"Then we had best start gathering lumber," said Kargen. "We are going to need a lot of it."

Kragor watched as the Humans drew closer—dozens of them, wearing an assortment of chainmail and gambesons, each carrying a sword, mace, or axe. He had spied them some distance off, but the men of Novarsk clearly had no intention of letting the Orcs remain where they were.

"*String your bows,*" he ordered as he stood, taking a step from the trees to make himself visible. The intention was to warn them off, but the sight of him must have brought fear to their hearts, for they increased their pace, converging on his location, all the while yelling and cajoling their fellow warriors to join them.

He briefly glanced over his shoulder, making sure his hunters were ready. "*Nock arrows, but pick your targets with care. You may draw and loose at your own discretion.*"

Kragor strung his own weapon, using the back of his leg to bend the mighty warbow so he could attach the string. The manoeuvre was a well-practiced one, carried out countless times, and took but a moment to complete. All the while, his eyes scanned the enemy, choosing a man who looked to be giving the orders.

He took an arrow from the quiver at his belt and nocked it, then, in one smooth motion, drew the bow and let fly. It sailed true, sinking into his target's chest, easily puncturing the shirt of mail. The man toppled forward without so much as a grunt, but Kragor was already loosing another arrow, a new target selected. Behind him, his hunters let loose with their own volley, several striking the same targets, but every arrow hit its mark. Twelve men went down, some writhing in agony, while the rest steeled themselves for the inevitable melee, screaming out a blood-curdling challenge.

The Humans in the lead were now no more than twenty paces away. Kragor let fly a final arrow, then threw the bow over his shoulder. Had he the time, he would have unstrung it, for the mighty warbow's strength would play havoc with the string, but he was far too occupied to consider such action.

Drawing his axe, he then waited as a man in a kettle helm rushed towards him, mace in hand. Kragor let his opponent swing first—a clumsy attack, easily parried. Then his axe came down onto the fellow's shoulder, digging in and crunching bone. His target fell to the ground as an eruption of blood sprayed into the air.

A roar behind him told him his fellow hunters had joined in the melee.

A surge of green exploded forth from the trees to flood across the field, slicing down with axes that gave no mercy.

Movement off to Kragor's left caught his attention, and he quickly parried, allowing the handle of his axe to catch the impending sword. He drove the weapon down, then twisted his wrist, sending the sword flying through the air. His opponent, now disarmed, backed up only to be cut down by another Orc hunter.

The enemy fell back under the ferocious assault, many turning tail and dropping their weapons. Off in the distance, however, a group of horsemen formed up into a rough line. It would only be a matter of moments before they were charging through his hunters.

"*Back!*" screamed Kragor. "*Back to the trees!*"

Had this been any other army, the men would have hesitated, but the hunters of the Red Hand knew their business, and more importantly, trusted their leaders. They turned and, as one, fled into the safety of the forest.

Only Kragor lingered, making sure all the hunters were accounted for, then ran, seeking refuge with his fellow Orcs. His hunters took up positions amongst the trees, their bows nocked but not drawn, waiting for the enemy to close once more.

The horsemen advanced yet remained outside of effective range. Instead, they maintained their distance, running parallel to the Orcs' position and riding north. Their intent was clear—flank the hunters and attack from behind.

Kragor turned to his tribemates. "*We must withdraw. Our position is compromised. Pass the word. We shall make a run eastward while the horsemen are out of sight.*"

The men of Novarsk rode around the top end of the woods, disappearing from Kragor's view.

"*Now!*" he called out.

The hunters began their withdrawal, working in pairs. One would rush forward, then pause, his bow in hand, watching for danger as their partner caught up. The tactic was repeated until all the Orcs cleared the field and were once more beneath the welcoming embrace of more trees.

He turned to Grundak. "*Take word to Kargen. Tell him we were attacked but have taken no losses. We shall hold here unless he sends word to do otherwise.*"

The Orc hunter grunted his acknowledgement, then turned and sprinted, heading east. It would take some time for him to reach their chieftain, but the enemy showed no signs of pressing their attack.

The horsemen finally reappeared, riding south, across the field with their attention firmly fixed to the west, and the forest that had, until recently, harboured Orc archers.

Natalia sat on her horse, working up the nerve to ride towards the gate. Beside her, Belgast looked decidedly unhappy in the saddle but appeared determined to be of assistance however he might.

"Now's as good a time as ever," he said.

She urged her horse forward, Belgast doing likewise while carrying a short spear upon which a makeshift white flag flew to show the defenders they wished to parley, but Belgast had his doubts.

They approached to within fifty paces, then halted, waiting as men scrambled along the gatehouse walls. The afternoon dragged on, and then someone finally called from the walls.

"What do you want?"

"Only to talk," replied Natalia. "We wish you no harm."

"Says the person with the army behind her."

Belgast chuckled. "He's got you there."

"I wish to parley," she called back. "Will you send forth a representative?"

"So that you can kill them? I think not!"

The Dwarf leaned towards her. "Ask to speak to Brother Yaromir. He's a Temple Knight of Saint Mathew."

"What good will that do?"

"You can tell him what transpired, and he and Stanislav can search for Oswyn. That is what you want, isn't it?"

"Of course, but how do I tell them that without revealing they hold my daughter's fate in their hands?"

"Simple. You just ask for Yaromir. Inform them you'll speak to no one else. It shouldn't surprise them. After all, he's a member of the Church. They're often used in dispute resolution."

Natalia took a deep breath, letting it out slowly. With her nerves now settled, she turned her attention once more to the gate.

"Do you know Brother Yaromir?" she called out.

"We do. What of him?"

"Send him out, and he can discuss matters on your behalf."

"I doubt he'll want to talk to you."

"Tell him Belgast sends his regards."

"Bel-who?"

"Bel-gast," yelled the Dwarf, emphasizing the syllables. "By the Gods," he said, under his breath. "These men are complete idiots."

"He's not here at the moment," came the reply.

The Dwarf face-palmed himself. "By the forge of Gundar, has this fellow no sense at all?" He stood in his stirrups, although it gave him little advantage. "Go and get him, then!"

Even from their present position, they could hear the grumbling.

"That will take some time."

"Then we'll wait," said Natalia.

Everything grew quiet. A bee buzzed by, heedless of the events unfolding around it. Off in the distance, Belgast spotted a hare rushing through a field, and his stomach growled at the prospect of a nice stew.

More time passed until the sun began to wane. Belgast, just about ready to ride back to their camp, noticed one of the doors open, and an armoured man rode forth, his chainmail glowing red in the receding light.

"Brother Yaromir," called out Belgast. "So good of you to come."

The Temple Knight rode right up to them, coming to rest only a few paces away. "Greetings," he said. "I expect you're Natalia Stormwind."

"I am."

"Good to see you too, Belgast," the knight continued. "I trust all is well?"

"As well as can be expected under the circumstances."

Brother Yaromir returned his attention to Natalia. "I assume you're here to demand the surrender of the city, but I fear the High Lord will not be so accommodating."

"I'm here on another matter entirely."

"Then speak freely, and I shall see if I can be of assistance."

"We seek a Therengian woman named Ethwyn, who's possibly a Fire Mage. She fled to Ebenstadt after abducting my daughter, Oswyn."

The Temple Knight removed his helmet, revealing a grizzled countenance. "I am sorry for your misfortune, my lady. You say she's a Fire Mage? Is she dangerous?"

"She's already killed two and seriously injured another. I hoped you could take word to Stanislav, and with his help, you might be able to locate her."

"I shall do what I can, Lady Stormwind, but the place IS under threat of attack. People may not answer my questions under such circumstances."

"Still, it would do my heart good to know that at least someone was looking out for her safety."

"You have my word. Is there anything else you wish to discuss? The fate of the city, perhaps?"

"No," replied Natalia. "Then again, I doubt your High Lord is willing to talk anyway, what with the army of Novarsk sitting outside his gates."

"He is not MY High Lord, but I believe you are otherwise correct."

"Then I bid you a good day, Brother Yaromir. May your Saint watch over you."

"And your Gods over you, my lady."

"My Gods?"

The Temple Knight gave her a puzzled look. "I just naturally assumed you worshipped the same Gods as the Therengians."

"I worship the Saints."

"Then I wish their blessings upon you."

He turned his horse around and rode back to the gatehouse.

"Do you think they can find her?" asked Belgast.

"They must," replied Natalia. "We've little choice at this point in time."

# ALLIES

## AUTUMN 1105

"**N**atalia must be frantic," said Stanislav. "You say this Ethwyn woman took the baby?"

"That's what I was told," replied Brother Yaromir. "Though I have no clue where to even begin to look for her."

"That's easy," said Evira. She had just returned to the table and placed two tankards before them.

They both looked at her. "Care to elaborate?" asked Stanislav.

"The child is young, yes?"

"Yes," he agreed. "Only a few months old."

"Then she's likely still nursing. This woman, Ethwyn, is obviously not the mother, which means she needs a wet nurse."

"And where do we find those?"

Evira smiled. "Leave that to me."

"Remember," added Stanislav, "she's a Therengian. That means—"

"Yes, I know," she interrupted. "Her eyes will be grey. It's not like I haven't seen people like her before."

"And you honestly believe you can track her down?"

"Of course. Ebenstadt is a close-knit community. If you know the right people, you can find anyone."

"And if she doesn't want to be found?" asked the Temple Knight.

"The city's in lockdown. Where could she go?"

"Still, she could be dangerous. We know very little about her."

"Not quite," said Stanislav. "We know she abducted Oswyn from under the noses of Athgar and Natalia. She's either incredibly stupid or extremely brave."

"I would agree," added Brother Yaromir, "but I don't understand why? What could she possibly hope to achieve?"

"I can answer that. She must be working for the family."

"I'm afraid I can't see the connection."

"The Stormwinds raised Natalia," said Stanislav. "They, along with their cousins, the Sartellians, have been trying to breed powerful mages for generations."

"And?"

"Well, Natalia was one of their most powerful students. They hoped for her to couple with a Fire Mage, but she rebelled, fleeing the country. They've been hunting her ever since."

"Are you suggesting," said the Temple Knight, "that they would force her to bear children? That's barbaric?"

"That's why I helped her escape. I came here looking for her, but the family got hold of me and used me as bait. I'm afraid they became aware of her pregnancy at that time. Her husband, Athgar, is a Fire Mage, you see, although not a member of the family."

"So, in their minds, this Oswyn is a powerful child?"

"Well, powerful in terms of potential, definitely."

Brother Yaromir was clearly out of his depth. "Can you explain to me this idea of potential?"

"Yes," said Evira, "please do. I find the whole thing utterly fascinating."

"Certainly," said Stanislav. "Let's see, where shall I start? Everyone knows mages can wield magic, and some know the ability to wield that power flows in the bloodline. What a lot of people don't know is it can often lie within someone, untapped and undiscovered."

"But if that's the case," asked Evira, "how would anyone ever know?"

"Ah, well, you see what happens is the person has a certain affinity for things within the scope of that magic. Natalia, for example, could call fish when she was young. A potential Earth Mage might find themselves getting along with all sorts of animals or be drawn to plants."

"And these people have magic within them?"

"They do, although it doesn't always manifest."

"There you go," said Brother Yaromir, "using those strange terms again."

"Manifesting is simply the way in which their power influences things around them. It's not a conscious thing—it just happens."

"And you believe Oswyn can manifest?" asked the Temple Knight.

"No, she's only an infant. Children usually manifest when they grow into adolescence, although Natalia herself displayed magical tendencies much earlier."

"And is Athgar powerful?"

"From what Natalia's told me," said Stanislav, "I would have to say yes, although I'm led to believe his magic is more controlled."

"Are you saying other mages are uncontrolled?"

"Yes," added Evira. "Do they turn wild or something?"

"No," replied Stanislav, "but Fire Mages are taught to unleash their full power whenever casting a spell, at least the Sartellians are. It's what makes them so dangerous."

"But Athgar doesn't?"

"No, he was taught discipline by the Orcs."

"Remarkable," said the Temple Knight. "So the very thing the family desired came to be—Natalia created a child with a powerful Fire Mage. No wonder they seek to claim her. Do you suppose the family is here, in Ebenstadt?"

"No," replied Stanislav. "I've kept an eye out for them since my arrival last year."

"That means Ethwyn is alone," said Evira, "and as a Therengian, she'll hardly be welcome at social events."

"Meaning?"

"Her quest for a wet nurse won't go unnoticed. That's good news for us."

"And if we find her," said Brother Yaromir, "what do you propose we do with her?"

"For now," said Stanislav, "we simply keep an eye on her. If an opportunity presents itself, we'll rescue the child, but I shan't risk her life on pure chance."

"I'll start making enquiries," said Evira. "I've got a lot of people to talk to, so don't expect me to find her right away."

"That sounds good. I'll look into lodgings. Maybe someone will remember taking in a Therengian woman." He turned to the Temple Knight. "What of you?"

"I'll keep my ear to the ground, but I really must visit Tybalt Kemp if we're to have any hope of ending this siege."

"Then might I suggest we meet up here tomorrow morning? We can catch up on each other's progress and coordinate any future actions."

"Sounds good to me," said Brother Yaromir. "I'll take my leave of you now and bid you a good evening." He finished off his tankard, then rose, nodding politely to Evira before leaving.

Stanislav looked up at the woman. "Shouldn't you get back to work?"

"And do what? You're the only customer left in the place."

He grinned. "Well, in that case, take a seat, and I'll regale you with tales of my youth."

. . .

Brother Yaromir looked down at the man with the blood-soaked shirt.

"How long has he been like this?" he asked.

"He started coughing up blood two days ago," replied Brother Laslo. "I tried everything I can, but I fear he's not getting any better. I hoped you might have some idea as to what it might be."

"You're the lay brother, not me. Have any others shown similar signs?"

"Not as yet, but the symptoms came on quite suddenly, at least according to his wife."

"This wife," asked Brother Yaromir, "is she here as well?"

"No. We haven't seen her since she dropped him off."

"Has the patient his full wits?"

"Alas, no. Why?"

"We need to make sure this affliction, whatever it is, isn't contagious. The best way to do that is to check up on his wife. Do you know where she lives?"

"I'm afraid I don't."

"Then ask around. Maybe one of our other patients knows her. In the meantime, I need to visit High Lord Kemp. He's summoned me."

The lay brother wore a look of shock. "One does not summon a Temple Knight. Has he no sense of decorum?"

"Apparently not, but in this case, I'll humour the man. Likely he wishes to know what I discussed with those besieging the city."

"You've been a busy man, Brother Yaromir. I trust this is all temple business?"

"I swore an oath similar to yours, Brother. I have no need for a lecture."

Brother Laslo bowed his head. "Please forgive me, Brother Yaromir. I meant no offence. Will you be long, do you think?"

"I doubt it. Meetings with the High Lord tend to be short and to the point, not to mention expensive."

"Expensive?"

"His Grace expects financial compensation for his time."

"That's outrageous!"

"I would agree, but it's not up to me. In any case, he's the one who's sent for me, so maybe I should demand payment in return?"

"You can't do that!" argued Brother Laslo. "You are a Temple Knight, sworn to a life of humility and poverty."

Brother Yaromir sighed. "I only meant it in jest, Brother. You may rest assured my oaths are still intact."

"I find your sense of humour to be most uncouth. You would be better off to concentrate on your duty as a Temple Knight rather than trying to make light of such things."

"In that case, I will bid you a good day. I shouldn't like to be late to meet His Grace, the High Lord."

Yaromir left the room, eager to find some fresh air. The Mathewite's mission had been founded some fifty years ago, but the structure itself was significantly older. Some said it used to house worshippers of the old Gods, but the Temple Knight suspected it was more likely an early monastery, especially considering the layout of the place. The rooms which housed their patients were more like cells than anything else.

The streets were bare as he stepped into the summer sun. Ordinarily, he would saddle up his horse, but the High Lord's 'estate' was ill-suited for stabling of late, so he elected to walk instead.

This gave him the time to contemplate the situation he now found himself in. The Temple Knights of Saint Cunar had ruled over Ebenstadt for years, but with their abandonment of the city, the place had quickly devolved into chaos. People were starving, and now, to make matters even worse, they were besieged, not by one but two different armies.

He had to wonder where all this was leading. Were the Saints looking down on him? Was this the time of his judgement? He quickly dismissed the thoughts. The Saints were mortal. To speak of them as if they somehow watched over everyone did them a disservice. It was their words that inspired—a matter often forgotten by senior members of the order. Part of him wanted to shake some sense into his superiors, but his sense of duty was strong, so he continued up the street, doing the work that was his calling.

It wasn't easy being a Temple Knight at the best of times, but here in Ebenstadt, he was one of only two left, making his job that much harder. If the mission came under attack, he had sworn to defend it, but he doubted two Temple Knights could hold off a determined assault. The fact was if Tybalt Kemp wanted the mission for himself, there was little Brother Yaromir could do about it.

What could he say to the High Lord of Ebenstadt? He certainly couldn't reveal the real reason for Natalia's visit, or Kemp would take pains to find the child himself. What, then, should he say? With Brother Laslo's words still echoing in his mind, Yaromir knew he must tread carefully. As a Temple Knight, he had sworn to tell the truth, but now that very same oath was a heavy burden around his neck. Should he lie to protect a young infant? It was a quandary. So deep in thought was he that he almost collided with one of the town guards.

"Sorry, Sergeant," he said.

"That's quite all right, Brother," replied the man.

Yaromir took another step, but then the soldier called out to him.

"Yaromir, isn't it?"

He halted, turning to face the fellow. "Do I know you?"

"I've seen you down at the mission. You helped my daughter when she hurt her leg."

"Ah, yes, I remember now—she was kicked by a horse. How is little Gertrude?"

"Right as rain now, Brother, thanks to you."

"No thanks are needed. I was only doing my duty."

The sergeant moved closer, lowering his voice. "They tell me you spoke to those people outside the gates. What is it they want?"

"Mostly to be left in peace, although I can't say the same for the army of Novarsk."

"So they're not here to raze the city?"

"Ebenstadt would be a prosperous source of taxes. I doubt anyone wants to see it burn."

"I don't know about that. Kemp would set it aflame in an instant if he thought he was going to lose."

Brother Yaromir found the concept difficult to accept. "Why would you say that?"

"I was a soldier here long before he came along. These are, by and large, good people, Brother, but Kemp is ruthless. He'll do whatever it takes to remain in power, and surrender isn't something he's likely to ponder. Have you ever had to deal with him?"

"I have, unfortunately, and I'm on my way to see him again right now. Anything else you'd care to share?"

"Yes, he trusts no one. Anytime someone looks to be gaining any influence, they get taken away. They say the cellars of the commandery are full of such prisoners. Mind you, I doubt even he'd consider arresting a Temple Knight."

"I shall keep that in mind," said Brother Yaromir. "Now, if you'll excuse me, I have an appointment to keep."

"Of course, Brother, pardon my interruption." The sergeant stepped aside, allowing the knight to continue his journey.

Tybalt Kemp was in a rage—that much was clear. Even Brother Yaromir, standing outside his office, could hear the sound of cups being hurled against a wall. The Temple Knight waited patiently, then the doors flew open, and three individuals fled the room.

"And don't come back until you have answers!" screamed Kemp. Moments later, the High Lord himself appeared at the door, casting his eyes around as if looking for someone else to blame. His demeanour only calmed as his gaze settled on Brother Yaromir.

"Ah, Brother. Come in, please."

They stepped inside to a scene of total anarchy—furniture upended while plates, knives, and tankards littered the floor. Kemp sidestepped some spilled ale.

"Mind your step," he warned. "I've just been making a few changes."

"You sent for me, my lord?"

"I did, as a matter of fact." Kemp sat, then placed his elbows on his desk, interlacing his fingers before him. "I understand you rode out the east gate and talked to the wildling woman."

"I did, Your Grace, although I would hesitate to use the term 'wildling'."

"If she's not a wildling, then what is she?"

"A Stormwind, my lord."

Kemp stared back. "Are you sure?"

"There can be no doubt. She confirmed it herself."

"But what would a Stormwind be doing this far to the east?"

Brother Yaromir decided not to reveal what he knew. Rather than lie, he simply shrugged. "Who can say?"

"Yet you spoke with her. What did she have to say for herself?"

"I believe she represents the wildlings."

"Don't be preposterous. Stormwinds grace the most powerful courts of the Petty Kingdoms. What in the Continent would they be doing amongst the wildlings?"

"Again, I cannot say, but it's clear the people she represents are upset with your treatment of them."

"And what about the King of Novarsk?"

"King Vastavanitch? What of him?"

"What does he want?"

"I don't know for sure," said Brother Yaromir, "but it wouldn't surprise me if they have similar grievances as those in the east."

The High Lord of Ebenstadt didn't look happy, but whether he was scared or angry was anyone's guess.

"What to do, what to do…" muttered Kemp.

"If I may, my lord. I have a suggestion."

"Go on."

"Let me approach the king on your behalf. Perhaps we can come to some resolution that doesn't involve bloodshed."

"I suppose that makes sense." Kemp stood, then began pacing. "Go and meet with King Vastavanitch, but be careful not to reveal too much."

"About what, my lord?"

"About the state of this city. If he suspects we're as ill-equipped as we truly are, they'll be within the walls in a couple of weeks."

"Is it that dire?" asked Brother Yaromir.

"I'd be lying if I said it wasn't. I'm hanging on by a thread here, Brother. One bad step, and the whole thing will come crashing down around me."

"Have you taken any steps to name your successor?"

"No," said Kemp. "Why? Thinking of applying for the job?"

"Alas, no. My vows prevent me from doing so."

"Pity. A Temple Knight would be just the thing this city needs right now."

"As to the king," pressed Brother Yaromir, "what would you have me say?"

"I don't care, so long as he leaves the area."

"They marched from Novarsk. I'm afraid they're not going to just march home without something in return."

"What would you suggest?"

"A treaty."

"A treaty?" said Kemp. "When they crossed the border and appeared like wolves at our door? No, it's much too late for that."

"There must be something you can offer?"

"I suppose we could promise to stop raiding his lands."

"That would be an excellent start, my lord."

"Of course, in return, he'd need to leave the vicinity of Ebenstadt immediately."

"Is this the message you wish me to convey to His Majesty, or will you tell him yourself?"

Kemp paled. "I hardly think that a reasonable suggestion. You take it. They wouldn't dare hurt a Temple Knight."

"I shall leave this very afternoon," said Brother Yaromir. "Is there anything else?"

"I don't believe so. What of you? Can you think of anything else?"

"It might be a good idea for you to write a letter, my lord, if only to identify me as your personal correspondent."

"I shall have my assistant draft one up immediately, not that it's likely to do you any good. I hear the king's particular about rulers being nobles. I doubt he'll take ME very seriously."

"Then it shall be my task to convince him of the wisdom in it," said Brother Yaromir.

"Do you think he'll listen?"

"In truth, I cannot say, but we must at least make an attempt. Too much is riding on it."

"Yes, it is," said Kemp. "Good luck with the king. Let us hope he sees reason."

# OVERTURE

## AUTUMN 1105

B rother Yaromir trotted out the west gate, his eyes on the distant soldiers of Novarsk. In the early morning, the mist still clung to the ground, lending it an eerie feeling as he rode his horse across the field. He carried no flag of truce, but his brown surcoat readily identified him as a Temple Knight of Saint Mathew, so he trusted in his Saint to keep him safe.

No shouts of alarm greeted his presence, but still, he saw them scrambling to arm themselves. Did they truly believe a single man could ride into an enemy camp and slaughter them? He halted some fifty paces from the nearest soldiers and removed his helmet.

"I come to speak to your king," he announced. "Would you be so kind as to inform him of my arrival?"

No one answered, yet, clearly, something was up, for one of them ran off in the direction of some distant tents. The Temple Knight waited, letting his eyes sweep the scene. A dog's bark echoed through the camp, breaking the silence, but it soon quieted.

Yaromir felt the sweat dripping down his back, although the sun had only just risen. It promised to be a hot day, made all the more so by this foolish errand. What did Lord Kemp hope to accomplish? The man was too obstinate to offer up anything other than empty promises. Was the King of Novarsk aware of this? He had to wonder.

A horse snorted, and then he noticed a rider making their way through the enemy's army. Moments later, the soldiers stood aside, allowing this newcomer to ride out to Brother Yaromir's position.

The messenger was well armoured. For a moment, the Temple Knight feared this might end in a test of strength, but then the rider removed their helmet, revealing the face of a woman with close-cropped hair. There was no denying the airs with which she presented herself—this was someone important, far more than a simple messenger.

"Greetings," she said. "I am Princess Rada of Novarsk, heir to King Vastavanitch. Who are you that comes seeking an audience with my father?"

"Brother Yaromir of the Temple Knights of Saint Mathew. I come representing High Lord Tybalt Kemp, ruler of Ebenstadt."

She gazed at him a moment, her eyes fixed on his, a look that might cause others to flinch but held no sway over a brother knight.

"Follow me," she replied. "I'll take you to him."

The soldiers parted once more, allowing them to ride into the Novarsk camp.

"I'm surprised to see a member of the Church," said Rada. "I was under the impression they had all fled Ebenstadt."

"That was the Cunars. My order remains."

"Does that mean you sided with the brigands who run the place?"

"I am here in the interest of peace, Highness. I wish only to avoid needless bloodshed."

"Then perhaps your order should have intervened sooner. The blood of Novarsk has already been shed. My father will not forgive that so easily."

"I regret the events that led to this confrontation, but we must look to the future, not the past, if we are to prevent further tragedy."

"Fine words from a supposedly neutral order. I wonder if you might think the same had some of your brethren died in the conflict?"

"Life is always to be preferred over death, but do not underestimate my resolve. I am a Temple Knight, willing to give my life in the performance of my duty if necessary. To believe otherwise would be a grave mistake."

"I shall be sure to keep that in mind. Tell me, Brother Yaromir, what is Lord Kemp like?"

"I'm not sure I understand what you're asking."

"What is your opinion of him, as a person, I mean, not a ruler?"

"He is a man much consumed by his responsibilities."

She laughed. "That's the most non-committal answer I've ever heard. Have you spent much time at court?"

"I'm no captain, merely a knight. My place is at the mission in Ebenstadt."

"Well, if you ever decide to take up the profession of a diplomat, let me know." She slowed as they drew closer to a group of tents. "Here we are."

Servants rushed forward, taking the reins and allowing her to dismount. Brother Yaromir followed suit, then accompanied her into the largest of the pavilions, where the interior was lavishly decorated. King Vastavanitch sat on a high-backed chair, his feet on a stool as he sipped from a goblet. To his side sat another individual, a soldier if his armour was any indication.

"Your Majesty," began Rada. "May I present Brother Yaromir, Temple Knight of Saint Mathew."

"Greetings, Sir Knight," the man replied. "I assume you're here to plead the case for this fellow…" He seemed to struggle to remember the name.

"Lord Kemp," offered the armoured man.

"Yes, Lord Kemp."

"I am here at his behest, yes," said Brother Yaromir.

"And what does he offer me to leave? Wealth? The keys to the city? I don't suppose he'd offer up his head on a platter, would he?"

"No, Your Majesty."

"Then I fear you've wasted your time."

"Yet still, you have agreed to meet me."

The king smiled. "You're perceptive; I'll give you that."

"It might prove more profitable to do away with the threats and blustering and talk of more reasonable expectations."

The king looked at his daughter. "You warned me about this."

"I did. Temple Knights are well-educated," she replied, "perhaps even more so than the diplomats in the Petty Kingdoms."

"But not noble-born. I find that most interesting."

"Some are," said Brother Yaromir, "but the sons of the wealthy elite tend to favour the Order of Saint Cunar."

"No doubt, but you made a valid point, nonetheless. Very well, let us talk of more reasonable demands." He leaned forward, taking his feet off the footstool. "I want Ebenstadt. With the city in my hands, my eastern frontier will be secure."

"And if Lord Kemp refuses?"

"Then my army will attack. He has little choice here other than the obvious. He can either hand over the city, in which case I will spare his life, or I will be forced to take it. If that happens, I can't guarantee his safety."

"The walls of Ebenstadt are high, Your Majesty."

"Yes, but all walls can be breached given enough persuasion. I'm confident we can do so here."

"Would you, by chance, consider leaving the city under Kemp's rule? Arrangements could be made to divert a large part of the taxes to you?"

"The High Lord must go," said the king. "The fact of the matter is he can't be trusted to keep his word. My troops must be permitted to enter the city. It's the only result I'll accept."

"You are not the only enemy who threatens Ebenstadt. How, then, would you react if the men to the east breached its walls first?"

"I think you overestimate their chances."

"Maybe, but it still bears some consideration. And if Kemp feels he is losing, he might consider throwing the eastern gate wide open."

"That's an empty threat. You know, as well as I, the Easterlings would massacre all within the city."

"What makes you say that?" asked Brother Yaromir.

"The simple fact is they're barbarians. They worship the god of death, for Saint's sake. You're a member of the Church. You should be the one warning US about such things."

"That's a fallacy, one which I'm afraid the orders did little to quell. While it's true they worship the old Gods, there's no evidence to suggest they support the practice of Necromancy."

"How can you be so sure?" asked the king.

"I spoke to their leader, a woman named Natalia Stormwind. Do you really believe a member of that august family would support someone who worshipped death?"

"Stormwind?" said Rada, visibly paling. "Are you suggesting the Volstrum is behind the defeat of the Church?"

"Not at all," said Brother Yaromir. "I'm told she's always been on good relations with my order. I am, however, telling you a member of a powerful and influential family has taken an interest in Ebenstadt. Now ask yourself, what would SHE do if the army of Novarsk took the city?"

"This complicates things, Father."

"It complicates nothing," said the king. "We only have this man's word the Stormwinds are involved. For all we know, he could be lying."

"Lying?" said Rada. "He's a Temple Knight. They don't lie."

"True, but it matters little. Influential they may be, but I'm the one who rules Novarsk, and I will have my way." The king stood. "Leave us, Brother Knight, and trouble us no more."

Brother Yaromir bowed. "As you wish, Your Majesty."

"I shall escort you back," said Rada.


Natalia stared down at the bowl of porridge. It had been a long day, but her appetite had not returned.

"You must eat," urged Shaluhk. "I even made it the way you like it—with maple."

"I'm not hungry," the mage replied. "It's hard to work up an appetite when all I can do is wait."

"The tunnel is proceeding as planned, tribe-sister. What more can you do?"

"I could demand the High Lord turn over my daughter!"

"That would only give him a weapon to use against you. You must trust in the tribes. They will not let you down."

"Where's Athgar?"

"Down in the tunnels, overseeing the progress along with Belgast."

"And have we any further news of when we might expect it to be complete?"

"No," said Shaluhk, "but not for some time, I imagine. It is not yet even with the walls and must go some distance beyond to be of any use. As to its construction, I am told it is wide enough for three Orcs to walk abreast."

"Why so wide?"

"Once we break through, we will need to get as many hunters as fast as we can into the city."

"Can we not dig faster?"

"I am afraid not," said Shaluhk. "The masters of earth would be willing, but as you know, the energy used in casting can only be replenished with time. It would be a different matter if we had more Orcs capable of using such spells, but we are forced to work with what we have."

"You're right, of course. Sorry, I should know better than to question you."

"There is no harm in asking." She placed her hand on the mage's arm. "We grieve with you, Nat-Alia. Oswyn is a member of the tribe, and we have asked the Ancestors to watch over her."

"I just wish I didn't feel so helpless."

Raleth appeared out of the darkness, an excited look on his face.

"General," he said. "We have a visitor, a woman."

"From the city?"

"No," the Therengian replied. "From the other camp, the one to the west of the city."

"And she wants to see me?"

"She asked for you by name."

Natalia handed the bowl to Shaluhk, then straightened her back. "Then bring her to me, and I shall see what she wants. Let's hope it will give us some idea what they're up to."

"I shall bring her directly," promised Raleth.

He ran off, leaving Natalia with her thoughts. Was this some kind of extravagant threat? Did this woman seek to do her harm? She turned to her tribe-sister.

"Shaluhk, I wonder if you might summon some of the other tribe members? I feel a show of force would help to demonstrate we mean business."

"Certainly. How many would you like?"

"A dozen would do, but make sure each tribe is represented."

"And Therengians?"

"Yes, some of them too, and see if Wynfrith is available, would you? Her presence might help."

"I shall be as quick as I can."

Rada stepped into the firelight, her armour glinting with the flicker of the flames.

"This," said Raleth, "is Natalia Stormwind, High Mage of the Alliance."

The princess nodded her head in greeting. "Good day to you, madame. I come as a representative of the King of Novarsk."

"And you are?"

"Rada, princess and heir to King Vastavanitch. Do you speak for this so-called alliance?"

"I do," replied Natalia, "though maybe the term 'alliance' is a little misleading. We are, in fact, a sovereign state."

The princess sneered. "Oh yes, and what do you call this country of yours?"

Natalia met her gaze. "Therengia."

Rada's eyes widened. It was one thing to claim to be a country, quite another to invoke the name of the Old Kingdom. She tried to laugh it off. "Surely, you jest?"

"Do I look amused?"

"But you aren't even a Therengian!"

"There's more to being Therengian than simply having grey eyes. I've embraced their culture, as have many others."

"What others?"

Natalia waved her hand, and a dozen Orcs stepped from the shadows. "These are the great tribes of the east. They are also part of Therengia."

"But this is outrageous. You can't simply claim to be the Old Kingdom."

Natalia kept her voice calm. "This is no simple boast. It is the truth, and whether or not you accept it is immaterial. The fact is Therengia is reborn, and nothing you can say or do will make it otherwise." She noticed the sweat building on Rada's forehead.

"Now," Natalia continued, "did you come here merely to insult us, or are you here to do something productive?"

"I'm sorry," the woman replied. "I merely thought—"

"What? That this was nothing more than a bluff? Did you not hear of how we defeated the Holy Army? Must we do the same to your own?"

"I'm not here to fight; rather, I'm here to seek common ground."

"Then speak," demanded Natalia. "What would your king want of us?"

"The king wishes the predations of Ebenstadt to cease. The best way to do that is to occupy the city."

"And by what means will he accomplish this task?"

"He means to reduce the walls to rubble using engines of war."

"Then why come to us?"

"To get you to agree to not interfere. This is a private matter between Novarsk and Ebenstadt."

"I'm afraid we have business of our own with this city."

"What if we could work together?"

"Go on," urged Natalia, "I'm listening. What are you proposing?"

"We've blocked the west gate, you the east. Let us then combine forces to assault the place. Tybalt Kemp will be hard-pressed to man all the walls at once, forcing him to thin out his defence."

"Your idea has merit. I shall consider it."

"Might I ask," said Rada, "what land you claim as your own?"

"Everything east of Ebenstadt."

"But that's all wilderness."

"Is that what you think? I hate to be the one to correct you, but the reality of the situation is that there are a number of towns within the great pine forest, not to mention Orc villages." She noticed the lines of worry creasing Rada's face.

"Just how many towns?"

"That," said Natalia, "is none of your concern. You should focus your attention on the fact a Stormwind represents them."

"I... beg your pardon, Mistress Stormwind. I meant no disrespect, but my father—"

"Your father, what, claims a city he has no right to? We shall not simply stand idly by while he takes Ebenstadt by force."

"Are you saying you'll help the defenders?"

"No, I'm saying we'll deny you the city."

Rada struggled to come to grips with the reality of the situation. She had come expecting a ragtag bunch of Easterlings eager to help plunder the city. Instead, she now faced the Petty Kingdom's worst nightmare—the rebirth of the ancient Kingdom of Therengia. Not only that, but it appeared the entire realm had risen in the east, even as efforts were made to suppress its people in other lands.

"We've no wish to go to war with Therengia," she said at last, "but my father, the king, cannot be stopped. I think, though, given the circumstances, if he discovered you had entered the city before him, he might consider withdrawing back to our border."

"That would be agreeable to us," said Natalia, "but how do I know your father would honour such an agreement?"

"I give you my word; I'll do all I can to persuade him. He can be a reasonable man, given the facts, and I'm sure he'd see the wisdom in withdrawing under those conditions."

"Then return to him and tell him of our agreement." Natalia turned to Raleth. "See her safely escorted to her camp."

Natalia waited until her visitor was well clear of the campfire before taking a deep breath and letting it out.

"That was inspired," said Shaluhk. "The rebirth of Therengia. Where did you ever come up with such an idea?"

"I don't know," she replied. "I was struggling for something to make her take us seriously, and I remembered how Therengia used to dominate the Petty Kingdoms."

"So you used their own fears against them? Brilliant."

"I'm not so sure about that. I might have just made things worse."

"How so?"

"Word will spread quickly of the rebirth of Therengia. I'm afraid it won't take long for warriors to flock eastward, determined to wipe us out."

"You worry too much," said Shaluhk. "We defeated a Holy Army. That alone will dissuade any further aggression."

"And if it doesn't?"

"Then we shall defeat all who come for us. We are one people now, Nat-Alia. You did what no one else could accomplish—gave us recognition."

# INFILTRATION

## AUTUMN 1105

A thgar fumed. "More stone?"

"It's to be expected," said Belgast. "We're beneath the very walls of the city now, and that takes more than simple dirt to support the weight."

"But this stone doesn't look natural."

"It isn't. Whoever built this place dug down deep, then used stone for the foundation. They definitely knew what they were doing. On the bright side, we're almost within the city itself. Another few spells from the Orcs, and you'll be able to breathe the air of Ebenstadt."

"That close?" said Athgar.

"According to my calculations, the walls here are likely less than ten paces in width. Your masters of earth can move significant amounts of dirt, even this rock, each time they cast their spells. I can say with a high degree of confidence that you'll be safely inside the city by nightfall. That being said, you should probably get some sleep. It's likely to be a long night."

"And how, precisely, will I get inside without being seen? I understand you can move the dirt, but how do we break the surface without someone noticing?"

"Once we're past the walls," said the Dwarf, "we'll start digging straight up but only on a narrow section. When we break the surface, Rugg will create a stone shelf to hold the dirt in place, then we can remove everything below it. You wanted to get into Ebenstadt before the actual assault, so once you're above, you'll be responsible for covering up the newly made hatch."

"Then I can make my way to the Elk. Hopefully, Stanislav will have news for me."

"It's important to remember you'll only have one day. At sundown tomorrow, the assault will commence in full. If Oswyn isn't in your hands by then, I'm afraid there's little we can do about it."

"Understood," said Athgar.

Having waited while the two of them conversed, Rugg used the lull in the discussion to intervene. "*Shall I continue with my spell?*" the master of earth asked.

"*By all means,*" replied Athgar in the Orcish tongue, watching as the master of earth resumed his casting.


King Vastavanitch waved his hand. "Let the bombardment commence."

A warrior stepped forward, igniting the pitch, and then the catapult operator pulled the lever, releasing its burden. The fiery ball flew through the air, landing just short of the wall.

It had not been expected to hit, but the ball split into smaller fragments, sending bits scattering around, illuminating their target, as had been the intent. Now, with something to set their sights on, the other siege engines began hurling their loads towards the walls.

A rather distinctive cracking sound echoed back to the king. "That was quick. They already have the range!"

General Spanov frowned, for one lucky shot meant little at this point, something the king should have been more than aware of. He turned towards Princess Rada.

"It looks like your father is in a fine mood."

"And well he should be," she replied. "This is everything he always wanted—a battle to stamp his name on."

The general watched her, trying to gauge her sincerity. There was little love lost between daughter and king, leading him to wonder why she was here in this Saint's forsaken place. Spanov half expected her to be watching the bombardment, but instead, she stared at her father.

"He is advanced in years," said the general.

"Men do not live forever, and as his heir, I must be prepared to assume the mantle of the Crown at any time."

"You fear his health?"

"Only insofar as he might never die. The man has the constitution of a bear."

"Even bears die eventually."

She swivelled her gaze to Spanov, her eyes boring into him. "The Crown must endure, General, even in the face of adversity. If some unfortunate accident befell the king, I would hope you would continue to serve?"

A smile crept over the general's face. "Of course, Highness. You may always count on my loyalty"—he lowered his voice—"and discretion."

"How long before a breach will prove tenable?"

"Now that we've switched targets away from the gatehouse, it largely depends on the construction of the wall, Highness. We'll know more come daylight when we can see the results of our present attack."

"And what would be your best guess at this particular moment?"

"Several weeks at least, I should think. The walls were built under the supervision of Temple Knights, and they know their business when it comes to such things."

"Why does my father insist on attacking along such a large section of wall? Wouldn't it be better to concentrate on one point?"

"It would, Highness, but he has dreams of leading the cavalry through the breach."

"You can't be serious? Has he completely lost his wits? You can't take horsemen through a breach. How in the Continent would they climb the rubble?"

"I tried to explain that very fact to him," said the general, "but you know how he gets. Perhaps you can put some sense into him?"

She pondered the distant wall. The initial flames had died down now, letting darkness once more engulf the target. "I wonder if he might be convinced to lead a foot assault?"

"It would be dangerous for him."

"True, but picture the glory. He would be forever enshrined as the warrior king of our people."

Spanov snorted. "He'd love that."

The princess smiled. "He would, wouldn't he? He's always wanted to leave his mark in the history books."

"And what of yourself, Highness?"

"I have no interest in such things. I will rule Novarsk one day, but not from the battlefield. I shall leave that burden in your hands, General."

"I wish your father felt the same. He named me general but orders me around like a common captain."

"Once I'm queen, you'll have all the recognition you deserve, General, but for the time being, I suggest you play along with my father's plans. He is, after all, the king."

General Spanov bowed. "Of course, Highness. And in the meantime, will you propose to your father that he leads the assault?"

"I would never do that myself, but I might mention the glory and honour that would be obtained from such an act. If he decides to do so after that… well, that's his prerogative, isn't it?"

"Indeed, Your Highness."

Kargen looked around the fire, taking in each face in turn.

"*We are the vanguard,*" he said in his native tongue. "*When the tunnel is ready, we must get into position. Once we are within the city, our job is to seize the eastern gate from the inside. Laruhk, you and the other tusker riders will begin the advance as soon as you see the gate opening. Kragor and the archers will accompany you, but you will quickly outpace them.*"

"*What kind of resistance is expected?*" asked Shaluhk.

"*On the streets? Little, but once we get to the gate, we can expect their warriors to put up a fight.*"

"*They are weak,*" said Kragor.

"*They are,*" said Kargen. "*We expect to have the advantage in numbers, but their armour is superior to ours.*"

"*Do they not have more warriors than us?*" asked Ushog.

"*They do, but there are a lot of walls to defend, and they can not be everywhere at once. In addition, they must contend with Novarsk's attack from the west.*"

"*Why can we not send in more hunters through the tunnels?*" asked Kragor.

"*More hunters means more noise, and stealth will be our ally in this. Do not fear; once the alarm is raised, Kirak will bring more of the Black Axes into the city. Until then, however, we must move quickly and quietly to the gate.*"

"*And Athgar?*"

"*His job is to find Oswyn and keep her safe, nothing more. Should any of you come across him during the attack, do what you can for him, but do not jeopardize our own objectives.*"

"*And if we are unable to seize the gate?*"

"*Then we will bring up the Stone Crushers and their masters of earth to gain entry. Remember, we can and have defeated this enemy before. Their morale is broken, their leadership poor—they will not put up much of a fight.*"

"*Do we know where the High Lord dwells?*" asked Laruhk.

"*We do. Why?*" asked Kargen. "*Did you want to visit him? Invite him to drink the milk of life?*"

"*No,*" said Laruhk, "*but if we fail to take the gate, then maybe we can take his chieftain's hut?*"

"*Do not be ridiculous,*" said Ushog. "*If we can not get in through the gate, how are we then expected to seize his chieftain's hut?*"

Laruhk blushed, turning a darker shade of green. "*I suppose that is something I had not considered.*"

Shaluhk looked at Ushog with a newfound sense of respect.

"*Now,*" said Kargen. "*Return to your tribemates and pass on these instructions.*"

"*Do we know when the assault is to commence?*" asked Kragor.

"*Tomorrow night, after sundown,*" said Kargen. "*Now off with you, and may the Ancestors watch over you.*"

They dispersed, leaving only the chieftain and his bondmate.

"*That Ushog seems to have made an impression on my brother.*"

"*It is about time,*" said Kargen. "*Laruhk is one of my closest friends, but he needs a guiding hand.*"

"*Is that what I am to you?*" asked Shaluhk. "*A guiding hand?*"

The chieftain smiled. "*That and so much more.*" He took her hands in his. "*You are the sun in my day and the moon at night.*"

"*You have quite the way with words, bondmate mine. You should consider becoming the tribe's bard.*"

"*We have no bard. That is a Therengian tradition.*"

"*They are beginning to adopt our ways. Perhaps we should adopt some of theirs?*"

"*It is an interesting observation, but I am content to be chieftain, providing you are by my side.*"

"*I am always by your side,*" said Shaluhk, "*even when distance separates us. Do you now doubt it?*"

Kargen grinned. "*No, but this attack holds great danger. Our people have never assaulted a city before, at least not to my knowledge.*"

"*In this, you are wrong, my love. Our tribe has not engaged in this type of battle before, but our cousins to the far west have. There, they fought beside Human allies, much as we do now. Our people are emerging from centuries in the shadows, Kargen. Can you not feel it?*"

"*I wish I had your enthusiasm, but I must bear the burden of leading our tribe. How many will die before we can finally live in peace?*"

"*I understand your hesitancy, but better a few should die now than many later.*"

Kargen straightened. "*I shall not hesitate,*" he said. "*I will do what is needed; have no fear.*"

"*I have none as far as your bravery is concerned. My only wish is you do not become one of the fallen. We have much to live for, you and I, and I would see you safely returned to me.*"

Natalia stared into Athgar's eyes.

"I fear for you," she said. "The city is a dangerous place, and your sister has proven herself to be deadly."

"No more so than I; I promise you. The woman who holds our daughter is no sister of mine."

"And yet she has you at a disadvantage. You cannot use your magic against her for fear of hitting Oswyn, but no such protection is afforded you."

"This is not the first time I'll be fighting a Fire Mage."

"True, but the first time you were badly burned, and the second, you would have died had I not been there. Let me come with you, Athgar, if only to help rescue our daughter."

"I wish I could, but you're needed here. Like it or not, you command the army of Therengia." He grinned. "Therengia," he said again, the name invoking images of days long lost to history. "Who would have thought I'd live to see the day the Old Kingdom was reborn?"

"I only mentioned the name to impress the Princess of Novarsk," said Natalia.

"You did well. I suppose it was inevitable, given the circumstances."

"I'm afraid I've put all of us in great danger. I fear the Church will launch another Holy War."

"If they do, this time we'll be prepared. And once word spreads, we'll have more Therengians coming to join us, making us even stronger."

"I would gladly trade all of that to have Oswyn safely back in my arms."

"As would I," agreed Athgar, "but we must deal with what fate has handed us."

"Have you no fear?"

"Of course, but something guided us here, and remember the dream? How can that possibly come true if Oswyn were to die? She'll live, Natalia. I know that now, and she'll lead our people to a bright future."

"Do the Gods tell you that?"

"No," he replied. "My heart does, and how can it not? Part of you is in her. I will not suffer her loss."

"You can't just change things by your beliefs."

"My people have always worshipped the old Gods," said Athgar. "I know you find the very idea strange, but look where it's brought me."

"Where?"

"To you, here, right at this moment."

"Since when did you start believing in the Gods?"

"Since our daughter's life depends on it. Think about it, Natalia. Did the Ancestors bring us to Ebenstadt, or was it the Gods?"

"The Gods don't talk to the Orcs. Only the Ancestors do."

"But even the Ancestors couldn't tell us why they sent us here. And what of the dream?"

"Shaluhk already explained that."

"Did she?" said Athgar. "Think on it for a moment. Both of us had the same dream. The only thing that makes sense is the Gods wished it."

"But I don't worship the Gods," said Natalia. "Why, then, would they send that dream to me?"

"An excellent question. Maybe your Saints had something to do with it."

"So now you're saying the Saints control our destiny?"

"I don't know how to explain it," he replied, "but I just know I'm going to find Oswyn. Whether that's because of the Gods or the Saints matters little to me."

She moved closer, cupping his face in her hands. "In truth, it matters little to me as well, providing our daughter is safe. Find her, Athgar."

"I shall. I promise."

They stood staring at each other.

"It's time," came Belgast's voice.

"So soon?" said Natalia.

"So it would seem," said Athgar. "It's time for me to go."

She folded her arms around him, hugging him tightly. "Come back to me, my love," she whispered.

He returned the embrace, then kissed her tenderly. He wanted to say more, to reassure her all would be well, but a great sadness welled up inside him, and he suddenly feared he would never see her again.

"I must go," he said at last, his voice strained. He forced himself to turn towards the Dwarf, clearing his throat to hide his distress. "Lead on," he said in as gruff a voice as he could manage.

"This is the exit," said Belgast, holding a torch, its flickering light illuminating a vertical shaft leading up to a disc of stone. He pointed upwards. "Above that lies a thin layer of dirt. Lift it, and you'll be inside Ebenstadt."

"Do we know where I'll emerge?" asked Athgar.

"Not precisely. I used the old ruined tower outside as a reference point for my calculations, but even my best estimate would only place us just at the inside base of the wall."

"And if you're wrong?"

"Well, we know for certain we're not beneath the wall, so I suppose it would likely mean we're farther in than expected. It's always possible you might emerge in someone's cellar."

"Let's get this over with, then."

Belgast retrieved the makeshift ladder, setting it against the side of the shaft. "Got everything you need?"

"Axe, bow, and knife," said Athgar. "What else could I need?"

The Dwarf dug into his pouch. "Here, take these coins. You remember where I told you the Elk is?"

"I remember."

"Good. If you don't see Stanislav when you first arrive, ask for Evira. She works there."

"Anything else I should know?"

"Not that I can think of. I'd go myself, but the unexpected sight of a Dwarf in a city of Humans would likely be remarked upon. Don't worry though. I'll be amongst the first ones out of this tunnel tomorrow night."

"And I will be leading," added Kargen as he stepped forward, placing his hand on the Human's shoulder. "Look after yourself, my friend, and find that daughter of yours."

"I will." Athgar began climbing the ladder, taking his time. Once he reached the top, he gazed back down. Belgast and Kargen watched with great interest, their eyes glittering in the torchlight.

"Douse the flame," he commanded. Darkness engulfed the shaft, forcing Athgar to let his eyes adjust before he felt for the disk of stone. He heaved upward, feeling a little resistance, then it parted way with the surrounding dirt, revealing the night sky.

Athgar climbed out, looking around to discover he was in the southeast corner of Ebenstadt, behind what looked like a tavern. He found himself wishing he had spent more time getting to know the town on his last visit, but such regrets would serve him little purpose now. Turning his attention back to the shaft, he pulled the stone disc into position, then used his hands to cover it with dirt.

Satisfied with the result, he stood, brushing off his clothes to make himself more presentable. Pausing for a moment, he strained his ears, trying to hear anything that might indicate he had been discovered, but all seemed peaceful. High above him, he heard the sounds of boots on stone as a soldier walked along the wall, so he waited and watched, although little could be seen of the guard. The footsteps soon receded, and Athgar made his way around the side of the building into the streets of Ebenstadt.

# POLITICS

## AUTUMN 1105

Thane Galan slowed his horse, turning to his companion. "And you're sure there is no connection to me?"

"How could there be?" said Magran. "Those who knew are either dead or fled."

"What about that fyrd captain, Harwath?"

"He is seen as a traitor, Lord. Who would trust his word against that of a thane?"

"You're right. I worry too much. The real problem before us now is how we turn this to our advantage? Do we wait for things to calm down or strike while the coal is hot?"

"Perhaps an opportunity will present itself?"

"I'm not one to rely on chance alone," said Galan. "Rather, I like to be kept well informed. Ride ahead, and see what you can discover."

"Yes, Lord." Magran galloped off, leaving Galan and the others to continue their journey. No sooner had his aide disappeared from view than Thane Aswulf made his presence known, pulling up beside Galan, matching his mount's pace.

"I don't like this," said Galan, noting his comrade's arrival. "Athgar marched his men to Ebenstadt without even consulting us."

"He's a headstrong individual, I grant you," said Aswulf, "but his heart's in the right place."

"Is it, though? I begin to wonder."

"What's that supposed to mean?"

"People talk of making him king, but a ruler must put the needs of the people before their own."

"And?" pressed Aswulf.

"And here we are, attacking the city because a woman has stolen his child, and not just any woman, his sister, no less."

"You can hardly blame him for that. Would you do any differently if the circumstances were reversed?"

"I most certainly would," said Galan. "I realize family is important, but children die all the time. You can't stop to cry over them all."

"How can you be so callous? This is a baby we're talking about."

"And would it be any different had it been a full-grown man? A king must make difficult choices, Aswulf. It's part of the burden."

"It seems we find ourselves in opposition on this."

"Oh? Tell me, which would you prefer to lose—a small child or a kingdom?"

"Come, now," said Aswulf. "We're hardly in that position."

"Aren't we? Think on it. What happens if we attack this city and are repulsed? I'll tell you—we'll become the laughingstock of the Petty Kingdoms. Every ruler from here to the western coast will send their soldiers here to wipe us off the face of the Continent. We can't afford that, Aswulf, as well you know. We only survived the Battle of the Standing Stones by the skin of our teeth. We can't do that again."

"Then what would you have us do? Replace Athgar? You know the people of Runewald would never allow that. They adore him."

"Yes," said Galan. "He and his skrolling wife. I wish they'd never set foot in our land."

"Had they not, we wouldn't be here to talk of it."

"Nonsense. We would have moved east, as King Eadred wished."

"And fought the Orcs?" said Aswulf. "Are you mad?"

"Better them than the men of the west."

"Well, I can see you won't be persuaded, but it matters little. We're here now, and nothing we do will change the past."

"You're right, of course, my friend. Let us look to the future."

Aswulf craned his neck, looking at the men who marched behind them, then returned his gaze to his companion. "These men and women are the future, my friend. It is they who will win the city for us."

"I suspect so," said Galan, "but my primary concern at this time is what comes next."

"Next? Why, peace, what else?"

"And who shall rule our land?"

"The Moot, of course."

Galan shook his head. "You and I both know the Moot has its limitations. We have always had a king. To do otherwise at this point is the height of folly."

"We offered the Crown to Athgar, and he refused. What else can we do?"

"It would appear it's time we took matters into our own hands."

"How?" asked Aswulf. "By forcing him to wear the crown? You know he'd never agree."

"Then someone else should take on that burden."

"Like who—you?"

"I was thinking more along the lines of you, Aswulf. It wouldn't be the first time a thane rose to the position of king, nor, I suspect, will it be the last."

"I have no desire to rule."

"You already do, to a certain extent. You are a thane after all."

"Yes, a man in charge of a village. That's a huge difference from running a kingdom."

"Only in terms of scale. It merely means you'd have to delegate to others."

"I see," said Aswulf. "And how do we separate the responsibilities of king and thane?"

"Along existing lines, as it was under Eadred."

"I might remind you Eadred is dead, killed by his own treachery."

"Oh, come now," said Galan. "Eadred was a bad king, I grant you, but we both know Athgar was responsible for his downfall."

"Eadred lost sight of what it means to be king."

"So he did, but someone like you would take that position seriously."

"You and I can argue the point as long as we like, but we are only two of four thanes."

"True," said Galan, "but I believe I could convince Wynfrith to come around to our way of thinking."

"Our way of thinking?" said Aswulf. "You mean of making me king?"

Galan smiled. "Of course. Let's face it, you're more than qualified. Why, you're ancient, far more so than I."

"I'm better suited to the part because of my age?"

"You know what they say—with age comes wisdom."

They rode in silence for a while, but it was obvious Thane Aswulf was working through things in his mind. They soon encountered the guards who manned the outer perimeter of the allied camp.

"Where is Thane Athgar?" asked Galan.

"Within the walls of the city," replied the guard. "He entered late last night."

Galan turned to his companion. "It appears fortune favours us this day."

"Who's in charge here?" asked Aswulf.

"High Mage Natalia," replied the guard.

"Then lead us to her. There is much to discuss."

Shaluhk watched as the thanes rode through the camp. "I sense trouble," she said.

"You had better go and take a look," said Skora. "Natalia may have need of you."

"And what of Agar? I can not take him to meet the thanes. Humans dislike such disruptions."

Skora chuckled. "Not all Humans, only the ones who are full of themselves."

"Full of themselves? I am not familiar with the concept."

"They think only of themselves. Such men are victims of their own pride."

"Ah," said Shaluhk. "This I think I understand. May I leave Agar with you?"

"With me?"

"Of course. Why would I not?"

The old woman looked at the ground. "I was responsible for Oswyn's abduction. Are you sure you want to trust me with your son?"

"It is Ethwyn who bears that burden, not you. You may rest assured I believe Agar safe in your company, else I would not suggest it."

Skora's face brightened. "In that case, I agree."

Shaluhk took her son by the hand and knelt before him. "Agar, I need to go and help Nat-Alia. You must stay here, with Skora. Do you understand?"

"S-Kora," replied the youngling.

The shaman smiled. "Close enough." Her eyes drifted back to the old woman. "I suspect I shall be gone for some time. These thanes seem to delight in wasting time."

"Don't worry, I have plenty to keep Agar busy."

Shaluhk waited until Agar ran across to his new nanny, then rose. With a nod to Skora, she turned and made her way towards Nat-Alia's campfire.

Had they been back in Runewald, she would need only cross to the other side of the great longhouse. But here, in the wilderness, Natalia had to constantly consult with her leaders, making it far too difficult to settle a youngling. As a result, they had set up separate campfires, although still within hailing distance of each other.

As Shaluhk drew closer, she heard the thanes making their introductions. She had met them before, of course, for the Moot met regularly, but to see them here, in this place, brought home the seriousness of the situation they now found themselves in.

"Ah, Shaluhk," said Natalia. "Good to see you. You remember the thanes?"

The shaman nodded her head. "Of course. I trust your journey was uneventful, Thane Galan? Thane Aswulf?"

Galan cleared his throat. "Yes, quite. Now, where were we?"

"I was telling you of our current situation," replied Natalia. "Athgar is presently within the city, and our warriors are ready to attack as soon as darkness descends."

"And by 'our warriors' you mean…" said Galan.

"The Orcs of the Red hand, led by Kargen himself."

"Are you sure that's wise?"

"Are you questioning my military judgement?"

"It's a Human city. Should our own people not be the ones to carry out the attack?"

"Tell me, Thane Galan, were I to make that change, how would they tell friend from foe?"

"Whatever do you mean?"

"Would they need to stop each person they see to examine their eyes?"

"No," said Galan, "that would be impractical."

"The Orcs were chosen because they are easy to identify by our own troops."

"And whose idea was that?" asked Aswulf.

"Chief Kargen's," said Natalia.

"And where is he?"

"He is busy," said Shaluhk.

"Too busy to welcome us?"

"He is preparing for the coming attack."

Galan turned his attention to Natalia. "Is there anything else we should be made aware of?"

"Yes," she replied. "I met with a representative of Novarsk, the army which lies on the western side of the city."

Galan paled. "Another army? Here? Surely, we must retreat!"

"They are not here for us. Their king wants to capture Ebenstadt."

"Then let them have it. It's of no use to us."

"I will not!" she replied. "Not while my daughter is within those walls."

"Your judgement is clouded."

"And what would you know of such things?" said Shaluhk. "Have you a child held captive?"

"No, of course not." Galan turned to Natalia. "Look, I don't know what she's doing here, but you can dismiss her. This is none of her concern."

"On the contrary," said Shaluhk. "I am shaman to the Orcs of the Red Hand. In the absence of my chieftain, I am empowered to speak on his behalf. We are of one mind, Kargen and I, and I can assure you I am fully aware of his wishes."

"If you say so," the man replied, "but this matter is none of your concern." He paused for a moment, collecting his thoughts. "Natalia Stormwind, I call for your removal as High Mage. Thane Aswulf here will second the motion."

"That still leaves you in the minority," said Natalia.

"Then go and fetch Wynfrith. I'm sure she'll see the reason in this."

"And what of the Orcs?" said Shaluhk. "Are we to be consulted as well?"

"This is a matter for the Therengian warriors and has nothing to do with you."

"In that, I believe you are mistaken. Natalia has informed the Princess of Novarsk that both Orcs and Humans represent the army of the Sovereign State of Therengia. Is that not true, Nat-Alia?"

Galan's face turned red. "You did what? How dare you! Do you realize what you've done?"

"I did what I thought was best," said Natalia. "How else was I to get Novarsk to treat us with respect? Oh, and by the way, I lent my name to your cause as an added incentive to be taken seriously."

"You what?"

"The Stormwind name carries great weight amongst the Petty Kingdoms," said Shaluhk. "They say the mere mention of them is worth a thousand warriors."

Wynfrith's voice carried to them. "What's going on here?"

"Ah," said Galan. "We were just talking about you. Come here and settle this, will you?"

The Thane of Bradon came closer, joining the discussion. "I presume you're having a disagreement about something?"

"Lord Galan doesn't like the fact I named our land," said Natalia.

"Then he's more than capable of suggesting an alternative."

"I move Natalia Stormwind be stripped of her title," said Galan.

"And I second the motion," added Aswulf. "Since Athgar isn't here, the motion carries."

"Not so fast," said Wynfrith. "You might have two votes, but that's far from a majority. Did you forget we're an alliance? That means the Orc tribes have a vote in who commands. What say you, Shaluhk?"

"The Orcs of the Red Hand stand with Nat-Alia."

"And the other tribes?"

"I can summon them if you wish, but there is no doubt how they would vote. They have cast their stones for Nat-Alia. There can be no other to lead them."

"There, you have it," said Wynfrith. "That's three votes to your two. Oh, did I say three? How silly of me, I forgot to add my own. Make that four votes to two. In other words, the motion is defeated. Natalia shall remain as Warmaster."

"High Mage," corrected Shaluhk.

"Oh yes. Pardon my mistake."

"Not so fast," said Galan. "As thanes of our respective villages, we still command our fyrds. You may rule here, but nothing is stopping us from withdrawing our warriors."

"Go ahead," said Natalia, "but when the city falls, and it WILL fall, to the victors go the spoils."

"Yes," added Shaluhk, "and if the Orcs are the only ones fighting…"

"Then they shall be the only ones to reap the benefits," finished Natalia.

Galan gaped. "This is outrageous!"

"You're more than welcome to assist," said Wynfrith. "My own warriors are participating. Yours can too."

"I'm in," said Aswulf, a little too quickly. Clearly, the prospects for profit were a great motivating factor.

"Not you too, Aswulf?" said Galan. "Can't you see what they're doing?"

"There's more, actually," said Wynfrith.

"More? What do you mean by that?"

"Didn't I mention it? We have a man in custody who testified to your part in the abduction of Oswyn. A man named Harwath. Are you familiar with him?"

"The Runewald fyrd captain?" said Aswulf. "What's he to do with this business?"

"Apparently," said Wynfrith, "he was approached by someone named Magran. Correct me if I'm wrong, Galan, but isn't that the name of your aide?"

Galan paled, and his mouth flopped open, but nothing came out.

Aswulf turned on him. "What's this all about? What have you been up to, Galan?"

"This is all a big mistake, I assure you."

"What is? What in the Gods' name is going on here?"

Wynfrith waved some warriors over. "Take Thane Galan into custody," she ordered. "He is charged with treason."

"Treason? I only plotted to abduct a filthy skrolling child!"

"No," said Shaluhk. "Your people abducted Oswyn, the child of a thane and a High Mage. Were you an Orc, you would be forever banished."

Galan straightened his back. "We Therengians have laws."

"Don't worry," said Wynfrith. "Just like the Orcs, we have a system of judging such crimes. Of course, we don't favour banishment so much as execution. You might have better luck if you throw yourself on the mercy of the tribes."

"It would be refused," said Shaluhk. "Athgar and Natalia are considered members of the Red Hand, as is their daughter, Oswyn. A crime against any of them makes him an enemy of the tribe."

"It appears your fate rests in the hands of your fellow thanes, Galan. What have you to say for yourself?"

"The child was only supposed to be taken long enough to force a vote of the Moot."

"That may be, but it led to death, a crime which cannot be overlooked." Wynfrith turned to the guards. "Bind his arms and take him away. He is relieved of his position as ruler of Thaneford."

"You can't do that!" said Galan. "Only the people of Thaneford have that right."

"Don't worry, they'll have their say at your trial. In the meantime, I propose he be kept locked up? What say you, Thane Aswulf?"

"I agree."

"And you, Lady Stormwind?"

"Me? I'm no thane."

"True, but your husband is. Surely, as a member of the Red Hand you can speak on Athgar's behalf? That is the custom, is it not, Shaluhk?"

"It is," said the Orc.

"In that case," said Natalia, "I agree with you, Wynfrith. This man should be placed under arrest. What do you think, Shaluhk?"

"The Red Hand agrees with your decision. Shall I consult with the other tribes?"

"Do you believe there's any chance they might vote differently from you?"

"Not at all."

"Well, then," said Wynfrith. "Let's dispense with the formality, shall we? High Mage Stormwind, since this is a matter of war, will you take charge of the prisoner?"

Natalia turned. "Raleth," she called out. Moments later, the new fyrd captain arrived. "Yes, Natalia?"

"Thane Galan is under arrest. I trust you can take care of his confinement?"

"Might I ask the charge against him?"

"Treason, in that he plotted the abduction of Oswyn and manipulation of the Moot."

Raleth moved to stand before the ruler of Thaneford. "Lord Galan, I hereby place you under arrest on the charge of high treason against the Realm of Therengia. You will be placed in confinement until such time as a trial can be arranged. I order you to surrender your weapons, or I shall take them by force."

Galan removed his sword belt, handing it over with a look of utter defeat. Raleth walked around behind the man and began binding his arms.

Natalia watched the entire procedure with an icy glare. "Remove him from my sight."

# THE PLAN

## AUTUMN 1105

A thgar edged around the side of the building, peering into the darkened streets. He knew geographically where he was in Eben-stadt, but this part of the city was unknown to him. How, then, would he find his way to the Elk, a tavern he had never visited?

From his present position, the road came down from the north, then turned west, following the general shape of the outer wall. His first instinct was to head north, for Belgast's description placed the tavern close to the eastern wall, yet the layout of the city overwhelmed him, just as it had on his first visit. He had grown far too used to the spread-out buildings of Runewald, but here they were packed so tightly together there was seldom any space to pass between them.

He stepped out onto the road when some movement off to the west caught his attention. An old man had exited a building and was refilling a brazier that hung on chains, illuminating the brown and white banner suspended there. Athgar immediately recognized the image of the axe that adorned it—the markings of the Order of Saint Mathew. The flame beck-oned him, and so he made his way down the street.

The old man, having completed his task, turned, his intent clearly to re-enter the structure, but the sudden presence of a visitor forestalled him.

"Can I help you?" he called out.

"Greetings, Brother," said Athgar. "I'm looking for a Temple Knight. He goes by the name of Brother Yaromir?"

"He's inside. Come out of the chill of the night, and I shall find him for you."

Athgar hesitantly drew closer but sensed no sign of deception. "I am

Athgar of Athelwald," he said, "and have travelled some distance seeking his help."

"Brother Yaromir is one of two Temple Knights who serve this mission," the man replied, then appeared to startle suddenly. "Pardon me, where are my manners? I didn't even introduce myself." He held out his hand. "My name is Brother Laslo. Welcome to our humble abode. Are you sick, perchance?"

Athgar shook his hand. "No, I'm here on another matter, although I regret it's not something I can discuss with others. It is for Brother Yaromir's ears alone."

"Of course. Now, let's see if we can find him for you, shall we?" He led the way indoors.

The mission was a strange-looking old building, having been initially much smaller and then been enlarged over the years, resulting in a mismatch of architectural styles. Athgar wondered if the original building was constructed by Therengians, but the stone walls seemed to suggest otherwise.

Brother Laslo led him into a large room filled with tables and benches, undoubtedly a dining hall. Inside sat a lone occupant, his chainmail armour reflecting the candlelight.

"Brother Yaromir," called out the lay brother. "You have a visitor."

The Temple Knight turned his head, revealing a well-trimmed beard. Upon noticing the newcomer, he stood, bowing his head slightly.

"Welcome. I'm Brother Yaromir. How can I be of assistance?"

"I'm a friend of Stanislav."

A grin broke out on the knight's face. "You must be Athgar." He moved closer, grasping his hand.

Relief flooded through the Therengian. "I need to get to the Elk, but I'm afraid I don't know where that is."

"I shall take you," said Yaromir. He turned to his fellow Church member. "I'll take it from here, Brother Laslo. You may resume your duties."

"Excellent. I shall bid you both good evening." The lay brother wandered off, his sandalled feet slapping against the stone floor.

"Come," said Yaromir. "I'll take you to Stanislav."

"Is it far?" asked Athgar.

"Not at all, although I suppose it is like threading a maze."

"A maze?"

"Yes, a..." He noticed the look of confusion on Athgar's face. "Never mind, we'll talk about that later."

They stepped outside, and the Temple Knight led them westward. "We'll turn north at the first chance," he said. "Ordinarily, I'd cut between some of the buildings, but you'd likely twist an ankle this time of night." He turned his attention to Athgar. "If you don't mind me asking, how did you get into Ebenstadt?"

"Through a tunnel, actually."

"A tunnel? That would take weeks, surely? Your army hasn't been here more than a couple of days."

"It's all due to magic," explained Athgar. "I don't know how much Stanislav told you, but the Orcs can wield the power of Earth Magic."

"Fascinating." They reached a crossroad and headed north.

"I presume you know this part of the city well?"

"Oh yes," said Brother Yaromir. "It's part of my regular patrol route."

"You patrol the city? I thought your job was to guard the mission?"

"It is, but ultimately the order serves the sick and poor. That means going out and visiting people. I typically accompany Brother Laslo on such trips."

"But you spoke of conducting a patrol?"

"Yes, that's a little more recent. Since Tybalt Kemp came to power, there's been more incidents requiring my intervention."

"Incidents?" asked Athgar.

"Yes. Many of his soldiers feel a need to supplement their income at the expense of others. The funny thing is, they choose to pick on the poorest residents, the very people who have so little to give."

"Not so strange, really. They most likely see them as weak, not to mention less risky. I would hazard a guess the more affluent might have private guards."

"I suppose I hadn't thought of that. Still, the sight of an armoured Temple Knight should be enough to deter them, even if it's only a Mathewite." Once more they turned, this time heading eastward. "We'll take the first road on the left, and that will lead us to the Elk."

Athgar's eyes took in the city, illuminated as it was by the moonlight, and he could see a myriad of styles. "I don't recall seeing those buildings before."

"Well, you wouldn't, from what Stanislav told me. I understand you stayed in the northwest quarter the last time you were here. That's far nicer."

"Is that where the theatre is?"

"It is. I'm surprised you're familiar with it. They say it's been closed for years."

"That's where I first met Stanislav."

"Ah, here's our last turn," said Brother Yaromir. They continued north, but the buildings here crowded in on either side. Athgar couldn't help but feel anxious, for the buildings were far higher than he could have imagined, some looking to be three stories in height.

"Are all the buildings so tall?"

"Pretty much," replied the knight. "The city can't expand because of the wall, so the only place to grow is up. I've seen this type of thing in other cities, although the building style here varies greatly, likely due to the influence of crusaders."

"Crusaders? You mean the Holy Warriors who tried to wipe out my people?"

"Yes, although I've never agreed with their cause. Warriors from far and wide flocked to Ebenstadt over the years, seeking glory in the name of the Church. Of course, anyone familiar with the teachings of the Saints knows that's the exact opposite of what they intended, but you know how people are."

"Let's just hope there are no more Crusades," said Athgar.

"A matter in which we are in agreement."

They passed between two buildings, although the term 'squeezed' might be more appropriate.

"How in the Continent would they get a cart through here?" asked Athgar.

"That's an easy one to answer—they wouldn't. Deliveries here are either brought from the north or on foot. We don't see much horse-drawn traffic in these parts, especially since Kemp took over."

"There's a shortage of horses?"

"Oh yes. Not only did the Cunars take all their breeding stock, but the High Lord has been butchering what's left for food."

"There's that much of a shortage?"

"Indeed," said Brother Yaromir. "The mission has seen a substantial increase in hunger amongst the poor. People are literally starving to death, or soon will be." They continued in silence, both deep in thought. Finally, they halted.

"This is the Elk," said Yaromir. "Let's go and find Stanislav, shall we?"

Inside they went, stepping into an empty taproom.

"No one seems to be here," said Athgar.

"Well, it is the middle of the night. Stanislav shares a room here with a woman named Evira. Take a seat, and I'll go and see if I can fetch him."

The Temple Knight disappeared up the stairs, leaving Athgar alone in the dark. He held his palm out, conjured a flame, and then used it to light a lantern that hung nearby. It bathed the room in a dull light, casting ominous shadows that flickered and danced against the walls.

He began to wonder if he was doing the right thing. Oswyn was out there somewhere, amongst strangers, and he felt an ache deep in his heart. Voices drifted down from above, and then Brother Yaromir returned. Behind him came Stanislav, his hair askew as only one woken from sleep would allow. Behind the mage hunter stood a woman of similar age, clutching a blanket over her shoulders, no doubt Evira. They all took a seat.

"Good to see you," said Stanislav. "This is Evira."

The last thing Athgar wanted was pleasantries, but then the woman spoke. "We have news," she said.

He leaned forward, resting his elbows on the table. "Of Ethwyn?"

"Yes," she replied. "I have word she's hired a wet nurse—a woman named Imelda."

"Have you an address?"

"We do," said Stanislav, "but I'm afraid the situation is a bit more complicated than we thought."

"How so?"

"Ethwyn is staying at Imelda's home, and other children live there."

"We cannot confront her there," insisted Brother Yaromir. "The risk is too great."

"The risk is great if we don't," said Athgar. "Every moment we leave her alone, we risk her making contact with other family members."

"The city is besieged," said Stanislav. "She has nowhere to go. If there were agents of the family here, she would have found them by now."

Athgar slammed his fist onto the table. "I didn't come here to sit idly by and wait. I must find her tonight!"

"Why the hurry?" asked Evira.

"Of course," said Brother Yaromir. "I should have realized."

"Realized what?" said Stanislav.

"He told me he came in through a tunnel. I imagine that same tunnel will allow his allies to get into the city. How much time do we have, Athgar?"

"The attack will commence at nightfall tomorrow."

"So we have one day," said Stanislav. "That should be more than sufficient."

"The city is not my element," said Athgar. "How would you recommend we proceed?"

"Let us go and keep a watch on this place. Sooner or later, she may step out, and then we can seize the opportunity."

"Agreed," said Brother Yaromir. "Or at the very least, some of the other residents may vacate the property. I'd prefer to go in with as few people inside as possible. What can you tell us about Ethwyn?"

"She is a wielder of fire," said Athgar. "We suspect she was trained by the family, although there's no way of knowing for sure."

Stanislav nodded. "That would make sense. They'd want Oswyn for her magic potential. They've been trying to breed powerful mages for generations."

"Aside from the magic, though," continued the Temple Knight, "what do we know about her?"

"She has a gift for charming people," said Athgar. "She used it to coerce some in our village to help her in her crime. She's also a Therengian, trained in weapons, so I doubt she'd submit willingly."

"The biggest issue is Oswyn," said Evira. "Would your sister use her to protect herself?"

"Most assuredly."

"That complicates matters immensely," said Stanislav.

"Children must sleep eventually," Evira added. "Perhaps that would give us our chance?"

"That would be preferable, but we have no way of knowing when that might be."

"But we do know who feeds her."

"How does that help us?" said Stanislav.

"Babies usually sleep after they eat. Didn't you know that?"

"Why on the Continent would I know that? I don't have any children."

"Well, maybe it's time you settled down and had some?"

The mage hunter grinned. "Any suggestions with whom?"

"Come, now," said Brother Yaromir. "There's no time for such games. Marry her and get it over with, will you? We have more important matters to discuss. Athgar here needs his daughter safely returned."

"Sorry," said Stanislav.

"Where does this woman, Imelda, live?" asked Athgar.

"To the south of the theatre," answered Evira. "There's a house that's tucked in amongst the shops there."

"Is there any place we can observe it without being seen?"

"Yes, a narrow alleyway across the street. I shouldn't imagine our presence there would arouse much suspicion."

"OUR presence?" said Stanislav.

"Of course," said Evira. "You don't think I'd let you go without me, did you? Who'd look after the child?"

"What makes you believe you'd be best suited for that? You don't have children."

"True, but I do have two nephews, and my sister keeps telling me I'll make a good mother, someday." She looked at Stanislav, the hint of a smile playing across her lips.

"We'll go there at first light," said Athgar.

"Well, then," said Brother Yaromir, "we won't have long to wait. By my reckoning, the sun will be up soon."

"Good," said Athgar. "Then I suggest Stanislav and Evira go get dressed. Walking through town in their nightshirts might attract a little too much attention. And as for you"—he looked at Brother Yaromir—"any chance you might forgo the armour?"

"Give up the trappings of my order? Why?"

"It's a little bit obvious, isn't it? We'll be trying to blend in. It's hard to do that with a man in chainmail amongst our numbers, don't you think?"

"You make a good point." Brother Yaromir rose. "I shall drop my armour off at the mission and meet you back here. That should give you plenty of time to prepare."

"And Evira and I will get dressed," added Stanislav.

"Then I suppose I'll just wait here," said Athgar.

"Help yourself to some ale," said Evira. "You'll find it in the back room."

"What if the owner of this place finds me?"

"I doubt he will. The fellow usually sleeps in till noon, but if he does happen to run across you, simply tell him I let you in." She grabbed Stanislav's hand. "Come on, it's time to put some clothes on."


The sun was just making its presence known as the group squeezed down the alleyway.

"Are you sure this is the way?" asked Athgar. "This city's so disorienting."

"Positive," said Stanislav. "I've spent the last few months here tracking down bounties. I know the place like the back of my hand." He halted, looking at a door that opened into the alley. "I don't remember that."

"It's here," called out the Temple Knight.

They all moved up to the end of the alley, keeping their backs to the wall. Brother Yaromir waved Athgar forward, and the Therengian peered out onto the street. Across from their position sat the target house, wedged in beside a carpenter's shop.

"I don't see any signs of activity," said Athgar. Off to the west, they heard a tremendous cracking sound.

"What was that?" asked Evira.

"Likely the catapults hitting the wall," explained the Temple Knight. "The army of Novarsk has been bombarding for some time."

"I'm surprised you haven't heard them before," said Athgar.

"She wouldn't," said Stanislav. "The sound is muffled by the other buildings. We're close to the western wall here, so it's more pronounced."

"So we need to rescue a child while they rain rocks down on our heads?" asked Evira.

"Novarsk wants to bring down the wall, not these houses."

Her look of worry did not diminish. "And that's supposed to make me feel better?"

"We can't all stand around here," said Athgar. "It'll draw undue attention."

"You cut across the street," said Stanislav, "then wander up one block and wait there. It should afford you a good view of the house. Yaromir, you stay here. Evira and I will take in a stroll and feign interest in some of these shops." He turned to the woman. "If that's all right with you, that is?"

She smiled. "I think that a grand idea. How do we know when to enter the house?"

"That remains to be seen. For now, let's just keep it under observation. If an opportunity presents itself, we'll try to get inside, but let's not rush in too soon. It'll only make things worse."

Athgar wandered out first, trying to look as nonchalant as possible. It felt awkward walking the city's streets without Natalia at his side, and he wondered what she was up to. They had only been together for a short time, yet he could barely remember his life before meeting her. He glanced at the house as he walked by, committing it to memory. Somewhere inside that building, Oswyn waited for him, and he swore she would soon be in his arms.

Reaching the corner of the carpenter's shop, he halted, turning to watch as its proprietor threw open the door. Inside he saw workers getting their tools ready to begin their day's labours. It made him reminisce about his days as a bowyer. Life had been simple, but then the slavers had come. Many would have regretted that loss, but in Athgar's mind, the destruction of Athelwald had brought significant change and the beginning of a life he wouldn't give up for anyone.

The thought of Natalia warmed him, and his mind turned once more to his present circumstances. Getting emotional wouldn't help. He must concentrate on how to deal with Ethwyn and her Fire Magic.

# SIEGE

## AUTUMN 1105

R ada watched as the catapult flung the stone in a graceful arc far into
the air, then descended, landing with a satisfying crack as it hit the
wall. Masonry went flying, lifting up a cloud of dust. After they struck their
target, the crew gave a cheer and then began working anew to load the
clumsy siege weapon.

A large crack was revealed when the dust finally cleared, blown away by
the morning breeze. Rada leaned forward as if the tiny motion might make
things easier to see.

"Is that what I think it is?" she asked.

General Spanov squinted against the early morning sun. "I believe it's a
crack. Hmmm, it appears the walls of Ebenstadt are not so mighty after all."

"I thought the Temple Knights built that wall?"

"They did, or at least they oversaw construction, but even the best-laid
plans of men are subject to the whims of nature."

"In what way?"

"Who can say? It's possible the local stone they used is weaker than they
surmised, or maybe the years of extreme weather have weakened it. The
cause matters little. What is of concern to us is the opportunity this
provides."

"Which is?"

"We will concentrate our efforts on that weakened portion. With any
luck, we'll have a section of wall down by nightfall."

"That soon?" asked Rada.

"Indeed. I've seen something like this before, back in ninety-one. Once
the integrity of the wall is broken, the rest won't take long."

"And we have enough catapults to bring it down?"

"Catapults aren't the problem," said the general. "Rather, it's the stones we're using. Each one we fire has to be brought down from the hills. It's a labour-intensive process." He looked behind him to where men were working, splitting rocks into manageable stones. "We should have enough. I originally planned to stretch this supply out over several days, but if what you've told me about the Therengians is true, we haven't the time, anyway. Might as well use it all up in one go."

"So we plan for a night assault?"

"That would be my advice, although who knows? These things have a way of being fairly unpredictable."

"What if the wall doesn't fall?" asked Rada.

"Then it won't make any difference, but it won't hurt us to prepare."

"The men are all ready to attack. What else is there to be done?"

"Lots," said the general. "I'll start sending flaming pitch into the city. A few fires will help."

"I fail to see how."

"The soldiers who man those walls live in Ebenstadt. If the city's aflame, they'll be more concerned with saving their houses than manning the walls." He glanced at the catapults once more, then back at the men behind him. "You must excuse me, Highness. There are things I must attend to."

"By all means," said Rada. She watched him go, then stared off at the distant walls, deep in thought. Her father was an unforgiving man, prone to outbursts of anger on occasion. For the most part, she managed to avoid such attention, but since the raids had started, he had become even more unmanageable. Was it time he was replaced? Even as the idea drifted through her mind, she had to acknowledge this wasn't the first time such thoughts had come to her. Maybe he was going senile? It wasn't unknown within the Royal Family. Well, if that were it, he might as well go out a hero, at least that's what she told herself. She turned and walked towards her father's tent.

King Vastavanitch tossed another morsel into his mouth, marvelling at the taste. It wasn't every day his meals were so extravagant, but the commencement of the bombardment made him feel like celebrating. He held out his goblet, waiting as a servant rushed forward to refill it. The tent flap pushed aside, and his daughter entered, resplendent, as she always was, in her plate armour.

"Ah, Rada," he began. "I understand the bombardment is going well?"

"It is, Father. In fact, that's the very thing I came to see you about."

"Oh? Is there a problem?"

"No, quite the reverse. We've been presented with the opportunity of a lifetime."

The king gulped down some wine, then wiped his mouth on his sleeve. "And what, precisely, is the nature of this opportunity?"

"General Spanov reports he has found a weakness in the walls."

"What kind of weakness?"

"A flaw in its construction," she said. "This morning, a crack appeared, one he believes runs deep into its foundation."

"Meaning?"

"If our luck holds, the entire section of wall will collapse."

"That would mean we could enter the city."

"My thoughts exactly," said Rada.

"Still, it's a dangerous business."

"Men die in battle, Father. It's their lot in life."

"I'm not concerned with lives but the reaction this Stormwind woman might have to our success. I shouldn't like to bring their wrath down upon us."

"How could it?" said Rada. "If we are the first in, then by rights, it's ours."

"Do you think that matters in the grand scheme of things? It's power and influence that's important, and we can't do that by taking on a Stormwind."

"She is but one person, Father, and you are a king! Are you suggesting a royal is outranked by a simple mage?"

"A simple mage? Can't you hear the words coming out of your mouth? The Stormwinds are no such thing. They're powerful, influential members of some of the most prestigious courts in the Petty Kingdoms."

"Exactly," she replied. "Let us hope after this, they'll consider sending representatives to OUR court. Saints know we've asked them enough times."

The king pondered her words, his meal all but forgotten. "You raise an interesting point. Should we succeed, they would need to acknowledge our military prowess, wouldn't you agree?"

"How can they not? Of course, to win them over, we'd need to set a good example. Maybe I should lead the assault myself? After all, I am a royal."

"And risk the heir to the Crown? I don't think so. Let Spanov do it. It's his job after all."

"An excellent idea, Father. I'm sure the general won't let the glory go to his head."

The king stared at her, his mind churning over possibilities. "Glory, you say?"

"Of course. Whoever leads that assault will be forever immortalized."

"Why would you say that?"

"History remembers the brave," replied Rada. "Armies may clash, but it's the heroes who earn their place in the tales."

"And you believe Spanov is worthy of that?"

"You did pick him to lead your army." She could almost see the jealousy writhing inside of him.

"Spanov is a simple soldier, not a hero!"

"I'm afraid we have little choice," she said. "Who else is there who could do such a thing?"

"Who, indeed?" The king stared into his goblet, swishing it around as he watched.

Rada rolled her eyes. Was he so dim as to not see the obvious? Perhaps his mind had gone after all?

"Send for the general," the king finally said. "I would have words."

"I shall fetch him immediately, Father."

General Spanov entered the tent to find the king sitting with his daughter.

"You sent for me, sire?"

"General, there you are. Rada here tells me we're making some progress on the walls."

"One section, yes, Majesty. With luck, it'll collapse by nightfall."

"Did you give any thought as to who might lead the assault?"

Spanov's eyes quickly shot to the princess, who simply nodded.

"I thought I might have that honour myself, sire."

The king quickly dismissed the notion. "You are far too valuable to risk in such an undertaking. No, your place is here, looking after the rest of the army."

"Then who will lead the attack? Princess Rada?"

"No, I shall undertake that burden myself."

"Yourself? Surely not, Majesty? You are the king. Such things should be left to others!"

King Vastavanitch rose. "You'd like that, wouldn't you!"

"Sire?"

"You want to claim all the glory for yourself! Well, I'm no fool, General. That would put you in a position of far too much influence for one of your standing. I will lead the attack, and I'll hear no arguments about it."

"Yes, Your Majesty."

"Are you sure, Father? It's not without risk."

"The greater the risk; the greater the reward," said the king. "I shall be forever enshrined as the hero of Ebenstadt! Now begone, the both of you. I must prepare myself."

"But, sire, it's barely past sunup. The catapults have much work to do before such a thing can even be contemplated."

"True," said the king, "but I must prepare, nonetheless. There are prayers to be said, and before I don my armour, I must bathe."

"Understood," said the general. "I shall look forward to watching you at the head of the attack, Your Majesty."

Rada stood, then took a step forward, hugging her father. "Your bravery shall not be forgotten, Father." She looked at Spanov. "Come, General. We should leave him to prepare in whatever manner he chooses."

They stepped outside, and Rada spared a glance at the general. As their eyes met, a smile creased both their lips. Spanov waited until they had put some steps behind them before speaking.

"It appears the Saints look kindly upon you this day, Your Highness."

"It wasn't the Saints who guided me," she replied. "Now, you need to make sure the wall is ready, or all my efforts will have been wasted."

"And if it isn't?"

"Then convince my father the assault should continue, regardless. Come midnight, I want to be the Queen of Novarsk."

"As you wish, Your Highness… or should I say, Your Majesty?"

Urughar crouched down amongst the undergrowth. Off in the distance, the men of Novarsk loaded more stones into their siege engines, a laborious task made even more so by the general weakness of the Human race.

"*What are they doing?*" asked Ogda.

"*What they always do,*" the hunter replied, "*wasting time.*"

"*I do not understand how those things work.*"

"*You mean the catapults? They act like a giant arm, hurling the rocks a great distance.*"

Ogda moved his great bulk forward, eager to get a better view. "*Yes, but how did they ever come up with the idea? It defies all logic.*"

"*Who can say? Maybe it was a Dwarven invention? Their minds work differently than ours. In any event, it is not the catapults that need concern us. It is the stones themselves.*"

"*How so?*"

"*Look,*" said Urughar, pointing at the city. "*See how the wall crumbles? The entire thing will collapse before long, and then the men of Novarsk will swarm into the city.*"

"*How long until they decide to attack?*"

Another rock hit, causing the crack to widen. "*Not long, I fear. The Humans are already gathering their men. They must feel the time is imminent. We need to return to our camp and tell of what we have seen.*"

"*You think it will affect our plans?*"

"*Most assuredly. If Kargen does not enter the city soon, it might be too late.*"

"*That would mean a daytime assault,*" said Ogda. "*We would lose the advantage of our night vision.*"

"*It seems we have little say on the matter.*"

"*What of Athgar's mission to save the child?*"

"*I fear that, too, is beyond our control.*"

"*Then let us be gone from this place and tell Nat-Alia of our discovery. I hope she will have a solution.*"


Shaluhk placed the axe in Agar's hand. The youngling tried raising it as he had done his old wooden weapon, but a steel axe was far heavier than his original, and he struggled with the unfamiliar weight.

"You will learn to use it in time," she said, using the common tongue of Humans.

"He adapts quickly," said Natalia. "Has he mastered the bow yet?"

Shaluhk chuckled. "No, although my brother thinks it time. Tell me, how long until Oswyn carries such a weapon?"

"Years yet," said Natalia, then her voice began to tremble. "Assuming we get her back."

"Protect Oswyn!" shouted Agar.

"He has mastered your language," said Shaluhk, "insofar as one his age can master anything. He will grow to be a master hunter one day."

"Like his father?"

"Kargen can hunt, I grant you that, but he is far from a master. His strength lies in his concern for our people, a trait he shares with Athgar." She leaned forward, placing her hand on that of her friend's. "He will find her, Nat-Alia. I am sure of it."

"I wish I had your faith," replied the mage, fighting to maintain her usually calm demeanour. "I just feel so helpless. It should have been me who went into Ebenstadt, not Athgar."

"Had you done that, Athgar would have stormed the city by now. You know this to be true. You are needed here, where your strength can hold this alliance together. Athgar might be the soul of Therengia, but you are its heart. Both are important, but the combination of the two is what gives life to the Alliance."

Agar brought his axe down onto a twig, easily cutting through it. He howled with glee, then struck again, fascinated by the results.

"He takes after his father," said Shaluhk. "Kargen was always fascinated by axes, even as a youngling."

"I wish I'd known Athgar when he was younger."

"Do not wish for that which you can never have. It is better to celebrate what you have than lament that which you do not."

"Are you a philosopher, now?"

"I am a shaman, but I suppose we perform the same function."

"Other than the magic," said Natalia. "I've never heard of a philosopher using spells."

"There is that, of course." She was about to say more but noticed the approach of Kirak. "It looks as if we have company."

"*Greetings, Kirak,*" said Natalia, switching to the Orcish tongue. "*What brings the chieftain of the Black Axes to us this day?*"

"*I come bearing news,*" replied the Orc, "*though not, I fear, something which you will look on favourably.*"

"*What is it?*" said Natalia. "*Please, speak freely. You are amongst friends.*"

"*I received reports that the men of the west successfully damaged the city's walls. They will be starting their attack* soon."

"*Already? I expected the bombardment to continue for a few days yet.*"

"*I had hunters watching their progress. They report the wall has begun to fail. Without a master of stone to repair it, I fear it will soon collapse. We all know what that means.*"

"*We shall need to move up our own attack.*"

"*Agreed,*" said Kirak.

"*Will that give Athgar sufficient time to find Oswyn?*" asked Shaluhk.

"*I have no way of knowing,*" replied Natalia. "*Maybe it would have been best if you'd accompanied him. That way, you could have relayed his progress through your magic.*"

"*An Orc in Ebenstadt would draw too much attention.*" Shaluhk saw the indecision on Natalia's face. "*He will find her,*" she soothed. "*In the meantime, we must accelerate our plans and prepare for the assault.*"

"*It appears so. We need to get the Orcs of the Red Hand into position. They'll exit the tunnel once everyone else is in place.*"

"*I shall inform Kargen,*" said Shaluhk. She turned to Kirak. "*How long until your hunters can be ready?*"

The Orc chieftain looked skyward, judging the time of day. "*When the sun is at its highest, the attack can commence. What of the Therengians?*"

"*You can rest assured they'll be ready when you are,*" said Natalia. "*When the assault comes, I'd like all our spellcasters here, with me.*"

"*I would suggest otherwise,*" said Shaluhk. "*Were we to spread the shamans throughout our groups, we could communicate our progress.*"

Natalia smiled. "*That's an excellent idea. I'd forgotten how easy it is for you to contact the others.*"

"*I shall accompany Kargen when he goes through the tunnel. I have arranged for Voruhn to accompany you, Nat-Alia, as she speaks your language. Laghul will, of course, be by Kirak's side.*"

"*You seem to have given this a great deal of thought.*"

"*I hope you are not upset?*"

"*Not at all. I only wish I'd thought of it myself. I'll let Wynfrith know the attack will commence at noon.*"

"*Then let us prepare for battle,*" said Kirak, "*and may the Ancestors guide our hands.*"

# ROOFTOPS

All was quiet on the street, although that likely had more to do with the threat of attack than anything else. Even as Athgar watched, another stone cracked against the walls of Ebenstadt, the sound echoing across the city.

He peered around the corner, willing Ethwyn to exit the house, but there was no sign of any activity. Panic rose in his chest, and he fought to keep it suppressed. It was bad enough dealing with another Fire Mage, let alone it being his only sister. The thought of Oswyn's presence only made it worse. How, then, would he rescue his daughter from her captor? Part of him hoped Ethwyn would emerge without her captive, but that seemed unlikely. Distasteful as it was to admit, his sister had always been a cunning individual. Clearly, her training at the hands of the family had only made her more so.

He heard the crackle of flames overhead and looked up to spot a great ball of fire arcing through the air, only to witness it smash into a house, tearing through the roof and scattering wood and thatch. Inside, it made a dull thud as it struck the floor, and then the shutters blew open as if a giant hand had hit them.

Moments later, the smouldering roof burst into flames, dark smoke spiralling into the sky. So surprised was Athgar that all he could do was stare at the destruction, his mind unable to grasp the consequences.

A sharp crack behind him caused him to turn around to see where a large stone had struck a building, tearing through a stone column and digging through a wall beyond. Low rumbles reverberated down the street, and then the building collapsed, sending dust outward in a large, choking cloud.

Screams filled his ears, and then another building collapsed, forcing Athgar to run for cover as chips of stone shot through the air. Out from the dust ran the townsfolk, abandoning their homes in a panic. The fire from the first hit now raged, quickly consuming the thatched roof and sending flaming bits of straw high into the air. These floated around, borne by the heat and flames, then descended to alight on other rooftops.

Ebenstadt was an old city, but much of the original construction had been replaced by newer wooden buildings, buildings with thatched roofs—the perfect fuel to feed a fire.

Smoke billowed out of several buildings, making breathing difficult, and Athgar struggled, the combination of dust and smoke stinging his eyes as well as his lungs. He stepped out onto the street, desperate to be away from any potential fire.

Ahead of him, the door to the house he had been watching opened, and a woman rushed out, clutching an infant. There could be no doubt who it was.

"Ethwyn!" he called out. She paused, looking directly at him.

"Stop this madness," he shouted.

In reply, she raised her free hand, directing it towards him. Flames leaped from her fingertips like dragon's breath rushing to engulf its prey.

Only instinct saved him as he dodged to the side, then held up his own hands, the words of power coming to him without conscious thought. Green fire erupted from his fingers to crash against the oncoming stream. The two rivers of fire struck each other, creating a shock wave that pushed the smoke and dust aside. Unable to proceed to its target, the fire splattered on either side, igniting wood and adding to the townsfolk's burgeoning panic.

Athgar poured everything he had into his spell, and the point of contact moved closer to Ethwyn. He felt heat coursing through him, his adrenaline rising as nature's most destructive element was funnelled by his power. It was often said Fire Mages never died of old age. Instead, they were destroyed by their compulsion to unleash their full power.

He wanted Ethwyn to die for her treachery, to suffer the horrible death his magic promised her, but then the words of his mentor, Artoch, came to him: "*Many have been the Humans who were consumed by their attempt to control the flame. It only leads to madness.*"

The flames crawled ever closer to Ethwyn. In his fervour, he had sought to punish his sister for her actions. But now he realized his mistake, for within her arms was something more precious to him than his need for revenge.

"Oswyn!" he called out, breaking the spell and allowing it to dissipate.

Ethwyn, relieved of the burden of magic, turned, intending to run in the opposite direction when the appearance of Stanislav and Evira quickly put an end to such thoughts. She cast her eyes around, desperate for an escape, only to find Brother Yaromir emerging from the alleyway. With no avenue available to her, she did the only thing she could and rushed back into the house.

Athgar dashed forward, determined to keep her in sight. He made it to the doorway, then ran in, expecting to confront his sister, but she had run up some stairs. He had a brief glimpse of her at the top, then a streak of flame flew down towards him, and he dove off to the side.

Had she wished it, she could have easily struck him with her magic, for the hallway was small, and there was little in terms of cover. Instead, she had targeted the stairs themselves, and now flames licked at the steps, blackening the wood and filling the entranceway with smoke.

Athgar cursed his luck. Upstairs, Ethwyn's footsteps echoed, yet here he was, unable to intervene. He closed his eyes, seeking a sense of calm, for panicking would do no good. His eyes snapped open, and he knew exactly what needed to be done. Words of power issued from his mouth, dampening a narrow path through the flames, then he rushed up the stairs, ignoring the fire licking at his tunic. He held his breath despite the urge to draw in air, emerging into a long hallway, but the real prize was above, up a second set of stairs that led to the rooftop.

Heedless of the danger, he followed, so close now he could hear Oswyn crying out, a sound that was like a dagger to his heart. There was a small landing here, along with several rooms, each with steeply angled ceilings, but Ethwyn had left through a window, its shutters still swinging wildly about. Out he went, onto the steep rooftop, Oswyn's wails acting as a clear beacon.

Ethwyn paused at the edge of the roof, looking down at the street below. Behind her, the city burned, reminding Athgar of tales of the Underworld he had heard as a child.

"Give me Oswyn," he called out, "and you can go free."

She turned to face him. "You know I can't do that, Brother. The family would never forgive me."

"Then return with us to Runewald. Let us help you avoid their grasp."

Her face settled into a look of grim determination. "And do what? Live as a peasant for the rest of my life? Or perhaps I should marry and raise a pack of brats to keep me busy? No, Athgar, I'm a Sartellian now, able to wield the most destructive force of nature. How can I turn my back on that?"

"I understand how seductive the spark can be," replied Athgar. "But without discipline, it will consume you."

"If that's our lot in life, then so be it. Better to glow briefly like a star than spend a lifetime grovelling in the dirt." She transferred Oswyn to her right hand, then shook out her left.

"You can't keep this up," said Athgar. "There's nowhere for you to run." He took a step towards her, but she raised her hand.

"Not one step closer," said Ethwyn, "or I'll burn you into ash."

"You already tried that. Come now, your training can't compete with my own. Come with me, Ethwyn, and I'll show you how you can properly harness your inner spark."

"Inner spark? Is that what your Orc friends call it? They're fools, Athgar. Fire Magic is a serpent that longs to be released. Bottling it up inside is simply a waste of your potential."

"Fire is dangerous," he warned. "Look around you and see for yourself."

She smiled. "Fire consumes everything in the end. Yes, the city is burning. See how glorious it looks!"

"Are you mad? People are dying."

"What if they are? It's of no concern to me. Power is what's important, Brother, and the magic of fire is my path to that power."

Athgar took another step. In response, Ethwyn placed her hand over Oswyn, igniting a small green flame that floated right above her palm. "One step closer, and I'll burn the brat."

"You wouldn't dare!"

"Wouldn't I? I mean to escape, and if I must give up my hostage to do so, then so be it."

"The family won't be happy about that."

"True, but at least I'll be alive. I'm afraid I can't say the same about your daughter."

"They want her alive," pleaded Athgar.

"Also true, but if I can't deliver her to them, then at least I can deny her presence to you and that turncoat."

Athgar felt sweat breaking out on his face as the heat rose, the fire below fed by the wooden building. He had to get Ethwyn to see reason, and quickly before the flames engulfed all of them, but how?

"You say you work for the family," he continued, "but the truth is, they don't trust you. If they did, they would have completed your training."

"And they will, in due course, but it takes years to master the magic of fire."

"Does it?" he replied. "It took me less than a year to master my inner spark, thanks to Artoch. The Orcs understand Fire Magic far better than the family, Ethwyn. You could learn much from them."

"Don't be absurd. The Sartellians have been custodians of Fire Magic for generations. Do you honestly expect me to believe a bunch of savage Orcs could do better?" She glanced down at Oswyn. "She is the future, you know. The epitome of all the family has worked for over the years. The demonstration of your own power only confirms that."

Athgar considered rushing her but had to weigh the risk. Would she kill Oswyn? He couldn't take the chance, so he decided to try a more pragmatic approach.

"Give up, Ethwyn. There's nowhere else to run. Soon the fire will engulf the rooftop, then what will you do?"

She laughed. "I shall embrace my destiny." She dismissed the magical flame, then clutched Oswyn to her chest with both hands.

Athgar had little time to react, for at that very moment, flames leaped up beside him, and part of the thatched roof collapsed, capturing his attention for but a moment. He returned his gaze to his sister just in time to see her leaping off the rooftop.

He rushed forward, but as he took his first step, his foot broke through the thatching, and his knees crashed onto the roof, releasing a rush of thick, black smoke that billowed up from below. He struggled to breathe, his eyes stinging while the heat beneath threatened to roast him alive, but he had to get to Oswyn.

Athgar pulled himself free, then crawled across the rooftop, trying to spread his weight out as much as possible. The roof behind him exploded into a blazing inferno, roasting his back. The pain was nearly unbearable, and he let out a scream, sure he would be consumed by the flames.

He reached the edge of the rooftop, expecting to see the bodies of Ethwyn and Oswyn below, but they were nowhere to be seen. Instead, they had likely made the leap to the next rooftop, a considerable gap to be sure. Could he do the same? One more look behind him was all the convincing he needed to make an attempt. The next building was shorter by one floor, and there was still a gap between the buildings to consider.

Athgar glanced at the ground for only a moment, but that was his undoing. The alley seemed to fall away to nothing as if he stood at the edge of an immense cliff. He felt the contents of his stomach heave, his legs going weak. As a Therengian, he had spent his entire youth in Athelwald, where even the largest building, the thane's hut, was only one story. Here, above the City of Ebenstadt, surrounded by smoke and fire, his legs refused to move. Instead, they felt useless as if he were old and feeble.

He tried to ignore the ground, concentrating, instead, on the distant rooftop, but a flame shot up behind him, and he felt his tunic catch fire. Athgar closed his eyes, calling forth his inner spark to quell the flames, snuffing out his clothes, but the building itself was now too far gone for the fire to be extinguished.

A quick look behind told him it was now or never, so he leaped, trusting the Gods to keep him safe. Time slowed as the wind rushed up at him, then he struck the thatched rooftop and immediately started sliding down the steep angle. His fingers dug in, trying to grasp something, anything, to halt his descent. The falling ceased only as his hands clawed through the roof to grab a wooden support in a death grip, his legs swinging down beneath him, crashing against the building's wall. The weight of his own body now worked against him, dragging him to his doom. He looked up to see Ethwyn standing over him, perched precariously on the rooftop, Oswyn still cradled against her.

"Time to die, Brother." She stomped down, heel meeting hand. He felt bones crack, pain lancing through his arm as he stared up at her.

"Don't do this," he pleaded. "Please."

"Too late for that." She raised her foot for the final blow, but just then, another catapult shot hit the adjacent building. The place was already aflame, but the stone sent fragments of burning wood flying everywhere, including the neighbouring rooftop. Ethwyn ducked as a large timber flew past, narrowly missing her, then turned and fled, leaving Athgar hanging on for dear life.

His arms ached terribly, his strength seeping from his limbs. Looking down did nothing but send his head spinning. He resolved, instead, to concentrate on the edge of the rooftop above him.

A sudden spasm of pain in his injured hand broke his grip, causing him to slide down a little more. For a moment, only a single hand kept him from plunging to his death, and then he reached out with the other, finding another wooden slat where the thatching was torn loose. He held on tight, then moved his other hand until it, too, felt the reassuring touch of the timber frame.

With his position now secured, he began the arduous process of hauling himself back onto the roof, an effort made all the more difficult by his smoke-filled lungs. With his safety finally secure, he leaned against the thatching for a moment, still unwilling to let go of the frame.

Ethwyn was no longer in sight, but it mattered not, for there was little choice as to where she could go. The rooftop he was on was too high for him to drop to the ground, but another building sat to the west, closer to the city's walls. He clawed his way to the peak of the roof, then peered over to get a better view. There, lit by the glow of burning buildings, was Ethwyn, making her way across the rooftops. She had jumped to the next building and was now running southward, where the roofs were pushed right up against each other.

Athgar dragged himself over the peak, then slid down the other side and leaped, easily clearing the gap. He struck the other rooftop quite handily, but the thatch gave way, and he fell through the roofing material to crash to the floor beneath. A pain shot up his leg as he landed, and he screamed out, more in anger and frustration than any real physical injury. He looked around the room, trying to get his bearings, but it was dark. Athgar rose to his feet right as more of the roof gave way, showering him with wooden slats and straw. A beam struck him as it fell, careening off his back to send him sprawling once again.

The west wall of Ebenstadt rumbled as a rock struck halfway up its height, cracking open their defences, the structure giving way across a gap of some fifteen paces. A second shot, aimed at the same point, careened past the new opening and slammed into the building beyond, the very same one Athgar now found himself in.

He felt the vibration, heard the crack and rumble, and then the entire floor gave way, sending him down into chaos.

# BREACH

## AUTUMN 1105

Kargen lifted the stone disc, letting light flood the tunnel. "*Come,*" he said. "*Let us make haste, and remember, our priority is the gate.*"

He tossed aside the cover, then hauled himself above ground. They were close to the wall, so close, in fact, he could hear the footsteps of guards above, but their attention was on distant matters. Kargen saw them looking west and followed their gaze to see smoke hovering over the city.

Others followed, and the Orc chieftain waited until a dozen of his hunters were clear of the tunnel before heading north. He broke into a run, confident the rest would follow. The tunnel had opened up between the wall and the first line of buildings, an opportune circumstance since it hid their initial emergence. For nearly a hundred paces, he moved along silently, his hunter skills serving him well, then a cry from the walls above sounded the alarm.

An arrow thudded into the ground nearby, but he ignored it, breaking into a full-out run. The walls of Ebenstadt were supported by towers spaced at regular intervals, and Kargen, running parallel to them, knew his luck could only hold for so long.

Before him, he saw soldiers descending the stairs from one such place, their swords at the ready. The Orc didn't slacken his pace. Instead, he pulled forth his axe and issued a roar of challenge.

It wasn't as if the Humans could understand what he said, for in his haste, he had used his native tongue, but the effect was quite pronounced, nonetheless. Even as he closed in on them, the men wavered, and then three hundred pounds of solid Orc careened into them.

Two went down immediately, driven to the ground by the sheer weight of the hunter. Kargen struck out with his axe, taking a third in the shoulder, feeling his weapon bite into bone. The guard screamed out in agony, but the chieftain was already pushing past him, leaving his hunters to clean up. He felt an arrow whizz by his ear but he ignored it, concentrating on getting to the gate as quickly as possible.

Natalia fretted. "Where are they?"

"They are entering the city even as we speak," said Voruhn, "but it will take some time to reach the gate."

"I see smoke," said Wynfrith. "Surely the Orcs are not setting fire to Ebenstadt?"

"No," replied Natalia. "I suspect it's the King of Novarsk's doing."

"But why? What does he have to gain by doing such a thing? Does he wish to capture a city that's burned to the ground?"

"He is likely seeking to sow fear and panic. How many soldiers would man the walls if their families were in danger?"

"He does this to strip the walls of their defenders?"

"Such a tactic is not entirely unexpected," Natalia replied. "Sieges are known to be brutal."

"Will that cause problems for us?"

"The smoke appears to be coming from the west. I doubt their engines of war have the range to threaten us."

"Still," said Wynfrith, "if we're going into the city, does that not mean higher casualties?"

"Not if I can help it. After all, what better way to put out fires than by the application of Water Magic?"

"You think you're powerful enough to put out that?" Wynfrith pointed at the thick cloud of smoke now hovering over most of the city.

"Likely not, but it may yet contribute to our own victory this day." Her eyes scanned the army assembled at her side. "Raleth, prepare to advance."

"Already?" asked Voruhn. "Do you not mean to wait until Kargen and his hunters are closer to their objective?"

"No, that would allow the defenders to converge on them. I intend to offer them a diversion. How do you expect they'd react if our army is moving in to attack?"

"I assume they would flood the walls with troops."

Natalia smiled. "Precisely. Have the archers move up, and begin peppering the gate with arrows. That ought to give them something to concentrate on."

"Anything else?" asked the shaman.

"Yes. Have Kirak move the master of flame up as well. I'm sure a well-placed streak or two of fire would do wonders to help."

"And the tuskers?"

"We'll hold those in reserve for the meantime, but once that gate's open, I want them within the city as fast as possible. They should be more than capable of putting down any further thoughts of resistance."

Rada watched as the wall came down, a smile creasing her features. She turned her attention to General Spanov, who was pulling on his gauntlets.

"You know what must be done, General?"

"Aye, Highness. The city will be yours by nightfall, as will the Crown."

"And my father?"

"Will be struck down by the enemy. One of the hazards of leading the attack in person, Highness."

"Excellent. I will remember your loyalty, General, and shall reward you accordingly."

"You are too kind, Princess. Now, if you'll excuse me, there is an attack to see to."

"Of course." She watched him run off, yelling orders as he went. The army of Novarsk was already formed up and ready to charge forth. It took only a command or two to see them off, and then the great press of men moved forward, making directly for the breach.

The princess watched the advance, but her thoughts were elsewhere. If truth be known, the City of Ebenstadt was of little consequence to her, except as a means to an end, an end that would see her wearing the Crown of Novarsk.

Men thought her weak. She had strived her entire life to prove them wrong, and what better way to do that than by seizing the Crown for herself?

Laruhk fidgeted in the saddle, trying to get comfortable. Beneath him, the great tusker shifted its feet as if picking up on its rider's discomfort.

"*Why do you fret so?*" asked Ushog. "*You are not afraid, are you?*"

"*Afraid? No, but I am eager. All of this waiting wears on me.*"

"*You should learn to relax more.*"

"*I am fully aware of how to relax, but now is not the time for such things. A hunter must remain alert at all times. It is what keeps him alive.*"

"*Agreed,*" she replied, "*but there is yet no danger. Keep up this worry, and you will soon have no hair left.*"

"*And how is it you are so relaxed? Are you not eager to come to grips with the enemy?*"

"*Of course, but worrying about it serves no purpose.*"

To their front, horns sounded. In response, Laruhk swept his gaze over his riders. There were twenty of them all told, a vast improvement over the few who had participated at the Battle of the Standing Stones. He raised his spear over his head to garner attention.

"*Riders, advance!*" he called out.

They slowly moved forward. Tuskers were immense beasts with massive muzzles, long and tapered like that of a horse, but there the similarity ended, for the tusker's head flattened at the top, more akin to a boar. Its short, stubby legs were built for endurance rather than speed, and the creature's body was covered in coarse, thick fur. Worst of all, though, was the sharp, pointed teeth that could easily strip flesh from bone. When the tribe had first encountered a tusker, it wreaked havoc with their camp. Only the combined might of the Red Hand had managed to bring the brute down at all. Fortunately, Rugg, the master of earth, had found a way of taming the beasts by using magic to communicate with them, allowing them to live amongst the Orcs in a symbiotic relationship.

Laruhk heard the sound of thunder, then realized his own tuskers were creating the noise. Before him marched the rest of the allied army, ready to assault the gate. Once that was done, it would be up to his riders to enter the city and crush any remaining resistance.

Kargen halted, peering around a building, while a group of hunters stood behind, waiting for the word to rush the last hundred paces to their target.

There had been little opposition so far, other than a few scattered guards who were easily overcome. Many of the townsfolk had witnessed their passing, the sight of Orcs on the streets driving them to seek cover as quickly as possible.

He glanced westward, where smoke still hung over Ebenstadt. The fires had not yet reached this part of the city, but Kargen knew it wouldn't take long for drifting sparks to alight on thatched roofs, leading to a full-scale inferno.

"*Where is Kragor?*" he called out.

"*I am here, Kargen,*" replied Kragor, who, as the best hunter in the tribe, was well known for his skill with the mighty warbow.

"*Do you see those guards there, milling* around *the gatehouse?*"

Kragor grinned. "*Which one do you wish me to kill?*"

"*Whichever one you believe is in charge.*"

The hunter stared for a moment, taking in the scene. "*It is the Human with the metal helmet.*"

He nocked an arrow, then drew back his bow, taking care to account for the breeze. Kargen watched the Orc tighten his stance, and then the arrow flew forth. The guard had just turned when the arrow pierced his back. He staggered forward, then fell to his knees before hitting the ground face first. The other soldiers looked on in astonishment, giving time for Kragor to loose another arrow. Other hunters soon joined him, taking down three more men.

Kargen raised his axe on high, letting out a primal scream, the sound echoing off the buildings. He charged out from behind the corner, followed by the rest of his hunters. The Humans raised the alarm, but it did little good, for the Orcs were amongst them before any defence could be organized.

Kargen directed hunters into the gatehouse, and they barrelled through the door, heedless of any danger within. When an arrow struck the ground near the chieftain's foot, he looked up to spot half a dozen bowmen preparing to let loose with a volley.

From behind him came the sound of arcane words of power, and he turned to see Shaluhk, weaving a spell of magic. A grey mist appeared on the wall, then coalesced into the images of Orc warriors in ancient armour and weapons. The spirits of the dead drove all before them, some by the force of arms, others by the sheer terror of seeing the ghostly apparitions.

"*It appears we have taken the gate,*" said Kargen.

"*The question now,*" said Shaluhk, "*is where can we find Athgar?*"

"The gates are opening," said Voruhn. "I believe the attack succeeded."

"Send in the Runewald fyrd," ordered Natalia, "then follow it up with that of Bradon."

"And the tuskers, High Mage?"

"Have them follow the Therengians. I want the people of Ebenstadt to see this as a liberation, not a conquest."

"Are they not our enemies?"

"The High Lord sent his troops against us, not the townsfolk. They only want to live their lives in peace. We will only take vengeance on those who oppose us."

"And when will you enter the city?" asked the Orc.

"I shall accompany Raleth's warriors."

"Then we had best get going, for they are already on the move."

Natalia spurred on her horse, easily catching the Runewald fyrd as it marched through the gates beneath the watchful gaze of Kargen's hunters.

Shaluhk called down from above. "Nat-Alia, there are fires to the west. I fear the men of Novarsk have already entered the city."

"Then we must hasten there at once," the mage replied. "Where is Kargen?"

"He is here, with me, helping to sort out the prisoners. It appears the defenders had little stomach for fighting."

"I need him and his hunters. I fear there is a tougher fight ahead of us to the west."

"I shall let him know."

Natalia turned her attention to Voruhn. "Contact Laghul and have her ask Kirak to send his hunters north, around the outside perimeter of the city. Hopefully, we can flush the men of Novarsk from the walls with a hail of arrows."

"I shall do as you ask," noted the shaman. She called upon her magic, weaving her hands in an intricate pattern as the words of power came forth. Her magic complete, she conversed with Voruhn, Shaman of the Black Axes.

Natalia noted a building up ahead on the right-hand side of the street. "Raleth, that is the old Cunar commandery. Take your warriors there, and I believe you'll find the High Lord inside."

Wynfrith appeared at her side. "Where do you want my soldiers?"

"With me," Natalia replied. "We're heading for the western breach. Let's hope we're not too late to prevent them getting into the city, or we'll spend days hunting them down."

The street cut across the north end of the city, showing off the finest buildings hereabouts, including the old commandery. To the south stood the packed buildings of the merchants, their doors barred and windows shuttered, fearful of retribution from the victors, no doubt.

Natalia wanted to gallop ahead but knew that to be foolhardy. The army of Novarsk was likely already on the streets, and such a move might prove dangerous, for even a mage could be slain by a quick knife or a well-placed arrow. Foremost in her mind was Athgar. He had entered the city to find Oswyn, but where had that search taken him?

The street curved south, and she brought her horse to a halt, overcome by the sight before her. Flames engulfed the entire street, while thick, black smoke threatened to blot out the sun. Several buildings had collapsed, strewing rubble into the street, and she struggled to see clear passage.

"By the Gods," said Wynfrith. "What's happened here? Could this be the work of Athgar?"

"On this scale?" said Natalia. "I doubt it, and magical fire wouldn't account for the collapsed buildings. I fear Novarsk is at the heart of this, hoping to eliminate any opposition before their attack."

"We can't go down there. The smoke will overwhelm the fyrd."

Natalia surveyed the area, her eyes coming to rest on the western gatehouse. "Have your troops take that gate. There should be little opposition from this side.

"And the army of Novarsk?" asked Wynfrith.

"We shall let Kargen's hunters take care of that." She looked back down the way they had come to see the Orcs quickly approaching.

"We are here," called out the Red Hand chieftain. "Where would you like us to go?"

"Follow me," replied Natalia. "We'll cross to the gatehouse and then follow the wall south till we find the breach."

General Spanov watched as his men climbed through the rubble. The wall had collapsed, the debris forming a ramp of sorts up which the soldiers now swarmed. Amongst them, the king, his sword held high, urged his men on to victory.

Spanov couldn't help but admire the fool's courage. Many rulers would never dare the danger of an open breach, yet Vastavanitch was there despite his advanced age.

The general increased his pace, drawing closer to His Majesty. In front of the king were hundreds of men, each eager to push back the enemy and gain entrance to the city. He watched as two men topped the debris only to be taken down by crossbow bolts. Those behind faltered, their fear overcoming their bravado.

"Onward!" shouted the king. "Onward to victory!"

As the general approached, he drew his sword and dagger. It would be hard work at the top, for the men of Ebenstadt had erected a makeshift barricade. All eyes were on the assault, glued to the actions of the defenders, and that's when Spanov seized his chance. Stepping behind the king, he grabbed him by his shoulder, twisting him around. His Majesty's eyes went wild, then the old man grinned.

"Oh, it's only you, Spanov. You should have said something."

"I'm sorry, Your Majesty," the general replied as he slipped his dagger under the king's helmet, driving into the old man's neck.

Vastavanitch staggered back as blood cascaded down his chest, staining his armour crimson, then fell to the rubble, wheezing as his very life fled his body. The general knelt beside him, the king clutching Spanov's arm with the grip of death.

"Why?" he wheezed out.

"Your time is nigh, my king. It's the moment for younger heads to prevail." He watched as the light left Vastavanitch's eyes, and then the king's head lolled to the side, and the body slumped to the ground. Spanov looked around. A group of men were hurrying past, eager to top the breach, and he called out to them.

"You, there," he shouted. "The king has been mortally wounded."

The men approached, a look of shock etched on their faces as they beheld their king. One of them knelt, stripping off the king's helmet, but there was no life to be found.

"I'm afraid he's dead, General."

Spanov did his best to look saddened by the revelation. "Take his body to the rear. We must see to his mortal remains."

The soldiers lifted the body of their liege lord, bearing him away. The general watched, a smile creeping across his lips. All was now as it should be, the king gone and Rada ready to assume the mantle of queen. He had no doubt he would be a noble by sundown.

He gazed up at the breach one more time, then began the slow descent to return to their camp. There was no use in taking the city now. The war was over, the king dead, and he had far more important things to see to.

# SHOWDOWN

## AUTUMN 1105

Athgar got to his feet, throwing aside the loose thatch that had fallen with him. He was in a small building, its roof now collapsed. Smoke and dust fought to overwhelm him, but he was alive and, apparently, undamaged, save for a few scrapes and bruises.

The sounds of fighting drifted to his ears, and he concluded he must be close to the wall. He thought of Ethwyn and realized her only hope lay in crossing that breach. Once amongst the warriors of Novarsk, it would be almost impossible to reach her. He must act fast.

He had just climbed out of the wreckage and into an alleyway when a familiar voice grabbed his attention. He looked to his left to discover Brother Yaromir.

"Behind you," called out the Temple Knight as he ran towards the Therengian. Athgar swivelled his head to see a startled Ethwyn. She had emerged from the next building over, but something about her appearance looked wrong. He struggled to make sense of it, his eyes still stinging from the smoke, and then it came to him—where was Oswyn?

Ethwyn turned to face him, looking far calmer than she should.

"Well, Brother. It seems our chase has come to an end."

"What did you do with Oswyn?"

She smiled, but the expression looked more grim than pleased. "She's there," she said, pointing. "Inside that building. Now you must make a choice—her or me?"

His eyes moved back and forth between the building and his traitorous sister. Something still didn't make sense, but his addled mind couldn't think clearly.

"I'd like to stay and chat," said Ethwyn, "but I need to be on my way. If you want your precious daughter, then go and get her."

She brought her hands up, and before Athgar could even react, the building erupted into flames, tremendous waves of heat emanating out of it. So powerful was the casting that a green flame shot high into the air, illuminating the entire area.

"Oswyn!" he screamed, running into the building.

"No!" yelled Brother Yaromir as Athgar disappeared into the raging inferno. He considered running in after the mad Therengian, but then new words of power echoed out of the alleyway. Up came his shield just as a streak of fire struck him, the heat so intense it burned the paint off his shield, leaving it charred and smouldering. Ethwyn, cursing her bad luck, turned and fled.

The Temple Knight tried to peer inside the house, but the temperature was unbearable. Stanislav and Evira appeared at his side.

"Where's Athgar?" asked the mage hunter.

"In there," replied the knight. "He went in to save his daughter."

"And Ethwyn?" said Evira.

"Gone, I'm afraid. We'll never catch her now."


The flames lit up the sky, drawing the attention of all in the area.

"By the Ancestors," said Voruhn, pointing. "Look!"

Natalia saw the green fire reaching up into the sky. "Magic," she shouted. "It has to be Athgar. We must hurry."

She spurred on her horse, the shaman doing likewise, eager to keep pace with the High Mage. They rode south, following along the base of the wall. The breach soon came into view. Soldiers swarmed along the top, although it was difficult to tell who was who. Natalia pushed it from her mind, for whether it was Kemp's men or the king's was of no interest to her. Her mind focused on one thing and one thing only—finding her family.

Past the breach they rode, then she spotted Stanislav, clutching a woman, Evira most likely, whose falling tears cleared away the dust and dirt on her face. Next, she spotted Brother Yaromir kneeling in prayer before a burning building.

"Where's Athgar?" she called out.

The knight looked up at her, sorrow in his eyes. "In there. He rushed in to save Oswyn."

Natalia felt a punch to her stomach as an icy hand gripped her heart. She dismounted, then somewhere deep inside her, the magic began to build.

Her eyes frosted over as she pointed her hand, letting loose with every bit of magic she could muster.

It poured out of her in the form of frost, a stream of frozen water so intense it instantly froze all it touched. It hit the door first, causing the wood to crack with the sudden drop in temperature, then spread to the building's interior. Natalia moved forward, everything around blurring as she concentrated on the fire before her.

Inside, the room was thick with smoke. She couldn't decide which direction to go, then saw a clearing in the flames where Athgar lay on the floor, clutching Oswyn to his chest. The fire raged all around them, yet a circle of frost surrounded them, denying entry to the fire. She struggled to comprehend what had happened, but of more import to her now was getting them out before the roof collapsed.

"In here," she called out. "Come and take them while I hold back the fire!"

Brother Yaromir ran in, as did Stanislav. They paused only a moment, taken aback by the horror before them, then the Temple Knight took command of the situation.

"Grab the child," he yelled to his companion. "I shall carry Athgar."

Natalia kept up the stream of frost, spraying it left and right, but she felt the effects of her exertions as blood streamed from her nose and ears, her eyes growing as cold as ice. All her efforts were concentrated on holding back the fire, and then she felt a hand seize the back of her dress, pulling her away. Stepping outside, she lowered her arms, collapsing to her knees.

"Come," said a woman's voice. "Let's get you out of here."

"Bring them over here," called out Voruhn. "I will see what my magic can do."

Natalia felt herself guided away from the flames and down an alleyway, deeper into the city streets. They finally halted, and then she sat, looking up only briefly as a group of Orcs ran by.

"Nat-Alia, are you well?" called out a familiar voice. Shaluhk looked down at her. "You are bleeding," she added.

Natalia was numb inside. Her daughter lay dead, her husband too, and now she was alone. All she wanted to do was cry but lacked the energy for even that simple act. She could only stare at the ground and curse the injustice of it all. A feeble wail broke through Natalia's misery, and her head snapped around.

"Oswyn!" she screamed.

"She is fine," said Voruhn, "though covered in soot. I have never seen such a thing."

"She is touched by fire," said Shaluhk, "as is her father."

"Here," said Evira, "take her."

Natalia, realizing they had placed her child in her arms, hugged her tightly, tears flowing freely, still feeling an immense loss. The air around her buzzed as magic was cast, but she only had eyes for Oswyn, then someone coughed, and Athgar spoke.

"What happened?" he asked.

Natalia rose, moving close and embracing him, their child between them.

"I thought you were dead," she sobbed.

"And so I should be. Did you save me again?"

She shook her head. "It wasn't me. I saw you lying on the floor with Oswyn. You weren't moving."

"It's the child," said Brother Yaromir. "She is blessed by the Saints."

"By the Gods more likely," said Athgar.

"Nonsense," said Shaluhk. "It is the Ancestors who looked over you this day."

"No," said Natalia. She looked down at their daughter. "Oswyn did it. She saved you."

"But how?" Athgar said. "She's only a baby."

"I don't know. Perhaps she reacted out of instinct? The flames didn't touch either of you. How else would you explain it?"

Athgar looked at her in shock. "Didn't you manifest your powers at a young age?"

"I did when I was three, but that's a far cry from being an infant."

Shaluhk drew closer, peering into Oswyn's eyes. "She is special, this one. I suspect she has the potential to wield the magic of both fire and water."

"But that's impossible," said Natalia. "The family has been breeding mages for centuries. There's never been anything like that before."

"It is not impossible just because it has not been seen before. You are one of the most powerful mages to graduate from the Volstrum, Nat-Alia. By your own admission, they wanted to breed you to produce gifted offspring, yes?"

"Yes, but—"

"But nothing," said Shaluhk. "Athgar is indeed a powerful Fire Mage. Your child is the very thing the family fears most—one capable of commanding both elements."

Natalia stared down at Oswyn. "Everything I've ever been told about magic says fire and water are opposites. In theory, they should just cancel each other out."

"Even the family does not know everything about the arcane arts."

"Well, I, for one, am delighted," said Athgar. "For without her, I wouldn't be here to hold you both."

"And I, too, am pleased," added Natalia. "Let us not argue the point but be thankful for what we have."


General Spanov knelt before Princess Rada. "It is done, Your Highness. Your father is dead, and you now rule Novarsk."

Rada drew her sword, a masterwork weapon fitting for a ruler, and held it up to see the light reflecting off its blade.

"Kneel," she commanded. "I would see you receive your reward."

The general bowed his head. "You honour me, Majesty."

The princess held the hilt with both hands, then looked at General Spanov. "You served me well," she said, "but the time for such service has come to an end."

He looked up in surprise as the blade swung out, severing his head cleanly from his body. She watched the blood spurt from his neck like a fountain, mesmerized by the macabre sight. Finally, it stopped, the body toppling to lay in a pool of its own blood.

"He killed my father," she announced to all. "Take the traitor away."

Guards sprang forward, eager to do their queen's bidding.

"Commander Korolev?" called out Rada.

The knight stepped forward, bowing deeply. "Yes, my queen?"

"You are hereby promoted to the rank of general."

"Thank you, Majesty. I promise to serve you faithfully. Have you any commands?"

"Yes. Withdraw the army."

"You don't wish to take the city, Majesty?"

"No, our work here is done. Let the Therengians have it."

General Korolev bowed again. "As you wish, my queen."

# HIGH THANE

Athgar stared across the table. The thanes were all there, as were the Orc chieftains, but he had gone one step further, insisting the tribe's shamans also be present along with Natalia.

"Will you now accept the Crown?" asked Wynfrith.

"I will," said Athgar, "though I have a few stipulations."

"Which are?" said Aswulf.

"I shall not rule as king, but rather as High Thane."

"I see no reason to object. Anything else?"

"Yes. From now on, this assembly will include all those present. It shall be their job to choose my successor should it become necessary."

"That would give the Orcs an advantage in numbers," said Wynfrith.

"For the moment, yes, but our villages grow with every passing day. It will not be long before more are added to the realm, and then Humans will outnumber them. Thus, each tribe will have two members, the better to represent their interests."

"I am in agreement," said Aswulf. "How about you, Wynfrith?"

"I agree, although I cannot speak for Scarburn. They still need to elect a new thane."

"My first act as High Thane is to appoint Natalia Stormwind as Warmaster of the Army." He turned to Belgast, who sat right behind them. "That is the correct term, isn't it?"

"Aye, it is," replied the Dwarf.

"What of Ebenstadt?" asked Wynfrith. "It's part of Therengia now. Who shall rule it?"

"I decided to appoint a tribunal," said Athgar. "I should like Stanislav

Voronsky and Brother Yaromir to rule alongside Master Belgast Ridgehand."

The Dwarf coughed. "Me? Are you mad?"

"Not at all. You have experience being an advisor to a king. The duties of a city councillor should pale in comparison."

"Are you sure it's a good idea," said Aswulf, "having a Temple Knight on the council, I mean? We've had nothing but trouble with the Church these past few years."

"He's a Temple Knight of Saint Mathew. I would trust him with my life."

"And if the Church sees fit to reassign him?"

"Then a successor shall be recommended by Stanislav and Belgast."

"Then the city shall remain under our rule?"

"Yes," said Athgar, "but there will be no more division between Therengians and outsiders. We are all one people now."

Wynfrith leaned forward, resting her elbows on the table. "What of Novarsk, Lord Athgar?"

The High Thane looked at Natalia.

"Queen Rada has sent word she recognizes the Kingdom of Therengia and wishes to send an ambassador to our court once things calm down a bit."

"So we finally have peace," said Kargen.

"So it would seem, at least for the moment," said Athgar, "but there is much to be done. Warmaster?"

"We need to rebuild the walls," said Natalia. "I hoped the Stone Crushers would be of assistance?"

"Of course," said Zahruhl. "With the help of Master Rugg, I believe we can eliminate the flaw that made entry so easy."

"A good idea," said Athgar, "and we should probably fill in that tunnel we built. We don't want it being used against us."

"What of Tybalt Kemp?" asked Kargen.

"He died fighting in this very building," said Natalia. She gazed around the room, taking in the furnishings. "Quite the structure, isn't it? You know it used to be a Temple Knight commandery. I daresay it would make a fine palace."

"I intend to return to Runewald," said Athgar, "and rule from there, although a palace would be useful for hosting visitors."

"Why don't we invite the Temple Knights of Saint Mathew to take up residence here?" said Natalia. "They can billet alongside the local garrison once it's raised."

"You think that wise?" said Aswulf.

"Not just wise," said Athgar, "but diplomatic. Few countries would consider war against a city defended by Temple Knights, even if they are only Mathewites."

"My goodness," said Natalia. "You're becoming quite the ruler. You've only been High Thane for a moment, and already you're thinking of the future."

"I must protect that which I hold most dear," he replied. "My friends"—his eyes swept the room, ending on Natalia—"and my family."

"Since you're now High Thane," said Aswulf, "does that make Natalia your queen?"

"No," said the mage. "I am content simply being his wife."

"And Warmaster," added Belgast.

"Well, yes, that's also true."

"I make a solemn vow to do my best to serve the people of Therengia," said Athgar, "and that means everyone, be they Orcs, Humans, or any other race. This is home now, for all of us, and I will not allow others to take that away."

Oswyn cried out in the distance. Moments later, a knock came at the door.

"And that, my friends," said the new High Thane, "is the sound of this meeting coming to an end. Come in, Skora."

The old woman entered, carrying Oswyn. Everyone filed out, save for Athgar, Natalia, Kargen, and Shaluhk. Natalia took Oswyn, gazing down into the babe's eyes, eyes which seemed to take in the entire room.

"You're home now, little one," she said. "No one will ever threaten you again."

# EPILOGUE

Winter 1105/1106 MC

E thwyn's feet echoed on the marble floor as she made her way to the High Magister's office. It had been a long trip back to Korascajan. She had, in truth, considered the possibility of not returning at all, but the lure of further training, of mastering even more powerful magic, was a call she couldn't resist.

She bore the weight of her failure as a heavy burden and feared it might lead them to refuse her any further training. What would she do then? Ethwyn had destroyed any chance of being accepted by her own people, the Therengians. How, then, would she survive?

Her path brought her to the desk of the High Magister's assistant. When she'd been given the task of recovering the child, the assistant was a man named Toras, but now a woman sat in his stead.

"Good afternoon," the woman said. "My name's Zaphena Sartellian. Are you here to see the High Magister?"

"I am," replied Ethwyn.

"May I ask your name?"

"Ethwyn, Ethwyn of Athelwald."

"Ah yes, he's expecting you." Zaphena stood, moving to the door, knocking before opening it a crack. "Ethwyn is here to see you, my lord."

"Send her in," came the reply.

The mage's assistant pushed open the door, standing aside to let the visitor enter. Once Ethwyn was inside, Zaphena left, closing the door behind her, the sound ominous.

"You're not Jendarth," said Ethwyn.

"No, I'm not. My name is Toras Sartellian. I'm surprised you don't recognize me. I succeeded to the position of High Magister last summer after my predecessor was removed."

"Removed?"

"Yes, for failing to live up to expectations. We serve at the will of the family, you see, and those who fail to perform are relieved of their responsibilities."

Ethwyn felt her mouth go dry. She had failed in her mission. Would she, too, be relieved of her responsibilities?

"I have returned from the north," she began.

"So I've heard. You were sent to retrieve the Stormwind child, were you not?"

"I was, but I'm afraid I failed the family, Magister."

He stared at her, causing her to pale.

"I suppose it couldn't be helped," said Toras at last. "Your training was incomplete, and you were woefully unprepared. Tell me, did you manage to lay hands on the child?"

"I did, my lord. She was in my care for several days, in fact. Had it not been for the interference of Novarsk, I would have brought her here, to Korascajan."

"And if you'd been properly trained, you could have utilized the ring of fire spell and returned directly. You did well, given the situation, Ethwyn. You proved your loyalty to the family, and that is not a small thing."

"May I return to my training, Lord?"

"I feel, under the circumstances, that would not be the best course of action."

Ethwyn felt the cold hand of fear grip her heart, but the High Magister was not yet finished.

"I think it better to put you on a more... individualized program. From now on, you shall be tutored one on one."

Hope began to rise once more. "My lord?"

"You have great potential, Ethwyn, and you share your brother's gift for magic. As a Therengian, I can't very well send you to the courts of the Continent. But there are other things at which I'm sure you'll excel, things that are of far more import than pandering to the rulers of the Petty Kingdoms."

"And the child?"

"She is yet an infant and will not come into her magic for years. We can try again later. After all, it's not as if we don't know where she can be found."

<<<<>>>>

Meet Athgar & Natalia in the Prequels

Continue the series with Maelstrom

———

If you enjoyed *Inferno,* then *Servant of the Crown,* the first book in the Internationally Best Selling *Heir to the Crown* series awaits your undivided attention.

Start Reading Servant of the Crown Today

# SHARE YOUR THOUGHTS!

If you enjoyed this book, I encourage you to take a moment and share what you liked most about the story.

These positive reviews encourage other potential readers to give my books a try when they are searching for a new fantasy series.

But the best part is, each review that you post inspires me to write more!

**Thank you!**

# A FEW WORDS FROM PAUL

Inferno completes a four-story arc that began in Ashes. Athgar and Natalia now have a home, and yet more is to come. Although they've managed to build a new life and lead their people to peace, the family is still out there, waiting in the dark. In a sense, the first four books of this series show the growth of Athgar and Natalia from naïve, well-intentioned individuals into two of the most influential people in the region. The threat to the Therengians might be neutralized, but the family is still out there with one goal in mind—taking Oswyn.

If you're worried that this will be the last of Athgar and Natalia, don't be. The story isn't done, but the focus of the following books will shift from building a home to revealing the family's true intentions and breaking the grip that they have on the Petty Kingdoms.

The story continues in Maelstrom, where Natalia must return to the Volstrum, where it all began.

While it's true that I am the author of these tales, it takes a lot of polishing to make them a finished product. I couldn't have done this without Carol Bennett, who is my guiding light as well as my editor, and her encouragement has been instrumental in bringing these stories to readers. I should also like to thank Brad Aitken, Christie Bennett, Stephanie Sandrock, and Amanda Bennett for their ever-present encouragement and support.

In addition, are those from my beta reading team who have contributed with their comments early on in the story process, so I would like to add thanks to them here:

Rachel Deibler, Michael Rhew, Phyllis Simpson, Don Hinckley, James McGinnis, Charles Mohapel, Lisa Hanika, Debra Reeves, David Clark, Michell Schneidkraut, Will Groberg, Wendy Francis, Joanna Smith, Brad Williams, Susan Young, Anna Ostberg, and Keven Hutchinson.

Last but certainly not least, I must thank you, my readers, for, without your interest, these tales wouldn't have seen the light of day. Reviews and comments are the lifeblood of modern authors, and I encourage you to take a moment and let me know what you thought of Inferno.

# CAST OF CHARACTERS

**Cast of Characters:**
Orcs
**Agar** - Youngling, son of Shaluhk and Kargen, Red Hand Tribe
**Artoch** (Deceased) - Master of flame, Red Hand Tribe
**Grundak** - Hunter, Red Hand Tribe
**Kargen** - Chieftain, bondmate to Shaluhk, Red Hand Tribe
**Khurlig** (Deceased) - Shamaness, Ancestor
**Kirak** - Chieftain, Black Axe Tribe
**Kragor** - Hunter, Red Hand Tribe
**Laghul** - Shamaness, Black Axe Tribe
**Laruhk** - Hunter, brother to Shaluhk, Red Hand Tribe
**Ogda** - Hunter, Black Axe Tribe
**Rugg** - Master of earth, Stone Crusher Tribe
**Shaluhk** - Shamaness, bondmate to Kargen, Red Hand Tribe
**Tonfer Garul**- Scholar at the great archives in Corassus
**Uhdrig**(Deceased) - Shamaness, Red Hand Tribe
**Urglan** - Hunter, Red Hand Tribe
**Urughar** - Hunter, Black Axe Tribe
**Ushog** – Tusker Rider, Red Hand Tribe
**Voruhn** - Shamaness, bondmate to Zahruhl, Stone Crusher Tribe
**Zharuhl** – Chieftain, Stone Crusher Tribe

Therengians
**Anweld** - Mother of Harwath and Raleth, Runewald villager
**Aswulf** - Thane of Thaneford, great uncle to Harwath
**Athgar** - Fire Mage, Thane of Runewald, son of Rothgar, bondmate to Natalia Stormwind
**Bergwith** -Niece of Wynfrith, Bradon villager
**Caladin**(Deceased) - Athelwald villager
**Dunstan** - Bard, Runewald villager
**Ethwyn** - Younger sister to Athgar, Athelwald/Runewald villager
**Freywith**(Deceased) – Mother of Melwyn, Athelwald villager
**Galan** - Thane of Scarburn
**Gunthar**(Deceased) - Athelwald villager
**Harwath** - Captain of fyrd, younger brother of Raleth, Runewald villager
**Hilwyth** - Member of the fyrd, Runewald villager

**Magran** - Trusted aide of Thane Galan, Scarburn villager
**Melwyn** - Athgar's ex-betrothed, Athelwald/Runewald villager
**Natalia Stormwind** - Water Mage, bondmate to Athgar, Runewald villager
**Oswyn** - Child of Athgar and Natalia, Runewald villager
**Raleth** - Member of the fyrd, older brother of Harwath, Runewald villager
**Rothgar**(Deceased) - Father of Athgar and Ethwyn, Athelwald villager
**Skora** - Friend of Athgar & Natalia, Athelwald/Runewald villager
**Weyland** - Runewald villager
**Wulforth**(Deceased) - Father of Melwyn, Athelwald villager
**Wynfrith** – Thane of Bradon, Aunt of Bergwith

Ebenstadt
**Barnbaum** - Baker
**Brother Laslo** - Lay brother of Saint Mathew
**Brother Mortimer** - Lay brother of Saint Mathew
**Brother Yaromir** - Temple Knight of Saint Mathew
**Evira** - Serving woman at the Elk
**Gertrude** - Young girl
**Grifken Skylar** - Member of the soldier's guild
**Imelda** - Nursemaid
**Sadron** - Murderer
**Stanislav Voronsky** - Former Mage hunter, friend of Natalia
**Tybalt Kemp** - Self-declared High Lord of Ebenstadt

Dwarves
**Belgast Ridgehand** - Entrepreneur, friend of Natalia and Athgar
**Haglarith**(Deceased)- King of Kragen-Tor
**Kieren Brightaxe** - Smith, cousin of Belgast Ridgehand
**Nodrim**(Deceased) - Dwarf King of Kragen-Tor prior to Haglarith
**Targan Hardhammer** - Smith, cousin of Belgast Ridgehand

The Family
**Eloran Sartellian** - Instructor at Korascajan
**Invidar Sartellian** - At the court of Reinwick
**Jendarth Sartellian** - High Magister of Korascajan
**Nezeroth Sartellian**(Deceased) - Fire Mage
**Toras Sartellian** - Chief aide to Jendarth Sartellian
**Verineth Sartellian**(Deceased) - Fire Mage
**Zaphena Sartellian** – Assistant to the High Magister of Korascajan

Others

**Beothric**(Deceased) - Nephew of ancient king of Therengia. Built Dunmere
**Duke of Holstead** - Lord Wilhelm Kohler
**Duke of Kriegoff** - Lord Freidrich Hartman
**Korolev** - Commander in the army of Novarsk
**Tristan Marhaven** - Attempted to seize Krosnicht Crown
**Maximillian** - Prince of Braymoor
**Olani** - Princess of the Kurathian Isle of Kouras
**Rada** - Daughter of King Vastavanitch of Novarsk
**Spanov** - General of the Army of Novarsk
**Vastavanitch** - King of Novarsk

**Places:**
Therengia
**Ashborne**(Destroyed) – Village west of Runewald
**Athelwald**(Destroyed) - Village near Ord-Kurgad
**Bradon** – Village north of Runewald
**Dunmere**(Occupied) - Village now occupied by Humans, called Ebenstadt
**Old Kingdom** - Another name for Therengia
**Runewald** - Near Ebenstadt, home to Athgar, Natalia, and Red Hand Tribe
**Scarburn** - Village northwest of Runewald
**Thaneford** - Village northeast of Runewald

Petty Kingdoms
**Abelard** - Kingdom on the northern coast
**Braymoor** - Principality on the northern coast
**Corassus** - City State on the southern coast
**Ebenstadt** - Independent city on the eastern border
**Eidolon** - Kingdom on the northern coast
**Finburg** - City in Novarsk, north west of Ebenstadt
**Grislagen** - Kingdom near the western border
**Halmund** - City in Novarsk, west of Ebenstadt
**Herani** - City in Halvarian Empire, known as birthplace of humanity
**Holstead** - Duchy on the eastern border
**Karslev** - City on the northern border, houses the Volstrum
**Krieghoff** - Duchy on the eastern border
**Novarsk** - Kingdom, west of Ebenstadt
**Ostermund** - Small village in the Duchy of Krieghoff
**Reinwick** - Duchy on the northern coast
**The Elk** - Inn in Ebenstadt

Orc

**Khasrahk** - Village, Stone Crusher Tribe
**Ord-Ghadrak** - Village, Black Axe Tribe
**Ord-Kurgad**(Destroyed) - Village, Red Hand Tribe

Other Places
**Korascajan** - Where the family trains Fire Mages
**Kouras** - Kurathian Island
**Kragen-Tor** – Dwarven Kingdom, birthplace of Belgast Ridgehand
**Kurathia** - A realm of princes on islands far to the south
**The Wildlands** - East of the Petty Kingdoms
**Volstrum** - Where the family trains Water Mages

**Other Information:**
**Battle of the Wilderness** - Human name for Battle at the Standing Stones
**Orcs of the Black Axe** - Kirak is chieftain, village of Ord-Ghadrak, shamans are masters of flame
**Orcs of the Red Hand** - Kargen is chieftain, in Runewald, shamans are Life Mages
**Skrolling** - Therengian term for a non-Therengian, often looked upon with disdain
**Stone Crusher Orcs** - Zahruhl is chieftain, village of Khasrahk, shamans are masters of earth
**Thane** - Elected ruler of a Therengian Village.
**Battle of the Pines** - Battle where Ebenstadt attacked Ashborne and Runewald
**Battle of the Standing Stones** - Battle where Therengian/Orc Alliance defeated the Holy Army
**Torkul** - Orc name for Therengians.
**Tusker** - Huge animal similar to a prehistoric entelodont

# ABOUT THE AUTHOR

Paul J Bennett (b. 1961) emigrated from England to Canada in 1967. His father served in the British Royal Navy, and his mother worked for the BBC in London. As a young man, Paul followed in his father's footsteps, joining the Canadian Armed Forces in 1983. He is married to Carol Bennett and has three daughters who are all creative in their own right.

Paul's interest in writing started in his teen years when he discovered the roleplaying game, Dungeons & Dragons (D & D). What attracted him to this new hobby was the creativity it required; the need to create realms, worlds and adventures that pulled the gamers into his stories.

In his 30's, Paul started to dabble in designing his own roleplaying system, using the Peninsular War in Portugal as his backdrop. His regular gaming group were willing victims, er, participants in helping to playtest this new system. A few years later, he added additional settings to his game, including Science Fiction, Post-Apocalyptic, World War II, and the all-important Fantasy Realm where his stories take place.

The beginnings of his first book 'Servant to the Crown' originated over five years ago when he began a new fantasy campaign. For the world that the Kingdom of Merceria is in, he ran his adventures like a TV show, with seasons that each had twelve episodes, and an overarching plot. When the campaign ended, he knew all the characters, what they had to accomplish, what needed to happen to move the plot along, and it was this that inspired to sit down to write his first novel.

Paul now has four series based in his fantasy world of Eiddenwerthe and is looking forward to sharing many more books with his readers over the coming years.

# HOW TO GET BATTLE AT THE RIVER
## FOR FREE

Paul J Bennett's newsletter members are the first to hear about upcoming books, along with receiving exclusive content and Work In Progress updates.

Join the newsletter and receive *Battle at the River*, a Mercerian Short Story for free:

PaulJBennettAuthor.com/newsletter

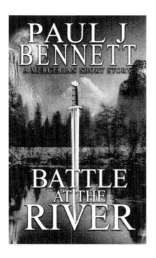

An enemy commander. A skilled tactician. Only one can be victorious.

The Norland raiders are at it again. When the Baron of Bodden splits their defensive forces, Sergeant Gerald Matheson thinks that today is a day like any other, but then something is different. At the last moment, Gerald recognizes the warning signs, but they are outnumbered, outmaneuvered, and out of luck. How can they win this unbeatable battle?

If you like intense battle scenes and unexpected plot twists, then you will love Paul J Bennett's tale of a soldier who thinks outside the box.

Printed in Great Britain
by Amazon

44833780R00169